Rosie GOODWIN

The Soldier's Daughter

CORSAIR

First published in Great Britain in 2014 by Canvas
an imprint of Constable & Robinson Ltd
This paperback edition published in 2014 by Corsair

A CIP catalogue record for this book
is available from the British Library.

ISBN 978-1-47210-172-3 (paperback)
ISBN: 978-1-47211-349-8 (ebook)

Printed and bound by CPI Group (UK) Ltd, Croydon, CR0 4YY

Corsair
is an imprint of
Constable & Robinson Ltd
100 Victoria Embankment
London EC4Y 0DY

An Hachette UK Company
www.hachette.co.uk

www.constablerobinson.com

Rosie Goodwin is the author of a number of bestselling historical fiction novels. Having worked in the social services sector for many years, she is now a full-time novelist. Rosie's writing career began when her husband submitted a short story to *Take a Break* magazine, which was later published. Rosie lives in Nuneaton, the setting for many of her books, with her husband and their three dogs. *The Soldier's Daughter* is Rosie's twenty-second novel.

Visit www.rosiegoodwin.co.uk to find out more about Rosie and to sign up for her newsletter.

Other titles by Rosie Goodwin

The Bad Apple
No One's Girl
Dancing Till Midnight
Moonlight and Ashes
Forsaken
Our Little Secret
Crying Shame
Yesterday's Shadows
The Boy from Nowhere
A Rose Among Thorns
The Lost Soul
The Ribbon Weaver
A Band of Steel
Whispers
The Misfit
The Empty Cradle
Home Front Girls
A Mother's Shame

Catherine Cookson titles
Tilly Trotter's Legacy
The Mallen Secret
The Sand Dancer

This book is for Christine Jarvis and Doreen Brownson, a much loved sister-in-law and auntie, with love and thanks for all your unfailing support. xx

Nuneaton, Warwickshire, November 1939

'Come on now, Sarah, if you keep crying like this you'll wake Alfie up and then none of us will get any sleep tonight.' As they lay curled up close together in their double bed, Briony Valentine hugged her young sister's slight body to her.

'B-but I don't want Daddy to go away,' Sarah sobbed as tears streamed down her thin cheeks. She had always been a frail child and her sixteen-year-old sister was very protective of her.

'You know that he has to go,' Briony told her gently but firmly. 'Lots of men are leaving home to fight the war. Mr Brindley from next door joined up months ago, didn't he? Try to look on the bright side, pet – it can't last forever, can it? Daddy will be home in the blink of an eye, you just wait and see.'

Yet despite her brave words, Briony's own heart was

aching too, and from along the landing she could hear the sound of her mother, Lois, crying and her father's voice as he tried to comfort her in their bedroom. Alfie was the only one who seemed unaffected by his father's imminent departure, but then at five years old he wasn't mature enough to understand the implications of their dad enlisting. As long as he was allowed out into the street to play football with his friends and his meals were on time, nothing much fazed her little brother, and Briony would not have had it any other way; she spoiled him shamelessly.

Many of Alfie's friends had already been evacuated, much to his disgust. Up to now, their mother had refused to allow them to go, making the excuse that they were unwell, but Briony wondered what would happen once their father was gone. James Valentine had always been the strong one, and the girl was more than a little concerned about how her mother would cope without him. Just thinking about her mother made the corners of Briony's mouth twitch into a smile. Lois was truly beautiful, and although her husband sometimes despaired of her, Briony loved her just the way she was and knew that deep down, he did too. Only the week before, he had scolded his wife because she had spent the money he had given her for new shoes for Alfie on a dress for herself.

'But darling,' Lois had said, batting her big blue eyes at him. 'You *know* I always like to look nice for you, and it was such a bargain I simply couldn't resist it. You wouldn't want to come home to find me in a wrap-around pinny with curlers in my hair, now would you?'

Briony had held her breath as she waited for her father's reply; eventually he had grinned and hugged her mother.

'No, I don't suppose I would,' he'd admitted. He could never stay mad at her for long, even when he came home to find the house a mess and no meal on the table, whilst she sat and painted her nails. Lois Valentine was a striking-looking woman and she knew it; fortunately, her naturally kindly nature made up for her sometimes selfish ways. She was a loving wife and mother, her only fault being that she liked to make the most of herself at all times, which had caused the neighbours to christen her 'Lady Muck'. Briony had heard them on occasion but it didn't trouble her. She was proud of her mother and felt sure that the other women in the street were just jealous of her, envious of the way their husbands' eyes would follow her each time she ventured out of the house – and it was no surprise really when she looked at them with their work-worn faces and their shabby pinnies.

Sarah had jammed her thumb in her mouth now and Briony knew that the worst of her weeping was over, for the moment at least. Hopefully the little girl would be asleep soon so she continued to stroke her hair soothingly as they lay in the darkened room. The blackout curtains effectively blocked out any light and normally she would have found the darkness comforting, but tonight her thoughts were too full of her father's departure to allow her to think of anything else. Once he was gone she was painfully aware that life as they had known it would change drastically. It was James who cooked for them the majority of the time when he came home from his shift at the local pit, although he had been teaching Briony to cook lately and now she prided herself on being able to make a simple but filling meal. She had also taken over the washing and ironing, which was just as well, because when it had been left to their mother, the children had often found themselves with no clean clothes to wear.

In the summer, Briony had left school and started work at the local Woolworths store in town, in the accounts department. She loved her job, even if Lois did take most of her wages off her – 'for bits and pieces', as she had put it. Of course, their father didn't know about it and Briony didn't want him to. She understood that Lois took a pride in her appearance, and as long as she herself had enough coppers for her bus fares and for a few treats for Sarah and Alfie, she was quite happy with the way things were, nor did she mind all the chores she often found herself having to do.

Once she was sure that the little girl was asleep, Briony eased her arm from around Sarah and swung her legs out of the bed, shivering as her feet made contact with the icy lino. Pulling her mother's old dressing gown about her, she set off downstairs for the kitchen. She could still hear her mother and father talking in hushed voices and thought they might be glad of a cup of tea. They obviously were not ready to sleep yet and she certainly wasn't.

Down in the kitchen she checked that the curtains were fully drawn to meet the blackout regulations before clicking on the light and gazing about the familiar room. She tried to envisage what it would be like without her father and blinked back tears – but then, squaring her shoulders, she filled the kettle and began to set cups and saucers out on a wooden tray. There would be plenty of time for tears once he was gone. After carefully spooning the right amount of tea leaves into the sturdy brown teapot, she placed the pressed-glass sugar bowl and the milk jug on the tray too. Then she glanced around again as she waited for the kettle to boil. There was nothing of any great value in the room, nor in the whole of the house for that matter; most of the furniture was second-hand and mismatched, but it was the only home Briony had ever known so she loved it just the same. Admittedly, her mother would never have won a Housewife of the Year competition, but the place was homely and cosy for all that, and it had been a happy home that regularly rang with laughter. She wondered if it still would be, once her dad had gone away, but thankfully the kettle began to sing at that moment so she had no time to brood.

A few moments later, she tapped on her parents' bedroom door and when her mother invited her in she carried the tray inside to them. They were sitting propped up against the headboard and Briony thought how pretty Lois looked in her pink silk nightgown, despite the fact that her eyes were reddened from crying.

'Come away in, pet.' Her father patted the side of the bed, and once she had put the tray down, Briony scrambled onto the eiderdown to join them. Her mother often teased her by saying that she and her father were like two peas in a pod, and it was true. She had inherited his coal-black hair and blue-grey eyes, whereas Sarah and Alfie were fair and blue-eyed like their mother.

James Valentine had met Lois Frasier after leaving the orphanage in Coventry where he had been brought up and was working his way around the country doing whatever jobs he could find. He had become quite a Jack-of-all-trades during that time, trying his hand at potato-harvesting or fruit-picking, fencing, building or any work that was available. He was a clever and personable young man. But then he had landed in the little Cornish village of Poldak where Lois had been raised, and he often jokingly told Briony that he had fallen in love with her at first sight.

'That were the end of my travelling days. There were no other lass for me once I'd clapped eyes on your mam,' he would reminisce and Briony's young heart would flutter at the romance of it all. Her dad could do no wrong in her eyes and she would listen entranced to the tales he told of his childhood. His early years had been happy ones, thanks to the Welsh housemother in the orphanage, after whom Briony had been named. Briony's eyes filled. Soon now, their jovial, kind father would be gone – and it was hard to imagine their life without him.

'Here you are, Mum.' Briony wriggled out of her father's arms, poured out the tea and passed a cup to her mother, who sniffed loudly as she dabbed at her eyes with a little lace handkerchief.

'There you are, Lois, our lass is looking after you before I've even left. Didn't I tell you she would?'

Lois nodded resignedly and James stroked her pale blonde hair. He was putting on a brave face, but Briony knew that he was hurting as much as they were at the thought of being parted.

He took a long swig of his tea, keeping the smile plastered to his face as he asked, 'When is it you're starting work, pet?'

Lois had taken a part-time job in a local corner shop not far from where they lived in Stockingford. It would be the first time she had ever done a paid day's work in her life and she wasn't looking forward to it at all. But she supposed she ought to show willing. Most of the other women thereabouts were already working and she knew that once James was gone, money would be tight even with Briony's wages coming in.

'Next Monday,' she answered, frowning.

'Well, there you are then,' James said cheerfully. 'You'll enjoy hearing all the gossip from the customers and it will keep your mind occupied till I come home.'

Briony wished wholeheartedly that she could be as optimistic as him; a knot of fear was wedged in her stomach and it refused to budge. Nuneaton had been more or less unaffected by the war up to now, but rumour had it that Hitler was just biding his time before the bombing of the Midlands started in earnest – and what would it be like then? Anderson shelters were being erected in people's back gardens, their own included, and blackout curtains were already in force. It didn't bear thinking about, especially as her mother was useless in a crisis. But now, not wishing to intrude any further on her parents' last night together, she kissed them both goodnight and made her way back to the room she shared with her little sister, where she tossed and turned until the first light of dawn streaked the sky.

Chapter One

'Just try and eat a few mouthfuls, Mum,' Briony pleaded as she placed some sausage and mash in front of Lois. 'You'll make yourself ill if you go on like this, and you'll feel better with something in your stomach.'

But it was soon apparent that her pleas were falling on deaf ears. Her mother had barely moved from the chair since early that morning following her husband's departure, and now her stunning blue eyes were red and swollen from crying. She hadn't even bothered to do her hair or put her make-up on for the first time that Briony could remember. The mood of depression in the house was so tangible that Briony felt she could almost reach out and touch it.

Sighing, she turned her attention to her younger brother and sister. Thankfully they had cleared their plates, so now she tried to inject a little cheer into her voice as she told them, 'Come on, you two, we'll get you washed and into your pyjamas, shall we? You can listen to the wireless for a while then before I tuck you in, if you're both good.'

Sarah scraped her chair back from the table and carried her dirty plate to the deep stone sink whilst Alfie scrambled down too and went to his mother for a hug. Normally she was very affectionate towards him – towards all of them, if it came to that – but today she hardly seemed to notice that he was there, let alone show him any attention. He found this thoroughly confusing. He knew that his daddy had gone away, but he had promised to come home again just as soon as he could – so why had Mummy been crying all day?

'Come on, sweetheart,' Briony urged, holding her hand out to him as he hovered at his mother's side. 'We'll get you washed first, shall we? And look, I have your clean pyjamas hanging on the clothes-horse by the fire so they'll be lovely and warm for you to put on.'

Alfie instantly cheered up and skipped towards his sister, who lifted him up and hugged him tightly before washing him from head to toe in the bowl of warm water she had ready.

Shortly after eight o'clock that evening, when Briony had Sarah and Alfie tucked safely up in bed, she told her mother, 'I might pop round next door for half an hour. Is that all right?'

'What? Oh yes . . . yes, of course, love. You go,' her mother said absently, so Briony pulled her coat on and stepped out into the back yard that divided the two houses. She shivered as she looked towards the dark shape of the Anderson shelter that was being erected in the back garden, then crossing the yard she tapped at the neighbour's door and without waiting to be asked, hurried into the kitchen and out of the cold.

Martha Brindley was sitting knitting at one side of the

fire whilst her youngest son Ernest, or Ernie as he preferred to be called, sat at the other listening to the wireless. Briony had hoped to find a slightly happier atmosphere here but she was instantly disappointed as Mrs Brindley raised reddened eyes to her.

'You'll never guess what this daft bloody ha'porth has gone an' done,' she said crossly, glaring at Ernie, who lowered his own eyes sheepishly. 'He's only gone an' signed up, ain't he? An' him not even eighteen till the New Year. For two pins I'd go down to that recruitin' office an' tell 'em he's lied about his age. I mean, he would have had to go soon enough anyway – so why hurry it along, eh?'

Briony's heart sank as she looked towards Ernie for confirmation; he shrugged as a lock of his thick dark-brown hair flopped onto his forehead. 'It wouldn't make much difference even if yer did, Mam,' he pointed out. 'They need all the lads they can get now an' I'm sure they wouldn't quibble over a couple o' months or so.'

'I think he's right, Mrs Brindley,' Briony said quietly, but her heart ached at the thought of him going as well. She and Ernie had grown up together but lately their relationship had changed and she had found herself looking at him through different eyes. Suddenly he was so much more than just the boy next door. He was handsome and kind, and although neither of them had actually acknowledged it yet, they both knew that there was something special growing between them. But Briony knew that now he was going away, that special feeling might be lost and it saddened her.

'*You* understand why I've done it, don't yer, Briony?' His deep-brown eyes held a silent plea for understanding as he gazed towards her. 'Nearly all me mates have gone already as well as me dad, an' I don't want people thinkin' I'm a yeller belly.'

Feeling as if she were caught between the devil and the deep blue sea, Briony wrung her hands together. Strangely, she *could* understand why he'd done it, but she didn't want to upset his mother further by taking sides, so she said tactfully, 'Well, as you say, you would have had to go in the New Year anyway.'

'Hmm!' Mrs Brindley's knitting needles clicked furiously, and rising from his seat, Ernie suggested, 'Why don't we go fer a walk?'

'In *this* weather?' His mother shook her head, exasperated. 'Why, you'll likely catch yer death o' cold – an' then it'll be that what kills yer instead o' Adolf!'

Despite the tension in the air, Ernie grinned as he towered over Briony and pushed his long arms into the sleeves of his coat.

'We won't be long,' he said, taking Briony's elbow and they left hurriedly before his mother had a chance to start again.

After feeling their way down the long whitewashed entry that was acting as a wind tunnel, they wound their scarves around their necks and set off down Eadie Street. Once at the end of it they turned up Church Road and had almost reached the Round Towers, the entrance to the grounds of Arbury Hall, before Ernie said quietly, 'Yer *do* understand, don't yer, Briony?'

'I think so.' If she had been a young man she would probably have done just the same, but it didn't stop the hurt from throbbing through her. 'I don't know how Ruth's going to feel about it though.'

'Ruth?' He stared at her through the gloom.

'Oh come on, Ernie. You must know that Ruth is nuts about you?'

'Is she *really?*'

Men could be really dim sometimes, thought Briony; how he could have failed to notice was anyone's guess. Ruth Teagles was Briony's closest friend and she had worshipped the ground that Ernie trod on for as long as Briony could remember, which was why she herself had held back. She sighed into the darkness now, wondering why everything had to become so complicated when you grew up. Not so very long ago they had all been at school together with not a care in the world – and now here was Ernie going off to fight for his King and Country.

A thick frost was forming on the deserted pavements, making them sparkle like diamonds, and as he felt a shudder ripple through Briony, Ernie drew her arm through his and said, 'Come on, that's blown a few cobwebs away. Let's get back an' see if me mam is in a better frame of mind, eh? I might even make yer a brew. Might as well make the most o' the time we've got left. I shall be off to start me trainin' in a couple o' weeks' time. Did I tell yer it were the RAF I've joined? I'm goin' to train to be a pilot. Just as well I got good marks at school, ain't it?'

Briony shivered again, but this time it was nothing to do with the cold. It was the thought of Ernie flying a plane that made fear pulse through her veins. No wonder Mrs Brindley was so upset. It was bad enough knowing that your loved ones were joining the Army, but everyone knew that the RAF pilots stood a chance of being blown out of the sky by enemy planes every time they took off. For some reason she had assumed that he had enlisted for the Army, as his father had. Briony was suddenly glad of the darkness that hid the tears that had sprung to her eyes. This was turning out to be one of the worst days of her life, what with her father leaving and now finding out that Ernie would shortly be going too. Suddenly she just wished that it could be over.

*

Ruth was waiting for her at the bottom of Church Road the next morning when Briony set off for work and they began the walk into town together as they normally did.

'Did yer dad get off all right?' the other girl asked conversationally.

Briony nodded miserably. 'Yes, but Mum's hardly stopped crying since he left.'

'Well, I think we expected that, didn't we?' Ruth plunged her hands deep into her coat pockets and shuddered. 'I ain't never known a pair like your mam an' dad. They're like a couple o' love birds. Not like mine.' She explained: 'Me dad were in the pub again last night after he finished his shift down the pit, an' me mam went fer him wi' the big umbrella when he finally came in.'

She chuckled as she slid her arm through her friend's. The two girls had gone all through school together, and although they were as close as could be, they were as different to look at as chalk from cheese. Ruth was short and dumpy, with wild mousy hair that tended to curl, and pale-blue eyes, whilst Briony was slim with straight hair that shone as black as a raven's wing. Ruth had always been envious of Briony's looks, not that it had affected their friendship. Briony often thought Ruth didn't have a nasty streak in her whole body and she wasn't far wrong. Ruth had a heart of pure gold and would have done anything for anyone, and Briony wondered how she was going to break it to her that Ernie was joining the RAF. Ruth had never made a secret of the fact that she adored Ernie and when they were younger she had followed him about like a puppy, which had complicated things when Briony suddenly realised that she had feelings for Ernie too.

They were almost at the top of Haunchwood Road when

Briony plucked up the courage to say bluntly, 'I heard that Ernie had enlisted too last night.' There didn't seem to be any easy way to say it so she decided to just get it over and done with.

Ruth stopped walking, and the ready smile she normally wore slid from her face as she asked hoarsely, 'You *are* kiddin', ain't yer?'

She looked so distraught that Briony felt a pang of guilt stab through her as she shook her head.

'Bloody hell!' The colour had drained out of Ruth's plump cheeks and Briony hugged her.

'I dare say he would have done it after his birthday anyway,' she said consolingly. 'He's just brought things forward a bit, that's all. But try not to worry; I'm sure he'll be fine. Before he left, my dad reckoned this war would be over before we knew it.'

Ruth swallowed deeply and nodded. 'Yes . . . course it will be,' she said, trying to be optimistic. Then: 'So when is he goin'?'

'In a couple of weeks, from what I could gather, but he'll have to complete his training before they send him off anywhere.'

They walked on into Tomkinson Road through the thick freezing fog, and for the rest of the way Ruth was very quiet.

The day passed slowly. In the accounts department, Briony was kept busy preparing everyone's wage packets and Ruth was almost rushed off her feet down on the shop floor. On the way home after work, Briony called into the corner shop in Cross Street and bought some vegetables before going on to the butcher's in Church Road, where she purchased some lamb chops. She doubted her mother would have bothered to cook for the children and had resigned herself to going home and cooking them a meal herself. The fog had lifted late that morning and now the frost was beginning to sparkle on the pavements again as she hurried through Stockingford. Everyone had closed the blackout curtains against the freezing night and Briony felt as if she were walking through a ghost town. Even the lamp-posts were no longer turned on now, and the odd car that crawled through the streets had its headlights dimmed. Ruth's mood hadn't lightened as the day progressed and now Briony just wished that this day could be over. It would be the first evening without her father's fond smile to welcome her after a long day at work, and she wasn't looking forward to it at all. Her spirits plunged even deeper once she stepped into their small terraced home to see Lois curled up in the chair at the side of a low fire still in her dressing gown. She clearly hadn't bothered to get dressed all day and her eyes were dull and swollen from weeping.

Sarah ran to meet her with a look of relief on her small face, saying, 'Mam hasn't stopped crying all day, Briony, but I got some coal in – look.'

'Good girl.' Briony stroked her sister's hair affectionately before she took her coat off and hung it on a nail at the back of the door. 'And have you and Alfie had any dinner?'

Sarah solemnly shook her head. 'Not yet, but I waited for Alfie after school and brought him home like you asked and I gave him some milk and a biscuit.'

'Then we'll have a nice warm cuppa, eh? And then I'll get the dinner started. While I'm doing that, you could help Alfie get into his pyjamas for me. I'll give him his wash later.'

Her brother was lying on his stomach looking at the pictures in his comic but he went willingly enough, and once the children were out of the way, Briony fixed a smile on her face and said brightly, 'I'm going to put the kettle on now, Mam. I've bought us some nice lamb chops for tea as a treat. We may as well enjoy them while we can. Once this rationing that they keep on about comes into force it might not be so easy to get hold of some things – and even when we can, we'll be limited in how much we can have.'

'I'm not hungry,' Lois said dully, and Briony felt a little stab of anger. Didn't her mother realise that they were all missing her father just as much as she was? Even so she kept her voice level as she turned to fill the kettle at the sink.

'Well, I still want you to eat something,' she answered firmly. 'You'll be no use to Sarah and Alfie if you get ill, will you?'

Receiving a sniffle as an answer she sighed inwardly and began to prepare the teapot and the mugs before starting on the vegetables. It looked set to be a very long evening.

By the end of the week, Briony was exhausted. Each day she would go off to work then each evening she would come home and see to the children and cook them all a meal. Then when that was done, she would tackle the washing and ironing whilst her mother sat curled in her chair, a mere shadow of her former self, locked in self-pity. Lois had always relied heavily on her handsome husband, and now that he was gone she didn't seem to be able to cope with anything.

It was Mrs Brindley who brought it all to a head one evening when she appeared at the kitchen door clutching a chipped cup.

Briony was up to her eyes in ironing the children's school clothes and she looked up as the woman entered the room.

''Ello, luvvie.' Mrs Brindley was dressed in her customary wrap-around flowered pinny. 'Yer couldn't lend me a bit o' sugar till in the mornin', could yer? I don't fancy goin' up the corner shop in this cold.' Then as her eyes settled on Lois she abruptly stopped talking and said, 'So what's this then? Why is young Briony doin' the ironin' when she's bin to work all day, Lois? Are you ill?'

'She's missing my dad,' Briony explained as her mother broke into a fresh torrent of weeping. Martha Brindley seemed to bristle before her very eyes.

'Is that so? Well, I'm missin' my Clal an' all, but it won't do no good to sit about weepin', will it? Then young Ernie will be off an' all soon, an' I'll be all on me own, not like you, Lois, who still have yer family about yer. Stop feelin' so bloody sorry fer yerself, woman, an' get up off yer arse, fer Christ's sake. You ain't bein' a bit fair on yer kids, especially young Briony 'ere.'

Lois was so shocked at being spoken to in such a manner that she stopped crying and stared at the older woman open-mouthed.

'That's better.' Mrs Brindley nodded approvingly. 'Now get yerself over to that sink an' wash yer face then go an' get yerself dressed, 'cos I'm tellin' yer now, I ain't goin' nowhere till yer do. Then when you've done that, yer can make us all a nice cup o' tea an' make yerself useful. Meantime I'll sit an' have a chat to young Briony 'ere.' And with that she plonked herself down in the chair opposite Lois and glowered at her until the woman stood up and hurried off to do as she was told.

Once Lois had washed her face and gone upstairs to get dressed, Briony smiled at Mrs Brindley gratefully.

'Thanks for that,' she said. 'I was beginning to get really worried about her, wondering if she was ever going to get out of that chair.'

'Hmm, trouble with yer mam is she's been spoiled,' Mrs Brindley said matter-of-factly. 'I reckon she had yer dad eatin' out o' the palm of her hand, waitin' on her hand an' foot. But he ain't here now so she's goin' to have to join the real world like the rest of us. Not that I don't like yer mam,' she added hurriedly, seeing Briony's face fall. 'It's obvious that she were brought up different to the likes of us.' She chuckled then. 'She's made many a head turn round 'ere, I don't mind tellin' yer, what wi' her lipstick an' her powder an' never a hair out o' place, but I reckon the majority o' the women are just jealous of her 'cos she's so attractive. Trouble is, yer dad's gone fer now, so she's goin' to have to pull her socks up an' look after them little 'uns – if they don't get evacuated, that is. Between you an' me I don't understand how she's managed to avoid it fer so long. But it certainly ain't right that you should have to come home an' do all this just 'cos you were the firstborn. You're still not much more than a slip of a kid yerself, even if yer have left school an' got yerself a job.'

She heaved herself out of the chair then and placed the kettle on the hob to boil. Soon afterwards, Lois reappeared dressed and looking slightly better than she had before.

'I didn't mean to bully yer, Lois,' Mrs Brindley apologised as Lois spooned tea leaves into the teapot. 'But sometimes, as me old mam allus used to say, yer have to be cruel to be kind. Now let's have that cup o' tea, shall we?'

Briony stared at her mother. Lois's eyes were still red and swollen, but at least she had stopped crying – which was a step in the right direction.

'Our Ernie'll be off next week,' Mrs Brindley glumly reminded them then, and Briony's heart missed a beat. It seemed that everyone she cared about was leaving – and there wasn't a single thing she could do about it.

Chapter Two

Much to Briony's surprise, soon after Mrs Brindley left that evening, Lois dragged in the tin bath that hung on a nail in the yard outside and began to heat up pans of water.

'I dare say I have let myself go a little,' she admitted reluctantly. 'And I'm sorry if I've put on you, darling. I know how hard you work, rushing about that office all day, and it's not fair that you've been coming home and having to see to all of us. But I will try harder in future, I promise. I'll make a start right now by washing my hair and having a bath. I shall be starting work at the shop on Monday and I don't suppose I can go in looking like this, can I?'

Briony's spirits lifted. 'I'll help you shampoo your hair,' she volunteered, flashing her mother a warm smile.

They filled the bath together and once Lois was soaking in the hot water and Briony had washed her hair for her, she sat down in the chair at the side of the fire, glad of a chance to rest her feet, which were throbbing nicely now.

It was a ritual they usually went through together on a Sunday evening, and Briony welcomed the feeling of things returning to some sort of normality.

After a while her mother glanced at her before saying quietly, 'I've got a feeling Mrs Brindley might have been right – about the children, I mean. I fear I won't be able to keep them here much longer. It said on the radio earlier today that Hitler is just waiting for the spring before he begins to bomb England. If that's true, it won't be safe for the kids to be here any more – but how will we bear it if they are sent away?'

Just the thought of Sarah and Alfie being whisked away to some unknown place filled Briony with dread, but not wishing to upset her mother again she answered sensibly, 'Well, from what I can gather from some of the ladies at work whose children have already been evacuated, they're doing fine. I suppose we won't have any choice in the matter. There isn't any other alternative, is there?'

'Actually . . . there is,' her mother said cautiously.

Briony blinked in surprise. 'Oh, and what's that then?'

Lois seemed to hesitate before saying, 'They could go and live with their grandparents in Cornwall until the war is over. I had a letter from my father today and he told me that you would all be welcome there.'

Briony's eyes almost popped out of her head. She hadn't even known that her mother's parents were still alive – so the information had come as a complete shock to her.

Lois sighed resignedly and, grabbing the towel that Briony had put ready for her, she hauled herself out of the tin bath while her daughter averted her eyes. After drying herself, Lois slipped on her dressing gown and sat down opposite her, a towel round her shoulders while her wet hair dried in the warmth from the fire.

'You are old enough to know the truth now,' Lois told the girl, and her eyes grew dreamy as her mind slipped back in time. 'I had a very privileged upbringing,' she began. 'My father has his own business – he's an undertaker in a town called Penzance – and I went to the finest schools and had the best clothes that money could buy. I'm afraid that Daddy always rather spoiled me. He's a wonderful, kind man but my mother . . .' She frowned. 'Well, Mother always made it crystal clear that my brother Sebastian was her favourite.' She smiled apologetically then as Briony looked taken aback, admitting, 'Yes, you have an uncle too. Our mother is a very strict woman and highly religious. We lived in a beautiful house with a cook and a maid. Obviously my parents both wanted the best for me and they expected me to make a good marriage – but then I met your father and needless to say, they weren't happy about me associating with him. They said he was a drifter and that he would never amount to anything, but the thing was, I loved him and I wouldn't listen.

Lois stood up and paced restlessly. She lit a cigarette and went on, 'Anyway, the long and the short of it is, eventually I became pregnant with you, and when they found out, Mother told me that I was to leave and never darken their door again. Your father and I ran away together in the dead of night with barely a penny between us, and eventually we ended up back here, in a part of the world he knew, and I had you. And I'll tell you something, Briony; I've never regretted it for a single second. Your father is a wonderful man, as you know, and although we have never been rich materially, I've been rich in other ways and I consider myself to be a very fortunate woman. It broke my heart to leave my father, and recently I wrote to him and asked him to help me. I knew it would be no good writing to Mother.

I explained that I now had three beautiful children and that I didn't want them to be sent to live with strangers, and he wrote back and said that of course you could all go there until the war was over.'

'But I'm too old to be sent away,' Briony objected. 'I'm almost seventeen and I'm working now.'

'I know, but you wouldn't want the younger ones to go alone, would you?' her mother answered cajolingly. 'At least if you were with them I'd know that my mother couldn't bully them. I won't be able to keep them here much longer. Most of the children hereabouts have already been evacuated and the school is working on a skeleton staff. Almost all the male teachers have joined up.'

Briony's mind was reeling as she tried to take it all in. It was a shock to discover that she had grandparents and an uncle that she had never known existed – let alone that she might now be expected to go and live with them. She had supposed that her grandparents were dead.

'But why didn't you tell me all this before?' she asked as things began to flash into her mind. The letters that had recently arrived and which her mother had hastily shoved into her pocket to open when she was alone. They must have been from her grandfather.

'Until now I didn't think you needed to know. And of course, it might not be for some time, if at all,' her mother hurried on, seeing her daughter's agitation. 'But if the Red Cross do call again, wanting to take the younger ones . . .' her voice trailed away. 'Just think about it and get used to the idea, eh?'

Briony could only nod numbly before she stumbled away to start emptying the dirty water out of the bath, trying to picture what these new members of the family might be like.

Later that night she lay under the bedclothes, her mind

working overtime, with Sarah's warm little body snuggled next to her. If she were to go and live in Cornwall, her life as she had known it would change completely. She would be sharing a house with strangers, even if they were her grandparents. But no doubt it wouldn't be forever. The war had to end sooner or later, and the thought of her young brother and sister going alone was unthinkable, especially if her grandmother was as strict as her mother had warned her. Eventually she drifted into an uneasy sleep, after deciding that she would worry about it if and when the time came.

Briony arrived home from work the following evening to find that her mother had made an attempt at cooking them all a meal.

'These taters have got lumps in,' Alfie whined as he pushed them about his plate.

'And my sausages are all red inside and black on the outside,' Sarah grimaced.

Lois glared at them. 'Oh, stop complaining,' she snapped. 'You know your father was a better cook than me, but it's better than going hungry, isn't it?'

'It's fine, Mum,' Briony said hurriedly, although her stomach was revolting at the stodgy mess in front of her. 'You just need to cook everything a little slower and for a bit longer tomorrow.'

Lois sniffed. 'I broke a nail while I was cooking all that as well,' she grumbled, staring down at her manicured hand as if it were the end of the world.

'Well, it will soon grow again. But now come on, kids; eat up while it's nice and hot.'

The children scowled but did as they were told, and once the meal was over Briony washed the dishes whilst her mother filed the offending nail and varnished it. Briony was pleased to note that Lois had curled her hair and put on powder and lipstick. Her eyes were still sad and she had lost some of her sparkle, but at least she was making an effort again – for which Briony was grateful.

They listened to Glenn Miller on the wireless after the dishes were all put away in their proper places, then Briony got the children washed and into their night things and took them up to bed.

'I'm going to pop next door and see Ernie for a bit, Mum,' she said when she came back downstairs and was surprised to see that Lois had fetched the sherry from the sideboard. It was usually kept for special occasions. Seeing the look on her daughter's face, Lois confided, 'I thought a drop of this might relax me. I haven't been sleeping properly.'

Briony didn't comment. After all, the way she saw it, if a drink could make her mother feel a little better – where was the harm in it?

Martha Brindley was standing at the sink washing the dinner pots when Briony tapped at her door and entered the kitchen. The woman smiled at her fondly. In her opinion, the poor girl had to do more than her fair share of housework and looking after her little sister and brother. That mother of hers was a right flighty piece – not that she wasn't pleasant, mind. Anyone would be hard pushed not to like Lois, but she was too vain by half from where Martha was standing, and that handsome husband of hers hadn't helped matters by pandering to her every whim. Still, he was off fighting now, so Martha hoped this might be the making of his wife. If there was no one there to wait on her hand and foot, apart from Briony, Lois would have to pull her finger out and learn to help herself, wouldn't she?

'If it's our Ernie you've come to see, he's just popped to the corner shop to get me ten Woodbine,' she told Briony, and saw the girl's face fall. 'But he shouldn't be long,' she added hastily. 'So why don't yer pour us both out a nice cuppa? I've just made a fresh pot and I've about done here now. I'll leave this lot to drain an' put 'em all away later.'

Briony obediently fetched some cups and saucers from the cupboard as Martha watched her from the corner of her eye. She had a sneaky suspicion that young Briony had a soft spot for her Ernie, and he made no secret of the fact that he fancied her – but up until now neither of them seemed to have done anything about it; no bad thing, in her opinion, now that he had been called up. Martha was a realist, and who knew what the future held for them? Up until recently she would have bet any money that young Ruth and Ernie would become an item eventually. After all, everyone knew that Ruth puppy-worshipped him. Martha liked Ruth; she was a gentle-natured lass and she wouldn't have minded at all having her for a daughter-in-law, but now it looked as if the feelings that were obviously developing between her son and Briony might throw a spanner in the works. But then from what she had learned, nothing ever went smoothly in life, so she was prepared to sit back and let nature take its course. What would be would be.

'So why the long face then?' she asked as she joined the girl at the table.

For a moment she thought Briony was going to ignore the question but then the girl blurted out, 'I've just found out from Mum that I have an uncle and grandparents living in Cornwall.'

'Really?' Mrs Brindley looked bemused as she scratched her chin. 'How come yer never knew about 'em before?'

'Because it seems they disowned Mum when she ran off to marry Dad, and she hasn't had anything to do with them since,' the girl answered solemnly. 'But now my grandfather has said that we – the grandchildren, that is – can go and stay with them until after the war rather than be evacuated.'

'And will yer be takin' him up on his offer?'

'Mum says we might have to, rather than let the younger ones go to strangers,' Briony told her. 'But I'm not too happy about it, to be honest. From what Mum's told me, our grandmother sounds like a bit of a tartar, and it will mean me giving up my job.'

'Hmm, I can see it would be a bit of a wrench for you,' Mrs Brindley agreed musingly. 'But then at least you'd all be safer there than here in the Midlands. Word is out that old Adolf could be droppin' bombs on us any time soon. It stands to reason, don't it, what wi' all the factories in Coventry that are makin' parts fer the tanks an' the aeroplanes. They'll be a prime target an' we're only a stone's throw away when all's said an' done, so no doubt we'll cop it an' all.'

'I suppose we would be safer,' Briony sighed. 'But how would Mum cope here all on her own?'

'She's a grown woman,' Mrs Brindley told her firmly as she spooned sugar into her tea. 'An' if push came to shove she'd have to manage same as the rest of us.'

'I dare say you're right.'

The door opened then, and Ernie rushed in, bringing a waft of icy air with him. 'Phew, it's bloody freezin' out there,' he grinned as his eyes settled on Briony. 'Is there any more tea in the pot? I could do wi' sommat to warm me up.' He tossed the cigarettes to his mother, who opened the packet and lit one.

'Young Briony here's just been tellin' me that she might be goin' away soon an' all,' she informed him through a cloud of smoke, and Briony then repeated her story as Ernie listened intently.

'Blimey,' he croaked when she had finished. 'An' yer say

yer mam's family are well-off. What do they do?'

'Apparently my grandfather has his own undertaking business.' Briony shuddered at the thought. It didn't seem like a very nice job to have to do, but then she supposed someone had to.

'Well, at least there's not much chance o' him ever goin' out o' business, is there?' Ernie quipped, hoping to raise a smile from her. She looked very glum and not at all excited to discover she had family she had never known about. There was another knock at the door then; it was Ruth, and the subject was closed as Ruth stared at Ernie from adoring eyes.

Mrs Brindley picked up her knitting and retired to her comfortable old chair by the fire, leaving the young people to it.

'Not long till you go now then?' Ruth said as she placed her gas mask on the table.

Ernie looked uncomfortable as he lowered his head and responded: 'No, not long at all – but then the war can't last forever, can it?' He was shocked to see that there were tears in her eyes and that she was blinking rapidly to stop them from falling. Briony noticed too and hastily rose from her seat as guilt shot through her. She knew how much Ruth cared for Ernie and wished that she could still look at him as merely a friend – but then it wasn't as if she'd ever intended to feel as she did, was it?

'I reckon I'll get off now,' she said quietly, trying to ignore the disappointment that had flared in Ernie's eyes. 'I've got to get my clothes ready for work tomorrow and check that Mum's got the children's outfits ironed too.'

'Shall I see you home?' Ernie scraped his chair back from the table but Briony shook her head and grinned.

'I hardly think you need to do that, seeing as I only live a few steps across the yard. No, you stay here and have a chat to Ruth, and I'll see you in the morning at the same time, shall I?' she asked her friend. Ruth nodded absently and snatching up her coat, Briony made a hasty retreat.

On entering her own kitchen again, she was dismayed to see that her mother had drunk almost half a bottle of sherry and looked a little bright-eyed.

'I'll have a tidy-up shall I?' she said, discreetly grabbing the bottle and shoving it hastily back into the cupboard. Then she got the ironing board out and began to press the children's school clothes. This was another job that her father had used to do each evening, and the thought of him standing there brought a lump to her throat. How could she blame her mother for feeling as she did, when she was missing him herself? Nothing seemed the same any more, and once Ernie was gone too she knew that she was going to feel even worse. Her thoughts returned then to the grandparents and the uncle she had never known about and now, without being able to stop herself, she blurted out, 'So tell me what my grandparents are like then, Mum. I know you said that Grandmother was strict – but what do they look like?'

Lois sighed. She had been expecting this, and now that Briony knew about them there was no point in trying to cover it up any more. 'Daddy was always smart,' she recalled. 'I suppose he had to be in the job he did. It was very rare not to see him in a suit and tie, apart from weekends. And even then he would rush away and get changed if there was a family who had suffered a bereavement. With his job, you were never really off duty. Mummy used to get quite angry with him sometimes when he was called away, especially if they were in the middle of entertaining guests. Death can strike at any time so Daddy was always on call, so to speak. He was a very tall, handsome man with brown wavy hair and lovely twinkling blue eyes.' Her lips twitched into a smile as she thought back in time. 'Often after school, if he wasn't busy, he would take my brother and me down to the beach and we would paddle in the sea and make sandcastles. He always made time for me, whereas Mummy believed that children should be seen and not heard, although she was much more relaxed with Seb, my brother. He could never do any wrong in her eyes and she made no secret of the fact that he was her favourite. He is three years younger than me, and from the day he was born she doted on him. We had a nanny who would bath me, but Mummy always insisted on bathing Seb herself.'

'You had a *nanny?*' Briony gasped incredulously, and Lois grinned.

'Oh yes, and the gardener-cum-handyman used to take us both to school each day in the pony and trap until Seb was old enough to go away to boarding school. Mummy was determined that he should have the best education possible.'

'Did you get sent away to boarding school too?'

Lois shook her head. 'No, although Daddy did put me into a private one, much to Mummy's disgust. She believed that girls didn't need an education and that he was wasting his money, but Daddy put his foot down on that score on one of the very rare occasions that I can remember and told her that I deserved a decent education too.'

'What does Grandmother look like?' Briony asked next.

'She looked a lot like me when she was younger,' Lois said thoughtfully. 'But Seb looked like Daddy, the same colouring and build. Mummy was beautiful, and sometimes when she came into the nursery to kiss us goodnight before an evening out with Daddy, I used to think she looked like a princess. She always smelled wonderful too. Daddy would buy her these lovely French perfumes that lingered in the room long after she had left. I dread to think what they must have cost him, but what Mummy wanted, she had. I don't think Daddy could ever say no to her. He was totally besotted with her, which was no wonder really as she was incredibly pretty. I dare say she still is.'

Briony was bemused. Whenever she had tried to imagine what her grandparents might have been like, she always thought of elderly, jolly people, nothing at all like the ones her mother was describing now. On occasions she had visited Ruth's grandparents with her in Priory Street. They were both elderly with a ready smile and a little treat and a hug for any of the family that came to visit them, and they sounded a world apart from these people. But perhaps her grandmother wasn't as bad as Lois was painting her? Perhaps Lois was just embittered because of the way her mother had turned her back on her when she met James Valentine?

'And my uncle?' she dared to ask.

Lois chuckled. 'What can I say about Seb?' she shrugged. 'He was spoiled rotten from the second he drew breath, and he soon learned how to make the most of it. He could wrap Mummy around his little finger, although Daddy did try to rein him in a little. When he finally got kicked out of the last boarding school he attended, Daddy set him on in the family business. Seb was not amused, I don't mind telling you, but I think Daddy gave him an ultimatum – either he knuckled down and learned the trade or he made his own way in the world. He had no qualifications and had failed all his exams, so needless to say he reluctantly did as he was told, although it was obvious he wasn't happy about it. I think he had every girl in the county drooling after him, and to say he was a bit of a Casanova would be putting it mildly. Seb could have charmed the birds off the trees, and I often wonder if he's settled down with anyone yet.'

Briony's head was spinning. There was so much to think about and she was glad when she could finally say goodnight to her mother and sidle off to bed, cuddling up to Sarah's warm little body for comfort as she tried to get her head around it all.

Chapter Three

It was the middle of the following week when Briony returned home from work one evening to find the house in chaos. The fire was almost out and the minute she stepped through the door the children complained that they were hungry.

'All right, all right, give me a chance to get in!' Briony sighed wearily as she took her coat off and hurried across to the fire, only to find that the coal scuttle was empty.

'I shall have to go out to the coalhouse,' she said irritably, snatching up the old beaten-copper coal scuttle. 'But where's Mum?'

'She went straight to bed once she'd fetched me from school. She said she had a headache,' Alfie informed her, glancing up from the *Beano*.

'Oh.' Lois had started her part-time job at the corner shop now, although she always finished in time to fetch Alfie from school. Briony had hoped that getting out would perk her up a little, but it didn't seem to have done much good. In fact, the house had slowly gone downhill, which only reinforced just how much their father had done for them.

Sarah was playing with her dolls on the hearthrug and Briony told her, 'Start to peel some potatoes, would you, Sarah, there's a good girl. I've got us some mince from the butcher's on the way home so I'll cook us a cottage pie when I've got the fire going again.'

It was over an hour later before Lois chose to put in an appearance. She was looking decidedly ill and dishevelled. Briony had the horrible feeling that her mother had been drinking again, but she forced a smile to her face as she asked brightly, 'Did we have any post today, Mum?'

'Only the normal pamphlets and leaflets,' Lois grumbled. 'If I saved them all we could keep the fire going for a week at least. One telling us to make do and mend, another telling us we should be putting tape across the windows. Can you imagine how unattractive that would look? Like spider webs!'

'Well, I've noticed that most people around here have already done it,' Briony responded. 'It's to stop the glass from flying into the room if we should have any bombs dropped nearby.'

'I know what it's for!' Lois said more sharply than she had intended and then she instantly felt guilty. The smell of the cottage pie and the vegetables Briony was cooking were wafting appetizingly around the room and she knew that she herself should have prepared the meal. But then the girl didn't seem to mind coming in from work and cooking, and she was so much better at it than Lois was.

'Mrs Brindley was saying earlier on when she popped into the shop that Ernie is going away to train this Thursday,' she told Briony then, and even though the girl had been expecting it, her heart fluttered.

'Did she say where he would be going?'

'I think she mentioned somewhere in Surrey,' Lois answered distractedly as she studied her hands. 'I have to say, this job at the shop is causing havoc with my nails. I broke another one today weighing potatoes for Mrs Miller, and my feet feel as if they're going to drop off.'

Briony was saved from having to answer when Sarah had a bout of coughing that shook her frail frame.

'I think perhaps you ought to be getting her to the doctor's,' she suggested. 'That cough is hanging on a bit too long for my liking.'

'Oh, you know Sarah always suffers with her chest in the winter,' her mother answered nonchalantly. 'I'll pick her up a bottle of cough medicine from the chemist's tomorrow and that should do the trick.'

Briony pursed her lips and frowned but she didn't bother to argue. As her mother had said, Sarah did seem to catch one thing after another each winter, but from now on she would be keeping an eye on her: if she hadn't improved by next week, Briony would take a couple of hours off work and take her sister to the doctor's herself.

When all the chores were finally done and the children were settled in bed with hot-water bottles, Briony slipped next door to say her goodbyes to Ernie. She found his mother in the process of packing a kitbag for him.

'Would you please explain to her that I don't need to take much?' he implored Briony. 'Soon as ever I get there I'll be issued with a uniform so I won't need any civvy clothes; just a couple o' changes of underwear an' some socks will be plenty.'

Martha waved her hand at him dismissively. 'I still say as

yer should take this nice warm pullover I've knitted yer for Christmas. Yer barracks could be freezin' fer all you know and happen then you'll be glad of it, come night-time.'

'Oh yes, an' what sort of a pansy will I look to the other chaps if I stick that on over me jim-jams?' he teased her.

'He does have a point,' Briony commented and Mrs Brindley sighed as she took the offending articles out of his bag again.

'Well, don't go complainin' to me then if yer get cold,' she grumbled, but despite her harsh words Briony could see how distressing this was for her. Once Ernie was gone, the poor woman would be completely alone and Briony felt for her. At least *she* still had her mother – for what use she was – and her brother and sister.

'Have you been to say goodbye to Ruth?' Briony asked as Ernie pushed a washbag containing his razor and a few toiletries across the table to his mother.

He paused to look at her before asking, 'Do you think I should?'

Briony nodded. 'Yes, I do. She'll be gutted if you go without so much as a by your leave.'

'In that case then I'll pop along as soon as this bit o' packin' is done. Do yer fancy coming with me?'

Briony nodded and ten minutes later they set off. However, they had gone no more than a few yards down the darkened street when they spotted Ruth hurrying towards them.

'Is it true what I've heard – that you're leavin' tomorrow, Ernie?' she gasped breathlessly and he nodded.

'Yes, it is. Matter o' fact, I was just comin' to say goodbye to yer,' he answered awkwardly. News travels fast in this neck of the woods, he thought to himself, trying not to see the misery on Ruth's face. She was wringing her hands together and even in the darkness he thought he could see tears sparkling on her lashes.

'Then in that case let's pop down to the Prince an' I'll stand you a drink,' she offered with a wobbly smile.

'I won't refuse an offer like that,' Ernie told her with a grin, and positioning himself between the two girls he linked his arms through theirs and they hurried along the chilly streets until the pub came into view.

Once inside, Ruth nervously approached the bar where she ordered a pint for Ernie and a shandy for herself and Briony, then she carried their drinks to the table. There were few in the pub apart from a handful of older regulars and they managed to find a table right beside the fire that roared up the grate.

'Phew, that hit the spot all right,' Ernie said after taking a long swallow of his beer. 'Best make the most of it, eh? Who knows how long it'll be before I get another.'

'You'll miss seeing Marlene Dietrich in *The Blue Angel* with us at the Scala on Friday an' all,' Ruth muttered, and then to Ernie's horror she promptly burst into tears.

Deeply embarrassed, he patted her hand before passing her a somewhat grubby handkerchief. 'Never mind,' he mumbled. 'There'll be lots of other pictures for us all to go an' see, once this war is over.'

'Y-yes, there probably will be, but how far away will that be?' she sniffed.

Ernie shrugged. 'No one knows the answer to that question at present, but what I do know is I have to go an' do my bit. Look how the war has affected our town already. There are shelters poppin' up like mushrooms in people's back gardens. There's sandbags all along the front of the shops in town, an' people are goin' mad, buyin' food before the strict rationin' comes in.'

'But nothing has happened here yet, has it?' Ruth argued. 'What I mean is, *we* ain't been bombed or anythin'. In fact, me dad reckons the folks hereabouts are callin' it the phoney war, an' some o' the kids that were evacuated earlier in the year are already tricklin' back.'

'Then yer dad ain't been readin' the same newspapers as me,' Ernie said, his lips set in a grim line. 'We ain't had much goin' on here yet admittedly, but not everyone has been so lucky. Only today I read that the Germans have been droppin' bombs on the Thames Estuary, and the paper was full o' pictures o' Jewish children arrivin' in London on Kindertransport trains from their homelands, poor little sods. No, by hook or by crook, this devil Hitler has got to be stopped in his tracks – an' I'll be doin' my bit to make sure as that happens.'

Despite her fears for his safety, Briony felt a measure of pride pulse through her as she listened to Ernie's words. He was very brave, and now all she could do was pray that he would survive the war and come back to them safe and sound.

Ruth reached out and gripped his hand, and suddenly feeling in the way, Briony rose hastily. 'I'd best get home and check on Mum and the kids,' she said with a lump in her throat, and although Ernie raised his eyebrows, she avoided looking at him and addressed Ruth, saying, 'I'll see you in the morning, eh?' And with that she was off, leaving them to it.

The door had no sooner closed behind Briony when Ruth's grip on Ernie's hand tightened and she gulped deep in her throat. It was now or never, so taking a deep breath she said tentatively, 'You must know how I feel about you, Ernie? What I should say is . . . I've cared about yer for as long as I can remember – and not just as a friend.' Noting his bemused expression, she rushed on, 'What I'm trying to say is, if you wanted me to be your girl, I'd wait for you . . . for as long as it took.'

Ernie squirmed uncomfortably in his seat. It seemed that Briony's suspicions had been right, but whilst he thought of Ruth as a dear friend, he had never considered her as anything else. The problem was, now, how could he get out of this without hurting her feelings?

Gently disentangling his hand from hers he smiled at her kindly before saying, 'That's a right nice thing for yer to say, Ruth. But to be honest, even if I were thinkin' of courtin' anyone, I don't feel now would be the right time to start. Who knows how long this war could go on for, and even if I'll ever come home? It wouldn't be fair of me to expect anyone to wait for me under these conditions. It could go on for years and people's feelings can change in that time, so let's just leave things as they are, eh? Good mates . . . for always.'

Swallowing her disappointment, Ruth nodded. She knew that her feelings for Ernie would never change, but she didn't want to put him under pressure. He would have enough of that in the days and possibly years ahead.

'All right then – but will you write to me?'

'Of course I will, when I'm able to,' he assured her. Then quickly draining his glass, he rose and asked, 'Would yer like me to see yer home?'

'Yes, please.' Ruth would have traded years of her life just for a few more moments with him but she followed him quietly and soon they were outside again and hastening through the bitterly cold streets.

It was almost two hours later, as Briony was damping down the fire for the night, that a tap came at the back door. When she opened it, she found Ernie standing on the doorstep.

'Come in,' she said, closing the door behind him. Then, feeling more than a little self-conscious, she said, 'You got Ruth safely home then?'

'Yes, I did – but why did you have to go scuttling off like that?' he answered irritably. He had found the whole incident with Ruth professing her feelings for him rather embarrassing.

'I thought you two needed a little time alone,' she replied. Her mother had gone to bed a while ago and now there was nothing to be heard but the sound of the clock ticking on the mantelpiece and the coals settling in the grate. In fact, had he come just a few minutes later she would have been in bed herself, and she wondered if that wouldn't have been better all round. After all, Ruth was her best friend – so how could she admit to Ernie that she had feelings for him herself? It would be a betrayal of Ruth.

Ernie sighed, then reaching out he took her hand. 'I couldn't go without saying goodbye properly,' he said, and the touch of his fingers caused colour to flame into her cheeks.

'Well, you know we will all be thinking of you, so take care of yourself, won't you?' The words sounded inadequate even to her own ears, but what else could she say?

'I'll do me best, but I'd leave happier knowin' that you were back here waitin' fer me,' he answered, then before she could say anything he rushed on, 'Ruth said almost the same words to me when you left us earlier on but I had to put her straight. I don't have those sort o' feelings for Ruth – but I do for you, Briony, so what do you say? Will you be my girl? I know I've left it a bit late in the day to ask, but it would mean the world to me to know that you cared.'

'I *do* care, Ernie. You are a very dear friend,' she said

cautiously. 'But the thing is, I could get shipped off to Cornwall at any time with the children if Mum decides it isn't safe for them to be here any more. And knowing how Ruth feels about you, it would be like betraying her if I agreed to be your girl. Can you even begin to understand how she would feel? And so, I have to say it's best if we stay just as friends for now. Who knows what the future has in store for both of us? But that doesn't mean that I won't think about you and worry about you, so take care – please.'

He was shocked at the irony of it. Briony was saying almost the identical words that he had said to Ruth not so long ago.

She saw his shoulders slump but held herself together, knowing that she was doing the right thing. Up until now, she, Ernie and Ruth had been like the Three Musketeers and it was better if things stayed that way as far as she was concerned.

Seeing the determined set of her chin, Ernie stayed silent. Briony could be as stubborn as a mule at times, as he had learned over the years, and he guessed that anything he said now was not going to sway her decision. And so he leaned forward, kissed her gently on the lips and whispered, 'Stay safe,' before going home and leaving her to dissolve into tears.

Chapter Four

It was the first week in December, and as the double-decker bus swayed towards the town centre, Ruth pointed out of the window.

'Can't see what good that's supposed to do in the pitch-dark,' she said glumly, staring from the upper deck at the workmen who were busily painting white lines along the edges of the pavements and around the postboxes and phone boxes.

'It's supposed to stop you slipping off the edge and falling onto the road, or stop you from bumping into them in the blackout,' Briony answered.

'Well, I know that, don't I? But like I said, what good will they be in the bloody dark?' Ruth grumped.

It was now two weeks since Ernie had left for his training and a week since the girls had been taking the bus to work. It was so cold now that they couldn't face the long trek into town on foot. Ruth had barely smiled since Ernie's departure, and Briony hadn't been able to tempt her to their monthly night out at the pictures.

Things weren't much better at home either, for Briony was getting increasingly concerned about her mother's drinking – not that she was able to do much about it. Only the night before, she had found an empty sherry bottle in the dustbin and another one under the sink behind the cleaning materials, but she hadn't said anything. It seemed to be the only thing that was keeping her mother going, and at least she wasn't bursting into tears at the drop of a hat any more, which was something to be thankful for at least. Briony was more concerned about Sarah than anyone else at present. The child's cough had worsened to the point that the week before, Briony had finished work early one afternoon and taken her to the doctor, who had informed her that Sarah now had whooping cough. This, of course, meant that the little girl could not attend school, and with both herself and her mother working now it presented a problem. Thankfully, Mrs Brindley had stepped in and offered to care for the child whilst Lois was at the shop. Secretly, Briony had felt that Mrs Brindley would take better care of her little sister than her mother did, and she was very grateful for the kindly neighbour's help. However, all the extra work was finally catching up on her, and over the last week, Mr Trimble, the office manager, had chastised her on several occasions.

'Miss Valentine,' he had said sternly only the afternoon before, as he returned a letter that was full of mistakes. 'Could you type this again, please, and *try* to keep your mind on what you are supposed to be doing! This really isn't good enough.'

Briony knew that she had deserved the reprimand but she was so tired that she could barely think straight. Her day began at six thirty each morning when she would get the children up and make them their breakfast before getting them ready for school, and then it would be a mad dash to get herself ready for work before she raced off to catch the bus and face a busy day at the office. After work she would rush home and start the dinner before tackling the housework and the washing and ironing – and by the time she tumbled into bed each night she was so exhausted that she would be asleep before her head hit the pillow.

But at least today is Friday, she thought to herself as the bus trundled along, and I don't have to get up for work in the morning, unlike Ruth, who was expected to work almost every Saturday. But then Ruth's job on the shop floor did have its perks. Lately she had been stocking up on lipsticks and other cosmetics, and being the kindly soul that she was, she was always happy to share them with Briony.

'I reckon they'll be harder to get soon,' she confided to her friend one day. 'And as for the food part of the shop – phew! Yer wouldn't believe how people are stockin' up on tinned stuff. At the rate we're goin' there'll be nothin' left fer Christmas – but then I suppose yer can't blame 'em, can yer?'

The bus continued along Tomkinson Road until it was forced to stop behind a lorry to allow some workmen to unload a cargo of great corrugated sheets; these would soon form the roofs of Anderson shelters in the yards of the rows of terraced houses they were passing. The sheets glinted dully in the early-morning light and made enough racket to waken the dead as the men threw them down onto the pavements.

Ruth sighed impatiently. 'I hope they get a move on else we'll be late for work,' she fretted and Briony could only nod in agreement. She was already in Mr Trimble's bad books and didn't wish to add poor time-keeping to her list of crimes.

Thankfully they made it just in time and Briony tried to concentrate on the work piled up on her desk. Friday was one of the busiest days of the week because she was in charge of handing all the employees their wage packets as they came to the office to collect them. At last it was six o'clock and with a weary sigh she placed the cover over her typewriter and went to fetch her coat from the staff cloakroom. Ruth was already there, and she stared at Briony and frowned.

'Are you feelin' all right, gel?' she asked. 'You've got bags under yer eyes that I could do me shoppin' in.'

'Oh, I'm just a bit tired,' Briony assured her, flicking her jet-black hair across her shoulder. 'But I'll get to have a bit of a lie-in in the morning, so that's something to look forward to.'

'Huh! Yer lucky bugger,' Ruth muttered as she wrapped her scarf around her neck. 'Wish I could say the same. But now, are we walkin' home or should we push the boat out an' catch the bus?'

'I reckon we'll get the bus.' Briony yawned, and arm in arm they set off for the bus station.

They parted at the end of Church Road to go their separate ways and as Briony trudged down the entry leading to her back door, she wondered what she would be arriving home to today. A peal of laughter reached her as she entered the yard, and she gasped with delight when she went in and saw her father standing at the stove flicking bacon in a pan and looking breathtakingly handsome in his Army uniform.

'DAD!' She flew to him and he wrapped her in his strong arms and kissed the top of her head.

'Hello, sweetheart. How's my girl?'

'B-but what are you doing here?'

'Well, if it upsets you I could always go away again,' he responded with a twinkle in his eye.

'Oh no,' she answered hastily. 'It was just such a surprise to see you.'

'We weren't told we would be getting a few days' leave till last night,' he explained, turning his attention back to the stove. It wouldn't do to let the dinner burn. Briony glanced towards her mother, who was grinning like a Cheshire cat.

'Isn't it just wonderful?' Lois said. Then she pouted and went on, 'But he has to go back in four days' time.'

'Never mind, we shall have to make the most of every second,' Briony responded brightly. And that's just what they did.

The next morning, it was her father who got the children up and prepared their breakfasts for them, and it began to feel like old times.

'I know it's a bit early but I thought we could catch the bus into town this morning and get a Christmas tree,' he suggested as he helped the younger two to get dressed. Sarah and Alfie hooted with delight, but unfortunately Briony knew that Sarah was nowhere near well enough to venture out into the freezing weather just yet.

'I think the cold would start her coughing again,' she told her father. 'But don't worry. I can stay here with her and while you're all gone, Sarah and I can get the box of baubles down from the attic, ready for when you bring the tree home. Then you can help me decorate it, can't you, Sarah?'

The little girl was disappointed at not being able to go with the rest of the family, but the thought of being allowed to help put the baubles and the lights on the tree mollified her a little so she nodded in agreement.

*

It was mid-afternoon and already getting dark by the time the family returned, with Alfie nearly leaping with excitement as his father dragged the tree into the kitchen.

'We got a smashin' tree,' he told Briony. 'An' look,' he showed her a twist of brown paper clutched in his small palm, 'Dad got us all a quarter o' sweets each. He got liquorice twists fer Sarah, 'cos they're her favourites an' we got pear drops fer you. Yer like them, don't yer? An' I had gobstoppers.'

Her father winked at Briony as he disappeared back out into the yard to find a bucket to stand the tree in.

'Then aren't we the lucky ones?' Briony smiled indulgently as she reached for the kettle, which was whistling its head off. She had guessed that her mum and dad would be ready for a hot drink when they got home and she wasn't far wrong. It seemed that Lois didn't need anything stronger than tea to keep her happy while she had her husband at her side, and Briony thought how sad that was. It just went to show how much she missed him.

Once her father had returned with a sturdy bucket full of earth, Briony quickly drew the blackout curtain across the windows and the next hour was happily spent dressing the tree while James Valentine cooked the evening meal. He had bought some sausages in the market and they all sat down to a steaming plateful of sausage and mash each.

'Cor! That were lovely,' Alfie declared as he rubbed his full stomach once he had cleared his plate. Even Sarah had made an effort to eat something this evening, for which Briony was thankful. The little girl was so frail now that she looked as if one good puff of wind would blow her away. Briony knew that her father was worried about her, but as they were washing the dirty pots together she tried to reassure him.

'Don't worry. I try to make sure that she eats,' she told him.

'You're a good girl, Briony,' he smiled. 'I really don't know what we'd all do without you.'

Briony glanced into the little sitting room where her mother was reading a story from a book James had bought the children from the market, and lowering her voice she said, 'Mum told me about our grandparents in Cornwall.'

'Did she now? Well, you had to know about them sometime,' he answered.

'Mum says that our grandfather has said that if things get bad, we can go and stay with them,' she added.

'I know, she told me.' James grappled with his feelings. Truthfully, he had no love for Lois's parents after the way they had treated her, but he knew that he would rather his children were somewhere safe if things became too dangerous, so he would just have to bite his tongue. 'And how do you feel about that?'

Briony sniffed. 'I feel I'm too old to be evacuated,' she admitted. 'And I would have to give my job up. But then I don't like the thought of the two little ones having to go away on their own. Especially Sarah. She needs someone who knows her to look out for her . . . but what are our grandparents like? Mum won't say too much about them when I've asked her anything.'

Checking to make sure they couldn't be overheard, his hands became still in the soapy water, and lowering his voice James confided, 'Actually, I rather liked your grandfather. He was a gentleman and he gave me work in the grounds of the house when I first landed there. It was more your grandmother that was the problem. She's a bit of a tartar, to be honest, and your grandfather is rather under the thumb if you know what I mean? She ruled him with a rod of iron from what I could see of it, and he was so besotted with her that he allowed it. There wasn't a problem until I became involved with your mum, and then the trouble started and she made him sack me. I wasn't good enough for her daughter, you see.' He grinned ruefully as the memories flooded back. 'Between you and me, your mum is a lot like her in some ways. She likes to be waited on and looked after, but I put that down to her upbringing. She was used to having servants do everything, and it was a bit of a shock when we first got married and she had to learn to do a few things for herself.' He chuckled. 'I don't think your mum had ever cooked a meal or lifted an iron in her entire life, and we had many burnt offerings and scorched shirts in the early days, but she did try.' He became serious then. 'I know she leaves you to do more than you should, lass, but it isn't because she doesn't love you – she does, I promise you. She adores all of you.'

'I know that,' Briony answered. 'And I don't mind helping out, really I don't. But I'll be glad when the war is over and you can come home. Mum is no good without you.' She briefly wondered if she should mention that Lois had taken to drinking to drown her loneliness and heartache, but then thought better of it. Her dad had enough to worry about as it was and she didn't want to make things worse for him.

'And what about Mum's brother, Sebastian – what is he like?'

James's face darkened as he slapped another dirty plate into the water, sending a shower of suds onto the wooden draining board.

'I never got on with him from day one,' he said tersely. 'And if you do end up going there, I'd suggest you keep your distance. There was something about him that I just couldn't take to, although he could do no wrong in your grandmother's eyes. She thought the sun rose and set with him. On the few occasions when our paths did cross he talked to me like I was something dirty stuck to the sole of his shoe – but then he thought he was a cut above everyone, from what I could see of it.'

'Oh, I see.' Briony didn't like the sound of this uncle at all.

Seeing that he'd worried her, James added hastily, 'Of course, this was all a very long time ago. He will probably have changed and settled down by now, so don't get worrying about it.'

She managed a weak smile whilst silently praying that she would never have to meet any of them. They went on to speak of the camp where her father had been training.

'It's hard work,' he said, 'especially the physical training, and you get shouted at as if you're still at school, but it's nothing I can't cope with. The accommodation leaves a lot to be desired as well. It's certainly not the Ritz. We sleep in Nissen huts and they're freezing for most of the time but then we're all in the same boat and you learn to just get on with it.'

Briony thought how brave her father was, but then he had always been her hero.

'Do you think there will be an invasion?' she asked.

He hesitated before answering. The last thing he wanted to do was frighten her. She had more than enough on her plate at present, but then he didn't want to lie to her either so eventually he said, 'Hopefully not – but we have to be prepared for one, just in case. Up to now we've missed the bombing, but I have a horrible feeling that we might cop it eventually because of the local munitions factories. They're always going to be a target – and if that does happen then I would sooner you lot were away from here.'

The thought was terrifying but Briony plastered on a smile. She was truly her father's daughter in every way.

On Sunday James cooked them all a wonderful roast-lamb dinner and Briony wished that time could stand still. Her whole family looked so happy – even Sarah seemed to have perked up considerably – and her mum was positively glowing. As she cleared the table after the meal she tried not to think of what it would be like when her father left again. Once the dishes were washed and put away, Mrs Brindley watched Sarah for them while the others all went for a long walk. They took the tow path from the Cock and Bear Bridge and walked along the canal for miles, and by the time they returned their cheeks were glowing and Alfie was hungry again.

'I swear that lad has hollow legs,' James commented as he prepared a pile of meat-paste sandwiches and hot buttered crumpets. They were one of the little boy's favourites and he tucked in as if he hadn't eaten for a month. It was nice to see him smile again. Many of his friends had been evacuated and he had been feeling miserable, but having his father home again, if only for a short time, had acted like a tonic on him.

'I saw Mrs Moreton on Friday on me way home from school,' he informed them, spraying crumbs all over the fringed chenille cloth. 'An' she reckons that she'll be fetchin' their Jimmy home again soon 'cos they're sayin' this is only a phoney war. She says she wishes she hadn't let him go an' be 'vacuated now. If that's true, you'll be home for good soon, won't yer, Dad? An' we won't have to keep cartin' our gas masks an' our identity cards round with us then, will we?'

A silence settled around the table as they all looked at James expectantly.

'Well, I'm afraid I can't rightly say, son,' he said quietly. 'But let's all hope that she's right, eh?'

Chapter Five

All too soon, it was almost time for Briony's father to return to his unit and as she made her way home from work that Monday evening, Briony's heart was heavy. A freezing fog had descended during the afternoon and it was impossible to see more than a few yards from the window of the bus.

'Cheer up, mate, it might never happen,' Ruth prompted.

'Huh! You're a right one to talk,' Briony responded. 'You've had a face like a wet weekend on you ever since Ernie went away.'

'I suppose I have.' Ruth sighed and blew on her cold hands. 'But I don't half miss him, don't you?'

'I suppose I do.' Briony said carefully. It wouldn't do to let Ruth know that she too had developed feelings for Ernie that went beyond friendship. 'But we're all having to get used to saying goodbye to people we care about because of this damn war.'

The bus swayed to a stop then and the girls clambered

down the steep metal staircase and hopped off into the chilly evening air.

'Right then, I'll see yer in the mornin',' Ruth shouted as she set off for home, and waved as the two girls went their separate ways.

The kitchen was bright and cheery when Briony entered a few moments later and an appetising smell hung on the air.

'Hello, love, I thought I'd do us all a nice chicken dinner seeing as it's my last night home for a while,' her father greeted her as Briony tugged her outer clothes off. There was a fire roaring up the chimney and she noticed that the clothes-horse was heaving with freshly ironed clothes, placed by the fire to air. Her dad had obviously been busy. The lights on the Christmas tree were twinkling and the two younger children were happily engaged in doing a jigsaw on the hearthrug. Lois looked immaculate, her hair freshly waved following a trip to her favourite hairdresser's that afternoon and there was a broad smile on her face as she watched her husband adoringly. Lois loved looking her best and Archie Carmen, her hairdresser, always ensured that she did. James would often tease her about going all the way down to Coton Road when there were other salons so much closer, but Lois insisted that none of them could hold a candle to Archie. 'Why do you think all the local businessmen's wives go to him?' she would say. 'It's because he's the best, of course.'

James was greatly amused by Archie, who was a well-known local figure and something of a curiosity to the townsfolk as he was the only man they knew who dared to walk out wearing make-up. He could often be seen strolling about the market with his rouged cheeks and his brass-topped walking stick, with not a whisker of his waxed moustache out of place. He was a dapper little man, but as James had found out long ago, his customers adored him pandering to them and he had long since accepted that Lois would go to no one else, even if Archie was considerably more expensive than the rest.

A large bowl of holly with shiny red berries was placed in the centre of the table and Briony glanced at it admiringly.

'Me and Alfie got that when I went to collect him from school this afternoon,' her dad informed her, and once again Briony's heart ached as she thought of him going away again. Lois was thinking much the same thing as she looked fondly at her family. She was under no illusions and knew that she wasn't always the best wife and mother. Sometimes she thought she had never been cut out to perform domestic duties but she did do her best and she loved them all dearly.

In no time at all they were enjoying the tasty meal that James had cooked, and even little Sarah did it justice tonight. Her cough finally seemed to be easing and there was a little colour back in her cheeks, but Briony had a sneaky suspicion that this was down to the fact that her dad was home. His presence had done her far more good than any of the medicine that the doctor had prescribed, and Briony just prayed that she would continue to improve even when he had gone again.

Once the meal was over, Briony helped her father to wash and dry the dishes and he told her quietly, 'I heard on the wireless this evening that HMS *Nelson* was struck by a mine off the coast of Scotland today.' He shook his head sadly. 'Between you and me, I think things are going to really hot up now. Rumour has it that Hitler is only waiting for the milder weather before he begins his raids. If that happens I want you to promise me that you'll get the children away to Cornwall to your grandparents, Briony.'

'I will, Dad,' she said sombrely, as she didn't relish the thought of going there one little bit.

They all settled down to a game of snakes and ladders, which Alfie cheated at abominably until it was time for the younger ones to go to bed.

'What time are you going tomorrow, Daddy?' Sarah asked with a catch in her voice and James kissed her forehead tenderly as he tucked the blankets beneath her chin.

'Oh, now don't you get worrying about that,' he soothed. 'You just be a good girl for your mummy and remember that I'll be home soon.'

Briony felt a huge lump form in her throat and scuttled away to the warmth of the little sitting room. James was subdued when he came back downstairs, and sensing that her parents would value a little time alone she told them, 'I think I might get an early night too. Night, Mum. Night, Dad.'

'Night, pet.' Her father hugged her soundly then tipped her chin to stare into the eyes that were so like his own. 'You take care now,' he said. 'And remember that I love you and I'll be thinking of you all, every single minute.'

Too full to speak, Briony could only nod as she hurried away up the steep narrow staircase.

A sound woke her early the next morning and she lay disorientated for a moment in the pitch darkness. Then she realised it was muffled sobbing, coming from below. Getting up and feeling her way to the door, she went downstairs. The sight of her mum crying uncontrollably met her when she opened the door leading into the little kitchen-cum-sitting room. Hurrying across, she placed an arm about her shaking shoulders and asked, 'What's wrong, Mum?'

Lois waved a sheet of paper at her as she rocked to and fro in the chair. 'It's your dad – he's gone,' she sobbed. 'He says in the note that it would have been too painful and upsetting to have to say goodbye to everyone again, so he slipped away whilst we were all asleep.'

Somehow Briony was not surprised. She had sensed that her father was saying goodbye to her the night before when she retired to bed, and it was just like him to try and save them any more heartache.

'He left a little note for you too,' her mother told her, passing over a small envelope with her name written on the front of it.

Briony quickly tore it open and began to read;

Dear Briony,

I'm sorry to take the coward's way out, but I just couldn't face seeing you all getting upset again. I know you will keep an eye out for the children and your mum for me, and if you look in the sideboard in the front room you will find I have left a little gift for each of you, to be opened on Christmas Day. Will you see that everyone gets them for me? God knows where I will be by then, but you can rest assured that I will be thinking of you all and that I will be with you in spirit. Let's pray that this will be the one and only Christmas that we will ever have to be apart.

Take care of yourself, my special girl, and know that I love you.

Dad xxxxxxxxxx

Briony swallowed deeply and blinked away the tears that were trembling on her lashes; bending down, she lifted the poker and jabbed some life back into the fire, then threw some coal on before saying, 'Well, sad as it is, I think Dad did the right thing, Mum. It would have been really hard for him to leave us all in tears again. At least this way he'll take away the memories of how happy we all were together last night. And now the least we can do is keep things going so that he has a home to come back to, so I'm going to make us both a nice strong cup of Camp coffee and then you can help me get the children up and ready for school before we set off for work, eh?'

'Yes, all right,' Lois sniffed, almost as if she were the child and Briony were the adult. James was gone and there wasn't a lot she could do about it now except to try to go on.

As Christmas raced towards them, the food in the shops became sparser. 'There's hardly anything to be had and the rationin' ain't even started yet. Gawd knows what we'll do for Christmas dinner,' Mrs Brindley grumbled when she popped round one evening. Briony had already invited the woman to spend Christmas Day with them rather than be on her own, and her offer had been gratefully accepted.

'Don't you worry about that – I have everything in hand,' Briony winked, and when their neighbour raised a questioning eyebrow she told her, 'I've ordered a nice plump cockerel off Charlie Mannering – you know, the man that has the large allotments off Church Road? He's been fattening the birds up for months and I got my order in early, guessing that everyone would be after them. He has some pigs as well so we're going to have a small joint of fresh pork too.'

Mrs Brindley's mouth watered at the thought of it and she grinned. In actual fact, she knew Charlie very well. They had been childhood sweethearts and whenever they bumped into each other she got the feeling that he still had a bit of a soft spot for her. Bless him, he had lost his wife, Maggie, only the year before and had taken her loss badly.

'There ain't no flies on you, are there, love?' she said approvingly. 'Yer mam should be proud o' you. I know I would be if you were my daughter. An' fer my contribution I shall be supplyin' the Christmas puddin'. I made it a few weeks ago an' it's got a sixpence and a threepenny bit in it.'

Martha Brindley's heart ached for this girl who seemed to be keeping the family going in her father's absence. Lois had gone completely to pieces again without James around. Just that very afternoon, she had watched Lois coming home after collecting Alfie from school and she could have sworn the woman had a sway on. But then she had told herself she must be mistaken. You'd have to be in a pretty bad way to drink during the day, surely? Although she'd had her suspicions for a while now that Lois might be hitting the bottle. There was no sign of her at present. Briony had informed her when asked that her mum had gone upstairs to have a lie-down because she had a headache, and now the poor kid was up to her neck in ironing the kids' clothes. It was all wrong to Mrs Brindley's mind, but then she knew better than to put her two penn'orth in.

Could she have known it, Briony too was concerned about her mother's drinking. Lois had taken to splashing a bit of whisky in her tea from very early in the day, and usually by eight o'clock at night she would be snoring in the chair whilst Briony got the children to bed. The girl had found bottles of spirits hidden all over the place, and each time she did she would discreetly tip them away down the sink and dispose of the bottle in the tin dustbin, but Lois never commented on the fact.

Briony had taken to reading the newspapers religiously and listening to the wireless whenever she could, which was something she had never done before. She had been terrified to read of the new magnetic mines that were taking their toll in the North Sea. The Admiralty had reported that submarines were finding it difficult to surface to mount attacks on the enemy, and several British ships had been lost as the sea war escalated. Briony wondered how long it would be before the fighting spilled over onto the land, and trembled inside at the thought of it.

If anything, the weather deteriorated further in the build-up to Christmas and the wireless reported that it was the coldest winter since 1888. Even so, the atmosphere was joyful on Christmas morning as the children excitedly opened their presents. They were especially thrilled with the gifts that their father had left for them. There was a skipping rope with wooden handles for Sarah and a small wind-up train engine for Alfie, which had him cooing with delight. For Lois he had left a bottle of Evening in Paris perfume and a bright red lipstick with matching nail varnish, and for Briony a lovely blue scarf with matching gloves that would be very welcome on her cold journeys into work. He had even remembered Mrs Brindley, and when she opened the large tub of Pond's cold cream her eyes welled with tears.

'Why, God bless 'im. You've got a good 'un there,' she told Lois, who nodded tearfully in agreement, missing him more than words could say. Even so, she made an extra effort to help Briony with the dinner and tried her best to make the day special for the children. She even did the drying-up when the meal was over, although she refused to wash up because of her manicure, much to Mrs Brindley's disgust.

On New Year's Eve the neighbours gathered together in each other's houses to welcome the New Year in, painfully aware that the women now far outnumbered the men, who were away fighting for their country.

Briony was grateful for an excuse to leave early, saying that the children were tired and needed to go to bed, because by eight o'clock it was more than obvious to everyone that Lois was drunk. Her eyes were unnaturally bright and there were two high spots of colour on her cheeks. On top of that she appeared to be having trouble walking a straight line from one house to another. In each home they visited, she accepted whatever drink was on offer.

'Right Mum, shall we be off then?' Briony suggested tactfully in the Douglases' home. 'The children are tired and ready for bed.'

'You get them home for me, there'sh a good girl,' Lois slurred, waving her hand distractedly as she took another gulp of the strong ale that old Mr Douglas had brewed himself. It was potent stuff and Briony was mortified to see her mother getting more sozzled by the minute.

Seeing Briony's distress, the kindly neighbour chimed in tactfully, 'I reckon young Briony is right, duck. Little Sarah is dead on her feet. An' look at your Alfie – he's yawnin' his head off, bless 'im. Come on, gel. I'll carry him an' you can show me what room yer want him in, eh? I reckon he'll be fast asleep afore we even get him home.'

Seeing no way to refuse, Lois rose reluctantly as Briony flashed him a grateful smile, and soon they were heading for home with Alfie tucked up nice and cosy in Mr Douglas's warm coat and Sarah leaning heavily into her side.

'Thanks, Mr Douglas,' Briony said when they reached their front door.

'No trouble at all,' he smiled, passing Alfie into her arms as Lois staggered through the door ahead of them. 'Happy New Year to you.' And Mr Douglas disappeared off into the foggy night whilst Briony carried Alfie inside, wondering what the New Year had in store for them all.

Chapter Six

In January 1940, temperatures dropped well below zero. To even step outside was like venturing onto a skating rink on the icy pavements, and people were further depressed when food rationing came into force. Everyone was issued with a ration book and they had to register at their local grocer, baker and butcher and queue to get their allowances, which were pitifully small. Even then, many found that the food had run out before they got their turn and tempers became frayed.

'They ain't allowin' us enough to keep a bird alive,' Mrs Brindley complained bitterly. She had always prided herself on keeping a good table and was struggling to eke out her allowances. 'God alone knows what my Clal would say if he was at home. I reckon there won't be a blade o' grass to be seen when the weather picks up. Everyone will be growin' veg in their gardens, but there's only so much yer can do wi' vegetables an' salad stuff. We'll all turn into a load o' bloody rabbits at this rate. An' the sugar ration is laughable! Why, my Clal likes at least three good spoonfuls o' sugar in his tea. The bit they're allowin' each person wouldn't last him more'n a day! An' then there's the bread, o' course – huh! It tastes more like sawdust now – an' whoever heard o' grey bread?'

Whilst Briony sympathised, she couldn't help but be amused at her kindly neighbour's outburst.

'Well, there isn't a lot we can do about it,' she pointed out sensibly. 'We're all in the same boat and we've just got to get on with it.'

'Hmph!' Mrs Brindley pulled her cardigan closer about her and stuck her feet out towards the fire. 'I thought I'd catch the train into Coventry the other day and see if there was any more food goin' over there,' she went on, 'an' you'll never believe what they're doin' now. Why, they're only coverin' up all the station signs, so if yer don't know where yer goin' yer wouldn't know where to get off.'

'Things are getting a bit grim,' Briony acknowledged, hoping to change the subject, but Mrs Brindley wasn't done yet, not by a long shot.

'I thought I'd get hold o' some wool to knit my Clal a nice new cardi fer when he comes home, but it's as rare as hen's teeth now so I've ended up unpickin' one of his old ones to reknit it. Things are bad when you're forced to do that, ain't they? I've taken to listenin' to *The Kitchen Front* on the wireless each mornin' an' all after the eight o'clock news, but all the recipes they're givin' out are about different ways to cook vegetables. I'm tellin' yer, I shall turn into a bloody turnip or a carrot at this rate.'

Briony stifled a giggle as she listened to the woman rant on, but deep down she knew that they didn't really have a lot to be happy about.

The newspapers weren't giving them much to smile

about either. Early in January, it was reported that two million young men in London between the ages of nineteen and twenty-seven had received their call-up papers, and things looked grim when the Germans gained ground in a fierce onslaught along a 120-mile front north of Paris.

'It'll be us they come after next, you just mark my words,' Mrs Brindley said with conviction, and a ripple of pure terror coursed up Briony's spine.

When it was further reported on 9 January that 152 people had lost their lives when the *Union Castle* liner was sunk by a mine off the south-east coast, the public began to realise that the threat of invasion by Hitler's army was drawing closer. The country now lived in fear.

Things were no better at work either; Woolworths was operating on a skeleton staff. Now that so many men had been called up, women were taking their jobs and many of them had left the store in order to work in munitions factories.

'It's hardly worth turnin' in to work,' Ruth told Briony one evening on their way home. 'There's nothin' worth sellin' anyway, an' I just wonder how much longer the place will stay open for. Yer can't even get a decent pair o' stockin's any more, they're like gold dust.' She looked down at her legs and the unbecoming lisle stockings, the only ones that were available, and Briony knew that she was right and could only nod in agreement. Since her father had returned to his unit her spirits were low and it felt as if all she ever did was work. She was missing Ernie too and this made her feel guilty because she knew how much Ruth cared for him. Life seemed to be very complicated at present and sometimes she wished she could just hide her head under the covers and stay in bed all day. But of course that wasn't possible. What would happen to her mum and the children if she gave in to her depression? Lois wasn't even trying to hide the fact that she was drinking heavily any more, and most evenings by the time Briony got home she would be in a stupor, leaving the children to fend for themselves. The girl doubted that tonight would be any different and she was proved right when she entered the kitchen to find a state of pandemonium.

The children were screeching excitedly about something whilst their mother dozed in the chair at the side of the fire.

'So what's all the excitement about then?' Briony asked as she took her coat off.

'We found this on our way home from school,' Alfie told her as he held up a tiny, furry body – and Briony's heart sank. It was a ginger kitten, very sweet admittedly, but the last thing she needed to take on at present.

'Oh, and what does Mum think about it?'

Alfie shrugged as Sarah hopped happily from foot to foot. 'Don't know. We asked her if we could keep him when we got in from school but she was asleep and she ain't woken up yet.'

'*What?* You mean you walked home from school all by yourselves?' Briony was desperately trying to keep the shock from her voice but failing dismally.

Alfie's face fell as he clutched the kitten to him. 'Yes, we did,' he muttered. 'Mum wasn't there to meet me so I waited by the gate for Sarah and walked home with her.'

'I see.' Briony forced a smile. The fire had almost burned out and she knew that she would have to see to it straight away else valuable time would be wasted having to relight it. As she had expected, the coal scuttle was empty, so after glaring at her mother's comatose figure she snatched it up and marched back out to the coal-house, telling Alfie, 'I need to see to the fire and get the dinner on the go then we'll talk about the kitten, all right?'

He nodded and her heart lurched as she saw the tears brimming in his eyes. She was filling the scuttle when Mrs Brindley's back door across the yard opened and she hissed, 'Is everythin' all right, luvvie?'

'Not really,' Briony answered, throwing some more coal into the bucket.

'Well, I could do wi' havin' a little word on the quiet with yer, pet,' Mrs Brindley said timidly. 'Would yer just step inside fer a minute?'

Sighing, Briony crossed the yard and walked into Mrs Brindley's kitchen, wondering what was so important that the woman had to speak to her straight away.

'The thing is . . .' Mrs Brindley looked decidedly uncomfortable. 'There ain't no easy way to say this but I'd rather yer heard it from me than somebody else so I'll just come out with it. It appears that yer mam got the sack from her job this morning.'

'But *why?*' Briony gasped.

'Well, from what I could make of what the women outside the shop were gossipin' about, it seems she turned into work smellin' o' drink an' wobblin' about all over the place. Apparently it weren't the first time, so Mr Finn told her he'd not be needin' her any more . . . I'm so sorry, love.'

'It's not your fault and I appreciate you telling me,' Briony said dully. 'To be honest I've been expecting something like this.'

Mrs Brindley patted her awkwardly on the shoulder. 'If there's anythin' I can do, yer only have to ask.' She felt desperately sorry for the girl and more than a little angry at her mother. From where she was standing it seemed that just because Briony was the firstborn, she had to take the weight of the family on her shoulders.

'I'd better get back,' Briony said. 'I've got the children's dinners to see to. Goodnight, Mrs Brindley.'

'Night, luvvie.' Mrs Brindley watched Briony cross the yard again and lift the heavy scuttle before closing her back door with a heavy sigh.

The meal, which was a hastily put-together concoction of mashed potatoes and corned beef, was a solemn affair and when it was over Alfie asked tentatively, 'So can we keep the kitten then, Briony?'

'I suppose we shall have to wait and see what Mum has to say about it. It's not really up to me, and you know Mum isn't really that keen on pets,' she answered. Lois had snored her way through the entire meal and Briony had left her dinner in the oven to keep warm. But then, seeing the children's crestfallen faces, she looked at the kitten, which was fast asleep in front of the fire, and relented. It was a lovely little thing and she supposed it wouldn't be too much trouble. 'Leave it with me and I'll see if I can't talk her round.'

'Oh *thanks*, Briony, you're the best sister in the whole world.' Alfie covered the space between them in two leaps and wrapped his arms about her neck, closely followed by his sister.

Briony chuckled. 'I'm very pleased you think so, but come on . . . it's time for bed now and if the kitten is staying I shall have to feed him and find him a box for him to sleep in while you two get undressed and have a wash. Oh, and you'd better start thinking of a name for him as well if he's going to be living here. We can't just call him "Cat", can we?'

Highly delighted, the children scooted away to do as they were told. Their bedrooms were bitterly cold but Briony had made them both a hot-water bottle.

'Tommy at school reckons it might snow this week,' Alfie

informed her as she tucked the blankets up to his chin and bent to kiss him. He slept in the tiny boxroom at the back of the house.

'I think your pal Tommy could be right,' Briony shivered. 'It's certainly cold enough and if it does, I'll have to get your sledge out of the shed for you.'

She then went to tuck Sarah in to the double bed that they shared. 'You won't forget to feed the kitten, will you?' the little girl asked sleepily as Briony kissed her goodnight.

'I certainly won't,' Briony promised, stepping out onto the landing. It was then that her shoulders sagged. They would miss the small wage that Lois had earned, and now it seemed they had a cat to care for too – but then, she asked herself, how much can one little kitten cost to feed?

Her mother was stirring when Briony got back downstairs and the girl glared at her as she began to clear the pots from the table. There was all the washing-up to do before she even thought of getting the children's clothes ready for school the next day.

'What time is it?' Lois asked groggily as she heaved herself up in the chair.

'It's evening,' Briony answered shortly as she headed for the sink with her hands full of dirty dishes. 'And if you want your dinner it's in the oven, although it'll probably be dried up by now.'

Lois stared at her daughter uncertainly. She had never heard Briony use that tone of voice to her before, but then as the events of the day slowly came back to her, she said guiltily, 'I'm afraid Mr Finn told me today that he wouldn't be needing me any more.'

'I know that,' Briony snapped. 'And I know *why* too.'

'Oh.' Lois looked so forlorn that Briony felt herself softening, but she wasn't done with her yet.

'You didn't meet the children from school either,' she accused. 'How would you have felt if anything had happened to either of them, Mum? Dad would go mad if he knew that they were having to make their own way home. Alfie is just five years old!'

To Briony's horror her mother promptly burst into tears. 'I know he would. Oh, I'm so sorry. I'm just a poor apology for a mother, aren't I? But I just can't seem to function properly without your dad.'

'We all miss him, Mum,' Briony said soberly. 'But we have to try and keep on and make him proud of us. And the thing is . . . Well, I'm worried about your drinking. It seems to be getting out of hand.'

Lois knew that she was right. Her head was thumping and her mouth felt like the bottom of a birdcage. However, desperate to make amends, she said, 'Leave that washing-up to me. If I'm going to be at home all day from now on, it's time I did my share of the work. You go and put your feet up, love. You've been rushing about all day.' It was then that her eyes fell on the kitten still curled up fast asleep on the hearthrug and she gasped in horror as her hand flew to her throat. 'What is that creature doing in here?'

'It's a kitten that the children found on their way home from school. Someone must have abandoned it and they've adopted it,' Briony said steadily.

'But . . . but it could have all manner of diseases. It might even have *fleas*!' Lois said in disgust. 'And animals need feeding and looking after!'

'I don't think you'll need to worry too much about that. The children adore him already and he can have our leftovers so he won't cost much to keep. I'm just about to find a box for him to sleep in.'

Lois gulped as she eyed the new family member. She

had no doubt that it would break the children's hearts if she made them give him up now, but then cats were known for wandering, weren't they? So perhaps it would be best to keep quiet and let him out when the children had gone to school. He'd no doubt wander off back to where he'd come from, with any luck.

'All right then, he can stay for the moment,' she said reluctantly and Briony heaved a silent sigh of relief.

'And I'm going to change from now on,' Lois added as she walked unsteadily towards the sink to tackle the pile of dirty pots. 'There will be a nice hot dinner on the table for you when you get in from work tomorrow, you just wait and see.'

Briony grinned ruefully. It was hard to stay angry with her mother for long because she didn't really mean any harm and the girl knew that she loved them all. It was just that Lois had not been brought up to put other people first. Perhaps this will be a turning point, she thought to herself as she settled down in the chair in front of the fire to read the paper. But she wouldn't hold her breath.

Over the next few days Lois did make an effort. Briony came home to find a meal of sorts ready, and although the children complained about the lumpy mash and burnt offerings, Briony praised her. 'You'll get better at cooking,' she said warmly. Lois had even tackled the ironing, although she had put almost as many creases in to the clothes as she had taken out of them, but still, at least she was trying. She appeared to be laying off the alcohol too, for which Briony was truly thankful, and she had resumed meeting the children from school as well.

The kitten remained, despite Lois's best efforts to shoo it outside each day, and the children had named him Tigger, which suited him somehow. So all in all, Briony was daring to feel a little better about things. Even Mr Trimble had stopped scolding her at work now that she wasn't so tired, and she had gone back to being the efficient worker he had known.

And then everything suddenly went pear-shaped again when she returned home from work one evening to find her mother in floods of tears, clutching a letter.

'It's from your father,' she told Briony on a sob. 'He says how much he is missing us all but he doesn't say when he might be able to come home on leave again, and what's more, there are rumours that they might be shipped out somewhere.'

'Does he have any idea where they might be sent?' Briony asked gravely, but Lois could only shake her head.

'No. None of them know, apparently, and they'd not be allowed to say, I expect – but what if he gets sent into the firing line? I won't be able to bear it if anything happens to him.'

Briony didn't think she would be able to bear it either, but she was wise enough not to say that to her mother. Instead she said stoically, 'Well, we've just got to get on with things here, Mum. There's nothing anyone can do about it.'

She then set about preparing a meal and while she was busy peeling potatoes, her mother slipped out. Briony had a sinking feeling that she might have gone to the local off-licence, and her fears were confirmed when Lois returned with a brown paper bag with two bottles in it.

'It's only something to get me through this evening,' Lois told her shamefacedly. 'I don't think I shall be able to sleep if I don't have a little drink.'

Briony sighed. They were back to square one.

Chapter Seven

On 9 April 1940 news reached England of the German invasion of Norway and Sweden. On 10 May Hitler's troops then also invaded Belgium and Holland. The newspapers were full of stories about the hardships that had been inflicted on the people there.

'I've got an awful feelin' that we'll be in the line o' fire soon,' Mrs Brindley commented as they clustered around the wireless listening to the evening news. 'So much fer us all hopin' that the bloody war would soon be over.'

Luckily the children were fast asleep in bed. Briony stared at her neighbour fearfully. It was unlikely that Lois had taken in a word of it, for as usual she was sitting in the chair staring into the fire from glazed eyes. Briony wondered what she would have done without Martha Brindley over the last few months. The kindly woman had been wonderful, coming round each day to get a meal on the go for when Briony got in from work, and often even taking the family's ration books to the shops to collect their rations for them. It was just as well. Lois was normally too drunk to even know what day it was lately, and Briony was at her wits' end. They had received one further letter from her father in February, heavily censored, but since then there had been no word from him and now Lois seemed to have given up. Mrs Brindley had heard nothing from her family either and she was worried sick.

Worse was to come. In May, news began to filter through of the British troops trapped on the beaches of Dunkirk. The navy was having trouble rescuing the ones that were still alive because the waters were too shallow for the huge ships to get in close enough to them. Horror stories were reported of the dead and dying which made the British people's blood run cold. The Allied Forces were being shot down like flies and it was rumoured that the sea had turned red with the blood of so many corpses. But then everyone rallied and soon boats of every shape and size were crossing the Channel, collecting the survivors and delivering them to the ships that lay at anchor in deeper waters, or bringing the men home themselves. Pictures of rescued soldiers appeared in the newspapers accepting cigarettes, tea and sandwiches from the WVS, their faces hollow but visibly thankful to be on home soil again. The injured were whisked away to the nearest military hospitals whilst the men capable of travelling returned to their families for a short, well-earned rest.

'I just pray our men are amongst that lot somewhere,' Mrs Brindley muttered fervently, but all they could do was wait for news.

And then sadly for Mrs Brindley, one bright May morning a young lad on a bike delivered a telegram to her door.

Briony was at home as she had been suffering from a raging headache, and when she saw the lad stop outside and prop his bicycle up against the lamp-post, her heart missed a beat. Nowadays every one dreaded the sight of the telegram boy and prayed that he would ride straight by. She saw him approach Mrs Brindley's front door and flew through the house and across the yard into her neighbour's kitchen, sensing that her friend would have need of her.

She watched the colour drain from the older woman's face as she opened the door and took the telegram, before walking back into the kitchen as if in a daze.

'Here, luvvie,' she thrust it at Briony. 'Open it for me, would yer? Me hands have gone all of a shake.'

Briony's weren't much better but she quietly did as she was asked and as her eyes scanned the page she experienced a sense of relief that it wasn't about Ernie, followed by a pang of guilt that she could have felt this.

'What does it say?'

Briony gulped deep in her throat. She croaked: 'It says that they regret to inform you that your husband, Clarence Brindley, was killed in action during the Battle of Dunkirk.'

The silence seemed to stretch on for ever with nothing but the ticking of the clock to be heard, and then suddenly Mrs Brindley swayed and Briony leaped forward to steady her and lead her to a chair. The woman sat down heavily as Briony wrung her hands together, at a loss as to what to say. What *could* she say after hearing such devastating news – and how would Mrs Brindley bear it? How could *she* have borne it, if it had been about her father or Ernie?

'Is . . . is there anything I can get for you?' she asked, but the woman didn't seem to hear her. She was staring through the window at a solitary daffodil that had managed to survive in front of the Anderson shelter in the yard. It seemed all wrong somehow to receive such devastating news when the world outside was blooming into life again.

Mrs Brindley turned to stare at her then although her eyes did not seem to be focusing. Briony was wearing a pretty navy-blue dress dotted with tiny forget-me-nots in a lighter blue that had belonged to her mother. It had a flared skirt with a wide belt at the waist, and Mrs Brindley thought it made the colour of her hair look even blacker. Briony was a good-looking girl, there was no doubt about it. And then she shocked Briony when she suddenly rose purposefully from the chair and went to collect her wicker basket and her ration book.

'I ought to be getting up to the baker's in Arbury Road otherwise all the bread will be gone again.'

'B-but you can't,' Briony stuttered. 'You're in shock, Mrs Brindley. Here, give the ration book to me and I'll fetch it for you.'

Mrs Brindley looked straight through her as she headed for the door so Briony scampered after her. 'All right then, if you won't let me go I'll come with you.' She would have liked to pop next door and tell her mother what had happened, but at present she daren't leave Mrs Brindley alone. Their neighbour was acting very strangely, but then she supposed it was to be expected. It was as if the news she had just received hadn't sunk in.

All the way up Church Road Briony had to almost run to keep up with the woman, who was striding along as if she were on a mission.

'Can you just slow down a bit, I've got heels on,' the girl implored, but Martha didn't seem to hear her. By the time they were at the baker's Briony was breathless and she stood at the back of the shop as her neighbour joined the queue.

'Lovely day, ain't it, Martha,' the woman in front of her commented and Mrs Brindley nodded in agreement.

'It is that, Lil. There ain't nothin' like the feel of a bit o' sun on yer back. It does yer the world o' good after the cold winter.'

The queue shuffled forward as Briony stood there not quite knowing what to do. And then some other women latched on to the back of them and Briony's ears pricked up as she realised that they were talking about what was happening in Dunkirk.

'They reckon it's like a bloodbath,' commented a plump woman in a scarf that was wrapped turban-style about her head. 'Our soldiers are bein' mown down like blades o' grass, by all accounts. Poor sods.'

Briony held her breath as she watched Mrs Brindley turn to stare at them. 'My old man's out there,' she whispered, and then to everyone's distress her face crumpled and she looked towards Briony as if she was seeing her for the first time. 'B-but he ain't there any more, is he? The telegram said that he . . . he was dead.' Suddenly she dropped her basket and her gas mask and she was pushing through the throng of women as sympathetic arms stretched out to her. When she finally managed to reach the pavement she gulped at the air as if she were having trouble breathing and Briony wrapped her arms about her as the tears suddenly gushed from her eyes.

'My poor Clal!' the distraught woman whimpered. In seconds the woman she had addressed as Lil had joined them, pressing Mrs Brindley's basket and a loaf of bread towards Briony.

'Here, let her have my bread and you'd best take her home, duck. It might not be a bad idea to get the doctor to come out to take a look at her. No doubt he'll be able to give her sommat to calm her down, God bless her.'

'Thank you. And yes, I'll do that,' Briony promised as

she turned Mrs Brindley about and began to lead her away. The short walk home seemed to take forever but at last they were back in Martha's cosy little kitchen.

Briony sat her in a chair before hurrying away to put the kettle on. She'd heard somewhere that hot sweet tea was good for shock, and her neighbour certainly needed it right now, even if it meant using up the whole week's sugar ration. Once the poor woman was sipping at the hot drink, Briony ran to the telephone box at the end of the road and spoke to the doctor's receptionist, who assured her that he would call to see Mrs Brindley after afternoon surgery. And then she went back and stayed with her neighbour until it was time to collect the children from school.

'Mrs Brindley has had a telegram informing her that Mr Brindley has been killed in action,' she told her mother curtly before setting off, and the news seemed to shock Lois out of her stupor. She had been sitting by the back door enjoying a bit of sunshine with a glass in her hand but she rose immediately.

'Oh no!' She looked genuinely distressed. 'Yes . . . you go and fetch the children, love, and I'll pop in and stay with her until you get back.'

'Why has Mum been crying? And why hasn't Mrs Brindley been round tonight?' Sarah asked later that evening as Briony was clearing up after dinner. She had taken a meal round to Mrs Brindley but it remained untouched. The sedative that the doctor had given her seemed to have knocked her out for the count, which Briony supposed was no bad thing.

'I'm afraid she has had some very bad news,' Briony said. There was no point in trying to keep it from them – the children were bound to hear it from someone – so she gently explained what had happened and hugged Sarah to her as the child's eyes brimmed with tears.

'Does that mean that Mr Brindley won't never come back?'

'I'm afraid it does, sweetheart.'

'But it ain't fair. Mr Brindley was a kind man. He used to give me an' Alfie pennies for sweets sometimes.'

Briony sighed. 'I know it isn't fair, love, but sadly there isn't much we can do about it apart from be extra kind to Mrs Brindley. She needs us right now.'

'Well, I shall go round an' fill her coal scuttle up fer her,' Alfie said with his chin in the air. 'An' I'll run to the shop fer her if she needs anythin'.'

'That's very kind of you. I'm sure she'll appreciate that,' Briony told him, then she hugged him too when he burst into tears.

The next few days were amongst some of the worst that Briony could ever remember as she watched Mrs Brindley suffering. The poor soul was consumed by grief and refused to either eat or drink, and Briony began to get really concerned about her. Much to Mr Trimble's disapproval she rang in and booked a few days off work, but she didn't care if he was annoyed. The way she saw it, Mrs Brindley had no one to care for her, and after all the kindly woman had done for their family she felt that she owed her this much at least.

And then, just when Briony began to think that Mrs Brindley was never going to get better, something wonderful happened.

She was dusting the furniture in her neighbour's already spotless front parlour when an ambulance pulled up right outside.

Hurrying into the back room she told Mrs Brindley,

'There's an ambulance outside. You haven't rung for one, have you?'

'Why would I do that?' the woman responded, but all the same she was curious enough to drag herself out of the chair and follow Briony into the parlour where they stood peeping through the white lace curtains.

Two ambulance men emerged from the front of it then hurried around to open the back doors – and then they saw them help someone whose leg was in a huge plaster cast to climb down.

'Oh my dear God.' Mrs Brindley's hand flew to her mouth and for the second time in a week Briony saw every vestige of colour drain from her face. 'It's me lad! It's our Ernie!' Then she was yanking the front door open, and before Briony knew what was happening, she was out in the street clutching her son so tightly that she almost had him over.

'Hello, Mam,' he grinned as he clutched his crutch with one arm and hugged her back with the other.

'B-but what are yer doin' here?' She was torn between pleasure at seeing him and terror at the sight of his leg.

'Well, if you'll let me get inside, I'll tell yer,' he said teasingly, and only too happy to oblige she stood aside as the ambulance men took an elbow each and steered him into the house. Once they were gone and he was comfortably settled on the sofa with his leg propped up on a stool he winked at Briony and she felt her heart race.

'I er . . . I'll go and put the kettle on while you two have a chat,' Briony mumbled, and as she turned away she could feel her cheeks burning.

'I'm afraid you're goin' to have to put up wi' me for a while till this heals,' Ernie told his mother, tapping the plaster cast. 'I've been in a hospital in Ramsgate after being rescued from the beaches at Dunkirk, but they're so desperate for beds they're sending home the ones who aren't too badly injured till we're fit to return to our base.'

Mrs Brindley stared at his leg worriedly but he assured her, 'It's just a straightforward break, Mam. I was one of the lucky ones.' His face became haunted then as he went on, 'I can't say the same for some of my mates though. They copped it good and proper, God rest their souls. Our plane was shot down. Thankfully we were flying low or I'd never have survived it. My co-pilot was killed straight out. I got away with this, which is why I ended up on the beach with the Army chaps. They found me in the wreckage of the plane and somehow managed to get me onto the beach.'

'Oh, son,' Mrs Brindley said brokenly, feeling his pain. 'I'm afraid I have some more bad news for you.'

As she began to tell him about the telegram that she had received, Briony quietly left, feeling they deserved some privacy. She would be able to catch up with Ernie later on when he had had time to come to grips with what his mother was telling him. But inside, her heart was singing. Life wasn't so bad, after all. Admittedly Ernie was injured but at least he was alive, which was a lot more than could be said for many of his comrades. She just wished wholeheartedly that he didn't have to return to his base. This time, as he had quite rightly said, he had been lucky; he had escaped with his life – but what if he wasn't so lucky next time?

Just seeing him again had made her break out in goose bumps and shown her how much she had come to care for him. And yet she knew that she must never let him know, for it would break Ruth's heart. She suddenly realised that she should let Ruth know that he was home; the girl would never forgive her if she didn't. But first she would allow mother and son to have some time alone together. They needed to talk – and Ernie was bound to be heartbroken when he learned of his father's death. She wondered if perhaps Mr Brindley had lost his life on the very same beach from which Ernie had been rescued. It would be ironic if he had.

Suddenly, what everyone had termed the 'phoney war' was well and truly over; it was now all too frighteningly real.

Chapter Eight

Ruth's mother answered the door to Briony that evening, and holding aside the heavy blackout curtain, she ushered her inside with a warm smile. The nights were drawing out now but Mrs Teagles didn't want to take the chance of a fine from the wardens if there was any light showing, so she had got into the habit of closing the curtains the instant she put the lamps on.

'Hello, love,' she said. 'Our Ruth is upstairs in her room if you want to go up to her. She's just washed her hair an' I think she was plannin' on havin' an early night, but I'm sure she'll be pleased to see yer.'

'Thanks, Mrs Teagles.' Briony climbed the steep narrow staircase and rapped on Ruth's bedroom door, 'Are you decent? Your mum told me to come up.'

'Come in,' Ruth invited, sounding genuinely pleased to see her. She was sitting at her dressing table rubbing her wet hair vigorously with a towel. Already it was springing into curls and she looked at Briony's hair enviously. 'I wish my hair was straight,' she sighed. 'If I don't keep attacking mine with the brush and sugar and water before it properly dries, I end up with ringlets and look like Shirley Temple.'

'Waves are fashionable,' Briony commented, perching herself on the end of the bed. 'It's me that's out of fashion.'

'Huh, out of fashion or not I'd swap with you *any* day. But what brings you round here tonight? There's nothing wrong at home, is there?'

'Oh no. Far from it,' Briony assured her quickly. 'In fact, it's just the opposite and I have some good news that I thought you'd want to hear.'

Ruth started to tug at her hair with a stiff wooden hairbrush. 'Well, come on then – out with it,' she said. 'Don't keep me in suspenders.'

Briony took a deep breath. 'It's Ernie. He was injured in the Battle of Dunkirk – his plane was shot down – so they've sent him home to recuperate until he's well enough to join his base again.'

Ruth's mouth dropped open. 'How badly injured?' The question came out on a breath.

'He's broken his leg and he's lost a lot of weight. Other than that he's going to be fine.'

'Oh.' Ruth sat there as a mixture of emotions flitted across her face. And then suddenly she was laughing and crying all at once as she grabbed Briony and hugged her tightly. 'That's *wonderful!* I don't mean that it's wonderful that he's injured . . . I mean it's wonderful that he's home and alive. I don't know what I would have done if anything had happened to him. I told him before he went away that I'd wait for him, you know, but he said it wouldn't be fair because he didn't know what was going to happen to him.

But now that he's back I'll make him see that I don't care. There'll never be anyone else for me. I must see him.'

She was suddenly scooting about the room snatching up the first clothes that came to hand and throwing off her dressing gown, and Briony's heart sank as she saw the look of pure joy on her friend's face. Now more than ever she realised just how much Ernie meant to Ruth, and she knew that she could never spoil it for her.

'I'm not so sure if you ought to go round there tonight,' she said tentatively. 'He's only just found out that his father has been killed and he looked worn out. Perhaps it would be better if you went to see him tomorrow?'

'What – and miss spending a precious minute with him?' Ruth snorted as she pulled a pale-blue jumper over her head. 'Not on your nelly! No, I'm going round there right now. I know he'll be pleased to see me. I've got to make him realise how much I love him, Briony.'

Briony twisted her fingers together and chewed on her lips as Ruth finished getting dressed in an amazingly short time.

Ruth glanced in the mirror and grimaced. 'What did I tell you – look! Ringlets! And they'll be even worse if I go out with my hair damp, but I don't care. Come on, let's be off.' She thrust her feet into a pair of shoes that she managed to drag from under the bed, then without a backward glance she raced towards the door, leaving Briony no option but to follow her.

They made the journey to Ernie's house in record time and Briony wondered if Ruth even remembered that she was there, she was in such a dither.

'Do I look all right?' the girl asked nervously as they hovered outside Mrs Brindley's back door. 'And are you coming in with me?'

'You look just fine and no, I'd better get in home and help Mum put the children to bed.'

'Right you are then. See you tomorrow.' And with that Ruth tapped on the door and disappeared inside, leaving Briony feeling as if the bottom had dropped out of her world.

'So how was Ernie?' Briony asked as they walked to work together the next morning.

'He didn't seem too bad,' Ruth answered, disgruntled, 'but I didn't get a chance to talk to him on his own. His mam stayed in the room with us the *whole* time. She was fussing over him like a mother hen.'

'I dare say that's to be expected. After all, now that she's lost her husband she's bound to want to spend as much time with Ernie as she can before he has to go back,' Briony said fairly.

'I suppose so.' Ruth kicked at a stone in her path but then brightened. After all, Ernie was going to be at home for some weeks yet whilst his leg healed, and his mother couldn't be with him every second of the day, could she?

Surprisingly, Lois seemed to have returned to some sort of normality since Ernie had returned and was sober as a judge over the next few nights. Her daughter wondered if it was due to Ernie or the fact that alcohol was becoming hard to get hold of now. Everything was becoming scarcer and the shelves in Woolworths were half empty.

'I'm fed up with customers' havin' a go at me 'cos we ain't got what they want,' Ruth grumbled one day. 'Anyone would think that I was personally responsible for stocks bein' low.'

'Well, I suppose they have to have someone to vent their

feelings on,' Briony said stoically and Ruth grudgingly agreed.

Since Ernie had been home, Ruth had spent every night round at his house, and as yet Briony had not managed to have any time alone with him herself. But then she supposed it was no bad thing. Even with Ruth and Mrs Brindley in the room with them, she felt as if a current of electricity were running between them – and she sensed that Ernie felt it too. And then on the second Saturday after he had returned she went round early in the morning to find that his mother had gone off to do some shopping. Ernie was sitting by the open window staring out at the Anderson shelter and strumming his fingers impatiently on the windowsill with his leg propped up on a stool.

When she entered, his face lit up. 'A lovely day, ain't it?' he said. 'It's just a pity I can't get out and about. I'm going mad, stuck in here all the time.' As he stared at her trim figure and her mane of black hair, his heart did a little flutter. Briony had always been a pretty girl, although he hadn't taken much notice back then, but now she was turning into a beautiful young woman.

Surprised to find that Ruth wasn't already there, Briony smiled pleasantly and said, 'I dare say I could put a chair out in the yard for you and help you get out there if you fancy a bit of sun on your face?'

'Huh! There ain't much left to look at out there, is there, apart from that ugly bloody shelter,' he grumped. Briony could understand his frustration. The last few months must have been a whirl of activity for him, so he would naturally resent having to be so confined and helpless.

'That's true, it is a bit of an eyesore,' she agreed. 'But with the way the war is going we might be glad of it in the not-too-distant future. It said on the wireless last night that Hitler is massing boats and landing crafts ready for invasion. Do you think it's true?'

Ernie shrugged. 'Who knows with that nutcase? The bloke wants to rule the world, but he won't if it's left to chaps like me! Thank God the factories in Coventry are working around the clock to make the planes. As long as we've got them we'll give that kraut bastard a run for his money.'

Briony shivered involuntarily, only too aware that Ernie was speaking the truth. She glanced around then and asked, 'So where is Ruth today? I thought she would have been here by now.'

'Had to go shopping with her mum apparently, and between you and me it's nice to have a break from her. I know she means well, but what with her and me mam I feel as if I'm being smothered. I reckon they'd cut me food up for me if I'd let 'em. At the end o' the day it's only me leg that's broke, ain't it? It's not as if I'm helpless.'

Briony giggled. 'Oh, how *awful* for you, being waited on hand and foot and having your every need pandered to,' she teased.

Snatching the cushion from behind his back he threw it at her and as she caught it she laughed.

But then he became serious and asked quietly, 'Did you give any more thought to what I asked you before I went away, Briony? About you bein' my girl, I mean.'

She lowered her eyes as she replied. 'Things have to stay as they are, Ernie, for more than one reason. For a start-off you know how Ruth feels about you, and she's my best friend. She'd think I'd betrayed her if anything happened between you and me. And anyway, like I said before, there's always the chance that I'll get shipped off to Cornwall with the kids if things get any worse here, and then we may never see each other again.'

'Don't say that!' His eyes were beseeching her but she was saved from having to say more when Mrs Brindley walked in and dropped her shopping bag on the table.

'Hello, pet,' she greeted her. 'Ooh, my feet are killin' me after trailin' round the shops all mornin'. I did manage to get us a nice bit o' brisket fer us Sunday lunch though, which is somethin', I suppose. I was beginnin' to forget what beef tasted like. Now I'll go an' put the kettle on, shall I? Oh, an' by the way, your little Alfie is howlin' his head off, bless him. He just slipped over an' grazed his knees while he were playin' wi' his marbles in the street. I've sent him in fer yer mam to clean him up.'

'I'd better get round there then. I don't think Mum is even up yet,' Briony said anxiously as she headed for the door.

When she'd gone, Mrs Brindley tutted. 'That ruddy mother of hers is useless at times,' she stated. 'If it weren't fer Briony, God alone knows what state them two little kids would be in. And Lois neglects herself too, these days. Before now I've hardly ever seen her wi'out her bein' made up to the nines and wi' not a hair out o' place, but then I suppose it takes all sorts.' And with that she set about putting the shopping away as Ernie watched.

The plaster cast was taken off Ernie's leg early in July and the doctor told him that he could return to his RAF base the following week. Mrs Brindley accepted this news with mixed emotions; part of her was thankful that her son's leg had healed but the other part of her was fearful at the thought of him flying again. Only the day before they had heard on the wireless that the Luftwaffe had launched their first large-scale attack on Britain, when seventy aircraft attacked the dock facilities at Swansea and the Royal Ordnance factory at Pembrey in Wales. Portsmouth, along with many other coastal shipping convoys and shipping centres, had also been the target of aerial attacks by the Luftwaffe. It was the largest and most sustained aerial bombing campaign to date and it was called the Battle of Britain.

'It'll only be a matter o' time now till they target the aircraft factories and the RAF airfields, you just mark my words,' Ernie forecast grimly.

Her mother shuddered. Now, more than at any other time, Ernie would be in the thick of the fighting, but there was not a single thing that she could do about it. Never in her whole life had she felt so helpless – and yet she also felt a sense of pride. Her lad was brave – there was no one could say differently.

On the morning that Ernie left, Ruth and Briony pinched a couple of hours off work and accompanied him to the station.

As they stood on the platform, none of them knew quite what to say, and it was a relief when the train chugged in.

'Right, this is it then. You two take good care o' yourselves now,' Ernie said in a choked voice as he opened a carriage door. There were many other men aboard in uniform, no doubt returning from leave, like Ernie.

'Don't you get worrying about us. It's you who'll be in the line o' fire,' Ruth sobbed as she kissed him tenderly on the cheek. She would have liked to throw her arms about his neck and kiss him soundly on the lips but she sensed that he wouldn't want that.

'Oh, I'm like a cat, me,' he told them with a cheeky grin. 'I've got nine lives.'

'Well, if that's the case you only have eight left,' Briony retorted. 'So just be careful and don't get taking any chances. We don't want a dead hero.'

'All aboard!' The guard was striding along the platform slamming the carriage doors shut so Ernie threw his kitbag in front of him and hopped onto the train before leaning out of the window.

'See you soon,' he shouted above the noise of the engine. 'And let's hope that the next time I come home, it will be for good.'

The train began to move away in a cloud of steam and for a few moments Ruth and Briony ran alongside waving until they felt as if their arms were about to drop off. Ernie waved back – and then the train turned a bend in the track and he was lost to sight.

'That's it then. We might as well get back to work,' Ruth muttered brokenly. Briony linked her arm through her friend's and the two girls left the station in silence.

Chapter Nine

The first bombs had been dropped on Coventry in June, and as the Battle of Britain escalated the people of Nuneaton began to wonder when it would be their turn.

'I'm gettin' the shelter ready just in case,' Mrs Brindley told Lois one fine morning in late July. Lois helped her to drag in a couple of worn fireside chairs that had been stored in the shed and Mrs Brindley also took in some tatty old blankets that she didn't use any more, explaining, 'It can still be nippy of a night an' yer never know. Better to be prepared.'

Lois took in some cushions and candles and Mrs Brindley made sure that a large flask was always at hand at the side of the kettle. 'I couldn't go all night wi'out me cup o' tea if the sirens should go off after dark,' she said stoutly. Lois eyed the reasonably comfortable little sanctuary they had prepared and prayed fervently that they might never need it. Britain was teetering on the edge of defeat as the German army stormed its way across Europe and the Battle of Britain raged in the skies above them.

Ernie, meanwhile, felt as if he were caught in the grip of a nightmare. Each day, he and his co-pilot took to the skies to fight the enemy, and each night when they returned to base they heard of yet more of their friends whose planes had been shot down and who would never return.

'I wonder if it isn't time I shipped you all off to your grandparents',' Lois told Briony musingly one day as she read the newspaper. She still had lapses when she was able to get hold of alcohol, but thankfully for most of the time now, Briony would return home to find her sober.

'No, not yet,' the girl pleaded. 'I'd be worried sick if you didn't come with us, Mum. Why won't you?'

'Because I have to stay here and keep the house going for you all for when it's over,' Lois answered. 'And anyway, I couldn't possibly live under the same roof as my mother again. We'd be at each other's throats.'

And then one Saturday morning early in August as Briony was scrubbing the front doorstep, the unthinkable happened: a telegram boy pulled into the kerb and, looking directly at her he asked, 'Are you Mrs Valentine?'

Briony feared she might vomit as bile rose in her throat, but she managed to keep her voice steady as she answered, 'No. I'm Miss Valentine.' Her hands were trembling uncontrollably as she gazed at the brown envelope in the boy's hand.

'I . . . is that for my mother?'

The boy nodded solemnly, and when she held her hand out for it, he rode away. Briony stood staring down at it as if it might bite her. Leaving the scrubbing brush and the bowl of soapy water where they were, she slowly rose, and after wiping her hands down the front of her apron she walked through the house as if she were in a trance. Lois was in the back room painting her toenails and she smiled as the girl entered the room. But then as she noted her daughter's white face and the envelope in her hand, the smile vanished.

Briony held the telegram out to her and Lois took it without a word. She read the contents, showing no emotion whatsoever until Briony's nerves were stretched to breaking point. 'For God's sake, Mum,' she hissed. 'What does it say?'

'It says that they regret to inform me that your father is missing . . . presumed dead.'

The next few days passed in a blur of misery as the Valentine family tried to come to terms with the loss of their loved one.

'It only says he's *presumed* dead. Yer mustn't give up hope,' Mrs Brindley tried to comfort them but there was no conviction in her voice and they all just stared dully back at her.

'Look at all the German prisoners o' war that they reckon are goin' to be held in the grounds of Arbury Hall,' she pressed on. 'It could be that your bloke is in sommat similar in their country.' Lately the townsfolk had watched curiously as row upon row of Nissen huts had been erected within the grounds of the stately home on the outskirts of town. None of them had been too pleased when rumours of what they were being built for had leaked out, but they needn't have worried. As they later discovered, the German prisoners who were eventually placed there for the duration of the war were classed as low-risk Wehrmacht troops who had formerly been tradesmen, professionals and teachers in their own country. Even so, many local people were nervous at the close proximity of men who were considered to be the enemy.

Mrs Brindley's optimistic words fell on deaf ears and eventually she went back to her own home and left the family to grieve. She of all people knew just what they were going through and she didn't wish to intrude.

The month progressed and sometimes Briony felt as if she were staggering through a thick fog. She couldn't or wouldn't accept that she might never see her handsome father again, and she began to fear for her mother's sanity. Lois seemed to be locked in a world of her own where no one could reach her. She would sit in the chair from dawn till dusk, rocking to and fro in her dressing gown staring sightlessly from the window, and had it not been for Briony, Mrs Brindley dreaded to think what might have happened to little Sarah and Alfie. They were bewildered, not truly understanding the finality of death, and every morning they watched for the postman, hoping for a letter from their father. Briony had gently told them that their dad had gone to a wonderful place called heaven where he was living with God. Sarah thought this all sounded very well and good, but one evening as Briony was tucking her into bed she asked, 'When will God let Daddy come home to see us?'

Briony blinked away the tears that were suddenly stinging the back of her eyes and told her, 'I'm afraid that once you go to live with God, He doesn't allow you to come home for visits.'

Sarah's small hands bunched into fists beneath the blankets. 'Well, I don't think that's fair then,' she said plaintively. 'He's *our* Daddy, not God's! Why doesn't God get His own Daddy?'

'Billy Norman's mum told him that his daddy had gone to live with God too,' Alfie piped up. 'But Billy knew that she was telling lies 'cos they had what they called a funral or somethin' like that for him an' planted him in the ground in a big box. How can he be with God in heaven, Briony, if he's in the ground? You said that heaven was somewhere in the sky behind the clouds.'

Completely at a loss as to how to answer such innocent questions, Briony merely kissed them both and sneaked out of the room with tears streaming down her pale cheeks. She was still managing to go to work, but most evenings she was in such a daze that she couldn't even remember what she had been doing all day. Thankfully, once he heard what had happened, Mr Trimble was being very understanding, and rather than bellow at her as he normally would if she made a mistake he would simply correct it and leave her well alone.

Ruth had been marvellous too, a true friend. Each evening after her meal she would turn up and pitch in to help Briony do anything that needed doing without a word of complaint. Briony didn't know how she would have coped without Ruth and Martha Brindley yet she could find no words to thank them, knowing that anything she said would be totally inadequate.

The days slipped one into another until August was drawing to a close.

'Christ, it's the twenty-fifth already, where does the time go?' Mrs Brindley said one evening as she sat at the Valentines' kitchen table reading the daily newspaper. She had tackled a pile of ironing for Briony and was now enjoying a cup of tea before returning to her own home. The children were fast asleep in bed when suddenly the sound that they had all been dreading echoed through the house.

'Dear God Almighty!' Mrs Brindley had paled to the colour of putty. 'It's the bloody air-raid siren.' Then taking control she barked at Briony, 'Run up and fetch the kids while I get yer mam into the shelter, lass.'

For a moment the girl stood as if she had been turned to stone but then gathering her wits together she raced up the steep staircase as sheer terror pulsed through her veins.

Sarah was already sitting up in bed knuckling the sleep from her eyes as her sister exploded into the room, and she asked sleepily, 'What's that funny noise, Briony?'

'Nothing for you to worry about,' her sister replied, keeping her voice as calm as she could. 'But I want you to come with me. We're going to have a little adventure and go and sit in the shelter for a while.'

'But it's dark outside!'

'I know it is, but we have candles in there so hurry up and put your dressing gown and your slippers on for me, there's a good girl, while I go and get Alfie.'

The sound of the siren wailing was deafening, but Alfie didn't wake even when Briony lifted him out of bed and put a blanket around him. She carried him out onto the long narrow landing where Sarah was waiting for her, looking a little fearful now, then quickly led the way downstairs and outside into the shelter. Lois was sitting in one of the chairs that Mrs Brindley had placed in there and Briony placed Alfie in her lap. He roused momentarily to jam his thumb into his mouth but then slept on blissfully oblivious of what was going on. Mrs Brindley was sitting in the other chair and she instantly lifted Sarah onto her lap, telling Briony, 'Get that door shut sharpish, luvvie.'

Briony did as she was told and they were instantly plunged into inky darkness but then she fumbled about for the candles and the matches that Mrs Brindley had also thought to bring into the shelter and within minutes she had managed to light a couple with shaking fingers.

'That's better,' her neighbour told her with an encouraging grin as she saw that Tigger had shot in there too, to cower beneath one of the chairs. 'We should be as safe as houses in here, so all we have to do now is sit it out.'

Briony sank cross-legged onto an old rug that her mother had been planning to throw out and shivered. Despite the balmy evening outside, the inside of the shelter felt cold and damp but hopefully the raid would not go on for too long.

Every minute seemed to last an hour as they sat there wondering what was going on outside. Then suddenly they heard the roar of planes overhead and as the noise subsided a little, there was the sound of an explosion in the distance.

'The bastards have dropped a bomb somewhere,' Mrs Brindley said with gritted teeth.

Briony wrapped her arms about her knees to try and stop herself shaking.

'I wonder who's copped it?' Mrs Brindley hugged Sarah more tightly to her but thankfully both children slept on. Eventually Briony slipped into an uneasy doze too and it was the sound of the all-clear that brought her eyes springing open.

'Is it over?' she whispered fearfully and Mrs Brindley nodded.

'Yes, it is. Now come on, help me get these children tucked back into bed – that's if it ain't time to get up. Lord knows how long we've been in here.'

They crept from the shelter into a misty dawn and once inside the kitchen, Lois and Briony carried the children upstairs while Mrs Brindley threw some coal onto the dying fire.

Later that morning, they discovered that an incendiary bomb had been dropped in the Gypsy Lane, Coventry Road area, but no one seemed to know as yet what damage had been done or whether anyone had been hurt. Briony had chosen not to go into work but she got the children up at their usual time and walked them both to school, feeling that it would be better to keep them in their normal routine. Even so, she fretted all day.

'What if the sirens go off and there's a raid during the day?' she asked Mrs Brindley. There were huge dark circles beneath her eyes and the kindly woman patted her hand reassuringly.

'Don't get worrying about that. They'd get all the children down into the cellars,' she assured her.

'But if they do that and the school gets bombed, then the children would be buried under tons of rubble.'

Mrs Brindley scowled at her and yawned. The sleepless night was catching up with her now and she was keen to get back to her own home and her own bed.

'You're just lookin' fer problems now,' she scolded, although the same thought had crossed her own mind. 'Now I'm goin' to go and grab a bit o' shut-eye, so I'll see yer both later. Oh, an' by the way, Betty Arkwright just told me there were no one hurt in the raid last night, so that's sommat to be thankful for at least, ain't it?'

She crossed the yard and disappeared into her kitchen as Briony looked at Tigger the cat, who had crept back in and was already fast asleep in the fireside chair.

The raid had deeply unnerved them all, for although they had known it could happen, when it actually had, it had been a different matter entirely.

Seeing her mother's strained face, Briony tried to force some brightness into her voice as she told her, 'I think Mrs Brindley was more upset about having to go without her cup of tea all night than anything else. Everything happened so fast she forgot to fill her flask.'

Lois nodded absently as Briony began to tidy the room.

*

They were all nervous as evening approached, but thankfully it passed without incident and they began to hope that the raid had been a one-off. Briony returned to work the next day, and on the way home Ruth remarked, 'It were nice to have a peaceful night, weren't it?'

Briony couldn't help but smile. Ruth was talking as if the raids had been a nightly occurrence rather than the first one. But she didn't say as much, instead she simply nodded.

'Yes, it was – and let's pray we have another peaceful time tonight.'

Her prayers went unanswered when shortly after she had retired to bed the sirens sounded. Grabbing her dressing gown, she yanked it on and carried Sarah down the stairs whilst her mother followed with Alfie in her arms. They met Mrs Brindley in the yard with her hair full of metal curlers and clad in a voluminous candlewick dressing gown.

She pointed to the flask beneath her arm as she ushered them all in the direction of the shelter, saying, 'I put some cups in the shelter earlier on so at least we'll be able to have a hot drink tonight.'

Tea was the very last thing on Briony's mind at that moment but she was too polite to say so. Now that August was drawing to a close the nights had become colder and soon Briony wished that she had thought to put her coat on over her dressing gown, but at least the children were warmly wrapped in the blankets that their neighbour had provided; once again, they slept through it all.

'The jerries are droppin' a fair few tonight,' Mrs Brindley muttered at one stage. The candles were flickering, making the walls of the shelter seem as if they were moving and Briony was absolutely terrified.

That night the raid seemed to go on for much longer and they all sat fearfully listening to the explosions and the roar of the ack-ack guns as they tried to shoot the enemy planes from the skies.

The next day, they learned that nine high-explosive bombs and twenty incendiary bombs had been dropped in Weddington Lane and in Caldecote Lane opposite the school, but miraculously once again no one was hurt and the school had remained intact.

'Them Jerries are bleedin' lunatics, the lot of 'em,' Martha Brindley ranted, and Lois and Briony could only nod in agreement.

Then on the following night came the worst raid to date. It began shortly after dark and seemed to go on all night. This time Weddington Road, Hill Farm and Boon's quarry in Tuttle Hill were the targets – and they were appalled to hear on the wireless the following day that this time, three people had lost their lives, and a further nine people had been injured.

'There's a bus up on the school playground; all the children that trickled back after bein' evacuated are bein' taken away again,' Mrs Brindley informed them after venturing as far as the butcher's to collect her meagre meat ration. 'I should expect a visit from the WVS or the Red Cross if I were you, Lois,' she warned. 'Happen they'll be wantin' to get Sarah an' Alfie away an' all, now that the bombin' has started.'

Briony held her breath, wondering if Lois would agree that it was time for her to take the children to Cornwall, but for now Lois merely chewed on her lip and shook her head in silent consternation. She still wasn't ready to let go of her beloved children, even in the face of the Luftwaffe's killing rage.

Chapter Ten

The next day, a Wednesday, Briony had just got home from work when she answered a knock at the front door to find a woman from the Red Cross standing there with a clipboard in her hand. She was a little stout woman with a hooked nose and the beadiest eyes that Briony had ever seen, but she was politeness itself when she asked, 'Would it be possible to speak to Mrs Valentine, dear?'

Briony felt like slamming the door in her face as it dawned on her why the woman might be there, but she smiled stiffly and held the door wider. 'Yes, of course, she's in the back room. Would you like to come through?'

Mrs Brindley and Lois looked up when the visitor followed Briony in, and the second they spotted the woman's uniform, their expressions became wary.

'Ah, Mrs Valentine.' The woman held her hand out and shook Lois's so hard that Lois feared it would drop off. She had the grip of a grizzly bear and was full of self-importance.

Narrowing her eyes, she squinted down at the list in her hand before going on, 'I believe we have two children here . . . Sarah and Alfred, isn't it?' There would have been no point in denying it as the children were both in the room, playing snap at the table.

'Following last night's raid,' the woman rushed on, 'we have decided to evacuate the next batch of children from the area this Friday for their own safety. They will be taken by bus at ten thirty a.m. from the school playground to the station, where they will travel to their destination. I have a list of things here that they will need to take with them. Will that be all right, dear?' She held a sheet of paper out to Lois who shocked them all when her chin suddenly set and she rose from her seat.

'Actually, no, it won't be all right,' she said calmly.

The woman looked flustered. 'B-but you can't possibly be meaning to keep them here, putting them at risk?'

'I have no intention of keeping them here.' Lois held her head high. 'They will be going to stay for the duration of the war at my parents' country estate in Cornwall, just as soon as I am able to arrange it. It will be so much better for them to be with family, don't you think?'

'Estate?' Briony croaked. From the little her mother had told her, the girl had guessed that her grandparents must have a wonderful house – but an *estate?*

'Oh, I see,' the woman said, looking utterly flabbergasted. 'So shall I take their names off the list then?'

Lois nodded imperiously as the woman, who seemed to have shrunk, backed towards the door. 'Yes, if you would be so kind,' she said, then to Briony: 'Would you show this lady out, please, darling?'

The woman seemed only too pleased to go and shot out as if Old Nick himself were snapping at her heels.

The door had scarcely closed behind her when Mrs Brindley erupted into gales of laughter that made her chins wobble as she clutched at her sides.

'Eeh, lass,' she chortled. 'Yer certainly put that pompous little so an' so in her place. I never knew yer had it in yer!'

Mrs Brindley's laughter was so infectious that soon they were all joining her.

'But you *were* joking, weren't you, Mum? I mean, when you said that our grandparents had a country estate?' Briony managed to ask eventually.

Lois smiled guiltily. 'No, I wasn't actually. Perhaps I didn't mention that as well as having his own business, my father also had two farms on his land that brought in a considerable income. The whole of the estate amounted to approximately three hundred acres.'

Briony was speechless. *Three hundred acres!* After spending her entire life living amongst rows of terraced houses she couldn't even begin to imagine how big that amount of land might be.

'Does the house have a name?' she asked next.

'Yes,' Lois answered, lighting a cigarette and speaking through a haze of blue smoke. 'It's called The Heights and it's situated near Penzance in a little village called Poldak. It's quite beautiful and I'm sure you'll fall in love with it. I shall write to my father this evening and tell him to expect you, and then I'll see about booking the tickets for you all. I'm afraid it's going to be a very long journey, and you'll have to change trains a few times to get there.'

Briony suddenly felt apprehensive and excited all at the same time. It would be like living in another world, having servants to do the chores and not having to go to work – and yet she knew she would miss her friends and her mother terribly. And although Lois was being strong at the moment,

Briony knew only too well how quickly she could slide into a depression – and what would happen to her then?

As if Mrs Brindley could read her thoughts she said, 'Well, I reckon yer doin' exactly the right thing, fer what my opinion's worth, Lois. The kids will be far safer down there, an' you an' me will rub along just fine together, won't we?'

She winked at Briony and the girl smiled at her gratefully. Of course her mother would be all right with Martha Brindley to look after her, and if she wasn't, then once the children were settled with their grandparents she could come back.

'But how will you manage without my wages coming in?' she asked then.

Once again her mother shocked her when she replied, 'As it happens I've found myself another little job down at the Haunchwood Colliery – I start next week. It's only cleaning the offices but I'll earn enough to keep the wolf from the door and pay the rent, so you don't have to worry about that.'

Briony's mouth gaped open and Alfie giggled. For a start-off she had had no idea that her mother had applied for a job, and secondly, she couldn't somehow imagine Lois Valentine as a cleaner. She didn't even like cleaning her own home, let alone offices! But then there was a war on and many people were having to do things they would never have dreamed of doing before. Briony didn't have much time to dwell on it though because then Sarah started to ask about her grandparents. She was obviously excited and fired questions at Lois one after the other, which Lois tried to answer as best she could.

'Fancy that,' the little girl said eventually as she stared dreamily off into space, trying to picture them in her mind, 'us havin' a *real* nanny an' grandpa. Florrie at school will never believe me when I tell her tomorrer, especially when I tell her that they're rich an' I'm gonna live with 'em in a big posh house at the seaside. She'll be so jealous.'

'Well, I don't wanna go even if they *are* rich,' Alfie piped up then with a mutinous expression on his small face. 'I wanna stay here wi' Mum an' Briony.'

'But it will be safer for you all there, darling,' Lois told him gently as she stroked a thick lock of fair hair back from his forehead. 'And it will mean that you won't have to keep going into that horrid cold shelter at night.'

'I *like* the shelter,' Alfie scowled, crossing his arms. ''Specially since Mrs Brindley put the bed in there. I pretend we're camping out!'

'Yes, well – how about we get some dinner on the go,' Briony said hastily, seeing how upset he was becoming. 'And then we can talk about this some more later on, eh? I don't know about you lot but I'm starving.'

Lois and Mrs Brindley went to play Happy Families with the children then, and for now all talk of their grandparents was put aside as Briony hurried away to peel the potatoes for dinner.

'What are our nanny and grandpa like?' Sarah asked a little later as they sat at the table eating the corned-beef hash Briony had cooked for them. They were all a little tired of corned beef, but seeing as it was the most readily available meat they could get, Briony had become adept at making different concoctions with it for them, and at least it meant they weren't going hungry.

'I'm not so sure they'll like you calling them Nanny and Grandpa,' Lois said cautiously.

'But why not? That's what Florrie calls hers!'

'Maybe she does, but it might be best if you address them

as Grandmother and Grandfather until you get to know them a little better,' Lois answered tactfully.

Sarah frowned but then brightened again as she said, 'Just think. We'll have servants to wait on us and I'll be just like a princess. *And* we'll live in a big posh house right by the sea.' She sighed, then added, 'Do you reckon we'll be allowed to play on the beach? And will we have to go to school?'

Lois glanced at Briony before saying, 'I'm sure you'll be allowed some time on the beach, and yes, of course you'll go to school. Probably the one in the village. But come on now – eat your dinner like a good girl before it gets cold.'

There were many more questions buzzing around in the little girl's head, but seeing as her mother obviously didn't want to talk about it any more for now, she did as she was told.

Meanwhile, Lois glanced across at the sideboard where the letter she had already written to her parents sat staring at her. It was all ready to be posted now and once it was done there would be no going back. It was daunting to think of being in the house all on her own, but she knew that for the sake of the three children, she would have to go through with this. They would definitely be safer in Cornwall away from the bombing – but she wasn't at all sure that they would be happier. She could only hope that the years would have softened her mother. Only time would tell.

As Briony lay in bed that night her head was spinning. Her mother had talked of beautifully manicured gardens and a huge house that the army of servants kept sparkling. It was a world away from what she was used to but she supposed she would adapt to it. She had already written out her letter of resignation and intended to hand it in to Mr Trimble the following morning. This didn't really concern her. She had learned that no one was indispensable and no doubt he would quickly find someone to replace her. But she was dreading having to tell Ruth that she was leaving, even though her friend had known for some time that there was a possibility of it happening. For now, her mother seemed to have acquired a reserve of inner strength from somewhere, but despite Mrs Brindley's assurances that she would keep an eye on her, Briony was still gravely concerned that she might lapse into drinking and a depression again. She sighed into the darkness, then snuggling into Sarah's warm little body she eventually drifted off to sleep.

'Oh!' Ruth said mournfully the next morning when Briony told her that she would be leaving. They were walking along Queen's Road and Briony was saddened to see that there were tears in her friend's eyes.

'We'll be setting off within the next week or so when my grandparents reply to Mum's letter,' Briony went on. 'As soon as she hears back from them she'll book the train tickets and tell them when to expect us.'

'I shan't 'alf miss you.'

'I shall miss you too, but I will come back to see you as often as I can, once the little ones are settled,' Briony promised and they walked on in silence, each locked in their own thoughts.

The following week, an envelope with unfamiliar handwriting on it plopped through the letter box and as Briony collected it from the doormat and carried it in to her mother, she guessed that this must be the reply from her grandparents that Lois had been waiting for.

Her mother quickly read it before telling her, 'Mother says

you may all go as soon as you like, but I'm to write again and tell her when to expect you so that she can arrange for someone to collect you from the station at Penzance.'

'I see.' Briony had been expecting this and yet suddenly it all felt very real and butterflies fluttered in her stomach.

'I shall go into town today and book the train tickets for early next week,' Lois decided. 'It should work out just right for you, working out your notice at Woolworths. But Briony, promise me one thing – try to keep away from your Uncle Sebastian. He's a nasty piece of work even if he is my brother.'

Briony nodded numbly, not quite knowing what to say. There was no turning back now, it seemed, so she was just going to have to make the best of it.

Chapter Eleven

The next few days were spent in a flurry of packing. Lois remained calm, centred only on the fact that she was doing the right thing for her children. They were to leave at six a.m. on Tuesday morning 11 September from Trent Valley railway station, and their tickets were tucked safely away in her handbag. She knew that there was no time for her parents to reply to her latest letter informing them of the children's date and time of arrival, but she had estimated that they would have had more than ample time to receive the letter and so hopefully there would be someone there to meet them from the train in Penzance. Her biggest worry was that, because the Germans had been targeting the railway lines incessantly, the children might have to be diverted, which would alter their estimated arrival time. However, there was nothing she could do about that. London was also being heavily bombed – what Hitler said was a reprisal for the bombing of Berlin – and

Lois prayed that the children would reach their destination safely. She tried not to think of the lonely time ahead once they were gone and instead kept up a constant stream of cheerful chatter.

'Just think, this time next week you'll be living by the sea,' she said to Alfie as she squashed his favourite teddy bear into the corner of his small suitcase.

'Don't *want* to live by the sea,' he whined. 'Want to stay here with you, Mam. Are you sendin' us away 'cos you don't love us any more?'

'Oh, darling, of course not!' Lois's breath caught in her throat as she stared down at the tears sparkling on the little boy's lashes. Alfie was at an age when he considered you were a cissy if you cried, but right at that moment he couldn't help it.

'I'm sending you away to stay with your grandparents because I don't want you here where you might get hurt with all the bombs being dropped,' his mother explained gently.

'But what about *you*? You'll still be here so you might get hurt. Why can't you come with us?' Alfie's lip was trembling.

'I shall be just fine,' Lois assured him, giving him a loving hug. 'But I have to stay here to keep the house nice for when you all come home again, don't I? And Tigger needs me here, doesn't he?'

He considered what she'd said then sniffed and nodded reluctantly. At least she had said they would be coming home – which was something, he supposed. He'd miss Tigger, though.

Sarah, on the other hand, was almost bursting with impatience and had bragged so much about where she was going to live that Florrie, her little friend at school, who was about to be evacuated to God knew where, was green with envy.

''S'not fair,' she sulked. 'I ain't got a clue where they'll be sendin' *me*.'

'It's bound to be somewhere nice,' Sarah said. She was a kind little girl at heart and despite her bragging she cared about Florrie.

And so the day of their departure raced towards them, and almost before they knew it they found themselves standing on the station platform with their mother, waiting for their train to arrive. They had already said a tearful goodbye to Mrs Brindley, who had promised to help their mum look after Tigger until they got back. Alfie and Sarah had wanted to take him with them, but Briony had managed to persuade them that Cornwall was such a long way away, he would be miserable locked in a cage during the journey.

All three were dressed in their Sunday best and they each had a small suitcase to carry as well as their gas masks and a basket full of sandwiches that their mother had packed for them to eat on the way.

'Now are you quite sure that you know where you have to change trains, and have you got the tickets safe?' Lois asked for at least the tenth time in as many minutes.

Briony patted her handbag and smiled. 'Yes, Mum, I'm *quite* sure,' she told her indulgently. She just wished that the train would come now so that they could be off. Saying goodbye was proving to be a lot more painful than she had anticipated. Could her mother have known it, she had every intention of coming back once she knew that the children were happily settled, but she hadn't told her that, of course. Briony was only too well aware of how Lois was prone to fall apart in a crisis and didn't want to leave her for a moment longer than necessary.

Alfie was clinging to the hem of his mother's pretty spotted skirt looking very smart in his little grey shorts and a matching blazer. Briony had polished his shoes until she could see her face in them but already one of his knee-length socks had slipped down to his ankle and she wondered what he might look like by the time they arrived at their destination. Alfie seemed to attract dirt like a magnet but then, as Mrs Brindley had always been so fond of saying, 'Show me a clean lad an' I'll guarantee there's somethin' wrong with him. Little boys were made to be mucky.'

Sarah, on the other hand, was standing primly, looking a picture in a white smocked cotton dress and a lovely pink cardigan that Mrs Brindley had knitted for her. She had a matching pink ribbon in her hair and was a miniature version of her mother. As Lois looked at her family now she wondered how she had ever managed to produce three such striking-looking children – although no one would ever have guessed at first glance that Briony was related to the other two. Her straight dark hair was a stark contrast to their fluffy blonde curls, and glancing at her now Lois felt a lump form in her throat. It was like looking at a female version of her husband, and the girl's likeness to James made his loss seem all the more unbearable. But just for today, Lois was prepared to put her children first and she fussed about straightening Sarah's ribbon and tugging Alfie's sock up until they heard the train come chugging towards them.

'This is it then.' Lois could barely hear herself as the train pulled into the platform in a hiss of smoke. The carriage doors opened and people began to alight, many of them men in uniform possibly coming home on leave and Lois found herself thinking how wonderful it would be if only one of them could be James coming back to her. But then that would be a miracle and she didn't believe in miracles any more. Just lately, life had knocked all the stuffing out of her. Briony was walking along peering into the carriage windows and when she found one that was empty she beckoned to her mother and the children.

She began to put the cases into the corridor as Lois kissed the little ones affectionately and now Alfie started to howl unashamedly. Cissy or not, he wanted to stay with his mum.

'Come on, darling,' Lois urged, knowing that she mustn't cry in front of him. 'You've never been on a train before. Think how exciting it will be – and when you get there, you can ask Briony to help you write a letter telling me all about it.'

He reluctantly allowed her to lift him aboard before she turned her attentions to Sarah. 'Now you be a good girl and be sure to collect me some pretty shells from the beach.'

The little girl nodded solemnly before climbing up the step to stand beside her brother, and now there was just Briony to say goodbye to. Lois wasn't sure how she would bear it. Her heart felt as if it were splitting in two but she kept her voice light as she hugged her beautiful daughter.

'I love you all, sweetheart,' she muttered into Briony's thick silky hair. 'Now take good care of yourselves and jump aboard otherwise the train will be going without you.'

Briony silently hopped onto the train as the guard hurried past, slamming the carriage doors shut as he went. He then glanced up and down the length of the platform and when he was quite sure that all the doors were closed, he lifted his green flag and blew on his whistle. The train instantly shuddered into life and a billow of smoke floated along the platform as it slowly began to draw away. The children clung to Briony with one hand as they frantically waved to their mother with the other, but within seconds she was swallowed up in the mist. Sarah was very quiet and Alfie was still crying, but as they stared from the window at the passing fields he wiped the tears and snot from his cheeks on the sleeve of his blazer.

'Cor, the train don't 'alf go fast, don't it?' The excitement of his first train-ride was kicking in now, and Briony smiled indulgently as the two children pressed their noses to the window and stared out in awe. She wished that their mood could last until they arrived in Cornwall but she doubted that it would. They were not due to reach their destination until very late that evening and she guessed that they would be tired and fractious by then. Still, for now at least she felt able to sit back and relax and that's exactly what she did.

Having lived in a town all their lives the children were enchanted by the sheep and cows that were dotted about the fields that they passed. Another field full of horses had them shouting with pleasure, and Briony began to hope that being away from home for a time wouldn't be as bad as she had feared. The children were certainly enjoying their first-ever journey on a train. The novelty began to wear off shortly after they changed trains at Exeter in the afternoon. By then they were getting tired so Briony gave them some of the sandwiches and squash her mother had packed, and encouraged them to lie down on the seats and have a nap.

The day had started as a beautiful misty September morning but now the mist had been burned off by the sun and it was uncomfortably stuffy in the small enclosed carriage. Once the children had dropped off to sleep Briony opened the small window and tried to read the book she had brought with her, but found that she was too apprehensive about what lay ahead of them to concentrate. Would they be greeted warmly, or were their grandparents only taking them in on sufferance? They would soon find out, and as the train ate up the miles her nervousness increased. Very late in the afternoon they changed trains again for the final leg of the journey. The light was fast fading by then and the children had become irritable after their long confinement.

'How much further is it?' Alfie asked every few minutes. And then suddenly they glimpsed the sea from the window and they were instantly excited again. Even in the fading light it was a deep shade of blue and Sarah hopped from foot to foot as she pointed to it.

'Cor, *look*, Briony – it just goes on *forever*!'

And then Alfie babbled hopefully, 'Will we have time to go an' have a paddle when we get there?'

'I doubt it,' Briony answered patiently. 'It's going to be very late by the time we get to Penzance. But I'll tell you what – if you're both really good I'll try and get you onto the beach tomorrow.'

Alfie pouted but then asked, 'Have we got anything else left to eat? I'm starving!'

Briony wondered if he had hollow legs. He always seemed to be 'starving', but thankfully after a quick rummage in the basket she found two more potted-meat sandwiches and handed one each to the children. 'I'm afraid that's it now until we get there,' she warned them. 'But I'm sure they'll have a meal ready for us.'

Again she tried to envisage what The Heights might be like. After what her mother had told her she had no doubt that it would be very grand indeed and she hoped that they wouldn't feel too out of place there. The scenery was changing now and Briony was soon as enchanted as the children. By peering from the window, she managed to make out majestic cliffs and could see waves breaking on the beach in great white sprays. It really was a different world to the one they had left behind, and she wondered how their mother had ever managed to settle in such a built-up area after being accustomed to having all this space about her. Slowly as they travelled further into Cornwall the children began to rub their eyes wearily.

'Not much further now,' Briony told them encouragingly as Alfie yawned. It was too dark to see anything out of the window now. It felt as if they had been on a train for days and she would be as pleased as the children to get to their destination. At last the train began to slow. Briony nudged the children, who had fallen asleep again, and urged them, 'Get your cases and put your coats on. I think we're there.'

Sarah and Alfie blearily did as they were told, and minutes later the train lurched to a halt. They found their way to the nearest door and Briony helped them both down onto the platform where they stood for a moment feeling totally out of their depth. They were the only ones to alight from the train, but as Briony peered along the dimly lit platform she saw the door of a waiting room open and an elderly man step out. He was a giant – well over six foot tall, Briony estimated – and he had a ruddy complexion, as if he spent a lot of time outdoors. As he walked towards them she saw that he was dressed in thick cord trousers, heavy boots and an old tweed jacket.

'Be you the Valentine children?' he asked in a broad Cornish accent, and Briony was suddenly so nervous that all she could do was gulp and nod.

'Arr, good. Then come along o' me. Your grandparents sent me to meet you. I have the trap outside.' She saw that his face was kindly as he smiled at the two younger ones, and she felt slightly better. But what had he meant by 'the trap'?

Clutching their suitcases, they followed him from the station and soon found themselves in a charming little cobbled street full of higgledy-piggledy thatched cottages that looked as if they had come straight off the cover of a chocolate box. Before they had gone more than a few steps Alfie sniffed at the air and asked nervously, 'What's that funny smell?'

'That be the sea salt you can smell, sonny,' the man said affably. It was then that Briony spotted a pony and cart and she suddenly realised that this must be their transport to The Heights.

'I er . . . thought we'd be going by bus or car,' she ventured as she eyed the horse warily and the man threw back his head and gave a throaty chuckle.

''Fraid not, my little maid,' he answered. 'There be a shortage of petrol even here in Cornwall, so you'll have to make do with Old Meg here.' He took a carrot from his pocket and fed it to the mare as he stroked her mane affectionately, and then suddenly remembering something he said, 'I'm Caden Dower, by the way. Worked for your grandparents for years, so I have, an' I knew your ma when she was just a little girl. In fact, that little 'un there gave me a rare shock when I first glimpsed her. Double of your ma when she were that age, so she is.' He patted Sarah's head gently and Briony felt herself warming to him.

'But come along now,' he went on. 'No doubt you're all hungry as hunters after your long journey, and the wife has got some food ready for you all.' He lifted their cases into the back of the trap then swung Sarah and Alfie up beside them, telling Briony, 'You can climb up in front with me if you've a mind to, young lady. 'Twould be a bit of a squeeze with you all in the back.'

Briony obediently clambered up beside him to sit on the hard wooden bench seat, then clung to the edge of it as the horse began to move away.

'Giddyap, there,' he said encouragingly, shaking the reins, and Old Meg broke into a trot that had all their teeth chattering as they rattled across the cobbles. Briony stared about with interest although there was very little to be seen, for even here in Cornwall the blackouts were in force and the whole place was shrouded in darkness. After a time they left the town behind and the road became smoother as they began to climb a steep hill. Soon they were on the cliff road and Briony shut her eyes at one point as she stared down at the sheer drop onto the beach at the side of them, lit by moonlight.

'My mate Jimmy reckons there are sharks in the sea here,' Alfie said at one point. 'Is that right, Mr Dower?'

'Arr, we do get the odd one from time to time,' the man replied genially. 'But don't you get worrying about that now. There's nothing better than a dip in the sea to blow the cobwebs away on a nice bright day.'

Alfie was very relieved to hear it and went back to staring about him.

'Is The Heights very far?' Briony asked when they had gone some distance.

'Only a couple of miles or so as the crow flies,' Mr Dower answered. 'It's close by the village of Poldak.'

Briony gawped nervously at the cliff-edge. It seemed dangerously close – but then the horse appeared to know where she was going so she supposed they would be all right.

Eventually, Mr Dower pointed ahead. 'That be The Heights,' he told her, and Briony felt her stomach cramp. Their long journey was almost over and very soon now they would be meeting their grandparents for the first time. Suddenly she just wanted to turn tail and run back home – but it was too late now.

Chapter Twelve

As Lois walked back into her empty kitchen after saying goodbye to the children at the station she looked about herself forlornly. The house felt so empty and quiet without them, and yet she knew that she had done the right thing in sending them away. She would never have been able to live with herself if anything had happened to them.

Somehow over the last few days she had managed to hold herself together, but now suddenly she allowed the tears that she had held back to roll from her eyes. She was still trying desperately to come to terms with the absence of her beloved James, and now the children were gone too and she didn't know how she could go on without them. Lifting a photograph of them all taken in happier times, she ran her fingers across their faces then placed it back on the mantelpiece. Coming to a decision, she ran lightly upstairs and dropped to her knees to reach beneath the bed. Her fingers closed about the bottle of sherry and the bottle of port she had been hiding there. It had seemed the safest place for them, and she had another two bottles stashed away beneath the towels in the airing cupboard too. If ever Lois had needed a drink it was now, so grappling the top from the sherry she took a great gulp straight from the bottle and sighed in relief as it burned its way down into her stomach. She drank some more. With any luck the pain would go away soon. It usually did after a good stiff drink – and who was there to care now?

'Lois, where are yer, gel?' Mrs Brindley entered Lois's kitchen later that afternoon. She had collected her neighbour's rations, which were pitifully small now that the children had taken their ration books away with them. Getting no response, she placed them on the table then called up the stairs: 'Did they get off all right? Are yer up there?'

Again there was no reply and she frowned as she looked about her. Lois's coat was chucked across the back of the chair where she had dropped it when she returned from the station, and the fire had gone out. Tigger was standing at the side of his dish waiting to be fed, and although it was getting dark Lois hadn't bothered to draw the curtains so her neighbour hastily closed them before switching the light on.

'I'm comin' up to check you're all right,' she shouted now and began to climb the steep staircase. She found Lois lying spread-eagled on the bed clutching a half-empty bottle of port, with an empty bottle of sherry dropped on the floor at the side of her.

'Oh, luvvie,' Martha muttered as she hurried across to the window and drew the bedroom curtains too. Lois was snoring, her mouth hanging slackly open, and the other woman could clearly see the tracks of the tears that had dried on her cheeks. 'Let's take yer downstairs an' get some strong black coffee into yer, eh? Drinkin' yerself into this state ain't goin' to help nothin' now, is it?'

She managed to get her arm beneath Lois and drag her up onto the pillows, but Lois was out for the count and in a very short time the other woman realised that she wasn't going to be able to wake her. Nor was she going to be able to get her downstairs in this state.

'Looks like I'll just 'ave to stay an' keep me eye on yer till yer wake up. I daren't leave yer alone in this state,' she muttered, and after drawing a blanket across Lois she sighed and settled herself into the chair by the window. It looked set to be a very long night and she wondered if this was just a taste of things to come.

Chapter Thirteen

Briony saw that they were passing through a wide opening that had clearly once had large gates attached to it at some stage. Perhaps the government had taken them, to melt them down to make aircraft parts. On either side was a wall that looked to be at least eight high, then they were clopping along a drive that was bordered by towering trees. Unfortunately it was too dark to see what the grounds were like so she peered ahead, keen to get her first glimpse of The Heights. The drive seemed to go on forever but at last they left the trees and ahead of them a huge building loomed up out of the darkness. Mr Dower drew Meg to a halt at the bottom of some stone steps that led up to two impressive oak doors.

'Here we are then, all safe and sound,' he said cheerfully as he lumbered out of his seat. He then reached up into the back of the trap and lifted Sarah and Alfie down as Briony hopped down to join them. They collected their suitcases and when Meg went to crop on the grass, dragging the trap behind her, the tall man led them up the steps.

'Will one o' the servants open the door fer us?' Alfie asked, his eyes like saucers, and Mr Dower chuckled.

'I reckon there's very little chance of that happening,' he answered, and pushing one of the doors open he ushered them inside.

They found themselves in the most enormous entrance hall they had ever seen. In fact, Briony was sure that it was almost as big as their school assembly hall. But for all that it was nothing at all like she had expected it to be. Scuffed black and white tiles covered the floor and a mahogany balustraded staircase swept up to a galleried landing. The balustrade was intricately carved and turned, and quite magnificent – but Briony saw that it was thick with dust and looked like it hadn't been cleaned for ages. A rich red flock paper covered the walls and to one side was a beautiful hall table in gilt with a matching mirror hanging above it, but again the items looked grimy and uncared for. She looked around, expecting their grandparents to be there waiting for them, but there was no one – and nothing to be heard but the loud ticking of a huge grandfather clock that stood on the opposite wall to the mirror.

'Leave your cases there,' Mr Dower instructed them. 'And then come along with me and we'll get the missus to rustle you up some dinner.'

They obediently followed him down the long hallway, their shoes making tap-tapping noises on the tiles until they came to a green baize door. He pushed it open and immediately the delicious smell of roast lamb met them, making their stomachs rumble with anticipation.

'So here you are at last, my lovelies,' a kindly faced woman greeted them. She was flushed from standing over the stove and her portly figure instantly put them all in mind of Mrs Brindley. Her hair was greying and pulled into a tight bun at the back of her head, and she was enveloped in a voluminous snow-white apron. She wiped her hands on it, then bustling forward, she hugged them each in turn.

'My goodness, you've a look of your mother about you,' she remarked in a soft Cornish burr, holding Sarah at arm's length and staring at her. 'Do you not think so, Caden?' she asked her husband, and he nodded as he took his cap off then washed his hands and sat at the large scrubbed pine table that took centre place in the room.

Briony risked a quick look around and was amazed at the size of the room. A huge stove stood against one wall, and a fire, above which were suspended a line of copper pans, was burning brightly. This room was cleaner than the hallway, Briony observed, but the whole place looked as if it would benefit from a good scrub. An enormous dresser was standing against another wall, loaded with china, and a rag rug lay in front of the fireplace with two easy chairs to either side of it.

'Now then, wash your hands and sit yourselves down,' Mrs Dower said bossily, 'and I'll have this dinner served up in the shake of a lamb's tail, excuse the pun!' In no time at all the woman was busily straining steaming vegetables into a vast Belfast sink.

Plucking up her courage, Briony asked, 'Will we not be meeting our grandparents tonight, Mr Dower?'

He scratched his chin, which she saw was in desperate need of a shave, and shook his head. 'I don't think so, my bird. No doubt your grandmother'll be settling Mr Frasier down for the night be now and she'll let nothing stand in the way o' that.' Seeing her crestfallen face, he added hastily, 'But I'm sure she'll make time to see you all, come the morning.'

Briony nodded and peeped at Alfie and Sarah, who were so nervous they had been struck dumb. Their eyes were on stalks and reaching out, she stroked their hair and smiled at them reassuringly. The meal that Mrs Dower served them was delicious. There were crispy roast potatoes and a selection of vegetables, which Mr Dower informed them had been grown in the kitchen garden, and the roast lamb was so tender that it almost melted in their ravenous mouths. It was followed by apple crumble and custard, and when they had eaten Briony thanked Mrs Dower.

'That was lovely,' she said. 'We haven't had a meal like that for a long time.'

'Ah well, there's some benefits to be had from living here,' the woman informed her. 'To tell the truth, the rationing has hardly affected us as yet. We have our own cows, sheep and chickens see, so we're never short of meat or eggs. Then Mr Dower here and Howel, our grandson, have both got green fingers, so there's always a supply of fresh fruit and veg.'

Briony suppressed a yawn as she began to collect the dirty plates together and carry them to the sink, but Mrs Dower shooed her away.

'No need to do that tonight, me lovely. The dishes can soak in the sink till morning. I'm thinking it's time you all turned in. You look fair worn out, but first let me get the little ones a nice bedtime drink.' She disappeared into an enormous walk-in pantry and returned with two glasses of frothy milk which the youngest two drank down in seconds, leaving white moustaches on their upper lips. 'Howel got that fresh from the cow this morning,' she told them, and then winking at Alfie, she bent to his level to tell him, 'I'm sure he'll teach you to milk a cow if you ask him nicely. Now Caden, you get the children's cases, would you, and I'll show them up to their rooms.'

She led them to a staircase that was hidden behind a door at the far end of the kitchen, and they began to follow her up some steep stairs. Eventually they reached a landing that had sloping ceilings either side of it and Briony realised with a little shock that they were up in the attics.

'This is where the live-in staff used to sleep,' Mrs Dower told the girl apologetically, seeing the confusion on her face. 'Your grandmother thought you'd all be better up here so you wouldn't disturb the master, but I've tried to make it comfortable for you.'

The housekeeper was secretly appalled that the missus had stuck the children up here so far away from the main house when there were so many decent-sized bedrooms, but she couldn't voice her opinion, of course; she was paid to do as she was told.

'I'm sure it will be fine,' Briony said uncertainly, following her into the first room Mrs Dower stopped at.

'I thought one of the little ones would be all right in here.'

Briony looked about the sparsely furnished room. There was a single metal bed standing against one wall with a small chest of drawers at the side of it, and on the opposite wall was a wardrobe. Drab curtains were tightly drawn, shutting out the night – but other than that the room was bare of any adornments of any kind.

After looking at the whitewashed walls, Sarah said bluntly, 'I don't like it here!'

Briony blushed. It did look clean at least, and Mrs Dower had clearly put fresh bedding on the bed.

'Start to put your things in the drawer and find your nightclothes,' she said, 'while I go and get Alfie settled in, and then I'll come back to tuck you in.'

'But I want to sleep with you! I *always* sleep with you.'

Briony ignored her as she hustled Alfie back out onto the

landing. The last thing she needed right then was for Sarah to fly off into a tantrum.

The second room was almost identical to the first, and once she had left Alfie reluctantly haphazardly unpacking his suitcase she then went to look at her own room. This was slightly larger than the other two and also had an old mirror hanging on the wall. There was a double bed in there too, but she saw with a sinking heart that it was equally as bleak. Even so she smiled gratefully at the friendly couple. At least they had both gone out of their way to greet them and try to make them feel welcome, which was more than she could say of her grandparents.

'Thank you,' she told them both sincerely.

Mrs Dower ushered her husband ahead of her along the landing then, saying, 'You're very welcome, pet. But now we must get back to the farm or Howel will think we've left home.'

There were so many questions that Briony wanted to ask. What did they mean – get back to the farm? And where were all the staff that her mother had told her about? She opened her mouth to ask but then clamped it shut again. She was just too weary tonight. There would be time for all the questions in the world tomorrow.

'Now I shall be back to cook your breakfasts for you in the morning,' Mrs Dower told her. 'Oh, and by the way, the bathroom is the last door on the left at the end of the landing. Goodnight, my dearies.' She and Mr Dower disappeared off down the stairs then, leaving Briony to check on the children. It seemed that there were a few compensations to being here at least. The meal had been wonderful and having an inside toilet would be a real treat after being used to an outside one.

She found both Sarah and Alfie sitting tearfully on the

end of their beds hugging the teddies they had brought with them and sucking their thumbs; a sure sign that they were upset. But at least they had both got changed into their nightclothes. She decided their washes could wait until the morning just this once.

Briony forced herself to sound cheerful as she tucked them in, promising she would try to get them to the beach the next day and reminding them what a lovely dinner Mrs Dower had cooked for them. Eventually they both settled down from sheer exhaustion and Briony went off to her own room to unpack. However she was so tired that after rummaging in her suitcase and finding her nightclothes she clambered into bed and snuggled down. Briefly she wondered how her mother was – and then started as an owl hooted into the night. Everything was so strange here, but then no doubt they would all adapt, and after all it wasn't as if it was forever. On this comforting thought she drifted off to sleep.

The following morning, Mrs Dower climbed the stairs to find Sarah's and Alfie's rooms empty. Guessing what had happened, she tiptoed along to Briony's room and sure enough when she inched the door open she saw the two younger children tucked up beside their big sister, fast asleep. They must have crept along the landing to join her during the night. Quietly closing the door she headed back to the kitchen, deciding to leave them where they were. They were obviously all worn out following the long journey of the day before, and a lie-in would do them good. She certainly had enough work to keep her busy until they came down for breakfast.

It was the sun shining through a slight crack in the curtains that woke Briony, and totally disorientated, she looked around wondering where she was. And then it all came back to her and panic set in as she glanced at the two little ones who were softly snoring on either side of her. What would Mrs Dower and her grandparents think of them if they had overslept on their first morning there? Gently shaking the children, she urged, 'Come on, you two, we need to get washed and dressed. I have no idea what time it is and I think we may have overslept.'

Half an hour later, with them all washed and neatly dressed she took the children's hands and led them down to the kitchen. Mrs Dower was standing at the stove flipping bacon in a huge frying pan and she smiled a greeting.

'No need to ask if you slept all right. You were all flat out when I came up to check on you a while ago,' she said merrily.

'I'm so sorry. We don't usually stay in bed this late,' Briony apologised. 'What time is it anyway?'

Mrs Dower nodded towards a clock on the wall. 'Its not late, my lovely. Only just gone nine. I've only just taken the breakfast through to your grandparents. Your grandad didn't have a very good night, apparently. But now, come and sit down and eat.'

Briony was embarrassed, not used to being waited on, but she did as she was told as Mrs Dower began to load their plates with thick juicy sausages, sizzling rashers of bacon and eggs.

'Cor,' Alfie muttered gleefully at the sight of the lovely yellow yolks. It had been a long time since he had been served with a fresh egg. All they had been able to get back in Nuneaton was powdered egg since rationing had been introduced, and it tasted nowhere near as nice as fresh ones.

'I went and collected them from the barn first thing this morning,' Mrs Dower told him. 'The chickens tend to lay where they've a fancy to. Perhaps you'd like to help me collect them each morning if I show you where to look?'

'Not 'alf!' Alfie answered enthusiastically and Mrs Dower laughed as she ruffled his hair. They were lovely children, there was no doubt about it, as she had remarked to her husband the night before. The younger two were the spit of their mother, while Briony was a dead ringer for her father. Mrs Dower could remember James and had always wondered why her mistress didn't like him. He had no money admittedly, but he had always seemed to be a nice enough chap and Miss Lois had been totally smitten with him. She could remember clearly the ruckus it had caused when the young woman had taken off with him and the way her parents had disowned her, or at least her mother had. Mrs Dower had a sneaky feeling that Mr Frasier would have accepted it, but he was so far under his wife's thumb that he went along with anything she said just for a bit of peace, which to her mind was a crying shame. And now after all these years, here were Lois's lovely children. Life was a strange thing when she came to think of it.

Alfie, and even Sarah, who was usually a delicate eater, cleared their plates in record time before asking Briony, 'May we go outside to have a look around now?'

'Well . . .' Briony looked towards Mrs Dower, who nodded.

'Of course you can. There's lots for you to explore. But don't stray too far from the house now. Once you get on to the moors there's old tin mines – and should you fall down one of the workings, chances are you'd not be seen again.'

Wide-eyed, the children scampered away while Briony stayed behind to help Mrs Dower with the washing-up, although the woman protested.

'No, please – I'd like to,' Briony implored, so eventually

the woman agreed and she washed the dishes whilst Briony dried them.

The questions that she had wanted to ask the night before were still buzzing around in her head so now Briony said tentatively, 'I expected there would be a lot of servants living here, from what my mother told me.'

'Ah, well, there were back then when she was living here,' Mrs Dower answered. 'But once the war started, everything changed. The master took ill, your Uncle Sebastian was called up, and along of him went most of the live-in staff. There's just me, my husband Caden and our grandson Howel now to keep things going in the house and garden, and it's not easy, I don't mind telling you. This place is far too big for me to cope with on my own, though I do my best. The gardens used to be a picture; the lawns were so well tended you could have played bowls on them. The house was the same, but most of the rooms are shut off now and even the Frasiers stick to just three rooms. I come along each day to do the cooking and what cleaning I can manage, then I have to go back and start on the farm.' She sighed wearily.

'Aren't there two farms on the estate?' Briony asked, remembering what her mother had told her.

'Yes, there are. We live at Kynance Farm, but the other one is empty now. Your grandfather has had to sell a lot of the land off, unfortunately. It was too much for Howel and Caden to keep up with. Not only that, but between you and me, I reckon they needed the money. Master Sebastian runs the undertaker's business down in Penzance – but that's about all he will do,' she ended somewhat scathingly.

Briony was confused. 'But I thought you just said my uncle was called up?'

'So he was – but he injured his hand in Singapore and was deemed unfit to return to his unit.'

'Oh, so is he here now then?'

'No, he's off on one of his jaunts to London, leaving old Morris Page to keep the business going,' the woman said, and then glancing across her shoulder to make sure that there was no one there, she advised quietly, 'I'd give him a wide berth if I were you, my lover.'

'Why is that?' It seemed that everyone was advising her to keep away from her uncle and she was curious to know why.

'He's a bad 'un, that's why, I don't think everything he does is above board.' But then, remembering who she was talking to, Annik Dower added hastily, 'But that's just my opinion, of course.'

Briony sighed, wondering what her mother would make of it all. The Heights was clearly no longer as Lois remembered it, and they still hadn't met their grandparents as yet. How much longer would it be before the latter sent for them? After helping Mrs Dower to finish tidying the kitchen she went off in search of her brother and sister and to get her first proper look at The Heights in daylight.

Chapter Fourteen

As Briony stepped out of the back door into a cobbled yard she was confronted by a number of outbuildings. Chickens were roaming freely, clucking and pecking amongst the cobbles, and seagulls were wheeling in the sky above her. The air was tangy with salt from the sea; it smelled clean and fresh – there were no smoky streets here – and she drew a deep breath of air down into her lungs. Immediately ahead of her were three stables, but she noted that only Meg, the old horse that had brought them here, was in one of them, contentedly chewing on a nosebag. The other two were empty and she decided she would ask Mrs Dower later on where the other horses were. She seemed to recall her mother telling her that her father had had quite a passion for horses.

At the end of the stable block were two large barns. The doors stood open on one of them and she glimpsed a hay loft and a number of gardening tools inside. The enormously high doors on the other one were firmly closed and heavily padlocked, and she briefly wondered what was stored in there. To one side of her was another door leading to what was clearly the laundry room, complete with deep stone sinks and a mangle, and next to that was yet another room that appeared to have been a dairy at some time. It clearly hadn't been used for some long while, if the heavy cobwebs hanging from the ceiling were anything to go by.

Beyond these rooms was a wall, and after entering through the wooden gate set into it, Briony found herself in what must be the kitchen garden. Only one side of it had been cultivated; the other half was overgrown with brambles, thistles and blackberry bushes. The brick walls were covered in ivy and other creepers, and she imagined that they would be a riot of colour in the summer. Back out again, she followed the wall round and found herself in an orchard. Again, the grass had not been cut and was ankle-deep, and the trees were heavy with fruit. She would have liked to linger here listening to the gulls and the birds in the trees, but she was keen to find the children now so she moved on.

After walking for some time she emerged from the trees and her breath caught in her throat at the sight before her. Miles and miles of moorland stretched out to one side of her, while to the other lay the sea. It was a truly magnificent sight. The water was crystal clear and sparkling in the sun beyond the cliffs, and way out on the waves she spotted a fishing boat. About a mile or so away she could see smoke curling lazily from the chimney of what appeared to be a farmhouse; she wondered if this was the Dowers' farm and made a mental note to ask Mrs Dower when she got back to the house.

Keeping to the edge of the cliff, she headed back towards

The Heights, and before she had gone too far she heard laughter and guessed that this was Alfie and Sarah. Smiling, she hurried on past the side of the enormous house into what had clearly once been a rose garden. The roses were still blooming profusely and the air was heavy with their perfume, but the whole sunken garden was clogged with weeds. The sight saddened her. It must have been a glorious spectacle when it had been tended, for even now it had a natural if somewhat unkempt beauty.

At that moment, Alfie appeared from around one of the overgrown bushes – they were quite high and clearly had not been pruned for some long time – and his little face was radiant. Briony was dismayed to see that his shirt was already hanging out and his clean grey shorts had grass stains on the backside.

'Oh Alfie,' she groaned. 'I'm sure you could manage to get dirty in a padded cell.' She was expecting a summons from her grandparents at any moment and had gone to great pains that morning to make sure that the children were as neat as new pins, but already they were both looking bedraggled. Even Sarah had somehow managed to pull the hem of her dress down, and her white socks looked decidedly grimy.

'Come on,' she said firmly. 'We need to get you two tidied up again. Heaven knows what Grandmother and Grandfather will say if they get their first glimpse of you looking like this.'

'Oh, do we *have* to?' Alfie complained. He was clearly having the time of his life but he came to her all the same, and turning about they were faced with the front of the house. It had been so dark when they had arrived the night before that they had been able to see very little of it, but now the sheer size of the place took their breath away.

'*Cor!* It's like a palace, ain't it?' Sarah said as she gazed at it in awe.

Briony smiled as she took them by the hand and began to lead them back the way she had come. They saw rabbits scurry across the lawn and a squirrel in a tree, and the children were enchanted.

'Why do we 'ave to go back?' Alfie complained. 'Why can't we go down onto the beach? There's some steps over there leadin' down to it. Me an' Sarah found 'em a while back.'

'Didn't I tell you not to go anywhere near the edge of the cliff?' Briony scolded, but it was hard to be mad at them when they were both looking so happy. Even Sarah, who was usually frighteningly pale, had a little colour in her cheeks already, and their eyes were as bright as buttons.

Mrs Dower was just about to leave when they re-entered the kitchen and she grinned when she saw the state of Alfie.

'Have our grandparents asked to see us yet?' Briony enquired hopefully.

Mrs Dower felt sad as she saw the expectant look on the girl's face. 'Not yet. But I'll tell you what – I'll pop along to see them now and ask if they're ready for you. Meanwhile you could perhaps clean his lordship up a bit, eh? Don't want to make a bad first impression, now do we?'

She disappeared off through the door leading into the hall as Briony grabbed a damp cloth from the draining board and started to scrub at Alfie's face.

'Gerroff!' he objected but his big sister ignored him and carried on. When his face was clean, she brushed the dust from the seat of his shorts as best she could, pulled his socks up and tucked his shirt in before turning her attention to Sarah.

By the time Mrs Dower returned they were all tidy again

and the woman forced a smile to her face. She didn't want to tell them that she had had to plead with her employers to meet the children. She had a sneaky feeling that the mistress would have been happier if she could have just kept them out of her way completely during their stay so that she could pretend they weren't even there.

'They'd love to meet you now,' she lied. 'Come along and I'll show you what room they're in.'

Alfie slunk nervously behind Briony as they followed Mrs Dower along the hallway.

She stopped and tapped at an elaborately carved wooden door, then told them, 'Go on in then, and I'll see you all later this morning when I'll be back to make your lunch.'

Briony nodded and smiled her thanks, then after taking a deep breath she pushed the door open and stepped into the room. The musty smell met her immediately and as the curtains were partly drawn the room was gloomy. But then as her eyes adapted she saw a man sitting in a wheelchair over by the fireplace and a stooped woman standing closely at his side.

'Well, don't just stand there like *morons*! Come in then,' the woman snapped, and Alfie shrank farther behind his sister's skirts as Briony tentatively took Sarah's hand and led her forward.

As the woman's eyes raked her up and down, she sneered. 'So *you* are the firstborn! No doubt whose daughter you are, is there?'

Briony was so shocked that she was speechless, but already the woman's eyes had settled on Sarah and again she looked as if there was a dirty smell under her nose. 'And you are *truly* your mother's daughter. I just hope you haven't inherited her ungrateful nature . . . But where is the boy?'

Briony tugged Alfie, who was looking absolutely terrified, from behind her and he clung to her hand.

It was then that a transformation took place, for the woman's eyes gentled.

'You must be Alfred,' she said softly. 'Come over here and let me look at you, child.'

'Me name is Alfie an' I wanna stay over 'ere wi' Briony,' he said defiantly, jamming his thumb in his mouth.

Briony held her breath, expecting the woman to shout at him, but instead she chuckled. 'Ah, so you have spirit! Not only do you *look* like your Uncle Sebastian but you sound like him too. But come . . . I won't bite, I promise you.'

Alfie looked up at Briony uncertainly and when she gave an imperceptible nod he inched his way across the carpet towards his grandmother, looking for all the world as if he were about to enter a den of tigers.

This gave Briony time to study the woman a little more closely and she was shocked at what she saw. She was nothing like her mother had described her, although the family likeness was undoubtedly still there. Her faded fair hair was heavily streaked with grey and straggled on her shoulders, and her blue eyes had a slightly wild look about them. Her clothes, a pale-blue twinset and a thick tweed herringbone-patterned skirt, although clearly of good quality, were creased and hung off her bony frame, and about her throat was a string of pearls that gleamed in the dull light. She put Briony in mind of a witch, so she quickly transferred her attention to the man sitting in the wheelchair. He looked very frail and ill, and his legs were swathed in a thick warm blanket, but when she met his eyes she saw that they were kindly and he gave her a gentle smile. She guessed that his hair must have been very dark once, although it was snow-white now. His face was deeply lined and haggard and the hands that poked from the sleeves of his thick brown jacket and rested on his lap looked almost skeletal, but as she returned his stare he said softly, 'You must be Briony?'

'Yes, sir.' She stuck her chin in the air, reluctant to let him see how nervous she was. There was a pungent smell in the room – of sickness and of something else that she couldn't identify – and suddenly she just wanted to snatch the children up and run back home with them. To calm herself, she looked around the room. Just as her mother had told her, it must once have been quite magnificent! Now it merely looked tired. The heavy velvet drapes were faded and moth-eaten and the fine Persian carpet was threadbare in places. Even so, there were some fine pieces of furniture dotted about – although they looked badly in need of a good polish – as well as some very valuable-looking pieces of china. Briony had only ever seen anything like them in the antique-shop window back in Nuneaton.

'So, girl!'

Her grandmother's voice made Briony's eyes snap back to her.

'I don't want you to think that this is going to be a holiday for you. We have been struggling to get help here since the beginning of the war, so once the children start their new school you will be expected to help Mrs Dower in the house and garden.' The words were said almost as a threat but Briony stared back at her with her head held high.

'I am quite happy to help with anything that needs doing,' she responded coldly and just for an instant she could have sworn she saw a spark of amusement flash in her grandfather's eyes.

'Good, then you girls go and find your way about. Alfred can stay here with us.'

'Don't want to!' Alfie responded, shooting back to stand at his big sister's side.

Briony watched conflicting emotions flit across her grandmother's face. She was clearly used to being obeyed but then her face softened again and she told him, 'Very well then, dear. But perhaps you could come back and speak to me and your grandfather later on?'

He sniffed and lowered his eyes as Briony turned and led the children towards the door. They were almost there when her grandmother said, 'Oh, and by the way, girl. It will be your job to keep the children quiet and under control. Your grandfather is not in good health and I do not want him disturbed. Do you understand?'

'I understand perfectly.' Briony's eyes were as cold as her grandmother's. 'And my name is Briony, not *girl*.' And with that she marched from the room as her grandmother gaped after her.

'It is just as I feared,' Mrs Frasier muttered to her husband once they were alone. 'Headstrong, impudent – just like her mother. I think we are going to have trouble with that one!'

He grinned, showing her a flash of the man he had once been. 'Give her a chance and don't be too hard on her, Marion,' he said gently. 'After all, she can't help looking like her father – and she didn't ask to be born, did she?'

'No, she didn't, William, and she wouldn't have been, had it not been for that common lout turning our daughter's head.'

'Well, lout or not he's done a very good job of bringing up his children. I thought they were all quite charming.'

Marion Frasier was so shocked at him standing up to her that she was momentarily speechless.

*

'I don't think I'm going to like it 'ere after all,' Alfie whined as they stepped back out into the bright sunshine. 'An' I don't think Grandmother likes us although Grandfather seemed all right.'

'Oh, you just have to give them a bit of time to get used to us,' Briony told him, keeping her voice light. 'Don't forget, it's strange for them too having us here.'

'Grandmother said I was truly my mother's daughter. What did she mean, Briony?' the little girl piped up. Her bottom lip was trembling and Briony could see that she might burst into tears at any moment.

'She just meant that you look just like our mum,' she said cheerfully. 'Which is a nice thing. But now what would you like to do? It's a wonderful day and it would be a shame to waste it. We don't have to be back for lunch for ages.'

'Go to the beach,' the children cried in unison, just as she had expected.

She smiled at them fondly. 'I think we'll save that treat for tomorrow, but for now how about we go for a walk into Penzance? We couldn't really see it properly when we arrived last night, and I wouldn't mind betting there'll be some boats in the harbour.'

Alfie was instantly all for it so they began to walk down the long drive away from the house with the children in a slightly happier frame of mind. The same couldn't be said for Briony, however, although she was determined to keep her fears to herself. The children were unsettled enough as it was, so the way she saw it, it was up to her to make sure that they were as happy as they could be for as long as they were there. She would take care to keep them out of their grandmother's way as much as possible. Deep inside she was stinging at the way the woman had looked at her and spoken to her, and her hopes of settling the children and returning home to her mother were already beginning to fade. But Grandfather didn't seem so bad, she consoled herself. Perhaps she would find an ally in him? She could only hope so.

Penzance was even more beautiful than it had appeared the night before, and as they walked around the narrow cobbled streets the children felt as if they were in another world. The little thatched cottages were so picturesque, and the people seemed friendly too, smiling at them and calling a greeting as these young strangers passed. It was so peaceful here, it was hard to believe there was a war on. They came to the High Street and walked past rows of tiny shops displaying their wares in the windows. There was a sweet shop full of big glass jars of sweets of every shape and size, and bars of chocolate and trays of home-made toffee. No shortages here! Briony promised the children that she would remember to bring some money with her the next time they came so that she could treat them, and was rewarded with two beaming smiles. Next to that was a butcher's. Sarah wasn't so keen on that shop after seeing the rabbits hanging in the window, so they hurriedly moved on. There was a baker's, and the smell of fresh-baked loaves and cakes made their mouths water; then came a hardware shop full of buckets and mops and everyday things. Further along the street was a blacksmith's – and then they came to a shop with Frasier & Sons on a swinging sign above a window in which stood a huge bowl of fresh flowers.

'This must be Grandfather's undertaking business,' Briony muttered, and shuddered. It was hard to believe on such a beautiful day that beyond the window, dead people could be lying, waiting to be buried. Glancing up, she saw a quaint church with stained-glass windows that twinkled in the sunshine. It was surrounded by a large churchyard and

Briony made a mental note to go and visit it just as soon as she could.

The three hurried on and came to an inn where some elderly men sat outside on a bench with pints of beer, smoking their pipes beneath the shade of a huge oak tree. The men touched their caps and smiled pleasantly at the three youngsters as they passed and they all smiled a greeting in return. The smell of the sea was growing stronger with every step they took, and as they emerged from the end of a cobbled lane there, spread before them, was a small harbour with boats of all shapes and sizes bobbing gently on a crystal-clear blue sea. A number of ruddy-faced seamen from the fishing boats were unloading their catch and the visitors gazed in awe at the huge buckets of fish, some of them still wriggling in protest. Women were sitting repairing large nets on the quay and the children were so fascinated by the scene that it was all Briony could do to eventually drag them away.

Suddenly nothing seemed quite so bad any more, and Briony determined to make the best of their stay in Cornwall.

Chapter Fifteen

By the time the children had climbed the hill back to Poldak, Mrs Dower was busily preparing a cooked lunch, and after the long walk in the fresh air they sniffed at the aroma appreciatively.

'I'm making you all a steak and kidney pie and some nice fresh vegetables out of the garden to go with it today,' she told them cheerily as she stood at the table rolling pastry.

'It smells delicious,' Briony said sincerely, glancing curiously at a young woman who was standing at the sink peeling carrots.

Mrs Dower followed her eyes. 'This is Talwyn,' she said. 'My granddaughter. She usually stays at the farm doing odd jobs there, but she wanted to meet you all so I let her come along with me today.'

The girl turned, and Briony thought how very beautiful she was. She looked to be in her early twenties and was quite striking, with long, dark-brown hair and the largest brown eyes that Briony had ever seen. Her hair curled down her back with golden glints shining in it where it had been kissed by the sun, and she had dimpled cheeks and a very sweet, shy smile.

'Why do your grandchildren live with you?' Briony asked and then immediately wished that she hadn't. 'I'm sorry,' she said, as a blush rose to her cheeks. 'It's really none of my business, is it?'

'It's all right, my lovely.' Mrs Dower's hands became still and a look of great sadness clouded her face. 'It's no secret, everyone hereabouts knows why. The thing is, my son Peder – Talwyn and Howel's father – was killed in an accident when my daughter-in-law, Gwen, was carrying their second child. Gwen was six months' gone at the time, and the shock of losing Peder sent her into early labour. It was touch and go for a time whether the baby would survive. Sadly, her mother died shortly after the birth so me and Caden were left to bring the two children up. The family lived at Chapel Farm – the other farm that you asked about last night.' She gave a gusty sigh. 'It was such a happy place. After that the Kerricks lived there for a time, but it's stood empty since then, and Talwyn – well . . .' she glanced towards the girl who had returned to peeling the carrots. 'She's a little bit slow . . . if you get my drift. The doctor reckons it was because she was born too soon. But she's a good-hearted girl for all that, and I wouldn't be without her, though we have to keep a close eye on her. There's those that could take advantage of a girl like her, and the fact that she's such a lovely-looking maid doesn't help.' She sighed again, then went back to rolling the pastry.

Briony was saddened. Talwyn was so lovely, and just by looking at her it was hard to believe that there was anything wrong with her.

'And how did your first meeting with your grandparents go then?' Mrs Dower asked, to change the subject. Seeing the girl's face drop gave her the answer she had been expecting.

'Not so good, to be honest.' Briony sat down at the table and rested her chin on her hand. 'Grandmother clearly didn't take to me or Sarah, but she did seem smitten with Alfie.'

'Ah well, that'll be 'cos he's the spit of Master Sebastian. Always was her favourite,' Mrs Dower said, loading the pastry into a dish and trimming it. 'Spoiled him rotten when he was a kid, she did – and now she's reaping the rewards.' Between you and me,' she went on, 'she never did pay your mum much attention. Lois was always much closer to her father.'

'Yes, Mum did tell me that her mother favoured her brother,' Briony admitted. After the picture that had been painted of him she was almost dreading meeting Sebastian, although she knew she would have to, sooner or later.

'Oh, you might be pleasantly surprised. He's a good-looking chap and he's got the gift of the gab. Problem is, he's not to be trusted.'

'But why does he keep disappearing off to London?'

'He *says* he's going to collect coffins.' The housekeeper rolled her eyes. 'Since old Mr Tollet the coffin-maker in the village died, that's the only way he can get them. He brings them back in a big van a dozen at a time, and stores them in the barn; the one that's locked up. But between you and me, I reckon he's a bit of a gambler and all. I think his mother has had to bail him out of his debts more than once, although the master wouldn't know about it. She tends to hold the purse-strings since Master William took bad, bless him. Your grandfather is a gentleman, and he'd have a fit if he knew half of what his son gets up to. Not so very long ago, a young maid from the village turned up here saying she was carrying his child, and when she told him, he dropped her like a hot potato! And she wasn't the first, may I add.'

'Really?' Briony's eyes stretched wide, 'So what happened?'

'Huh! I reckon the missus must have paid her off, 'cos next thing you know she's disappeared and she hasn't been heard of since. Fair broke her mum and dad's heart, it did. She never even told them where she was going.'

'Poor girl,' Briony muttered with feeling. She couldn't begin to imagine how awful it must have been for her to be cast aside and left to bear the burden of shame on her own. Mrs Dower bustled away then to fetch the meat she had cooked for the pie, and when she came back, Briony said, 'Grandmother has told me that once Sarah and Alfie are at school I'm to help you about the house and garden. You will tell me what you want me to do, won't you, Mrs Dower?'

Mrs Dower frowned. 'Doesn't seem right that you should have to work,' she said. 'You're family!'

'Oh, I don't mind,' Briony said truthfully. 'I'm used to working. I worked in the offices at Woolworths back at home as well as helping my mum about the house. And I'd get bored if I had nothing to do, so I'm quite happy with the arrangement.'

'Well, an extra pair of hands *would* come in very nicely,' Mrs Dower admitted, but she still didn't think it was right.

'I could start now, if you like?' Briony offered, but Mrs Dower shook her head.

'No, there'll be no need for that. You have a few days to settle in and get to know your way about first. The children should start at school next week and that'll be plenty soon enough to pitch in and help. In the meantime I'll have a word with the mistress about her giving you a small wage each week. 'Tis only fair. She'd have to pay if she could get someone in from the village, so leave it with me.'

Briony chewed on her lip but didn't say anything. Her grandmother clearly had no time for her as it was, and she just hoped that Mrs Dower asking her for wages wouldn't make things worse. Not that the money wouldn't come in handy. There were bound to be things that the children would need and her small amount of savings wouldn't last for long.

They enjoyed a delicious meal and when it was done Briony insisted on helping with the washing-up again. She had spoken to Talwyn by then and realised what Mrs Dower had said about her was right. The girl was very quiet and there was a vacant expression in her eyes. She also had a terrible stutter which made it very hard to understand her even when she did speak.

'Can we go down to the beach now?' the children asked when the pots were dried and put away.

'I think that's an excellent idea,' Mrs Dower beamed at them, 'In fact, I'll pack you up a crowst so as you don't have to rush back. Best make the most of the weather now, 'cos when it turns, it can get really bad here.'

'Er, what's a crowst?' Briony asked, looking confused.

Mrs Dower chuckled. 'Sorry, my lovely. I forgot you're not from these parts. I think you call a crowst a picnic in your neck of the woods.'

'Cor, that'd be lovely,' Alfie said. He had wonderful memories of times when he had gone on a picnic with his family back at home. Sometimes his mum would pack a basket and they would go to Hartshill Hayes or tramp across the fields through Galley Common and on to Ansley. They had used to pick wild flowers on the way back for his mum to put in jam jars on the windowsill, and when he got tired his dad would carry him on his shoulders. He was saddened to think that this would never happen again now. His dad was in heaven, and it was only just beginning to sink in that he was never coming back.

'Right we are then. I've got a nice bit of ham in the pantry,' Mrs Dower said good-naturedly. 'And there's some saffron cake I can pack you up as well, and a bottle of lemonade with a marble stopper. That should keep you all going till suppertime.'

Briony noticed that Talwyn was listening. She asked, 'Would it be all right if Talwyn came with us, Mrs Dower?'

The woman looked doubtful. 'Well, I'm not sure that would be a good idea, my little maid. She tends to wander off, you see. You need eyes in the back of your head with her.'

'Oh, I promise I'd take very good care of her,' Briony said hastily and after a moment the woman nodded.

'Very well then. But don't say that I didn't warn you.'

They set off for the steps leading down to the beach half an hour later armed with a heavy basket full of goodies that Mrs Dower had packed for them. Briony eyed the steps warily. They were very steep, cut into the face of the cliff, and it looked a long way down.

'You all follow me,' she ordered and they began the slow descent. Briony was actually quite afraid of heights and her heart was in her mouth, but eventually they reached the bottom safely, and, suddenly the effort was all worthwhile. The sand underfoot was silver-white, and she saw that they were in a little cove. Azure-blue waves were lapping onto the beach, and before she could stop them, Sarah and Alfie had stripped off their socks and shoes and were splashing in the sea. Talwyn held back, sticking close to Briony, who held her hand and led her to a sunny spot where she put down the basket and settled to watch the children. She had the impression that Talwyn didn't get to visit the beach very often but then she doubted that the Dowers had much free time for pleasure. They always seemed to be working, which Briony thought was a shame, living in such a beautiful place.

'Would you like to take your shoes off and go and paddle with the children?' Briony asked kindly, but Talwyn shook her head. She seemed quite content for now to sit with her. Sarah and Alfie ran back and forth, gleefully showing them the shells and pretty pebbles they had found. Soon they began to search the rock pools and Alfie squealed with delight when he saw his first crab.

I shall have to buy them a bucket and spade each, the next time we go into Penzance, Briony thought, and she was so pleased to see the children enjoying themselves that gradually the hurt feelings about the harsh way she had been treated by her grandmother faded away. After all, it was a lot to have three children suddenly descend on you, so she ought to make allowances.

As the sun moved round in the sky, Briony took Talwyn's hand and went for a gentle stroll around the cove, keeping a close eye on the children. The girl went without protest but remained very quiet and merely nodded as Briony handed things of interest to her. From the way she touched them and studied them curiously, Briony wondered if she couldn't have perhaps done more than she was allowed to, had someone had more time to spend with her. But then poor Mrs Dower barely had enough hours in a day as it was, and she had no doubt she was doing her very best for the girl. Talwyn clearly wasn't used to strangers; Briony doubted she would ever see anyone but her family, which was a shame. The girl was breathtakingly pretty. Her long slim legs and her arms were tanned and her hair shone like copper. She was very simply dressed in a flowered cotton dress that looked to be homemade, and her feet were encased in sandals.

Occasionally when Briony showed her something of interest, her face would break into a smile showing off her dimples, and Briony would see a flash of the young woman she might have been, had she not been damaged at birth. There was a light spattering of freckles across her nose and she had the longest, darkest eyelashes that Briony had ever seen – making her feel quite envious. Briony continued to encourage her to touch and feel things – seaweed that had been washed up on the beach, the smoothness of a shell . . . and eventually she led her back to the basket and they all gathered to eat their picnic. On more than one occasion Alfie dropped his sandwich, but he merely shook the sand off it and ate it anyway, assuring his big sister that it was delicious. He had always liked his food, but she had never known him to have such an enormous appetite; the fresh air must be doing him good. Home and the air raids seemed a million miles away, and could her mother and father have been there with them, Briony felt it would have been just perfect. But the sad fact was, that was never going to happen now.

By the time they climbed the steep steps back up the cliff, the sun was sinking into the sea and the children were tired and yawning. There was a nip in the air now too, despite the mild climate of this part of Cornwall, that reminded them all they were now into mid-September. Briony promised herself that she would bring them to the beach as often as she could while she still had the chance. It might be too cold to venture down there soon.

They made their way around the side of the house and entered by the back door – but not before Briony had noticed a young man digging in the kitchen garden. He looked up as they approached and Talwyn instantly ran to him and wrapped her arms about his waist. He responded by dropping a kiss on the top of her head, then turning his attention back to the others, he said, 'Hello. You must be Briony.' He was remarkably like Talwyn to look at, and Briony guessed that this must be her brother, Howel.

Her hunch was proved to be correct when he held his hand out, but then noticing how dirty it was he instantly withdrew it and smiled apologetically. 'I was just digging a few potatoes for my mother before packing up,' he explained. 'I'm Howel, by the way. It's very nice to meet you.'

'It's very nice to meet you too.' Briony smiled back, thinking what a handsome chap he was. He was at least six foot tall and had the same dark eyes and coppery coloured hair as Talwyn. His shirtsleeves were rolled up and his arms were muscled and deeply tanned, as was his face. Suddenly realising that she was staring she blushed.

'This is Sarah and Alfie,' she introduced the younger two and he winked at them.

'You all right, my lovers? Mum said you'd gone down to the beach. Enjoy it, did you?'

'Not 'alf!' Alfie said, trying to wink back. He and Sarah took to Howel instantly. He was so friendly that it would have been hard not to.

'Well, I'd better get these inside and cleaned up,' Briony said eventually, and gently putting Talwyn away from him, howel ruffled his sister's hair affectionately before returning to his task.

Once back in the kitchen they found Mrs Dower stirring

a large pan of thick chicken soup and the smell of that and freshly baked bread hung on the air, making Alfie feel hungry all over again. The woman smiled a welcome before asking, 'Did you meet my grandson on the way in?'

'Yes, we just spoke to him,' Briony responded as she sank into the nearest chair. 'He seems very nice.'

'Oh, he is,' Mrs Dower agreed proudly. 'Lovely lad, Howel is, none better. He's got a heart as big as Land's End. Though I dare say I shouldn't refer to him as a lad any more. He'll be twenty-three next birthday and I keep nagging him, telling him he should be thinking of settling down by now.'

'Has he got a girlfriend?' Briony asked, and then instantly wished she hadn't. It was no business of hers really but she was curious.

Mrs Dower paused as if she were thinking about the question before answering. 'Well, he's been walking out with a maid from the village, on and off for the last couple of years. I reckon she'd marry him tomorrow if he asked her. As I keep telling him – he could do far worse, but he doesn't seem that interested.' She sighed before confiding, 'Between you and me, he wanted to join up, and he would have done but he was needed to help me and Caden to run the farm. But I know it bothers him. He feels that he isn't doing his bit towards the war, unlike all the other men of his age.'

Briony suddenly thought of Ernie and wondered where he was and what he was doing now. But then she shepherded the children towards the sink and made them wash their hands before tea, asking herself why she felt so guilty.

Chapter Sixteen

That night, Briony lay tossing and turning. The children had dropped straight off, worn out after their day in the fresh air and all the unaccustomed exercise, and she wondered if they might actually last the night in their own rooms. They had certainly seemed a lot happier when she tucked them in and had spoken of nothing else but the time they had spent on the beach. Briony was tired too, but for some reason didn't seem able to sleep. After making sure that the lights were off she had opened the window and now the curtains fluttered in the chill night breeze as she stared up at the star-lit sky. Strangely enough, there seemed to be far more stars in the sky here than there had been back at home, and she wondered if she was imagining it. Eventually she rolled to the edge of the bed and after putting her dressing gown on she rummaged in the drawer for the notebook and pen she had brought with her and headed for the door. The house was in silence so she decided she would go down to the kitchen and write a letter to her mother and Mrs Brindley. They would no doubt be worrying about whether the three of them had arrived safely, and she wanted to put their minds at ease as soon as she could.

After creeping down the stairs she found the kitchen was in darkness and the curtains tightly drawn. She clicked the light on and settled herself down at the table. Tapping her chin with the end of her pen, she wondered what to write and then began:

Dear Mum,
I just wanted to let you and Mrs Brindley know that we have arrived safely. Thankfully there were no diversions on the way and we arrived in Penzance last night as planned. Mr Dower met us at the station and he and Mrs Dower asked me to send you their love.

She tapped her chin thoughtfully again then, debating whether to tell her mother about the meeting with her grandparents. She had no wish to worry her, so eventually she went on:

We met our grandparents this morning. They are hoping to get Sarah and Alfie into school here very soon.

She omitted to mention their harsh reception – after all, she wasn't really telling any lies, the way she saw it. She was merely dusting over the truth.

The children love it here, they are eating like little horses and we spent the afternoon on the beach with Talwyn, the Dowers' granddaughter. I'm going to write to Ruth too when I have finished this letter and then I shall walk down and post them in the village tomorrow. Has Mrs Brindley heard anything from Ernie yet? We are really missing you and hoping that you are taking good care of yourself. I hope there haven't been any more air raids? And are you eating properly? Please give Mrs Brindley and Ruth our love when you see them and I will write again very soon.

Love you,
Briony xx

P.S. Please write back soon!

Reading back through it, Briony sighed. It wasn't a very long letter but she couldn't think of anything else to write for now. She then wrote a similar letter to Ruth and began to address the two envelopes. She would buy stamps for them in the local post office.

She had almost finished when the door creaked open and her grandmother appeared. For a moment it would have been hard to say who was the more shocked of the two, but then Marion Frasier barked rudely: 'What are *you* doing here?'

'I – I couldn't sleep,' Briony stuttered. 'So I thought I'd write to Mum to let her know that we'd arrived safely.'

The woman swept towards the stove with her dressing gown billowing out behind her like a sail. 'Well, don't be down here too long. I don't want your grandfather disturbed. I've only come in to make him a cup of cocoa. And all this extra electricity you're using with all these lights on has to be paid for, you know!'

Briony wondered how she could possibly disturb anyone, seeing as she and the children had been banished to the former servants' quarters, but she didn't argue. Instead she said placatingly, 'Would you like me to make the drink for him? I could make you one too, if you liked. Mum and Dad always said I made a good cup of cocoa.'

The offer seemed to have the opposite effect to what she'd hoped for, since the older woman glared at her and said in an icy voice, '*I* alone see to my husband's needs. You are only here to do the more menial jobs. You have to earn your keep somehow.'

'But I did bring our ration books, I gave them to Mrs Dower,' Briony muttered in a small voice. It seemed there would be no pleasing this woman, and she was finding her thoroughly disagreeable.

'Pah! Fat lot of good *they'll* be,' Mrs Frasier spat, and realising that for now at least she was fighting a losing battle, Briony began hastily to gather her things together. Perhaps it would be better if she just kept out of the woman's way until the latter was more used to them being there. She was almost at the door when her grandmother said suddenly, 'Bring Alfred to me tomorrow morning in my sitting room at ten o'clock prompt. And I dare say you'd better bring the girl too,' she added as an afterthought.

When Briony turned to look at her she explained sharply, 'I shall be taking them to the village school to enrol them and meet their teacher.'

'Oh, I see. Then perhaps I might come too? The children are a little nervous at present with being so far from home, and if I'm there they—'

'There will be no need for that. I am *more* than capable! You can stay here in case your grandfather needs anything whilst I am gone.'

The words were spoken so brusquely that Briony simply shot off up the stairs without so much as another word. Once in the privacy of her room she gulped and blinked to stop the tide of tears that were threatening. Why was her grandmother being so horrible to her? She had apparently made up her mind to dislike her before they had even met, which was very unfair to Briony's way of thinking. She didn't appear to be too keen on Sarah either, although she had taken to Alfie – and Briony wondered if that was such a good thing. She would just have to wait and see.

By the following morning, Briony was calm again and hopeful that she and her grandmother might get off to a better start that day. She got the children washed and dressed before marching them down to breakfast where she found Mrs Dower laying the table.

'Look, I was thinking, if you were to let me take over cooking the breakfasts each morning it would give you a little more time over at your farm. I can manage it, honestly,' she told the woman.

Mrs Dower straightened to stare at her for a moment. Mornings were a rush, admittedly, and it would be a wonderful help. 'But who would take the breakfasts in to your grandparents?' she questioned worriedly. 'The missus is a stickler for having things just so.'

'Well, you could show me just how they like things and I'd make sure that I got it right.'

'Hmm . . .' The idea was very tempting and the offer kindly meant, she was sure – but how would Mrs Frasier react to Briony serving them their food? 'How about I have a word with her first, and see how she feels about it before I agree, eh?' she said cautiously. Then seeing Briony's face drop, she added swiftly: 'I think it's a grand idea and it would certainly free me up to do more at the farm.'

She ladled some thick porridge made with fresh cream and honey into their bowls and the younger two enjoyed it so much that they both had seconds. Even then Briony was sure they would have licked the dishes clean if she'd let them, but she put her foot down there, saying, 'Now don't you two go and get yourselves dirty, please. You're due to visit your new school with Grandmother in less than an hour.'

'Are we?' Sarah asked. 'And are you coming too?'

Briony said lightly, 'Actually I thought I might stay here in case Grandfather needs anything while you're gone.'

'But we don't wanna go wi'out you,' Alfie protested, suddenly nervous. He hadn't liked the lady he had been introduced to the day before one little bit, and he certainly didn't want to go out with her, even if it was to see his new school.

'Oh, you'll be fine and you won't be gone for that long,' Briony replied as she carried the dirty dishes to the sink. Then addressing Mrs Dower and pointedly ignoring the children's crestfallen faces, she asked, 'Would you show me where you keep all the cleaning things, Mrs Dower? I might as well make myself useful whilst they're gone. I can still listen out for Grandfather.'

Before the clock struck ten Mrs Frasier appeared in the kitchen doorway dressed in a smart lilac costume that hung on her frame, with an elaborately trimmed hat on her head. It was a concoction of feathers and flowers, and the children stared at it open-mouthed. She was wearing white gloves and carried a black handbag which matched her black court shoes. Briony thought that the outfit was more suited for a wedding than a trip to the village school but she said politely, 'You look very nice today, Grandmother.'

The woman simply glared at her before addressing the housekeeper. 'Sebastian informed me on the phone that he will be home later today, Mrs Dower. Could you make sure that his room is aired and that you have his favourite meal prepared. The poor dear will no doubt be tired after his journey.'

Mrs Dower's lips set in a grim line. As if I don't have enough to do already, she thought to herself, but she nodded just the same.

'And you, girl,' her grandmother snapped, staring coldly at Briony, 'make sure that you stay close. If your grandfather needs anything, he will ring the bell. Otherwise stay out of his way and don't trouble him or you will have *me* to answer to when I come back.'

Briony bit back the hasty retort that sprang to her lips and nodded, not trusting herself to speak.

Mrs Dower had watched this exchange without saying a word, but when her employer had left, taking two very reluctant children with her, she said in annoyance, 'I can't see why she has to speak to you like that.'

Briony shrugged. 'To be honest I think she'd made her mind up to dislike me before she even met me, but I do have to be grateful that she allowed us to come here. At least the children are safe, or safer than they would have been at home.' She gave Mrs Dower a cheeky smile then and added, 'Don't worry. I can handle her and I'd much sooner she was horrid to me than to Sarah and Alfie.'

She helped Mrs Dower to finish tidying the kitchen, and soon after that, the woman left to begin the chores on her farm. Briony felt quite sorry for her and wondered how she managed to fit everything in. The woman must be in her sixties; she was no spring chicken. But at least now that she was here she could give her a hand, and on that thought Briony collected a large mop and bucket and headed for the hallway. She had noticed when she arrived how grubby the hall floor tiles were, and if she were to give them a good clean and open the front doors, they might be dry by the time her grandmother and the children were back.

Despite the cool breeze wafting through the open doorway, Briony was soon sweating. The tiles had clearly not been washed for a long time and she had to keep going backwards and forwards to the kitchen to change the dirty water in the bucket. She was almost halfway through when suddenly a bell sounded and she froze. It must be her grandfather needing something. Looking down in dismay at the large apron she had put on, she then glanced into the mirror. Her face was flushed and there was a smudge of dirt on her cheek. She didn't look very tidy at all. But still she decided there wasn't much she could do about it and so she placed the mop back in the bucket, ran her hands down the front of the apron and went towards the door. She felt as if she were approaching a den of lions, but she tapped firmly – and when a voice shouted for her to come in, she pushed the door open and entered with a smile fixed on her face.

'Good morning, Grandfather. Is there something I can get for you?' she asked pleasantly.

He was sitting by the fire and once again the curtains were almost drawn, which Briony thought was a shame when it was such a beautiful day outside.

He smiled at her as she approached him and once again she was struck by his eyes. They were kindly, quite unlike her grandmother's, and made her feel welcome.

'Actually, I don't need anything,' he said softly. 'I just thought it might be nice for us to have a few minutes on our own before my wife comes back. Come and sit over here by me.'

Briony went and perched on the edge of a spindly little gilt chair, feeling very uncomfortable and out of place before saying, 'I'm sorry I look such a mess. Grandmother said I was to help out in the house so I thought I would make a start by giving the hall a good clean while she's at the school.'

His face became sad then, and leaning forward in his wheelchair he told her, 'Don't you let her turn you into a servant, Briony. You are our granddaughter and I want you to feel welcome here.'

Briony thought there was very little chance of that, but she was too polite to say so and remained silent as he went on, 'Tell me about your mother. Is she keeping well? She wrote to me and told me that your father was reported missing and presumed dead. It must have been a great blow to you all.'

'It was,' Briony muttered, angry at the sudden prick of tears at the back of her eyes. 'He was a wonderful dad to us and we all miss him terribly. But of course, it's so much worse for Mum. She hasn't taken the news at all well.'

'Hmmm.' Mr Frasier frowned sympathetically and then shocked her when he said, 'I really liked your father, my dear. From what I can remember of him, James was a decent hard-working chap. The trouble was, your grandmother had very high hopes of a substantial marriage for Lois and she felt that your father wasn't good enough for her. It's surprising really because she and your mother didn't always see eye to eye; and whilst she spoiled Sebastian shamelessly, she was rather strict with poor Lois.'

He glanced towards the darkened windows and Briony asked, 'Would you like me to draw the curtains and open the window for you? It's a beautiful day and if you were to sit over there I'm sure the fresh air would do you good.'

He thought about it for a moment then answered, 'Do you know, I rather think I would.'

Sunlight flooded into the room as Briony threw the curtains aside. It took slightly longer to open the heavy sash-cord windows as they clearly hadn't been opened for some time, but at last she managed it. Then, crossing to her grandfather, she pushed his wheelchair as close to the window as she could. The mild air couldn't possibly hurt him.

He breathed deeply and stared out across the overgrown gardens to the sea, saying, 'I think I'd quite forgotten what fresh air smelled like. Thank you, my dear.'

Briony then went on to speak of what their life had been like back in Nuneaton and he listened avidly, keen to have news of his daughter. In no time at all they were chatting away ten to the dozen but then glancing at the clock, Briony rose and said reluctantly, 'I ought to be getting on now. I'd like to finish the hallway before Grandmother gets back.'

A hint of disappointment shone in his eyes but he said immediately, 'Yes, of course. You get on, my dear. But if you should need anything, come and see me – and don't let my wife make you work too hard now.'

Briony skipped away feeling a million times better than she had since first arriving, and soon she was hard at work again.

She was just washing out the mop bucket when Alfie and Sarah came hurtling in, their faces alight.

'Our school is really nice, Briony,' Alfie told her, his little face animated. 'An' our teacher, Mrs Fellows, is really nice an' all. We're to start next Monday.'

'There are some other children there who 'ave been evacuated too,' Sarah rushed on. 'An' I met a girl called Annie who's from London. She's gonna be my friend.'

'Well, how nice is that then?' Briony grinned and hugged them both, but then the happy moment was spoiled when their grandmother barged into the kitchen, her face flushed with anger.

'Just *what* did you think you were doing girl, leaving my husband sitting at the side of an open window?' she stormed.

Briony flushed. 'I thought the fresh air would do him good,' she answered quietly.

'Well, in future *don't think*! Your grandfather is a very sick man – and if he catches a cold now, it will be your fault!'

Briony bit her tongue, sensing that nothing she said would make things any better. The woman was clearly determined to pick fault with her and she hadn't even mentioned the hall tiles, which were now at least three shades lighter than they had been.

'Very well.' Her eyes were mutinous as she stared back at the woman, who bristled before turning about and stamping from the room, making the feathers on her hat wobble all over the place.

'I don't like her, especially when she shouts at you,' Alfie said, his happy mood gone. 'When can we go home, Briony?'

She forced a smile to her face. 'Oh, don't you get worrying about me – and why would we want to go home yet? You have your new school to look forward to, and I for one want to go back down onto the beach again.'

As Alfie recalled the jolly time they had spent on the sand the day before, his smile slowly returned. Briony was right: although he wasn't that keen on his grandmother, there were lots of pluses to living here too, so he supposed that they would just have to make the best of things.

Chapter Seventeen

When Mrs Dower returned at lunchtime to prepare the meal, her face was grim. 'Caden was reading in the newspaper this morning about the total number of people killed and severely injured in London from August up till now,' she reported to Briony, keeping her voice down. The children were outside, but she didn't want to risk them overhearing. 'Those wicked German bombers are murderers, that's what they are. Those poor Londoners must be going through hell.' The housekeeper had never been to London, but she was very patriotic, and full of praise for Queen Elizabeth and her visits to the East End. 'It also said that Southern England Commands are on full Invasion alert now.'

Briony was shocked. Her thoughts turned to Ernie and she prayed that he was safe. She hoped that there had been no more bombs dropped on Nuneaton either. Seeing how distressed Mrs Dower was, and hoping to change the subject she said, 'That's just terrible, isn't it. Look – I've been thinking. If you were to tell me what you were going to cook each day and get the necessary food over to me, I could do the midday meal for us all.'

'Your grandmother's not going to be too keen on that,' Mrs Dower said uncertainly.

'I can manage,' Briony promised her. 'And as I said before, I could do the breakfast for everyone too. Surely that would be a help to you – and it would keep me busy while the children are at school. I'm not going to have anything else to do, am I? So you'd be doing me a favour really and stopping me from being at a loose end.'

Mrs Dower thought it over. She had refrained from putting Briony's offer to Mrs Frasier up until now but she supposed the worst the woman could do was say no.

Two hours later, as she was just about to leave again, she told Briony, 'The missus says you can give it a try for a day or two and see how you do. But if it gets too much for you, just say. Meantime I'll send Howel over with the milk, bread, meat and cheese, and anything else you'll be needing, early each morning. How does that sound?'

'It sounds marvellous.' Briony quite enjoyed cooking and was looking forward to it, although she wasn't quite so happy at the thought of having to serve her grandparents their meals. Marion Frasier was bound to pick fault, but she decided she would cross that bridge when she came to it. At least it would allow her to see a little more of her grandfather.

She spent the next hour scrubbing the kitchen floor, another job which was long overdue. Not that she blamed Mrs Dower. The poor woman did her best but there was only so much that one person could do. She could hear the children laughing as they played outside in the sun, but then Alfie came dashing in to tell her, 'There's a big lorry comin' up the drive, Briony. Who do yer suppose it is?'

'I should imagine it's your Uncle Sebastian,' she answered. 'Grandmother told Mrs Dower he was coming home today.'

The little boy shot off again, keen to catch his first glimpse of his uncle and Briony suddenly felt nervous. After all the things she had heard about him, she wasn't sure quite what to expect. The large van pulled around to the back of the house and drew up in front of the locked barn. From the kitchen window, Briony saw the driver get out but she couldn't see his passenger. The driver was a great bear of a man with an ugly scar that ran from the corner of his right eye to his chin. He looked as if he hadn't shaved for days and his dark hair was heavily oiled.

To Briony, he looked like one of the gangsters she had read about in crime novels borrowed from the library back home. She watched as he unloaded some large boxes and went off into the barn with them. Then he came back and she shuddered as she saw him checking a number of polished wooden coffins before carrying them into the barn too with the help of another man. He glanced towards the house and afraid of being seen spying on him, Briony hastily left the window and went back to polishing the large dresser, which was thickly coated in dust. After a time she heard the van pull away and then Alfie and Sarah came back into the kitchen again accompanied by the second man she had seen, who looked remarkably like her mother. He had the same fair hair and the same blue eyes – but his were wary.

'So you're Lois's firstborn then?' he said.

She nodded.

'Yes, and you must be our Uncle Sebastian.'

'Just call me Seb, everyone else does,' he answered as he eyed her up and down. Briony squirmed uncomfortably; she felt as if she had been put under a microscope.

Alfie broke the uncomfortable silence when he piped up, 'Me an' Sarah saw you unloadin' big boxes. They're called coffins, ain't they? An' they're what yer put dead people in.'

Sebastian smiled, totally transforming his face as he nodded in reply, saying, 'They are that. Sadly we'll all end up in one eventually. But not for a long time, I hope.'

He was remarkably handsome when he smiled and Briony felt herself beginning to like him. He looked so like her mother that it would have been hard not to. He, on the other hand, could scarcely believe that Briony was his sister's child. She was absolutely nothing like Lois – although the other two were the spit out of her mouth.

Sebastian had very mixed feelings about the children being there. His mother had washed her hands of Lois years ago when she'd run off with James Valentine. Now his father had relented and accepted the children back into the fold. He just hoped that this would not affect his inheritance. When the old dears snuffed it, he intended to be their sole beneficiary now – and the last thing he needed were these kids worming their way into his parents' affections. However, he couldn't really see that happening – not with his mother at least. If truth be told, Marion Frasier had been glad to see the back of Lois when she went. His father was a different kettle of fish entirely though. Lois had always been a Daddy's girl, which was why he himself had also been glad to see the back of her. Thankfully he couldn't see the old man outliving his mother, and she was putty in his hands. He sighed. He'd certainly have to soften his mother up this evening because he had yet another gambling debt that he needed her to settle. Oh, he knew she'd complain and tell him that money was tight, and that he had to stop this way of life, but he'd get round her, he always did.

As for these kids . . . he glanced at them all thoughtfully.

They seemed nice enough and the oldest might even be a help about the place. He couldn't see his old dear not taking full advantage of her. They'd be going home once the war was over and if his parents died before then, this place and all they owned would be his anyway and he'd simply chuck them out. Feeling slightly better about things, he smiled disarmingly at Briony, noting that she was trying not to stare at his damaged hand.

'I copped this in Singapore,' he told her. 'Shot straight through, it was, and a lot of the nerves were damaged. Can't use all my fingers now sadly, but worse still they invalided me out of the service. Still, shouldn't grumble really, you learn to live with it.' He shook his head as if this were some great tragedy and saw the sympathy in her eyes. Women were so easy to fool. He wondered what she would think if he were to tell her the truth: that he had deliberately shot himself so that he could come home. The way he saw it, he would rather be a live coward than a dead hero, and by doing this he could hold his head up and be admired.

Turning towards the door he told her, 'Right, I'd best get off and go and see the parents. Nice meeting you all. Bye for now.'

'Crikey! Uncle Sebastian is *really* brave, ain't he?' Alfie's eyes were like saucers. He had never met anyone who had been shot by a real live bullet before.

'Not so brave as our dad was,' Briony said chokily, and instantly wished that she could retract the words when Alfie's face fell and Sarah's eyes filled with tears.

'Sorry, I didn't mean to say that. Of course Uncle Sebastian is very brave and you two must be very good and not get under his feet. He runs Grandfather's business in Penzance so I would imagine he's very busy when he's at home.'

'I wish we could get a proper look at the coffins,' Alfie

commented and Briony couldn't help but smile. Why was it that little boys liked to be so gory? Show them anything to do with guns or blood and guts and they seemed to be happy.

Martha Brindley was standing in her front window waiting for Lois to return from her shift cleaning the pit offices. She had cooked them both a meal and hoped that if she could catch Lois before she went into her own home, she could stop her from drinking. She was really worried about her. Since the children had left she seemed to have sunk into a deep depression and lost the will to live. Her neighbour sympathised with her, but at the same time she wanted the children to have a home to come back to after the war – and if that meant keeping a beady eye on their mother, then so be it.

She had been standing there for some time when she saw Lois turn the corner, and quick as a flash she was out of the front door and waiting on the pavement for her. Lois looked nothing like the glamorous woman she used to be. Her hair, in which she had always taken such pride, was now lank and scraped back to the nape of her neck with a thin ribbon. She was wearing flat shoes instead of her customary high heels, and devoid of make-up she didn't stand out from the other women in the street.

'Hello, luvvie,' her neighbour greeted her. 'I was hopin' to catch yer. I've done us both a bit o' Spam an' mash fer us tea. It ain't much fun cookin' fer yerself, so come an' join me, eh?'

Lois hovered uncertainly, like a butterfly that was about to take flight. 'Well I er . . . I was hoping to go and check if a letter from the children had arrived,' she answered lamely. She really did appreciate how kind Mrs Brindley was, but she wasn't very good company at the moment and would have preferred to be alone.

'The postie didn't bring nothin' fer neither of us today. I know 'cos I was out cleanin' me doorstep when he went by.' Then seeing Lois's face fall, Mrs Brindley went on in a gentler voice: 'They've only been gone fer a few days, duckie. You've got to give 'em time, an' yer know how the post is at the minute. It's about as regular as my bowels – which ain't sayin' a lot.'

Crossing to the door she held it wide and let Lois step by her into her tiny immaculate front room. Lois sighed as she glanced about her. She knew when she was beaten. The floor was covered in brown linoleum, and the edges round the carpet were so highly polished you almost risked your life or at least a broken leg if you trod on it. A large, rather faded patterned rug covered the centre of the room and that was taken out weekly, thrown across the line and beaten to within an inch of its life. A small dark grey moquette two-seater settee stood against one wall and on either side of it were matching armchairs, their cushions plumped up and placed just so. Next to the fireplace was a tall wooden plant stand with turned legs housing a huge aspidistra plant. The leaves on it shone; Mrs Brindley washed them almost daily with a drop of watered-down milk from her precious ration. Snow-white lace curtains hung at the window, and were taken down to be washed on the first of the month, be it rain or shine.

This was what Mrs Brindley termed her 'best room', only to be used on high days and holidays and very special occasions. The only thing that marred the look of the room was the tape that criss-crossed the inside of the window – a stark reminder that the glass could implode into the room should the bombs drop too close to them. Lois wondered how her friend managed to keep everything looking so immaculate. She had never had either the time or the inclination to bother too much about her own home. In fact, it was only now that James and Briony had gone that she realised just how much they had used to do. If she had a meal or a drink now she would find the dirty pots exactly where she had left them the next morning, whereas before she would have come down to find them washed and put away. It was all very depressing and made her more aware than ever of what a failure as a wife and mother she had been. Perhaps the children would be better off with her parents after all?

As she squeezed by Mrs Brindley the older woman thought she smelled a waft of sherry on her breath. I bet she had a tipple afore she set off for work, she thought to herself, but she kept her voice cheerful as she ushered her neighbour through into the back room and motioned towards the table which was all set for two.

'Sorry it's only Spam again,' she said as Lois shrugged off her coat and took a seat. 'I don't know about you but I'd kill fer a decent joint o' meat, but then I suppose we should be grateful that we ain't starvin'. There's a lot worse off than us.'

Lois nodded, her eyes dull as she thought of all she had lost. The house felt so empty now. It was funny when she came to think of it. They had never seemed to have enough room when they were all at home and yet now it seemed enormous. But the silence was the worst. The place used to ring with the sounds of the children laughing or squabbling, and there had been times when she had felt like banging their heads together and begging them to give her a bit of peace, but now the silence was ominous – until she'd had a few drinks, that was, and then nothing seemed so bad.

She tried to look enthusiastic as Mrs Brindley put a plate in front of her but her stomach revolted. The woman had fried the Spam and the potatoes had been mashed with milk, for gone were the days when butter could be spared. All Lois really wanted to do was go home and finish the half-bottle of sherry she had left at the side of the chair that morning. But even so she forced most of the meal down, wondering how long she would have to wait before she could politely excuse herself. Mrs Brindley had a heart of gold, but Lois longed to be left alone to wallow in her misery. James was never coming back, she had accepted that now, and she might never see her children again – so what was the point of anything?

Chapter Eighteen

Mrs Dower had just fetched the dirty dishes from the Frasiers' dining room that evening when the telephone rang in the hall.

Alfie wriggled in his seat, his eyes wide. The nearest he had ever got to a telephone before was the one in the big red box at the end of their street back home, and he'd decided that his grandparents must be very rich indeed if they could afford to have one in their house.

'That'll probably be someone who's lost a loved one,' Mrs Dower said quietly. 'It's a good job Master Seb is home, isn't it?'

'Why would they ring here?' Briony asked.

'Because the shop is shut. During the day Mr Page would deal with it but after closing time the calls come here. No doubt he'll get the hearse out shortly and go and pick up Morris Page to help him collect the body and take it down to the funeral parlour.'

'How sad.'

'It is that,' Mrs Dower agreed. 'And not the nicest of jobs – but then someone's got to do it, haven't they?' The words had barely left her lips when Sebastian walked through the kitchen, heading for the back door.

'Tell Mother there's been a death up in the village, would you, Mrs Dower?' he said. 'It's old Ned Clark. His wife just telephoned.'

Mrs Dower looked sad. She had known the Clarks all her life, though Ned's death wasn't entirely unexpected. He had been ill for a long time. 'Shall I tell her how long you're likely to be?' she asked.

'Oh, not long,' he answered. 'We'll chuck him in the morgue and see to him in the morning after I've got a coffin out of the barn. I haven't had time to get any down to the parlour yet and I'm not going to attempt it in the dark.'

She tutted as he strode towards the barn where the hearse was kept.

'That young man hasn't got an ounce of compassion in him,' she muttered. 'You'd not have heard his father speak so disrespectfully of the dead when he did the job.'

Glancing at the children, Briony saw that they were looking nervous. All this talk of death was unsettling for them so she told them, 'Go on up to the bathroom, you two, and have a good wash for me, will you? Remember to brush your teeth. I'll be up in a minute then to tuck you in and if you're very good I'll read you a story.'

They scuttled away and once they were gone Briony set to and helped Mrs Dower to put the kitchen to rights. The woman was keen to get back to the farm as Talwyn wasn't so well.

'Her tonsils are right up,' she told Briony as they washed and dried. 'She's prone to tonsillitis and I wish now I'd let the doctors take them out for her when she was a kid. Trouble is, she's terrified of hospitals, bless her.'

'Then you get off and I'll finish up here,' Briony said immediately.

'Right you are then, if you're sure. I'll have Howel bring over all you'll need for tomorrow first thing in the morning. But I'll still be back to cook the main evening meal just till you're feeling in the swing of things.'

'Thank you,' Briony answered gratefully and as Mrs Dower collected her coat and left the kitchen she finished the tidying and made her way upstairs.

Once again the children were asleep within seconds of their heads touching the pillow, and feeling slightly at a loose end, Briony went back down to the kitchen. The evening stretched endlessly in front of her so she decided to go for a walk. Pulling her coat on, she slipped out into the yard. It was dark now and once again the sky was alight with millions of stars. She headed for the gates and stood there admiring the view of Penzance far below her. The whole place was in darkness because of the blackout but the moon and stars were so bright that it was possible to see almost every building. Moving along, she took the path along the cliff, being careful not to get too close to the edge. Far out to sea she could just make out the shapes of some fishing boats, but there wasn't a soul in sight and she felt as if she were the only person left in the whole world. The night was turning chilly now so eventually she headed back to the kitchen and was just about to turn into the yard when voices stopped her.

'Come back tomorrow. I haven't had time to get it yet.'

Recognising Sebastian's voice, she peeped around the edge of the barn, keeping to the shadows. The large van that he had arrived in earlier on in the day was there again, as was the unsavoury-looking character who had been driving it.

'Whadda yer mean, yer ain't had time to get it?' The man sounded angry and Briony's heart began to pound. She didn't know what to do for the best. If she was to move forward now they would see her and it might look as if she had been eavesdropping on them. She decided to stay where she was and flattened herself against the wall of the barn.

'I've just told you – I got called out on a job. I had to collect a body and take it to the funeral parlour so I haven't had time to get the old dear on her own yet. But she'll cough up, she always does. Your money is as good as in the bank.'

Briony surmised that the old dear Sebastian was talking about must be her grandmother.

'It'd better be,' the other man snarled. 'If I ain't got that dosh to the guvnor by tomorrow night I wouldn't wanna be in your shoes.'

'You'll have it,' Sebastian replied shortly as the large man turned about and climbed into the cab of the van.

'I'll be back here at six o'clock sharp tomorrow night,' he threw from the window and then he started the engine and Briony heard the van drive away. She held her breath until the sound of the engine had faded into the distance, and then cautiously peeped around the corner again. Much to her relief the yard was empty so she quickly picked her way across the cobbles and slipped back into the kitchen.

Now her mind began to work overtime. Sebastian apparently owed someone money and the man had come to collect it. Suddenly recalling what Mrs Dower had said about her suspicions of Sebastian gambling she wondered if he had perhaps run up another debt. It certainly sounded like it and it had also sounded as if he expected his mother to pay it for him. She poured some milk into a pan and placed it on the stove to heat up. She was feeling tired now and decided that she would have a hot drink before going to bed. Perhaps her grandparents might like one too? Before she could change her mind about asking them she went into the hallway and approached the sitting-room door. Mrs Dower had informed her that the drawing room had been turned into a downstairs bedroom for her grandfather, now that he was no longer able to tackle the stairs, and he would probably have retired for the night, but her grandmother might appreciate a drink. Briony still hadn't given up hope of winning her round.

She lifted her hand to knock but then stopped as raised voices came from the other side of the door.

'Oh Sebastian, not *again!*' she heard her grandmother wail. 'Haven't I explained clearly enough that money is tight at present? And you *still* haven't shown me the funeral parlour accounts. You know that I like to keep up to date with them.'

'The accounts *are* up to date and I'm only asking for fifty pounds, Mother. If you'd let me have access to the safe I wouldn't have to keep coming to you for every penny I need like a child asking for pocket money.'

'*Only* fifty pounds,' the woman groaned. 'If your father knew, he would be furious, you know he would, and you also know that the only people who have access to the safe are him and me.' But then, 'What's the matter? Oh, darling, is your hand paining you again? Sit down here. I'm sorry I was so sharp with you. I sometimes forget what you've been through and *of course* I'll give you the money. You do run the shop, after all, but you must promise me that this will be the very last time. I shall get the money out of the safe for you and you shall have it first thing in the morning. But whatever you do, don't tell your father.'

Briony turned and tiptoed away with a sombre expression on her face. It seemed as though Sebastian could play his mother like a fiddle. But then it was none of her business and she was only too happy to keep well out of it.

They woke to another clear, bright day with the sun riding high in a cloudless blue sky. Briony got the children washed and dressed and grinned to herself as they skipped away and she heard them giggling in Sarah's room. They were still not over the novelty of having a proper bathroom and an inside toilet. It seemed a world away from the outside lav with its little squares of cut-up newspaper and the tin bath they were used to. The bath in this bathroom was cast iron and sat on funny little legs that reminded the children of lion's feet, and the sink was so large they could almost have swum in it, but they loved it just the same.

As she got herself ready, Briony glanced at the pile of dirty washing that was building up in the corner of her room. She decided that she would take it all out to the laundry room and wash it after breakfast rather than bother Mrs Dower with it. The other woman had enough to do already without having to add their laundry to her duties. Once she was dressed in a pale-blue cotton dress with a full skirt she brushed her hair until it shone, leaving it to swing loosely down her back, then went to collect the children and shooed them down the stairs.

Although she had assured Mrs Dower that she could manage breakfast and lunch on her own, Briony was nervous at the thought of having to serve Sebastian and her grandparents. Still it was too late to go back on her word now, so she gave the children a basket each and told them to go and let the chickens out of their coops and collect some eggs for breakfast. They were only too happy to oblige as Briony made the fire up with logs that were piled at the side of it. This was another job that Howel usually did, but she was sure that the children would be happy to take it over if she showed them where the logs were stored.

She had just put the kettle on when Howel appeared in the doorway loaded down with two enormous wicker baskets. He was so large that his frame blocked out the light but when she looked towards him he smiled pleasantly.

'Morning. Did you sleep well?'

'Very well, thank you.' She returned his smile. 'I think it must be all this fresh air. We're not used to it.'

Crossing to the table he carefully began to unpack the baskets. In one of them were two fresh loaves, a large jug of milk, still warm from the cow, a dish full of butter and a thick sponge cake oozing jam and cream. In the other there was bacon, sausages and a number of other things that Mrs Dower had thought might come in useful. She had already shown Briony where a selection of food was stored in the pantry but Howel assured her, 'I shall be bringing the fresh supplies over every morning but should you need anything just get one of the little ones to pop over to the farm. There's usually one of us about. And you know where all the vegetables are in the kitchen garden, don't you?'

Briony nodded. 'Yes, I do, thanks. In fact, I might go and dig a few up this morning if you don't mind, then I can make a vegetable soup for lunch. I could use some of the cooking apples from the orchard to bake an apple pie for afters. Your mum said she would still cook the main meal in the evenings for the time being.'

'I could go and fetch the apples for you now,' he volunteered, but she shook her head.

'No really, the children will enjoy helping me and from what I've seen of it, you and your family already do more than enough around this place. I bet you've been working already this morning, haven't you?'

'I have, as it happens. I've milked the cows and put them back out to pasture and now I'm going off to clean the pigsties out.' He chuckled. 'Not the nicest of jobs, but I think the pigs appreciate it.'

Briony wrinkled her nose. She was more than happy to help and take some of the jobs over but she wasn't ready to volunteer for that particular one just yet.

It was then that a thought occurred to him and he suggested, 'You could bring the children along to the farm this afternoon if you've nothing else planned. I dare say they'd love to see all the animals.'

'Oh, they would,' Briony agreed, thinking how kind he was. 'The nearest they've ever been to a sheep or a cow is seeing them from the train window on the way here. They'd love it.'

'That's sorted then. See you later.' And with a cheery wave of his hand he was off, leaving Briony to start the breakfast.

The children scampered back in a few minutes later, beaming from ear to ear.

'I found six eggs an' Alfie found five,' Sarah informed her proudly, holding out her basket for the eggs to be admired. The hens were clucking in the yard now as Briony smiled her approval.

'Well done, both of you.'

She made a large pan of porridge although she had to admit it wasn't quite as nice as Mrs Dower's, then after serving the children she took some through to the dining room where the rest of the family were assembled.

Her grandmother didn't seem overly thrilled with the arrangement although she had grudgingly agreed to it with Mrs Dower. But only for a trial period, of course.

'Where are the children?' she asked with a sour expression on her face. Today she was dressed in yet another smart two-piece costume, but her hair was still slightly straggly and Briony thought she had a vaguely wild look about her.

'They're having their breakfast in the kitchen.'

Her grandfather smiled at her warmly. 'Perhaps they could start to eat in here with us, Marion?' he said to his wife.

She looked affronted at the very idea. 'I don't think that is such a good idea, darling. They're probably much happier in the kitchen with *her*.'

The *her* was pronounced so spitefully that William Frasier frowned as he placed a snow-white napkin across his lap. He wasn't at all happy about the children being shoved up in the old servants' quarters as it was. After all, these were their grandchildren, and from what he had seen of them they were very polite and well behaved.

'I suppose Alfred could join us,' she surprised them all by saying then. 'I'm thinking of sending him to boarding school when he is a little older and it would be nice if we were able to teach him some proper manners before he went.'

Briony was so shocked at the suggestion that she almost dropped the jug of milk she was unloading from the tray. Anger seethed through her, and her eyes as she stared at her grandmother were as cold as ice.

'Alfie already has very good manners for a five-year-old,' she said. 'And I sincerely hope we won't be here long enough for you to send my little brother away to boarding school. You would need our mother's permission to do that anyway.'

'Whilst you are all here under my roof *I* shall make the decisions on what is best for you,' the woman answered, her lips set in a thin line.

'Look, perhaps we should continue this discussion at a more appropriate time,' her grandfather put in hastily, hoping to avoid what looked in danger of turning into a row. Then to Briony: 'You get back to the children, dear. And the porridge is delicious, by the way.'

She smiled at him gratefully before walking briskly from the room, slamming the door resoundingly behind her. Well, at least the girl has spirit, her grandfather thought as he studiously avoided his wife's eyes. He rarely disagreed with her, but on this occasion he had felt she was out of order and needed to be curbed.

Briony's temper had simmered down a little by the time she got back to the kitchen, and not wanting to upset the children she smiled at them before starting to fry the bacon and the eggs that they had collected. It was a novelty to have fresh eggs again instead of the disgusting powdered variety they had been forced to eat back at home, and the children cleared their plates, mopping up the sunny yellow yolks with some of Mrs Dower's wonderful home-baked bread.

By late morning Briony felt as if she had already done a full day's work. After struggling with the boiler in the outside laundry room the children's clothes had been washed and rinsed before being put through the mangle and they were now flapping gently on the line strung across the yard. Mrs Dower had informed her the day before that she took the family's laundry back to the farm once a week to wash and iron it, so at least Briony knew now that she would only be responsible for her own and the children's washing, which was a relief. She had an idea that her grandmother wouldn't have appreciated her doing something as personal as washing her clothes for her. Now the soup that Briony had made was simmering on the stove and the apple pie was browning nicely in the oven.

She had glimpsed Sebastian briefly, just after breakfast when Morris Page had called to pick him up in a little Austin Seven. She guessed that they would be going to the funeral parlour to prepare the body of the man who had died the night before for burial, and the thought of it made her shudder.

At lunchtime she served the family their meal and left the dining room as quickly as possible. She had no wish to have another confrontation with Marion Frasier. In fact, she had once more determined to keep out of her way as much as possible in future.

By mid-afternoon the kitchen and the dining room were gleaming, and Briony looked about with a sense of achievement. The flagstone floor had been scrubbed and she had even washed the windows with vinegar and water – not that she expected her grandmother to notice. The latter was treating her more like a servant than a member of the family.

But now she wanted to give the children a treat, so stepping out into the yard she called them to her and they set off for the farm. With luck they would be able to spend a couple of hours there exploring before it was time to come back and help Mrs Dower prepare and cook the evening meal.

Chapter Nineteen

'I've had a letter from the children!' Lois brandished the envelope in the air as she barged into Mrs Brindley's kitchen with a rapturous smile on her face. It was mid-afternoon and luckily she was sober, although Martha wasn't sure how long that state might last. Still, it was nice to see her neighbour smiling so she ushered her to the table.

'Wonderful! Yer could per'aps read it to me while I pour us both a cuppa. It's been mashed a while so it might be a bit stewed, but at least it's wet an' warm, eh?' Gone were the days when precious tea could be tipped away if their rations were to last for a week.

Whilst she filled two cups with the dark-brown lukewarm liquid Lois read out the letter.

'Hmm, don't tell you much, does it?' the other woman said thoughtfully when Lois had finished. 'About what sort o' greetin' they got from their gran'parents, I mean.' Then, seeing Lois's face fall, she added hastily, 'But then it certainly don't say anythin' bad so that must be a good sign, an' they sound 'appy enough, bless 'em. I dare say yer dyin' to write back to 'em now.'

Lois stirred half a spoon of sugar into her drink and grimaced as she sipped it. 'Yes,' she agreed. 'I shall do it just as soon as I get back from work this evening. With any luck I'll be able to get it in the last post.'

'I might write to 'em an' all, though I ain't that good at letter-writin' an' me spellin' is atrocious. Still, at least they'll know I'm thinkin' of 'em, won't they? Mebbe yer could let me slip mine in the envelope wi' yours? Saves a stamp, don't it?'

Lois nodded as she quickly rose and headed for the door, telling her, 'Of course you can. But I shall have to get off now or I'll be late for work. See you later, Martha.'

'Bye, luvvie.' Mrs Brindley lifted the cups and was just carrying them to the sink when her second visitor of the day arrived.

'Afternoon, Mrs Brindley.' Ruth stuck her head round the door and Martha beckoned her in. The girl had been coming regularly in the hope that there might have been a letter from Ernie, but up to now she had been sadly disappointed.

'Before you ask, no, I ain't heard nothin' from me laddo,' she told her teasingly. 'But Lois 'as 'ad a letter from Briony. She just read it out to me afore she set off for work. Speakin' o' which, why aren't you there today?'

'I've got toothache,' Ruth answered, then coloured slightly as she admitted, 'Well, that's what I told me mam but truthfully I just couldn't face another day standin' in the shop starin' at bare shelves with hardly any customers to serve. I wonder if it's even worth the place openin' sometimes – an' after the air raid last night I'm dead on me feet.'

Mrs Brindley yawned. She had had a sleepless night too,

much of it spent stuck in the shelter with Lois who had snored her way through the whole raid. But then she had been so drunk Mrs Brindley suspected she could have slept through anything.

'I had a letter from Briony too this morning,' Ruth now informed her. 'And it doesn't sound like the war is affecting them much where she is, lucky devil.'

Taking the letter from her coat pocket, she read it aloud.

'It's almost identical to the one she sent 'er mam,' Mrs Brindley commented. 'Don't say a lot, does it?'

'Ah well, at least we know they're all right now and that they arrived safely.' Plonking herself down at the table, Ruth began absentmindedly to play with the fringe of the chenille cloth.

'I just wish we could hear from Ernie now and know that he's safe too,' she muttered worriedly. 'Every time I hear a plane go over I wonder if it's him and if he's going to come back and land safely. I don't think I could bear it if anything happened to him.'

'I know what you mean, luvvie, I feel just the same.' Mrs Brindley squeezed the girl's shoulder. Only now was she beginning to realise just how much her son meant to this girl, and she thought it was a shame, because she had a sneaky suspicion that Ernie's affections – if he had ever had any for Ruth in the first place, that was – had now shifted to Briony. Not that Briony wasn't a lovely girl too, of course, she told herself.

It was time to change the subject. 'I've joined the WVS,' she told Ruth proudly, hoping to shift the anxious look from the girl's face. 'I got to thinkin' I ought to do me bit, an' it's gettin' me out o' the house. Whenever there's a raid I make me way to the nearest church hall where they take the poor sods whose houses 'ave been bombed. It's 'eartbreakin', I don't mind tellin' yer. Some of 'em are left wi' nothin' but what they're stood up in, but we give 'em a place to sleep an' make 'em food an' drink.'

'How awful for them,' Ruth sighed, and in her gentle heart she prayed that this dreadful war might soon be over.

In Cornwall, Briony was heading inland to the farm with the children skipping ahead of her. Seagulls were wheeling in the sky above her and behind her she could hear the waves slapping onto the beach. This, she thought, must be as close to heaven as you could get. Already there were roses in the children's cheeks and their arms and legs were lightly tanned from playing outside.

As they drew closer to Kynance Farm she was surprised to see that it was much bigger than she had imagined it to be, with a number of outbuildings, including a Dutch barn, set around it. A tractor was parked beyond the barn and sheep and cows were contentedly grazing in the fields, which were bordered by drystone walls. She could hear pigs grunting and chickens clucking in the yard beyond a door, which Briony assumed backed on to the kitchen. A large black and white sheepdog bounded towards them, barking furiously, and for an instant they froze. But then as he reached them he began to wag his tail and in no time at all the children were petting him. A large ginger cat was curled up on a wall enjoying a nap in the late afternoon sun and for an instant the children were sad as they thought of Tigger back at home.

'I hope Mam's rememberin' to feed him,' Alfie said to Briony.

'Oh, I shouldn't get worrying too much about that. If she doesn't, Mrs Brindley will – and anyway, cats are more than able to catch their own food. Think of all the mice he used to bring home.'

Happy again, he and Sarah scooted ahead, and after they had all let themselves into an enclosed yard through a double farm gate, the younger ones headed for some pigsties set at the far end.

As Briony approached the kitchen door she heard the wireless, and peeping inside, she saw Mrs Dower rolling pastry at the table. When she saw Briony, the woman swiped her floury hands down her apron and hastily switched off the news and beckoned her inside.

The girl glanced about her appreciatively. The kitchen here was nowhere near as big as the one back at The Heights but it was still a good size and very warm and homely. An inglenook fireplace stood in one wall and the smell of freshly baked cakes and bread hung on the air. On another wall were a number of shelves that had been painted a soft cream colour; on these were arranged Mrs Dower's blue-and-white china. Briony recognised it as willow pattern and noticed that quite a few pieces were chipped, but even so from the way it was displayed it was clearly much cherished. Pretty flowered curtains lined with blackout material hung at the windows. The same material as the curtains had been used to make cushion covers that were strewn along a settee and two easy chairs, and a pipe rack containing a collection of pipes sat in the hearth. It was so much cosier than the kitchen she had just left that Briony was enchanted with it. Mrs Dower clearly had the gift of being able to make a house into a home.

At one end of the table, a tray of scones was cooling. Pointing to them, the woman told Briony, 'The butter and jam are over there, and the clotted cream. Butter a couple for me, would you, and take them out to the children. They should fill a hole till dinner tonight. I've cooked you all a nice leg of pork.'

Briony almost drooled. *A leg of pork!* Back home they were lucky to see a pork chop once a month now, but here no one would have believed that rationing was in place. Again she wished that her mother could be there to enjoy it with them, but if the way her grandmother had received her was anything to go by, the chance of reconciliation between the two women was highly unlikely.

'So how did your first day of cooking the breakfast and the lunch go?' Mrs Dower asked, watching Briony's face closely.

The girl split two scones in half and began to butter them. 'Well . . . put it this way: no one complained.'

'Hmm, but I bet you never got a word of thanks either,' Annik Dower said drily with a toss of her head. 'I reckon it's a disgrace, the way your grandmother is carrying on. You'd think she'd be over the moon to have you young 'uns staying with her.' She winked then and went on, 'I believe your grandfather is secretly pleased you're all there though.'

The kind words were Briony's undoing. She had buried the hurt she had felt at her grandmother's reception of her and put a brave face on things, even standing up to her, but now tears stung at the back of her eyes as she muttered, 'I don't think my grandmother likes me at all, Mrs Dower. I don't think my uncle is too keen on me either.'

'Ah, my poor little maid.' Mrs Dower was round the table in a breath and drawing the girl into her arms. 'Your grandmother won't like you because you're so like your father, God bless his soul. And she won't take to little Sarah either if I'm any judge, because she's too much like your mother. Those two never did get on. Your grandmother was jealous because Lois and her father were so close. And your Uncle Sebastian is scared of anyone replacing him in her affections. Inheritance, see?' She nodded wisely. 'Between you and me, I reckon he was pleased as Punch when your mum took off with your dad. It left the road clear for him to claim the lot when anything happens to his parents. So he's going to be very worried now you lot have turned up, isn't he? Stands to reason, though, the only one she'll take to is little Alfie. He's the double of Sebastian at that age, and your grandmother always doted on him. I think that's why he's such a selfish bugger now. But now come on. There's no point in upsetting yourself. You just stand up to her and you'll be fine.' She cleared her throat and said comfortably, 'Right, lass, get those scones out to the children and then we'll have a nice hot drink.'

Briony sniffed and pulled herself together, then plastering a smile on her face, she went out into the yard. The children were leaning over the wall of the sty laughing uproariously at the antics of the pigs, and she gave them each a scone which disappeared in seconds.

'Look at the little piglets, Briony.' Sarah pointed excitedly, spraying crumbs everywhere. 'I wish we could have one.'

'But you don't have pigs as pets.'

'Why not?'

Briony was lost for words for a moment. How could she tell them that these sweet little creatures would likely end up on their plates one day? 'Because they grow too big,' she said instead and thankfully the children seemed happy with that explanation. In all fairness the piglets were delightful with their little pink snouts and their curly tails, and suddenly the thought of the roast pork they were going to have for dinner that evening wasn't quite so appealing.

While they were standing there, Talwyn appeared from nowhere, and sidling up to Briony, she slipped her hand into hers and smiled shyly.

Briony was touched and squeezed the girl's hand affectionately.

'We'll be going home to The Heights soon with your gran to cook the dinner. Would you like to come with us?' she asked.

The smile froze on Talwyn's face and she snatched her hand away before Briony could say another word. Then she was off like the wind across the yard and vanished into one of the barns.

The children stared at Briony in amazement.

'What was up with her then?' Alfie asked in his usual forthright way.

'I have no idea,' his sister admitted. 'But I'm going back in to Mrs Dower so you two behave yourselves and don't get disappearing. We'll have to be heading back soon.'

When she told Mrs Dower what had happened with Talwyn, the woman said, 'I'm not surprised. She rarely ventures over there because she's scared of Master Seb. She only came with me yesterday because she was curious to see you. She doesn't often get to meet strangers out here. But now I'm just about done here so I'll cut a few sandwiches for Caden and Howel to keep them going, then we'll be off. We don't have our dinner till I've seen to that lot over there. The men are picking the late potatoes down in the bottom field at present, so no doubt they'll be starving by the time they get back in.'

As they meandered through the orchard and entered the yard of The Heights, Briony saw Sebastian outside, talking to the man who had been there the night before. As she watched, her uncle handed the man a large envelope, which the shady-looking character instantly put into the inside pocket of his overcoat, and then both men headed to the barn and proceeded to carry some large boxes out to a waiting van.

'Now you know whereabouts in Bristol you're taking

them to, don't you?' they heard Sebastian say before Mrs Dower shooed them all into the kitchen. Luckily they hadn't been spotted returning from Kynance Farm because it was already getting dusk.

'Best keep well away from some of the blokes Master Seb has coming here,' Mrs Dower advised as she reached for her apron. Then lowering her voice she confided to Briony, 'I don't think your grandparents know the half of what he gets up to. Personally, I wouldn't trust him as far as I could throw him. But that's just my opinion.' She then lit the oven, grateful to see that Briony had already peeled the potatoes and prepared the vegetables, whilst the girl made an attempt to clean the children up a little.

Later that evening, when the children had had a bath and were in bed, Briony sat at the kitchen table and read the newspaper that her grandfather had discarded. Mrs Frasier went into the village each day to get one for him so they were a day old by the time Briony got to read them. But at least it helped her to keep abreast of what was happening in the war and in other parts of the country. It seemed that London was still being heavily bombed, but worse still, the Jerries were targeting Coventry now too. The fact terrified her because it was so close to Nuneaton, but all she could do was pray that her mother and the other people she cared about back home were safe.

A tide of homesickness swept over her. She missed her mother and Ruth and their trips to the cinema. She missed Martha Brindley and her kindly ways. She missed Ernie, who was never far from her mind – but most of all she missed her father, whom she now knew she would never see again. The pain of that pierced through her like a knife and lowering her head, she wept with all her heart.

Chapter Twenty

'But *why* can't you come with us, Briony? I don't wanna go with *her!*'

As Briony straightened Alfie's tie she smiled at him encouragingly. It was Monday morning and the children were just about to set off with their grandmother for their first day at school. Personally, Briony could see no reason why she couldn't accompany them – but the woman was adamant that she would take them herself.

'I suppose she wants to take you on her own because she's so proud of you.' Briony didn't want to make things any worse for the children so she was putting a brave face on it. 'And anyway, there's nothing to worry about. You've already met some of the children there and your new teacher, Mrs Fellows. You're going to love it.'

At that moment their grandmother strode purposefully into the room, once again looking like she was about to attend a wedding in yet another big hat that was adorned with peacock feathers; these wobbled about when she moved as if they were alive.

Briony saw Sarah blink in amazement and hoped that she wasn't going to break into a fit of the giggles.

The woman's eyes raked up and down the children critically as she pulled on a pair of soft kid gloves.

'Ah, you're all ready to go,' she said approvingly. Like her other clothes, the smart dress she was wearing hung off her, and Briony thought that she must have lost a lot of weight. It was the ill-fitting clothes that gave her such a strange appearance; had they fitted properly, they could have looked wonderful. They were obviously of very good quality.

The woman swept towards the children and grasped their hands, then almost dragged them from the room as they shot appealing glances at their big sister.

'Good luck. Have a lovely time,' Briony shouted, but her words were drowned out by the slamming of the door. Sighing, she set about her chores. Once she had finished in the kitchen she intended to polish the banisters in the hallway today. She had made a start on them the day before, but there were so many that she hadn't managed to get them all done in one day. However, her plans were altered some time later when her grandmother reappeared and told her, 'I would like you to tidy yourself up and go down to the funeral parlour this morning. Mr Page has an appointment and Sebastian has to go to London again so I need someone to be there to keep the place open.'

The idea didn't appeal to Briony one little bit. She asked nervously, 'But what will I have to do there?'

Her grandmother rolled her eyes. 'Just *be* there of course!' she snapped. 'In case a call of a bereavement comes in. If it does, you will telephone me here and I shall have to get Mr Dower to come and fetch the hearse and collect the body.

I'm sure even *you* are capable of doing that aren't you?'

Briony's chin came up and she answered calmly, 'Yes, Grandmother, I am *perfectly* capable. I used to work in an office and am quite used to dealing with people, although the majority of my work involved accounts.'

Marion Frasier narrowed her eyes at this snippet of information. 'Did it now? And would you happen to know how to keep books up to date?'

Briony nodded. 'I certainly would. That was part of my job.'

'In that case I might allow you to look at the ledger for the funeral parlour.' She said it as if she were bestowing some great gift. 'My son Sebastian is always so busy, you see. And keeping the records up to date has never been his strong point. Perhaps if it is quiet you could go over the accounts to make sure that all the figures tally? You could then tell me what the profits for the last year are.'

'I suppose I could, if you tell me where the books are kept,' Briony said somewhat reluctantly.

'Very well.' The woman eyed her clothes disapprovingly. 'And *do* change into something a little smarter. I can't have you greeting people in the funeral parlour looking like that. Do you have a black dress?'

'I have a black skirt and a white blouse.'

'I suppose that will have to do. And *do* tie your hair back too, and then come through to the sitting room for the keys.'

Briony got washed and changed in record time. She brushed her hair and tied it with a thin black ribbon into the nape of her neck before presenting herself to her grandmother in the sitting room. Her grandfather was sitting in his wheelchair at the side of the fireplace and he winked at her over his wife's shoulder as she entered the room.

'You look very smart, dear,' he told her.

Briony's grandmother glared at him before saying acidly, 'I would hardly call that outfit very smart, but I dare say it will have to sufffice.' She then went on to tell Briony in detail what she expected her to do and where the accounts records were kept, and as Briony took the keys from her and turned to leave the room, she added, 'And if someone should call to tell you that they have lost a loved one, be sure to be sympathetic. The reputation of our business is second to none, and I do not want *you* spoiling it. Tell them that someone will be with them just as soon as possible, then take their details and telephone me *immediately*, girl.'

Briony didn't even bother to respond but strode from the room with her lips set in a grim line. The woman was utterly . . . she searched her mind for the right word. *Insufferable!* Yes, that would do very nicely. Mrs Frasier had agreed with Mrs Dower – albeit very reluctantly – to pay Briony a small allowance each week. It was a fraction of what the girl had earned in her job at Woolworths, but at least it would keep the children and herself supplied with a few treats and necessities. The trouble was, that ever since then, Mrs Frasier had treated her granddaughter even more like a hired skivvy and sometimes Briony felt like Cinderella, locked away in the kitchen at her wicked stepmother's beck and call.

As she approached the funeral parlour down in Penzance, Briony's stomach tightened into a knot. Hopefully Mr Page would be back for one o'clock at the latest, but she wasn't looking forward to the next few hours at all. Up to now she had never seen a dead body – and she hoped it would remain that way.

As she slotted the key into the door her hands began to shake, and once inside, the silence closed in on her. Outside was the squawking of the gulls and the sound of the sea in the harbour, but in here there was nothing to be heard but the ticking of a clock on the wall. She gulped as she stared at the telephone standing on a highly polished mahogany desk and prayed that it wouldn't ring. A thick Turkish carpet covered the floor, and on the walls were illustrations of various caskets and urns that the families of the departed could choose from. The walls were painted a deep dark red colour, making the room feel quite claustrophobic, and although Briony didn't particularly like the colour she wondered how they had managed to obtain it. Back home, the choice of paint colours for some long time had been restricted to khaki or Air Force grey, which were the colours they painted the planes. A potted fern stood on a table at the end of a row of easy chairs.

A large guest-book was open on the desk, and after giving it a quick glance she moved towards a door at the back of the room that was concealed by a thick purple velvet curtain. Her grandmother had told her that this would take her into a corridor. One of the rooms leading off it was the Chapel of Rest and Briony couldn't resist a quick peek inside. It was a small room with a stained-glass window set high in the wall, before which stood a small altar with a highly polished brass cross upon it. To either side were a number of hard-backed wooden chairs, and resting on two trestles in the centre of the room was an oak coffin with brass handles. Guessing that this must hold the body of the man that Mr Page and Sebastian had been to fetch a few nights ago, she hastily shut the door again without even venturing inside. She vaguely remembered Mrs Frasier mentioning that he was to be buried the following day, and she shuddered.

The next room proved to be a small office and the place where her grandmother had told her she would find the accounts. There was nothing very special about this room. It contained a small, rather battered desk and chair and a number of metal filing cabinets, but other than that it was bare. A dark blue blind covered a window that looked out onto a tiny yard bordered by a high brick wall. Briony knew that she should find the accounts ledger and start to look at it, but her eyes were drawn to the final door . . . Overcome by curiosity, she approached it and inched it open. She instantly wished that she hadn't. On the far wall of the square, whitewashed room were a number of small doors which she guessed opened on to shelves where the dead bodies were stored – and in the centre of the room was a raised concrete slab that looked remarkably like an operating table. Etched into the floor on either side of it were deep grooves that led to a drain. A chrome table on high legs containing scalpels and other equally daunting-looking equipment was placed at one side of it, and a number of white shrouds in various sizes hung on a wall. The smell in there was awful too – a mixture of strong disinfectant and the various chemicals that were used when the bodies were prepared for burial.

Briony slammed the door shut as quickly as she could whilst she tried to catch her breath and then tried to block the sights from her mind.

She sped back to the office, and once she had found the ledgers in the desk where her grandmother had told her they would be, she located the one for 1939–40, and began to go over the last year's accounts. Thankfully everything appeared to be in order and all the figures matched, so she tucked the book into her bag to take it back to The Heights as requested. She then wandered back into the front shop where she tried to while the time away. She thought of Ernie and wondered what he was doing, then of the children, hoping that they were enjoying their first day at their new school. She began to wish that she had brought a book with her to read. The time passed very slowly but then to her relief, just before one o'clock Mr Page appeared, looking every inch the undertaker in a smart black suit, white shirt and black tie. She saw that he was quite elderly. His hair, when he removed his bowler hat, was white as driven snow and his face was heavily lined, but his faded blue eyes were kindly.

He held his hand out, saying, 'Ah, you must be Briony. Thank you so much for stepping into the breach at such short notice, my dear. I'm afraid I had to rush off to the dentist.' He tapped the side of his face which she saw now was slightly swollen. 'I've been awake all night with a raging toothache so Mrs Page rang up and got me an appointment this morning. Nothing to be done at my age, of course, but to have it pulled out.' He grinned lopsidedly before asking, 'Has it been quiet?'

'Oh yes,' she assured him. 'Not a single call, so I'll get off now if you don't mind.'

'Not at all, and thank you again.' He leaned slightly towards her then and confided, 'Between you and me, I'd like to retire, but I don't like to let the family down. I'm not so very far off your grandfather's age, after all. I'm just hoping that Sebastian might take a bigger role in the business soon and then I'll have more time to spend in my garden. But hark at me, you have better things to do than listen to me rattling on. Goodbye, my dear.' He gallantly opened the door for Briony and as she stepped past him and out into the sunshine, she let out a sigh of relief.

As she was walking back through the town she passed the railway station, where a queue of children carrying cardboard suitcases and gas masks were being marched along the platform by two Red Cross workers with clipboards under their arms. Each child had a brown label with their name and address on it attached to their coat with a safety pin. They looked to be from the ages of about five to ten years old, and whilst a number of the little ones were whimpering for their mums the older ones looked to be quite excited at the prospect of being at the seaside. These must be the latest evacuees that Mrs Dower had been talking about, Briony thought as she smiled and hurried past them.

She had barely entered the kitchen when her grandmother appeared and asked, 'Did you bring the account book I asked for?' Briony supposed she must have seen her walking up the drive and round the side of the house to the back entrance. Somehow she got the impression that her grandmother would not appreciate her using the front entrance.

'Yes, I did.' Briony's eyes strayed to the dirty crockery left for her to clear away on the table but she made no comment. The other woman had made it perfectly clear that she was expected to earn her keep during her stay at The Heights, and she had accepted that.

Taking the heavy ledger from her bag, Briony handed it to her and the woman instantly began to flick through it with no word of thanks. No surprise there.

'I had a quick look at it and everything seems to be in order from what I could see', Briony said. 'All the figures for this year tally.'

'But this can't be right.' Her grandmother was frowning. 'We had far more funerals in the last year than have been recorded here.' She snapped the book shut and stuffed it under her arm. She was clearly not at all happy.

'There must be some mistake,' she muttered. 'Unless, of

course, Sebastian has another ledger somewhere. Anyway, you get on with your work, girl. It is no concern of yours. Oh, and by the way, *I* shall collect the children from school.' With that she stalked out of the room.

Briony knew that it was childish, but as Marion Frasier's thin frame disappeared through the door, she stuck her tongue out. Miserable old witch, she thought, then hurried away to get changed.

The children were bubbling with excitement when they got home from school despite being escorted back by their grandmother.

'It's ever so nice there,' Alfie informed his sister as she smiled at him indulgently. He had been as neat as a new pin when he had left this morning, Briony had made sure of that – but now the little boy looked as if he had been dragged through a hedge backwards. His socks were round his ankles and his tie was askew.

'The kids there are really friendly,' he went on, his words coming so fast they were almost falling over one another. 'An' Mrs Fellows is ever so nice too. She's goin' to have a baby. Ruby Dickenson told me so. That's why she's fat, see?'

Sarah stood back, content to let her brother warble on, and Briony winked at her. The little girl looked tired, but then she had never been the strongest of children and Briony guessed that she must be worn out.

Mrs Dower had arrived and was making pastry as she listened to them with amusement. Eventually they went off to their rooms to fetch a jigsaw; Briony had a fear of them venturing too close to the edge of the cliff in the dark, so she had told them they must entertain themselves indoors. The nights were drawing in surprisingly quickly and just that afternoon Briony had found some leaves off the trees in the orchard blowing across the cobbled yard. It was a sure sign that autumn was well on the way.

'Didn't I tell you that they'd be as right as rain,' Mrs Dower said as she placed a pan of potatoes covered in goose fat into the oven to roast.

'You did,' Briony agreed, but then there was no more time for chatter as they each got on with their jobs.

Much later on, when Briony was clearing the dining-room table, her grandmother handed her an envelope.

'This came for you this morning. I should imagine it's from . . . *her*.'

Briony knew that *her* meant her mother, and she bit her tongue as her grandfather gave her a warning look. She took the envelope and stuffed it into the pocket of her apron, then without another word she loaded the large wooden tray and left the room before her temper got the better of her.

Once in the kitchen, however, she let rip. 'Can you *believe* she's only just bothered to give me this!' she ranted to Mrs Dower in a hiss. She kept her voice down because she didn't want to upset the children, who were now sitting colouring at the kitchen table. They had full stomachs and were pleasantly tired. 'She must have had it all day!'

'Oh, she always grabs the mail first thing when the postman comes,' Mrs Dower answered. 'I reckon she must watch for him from the window because I've never yet found a single letter on the doormat in all the years I've worked here. From your mother, is it?'

Briony nodded, her lip quivering as she stared at the familiar handwriting.

'Why don't you save it till you've got the little ones to bed, then you can sit and enjoy it, eh?' the housekeeper said gently.

'I will,' Briony promised her. 'But you get off now, Mrs

Dower. It gets dark so quickly here and I wouldn't want anything to happen to you on your way home.'

'There's no fear of that, my bird,' the woman told her. 'I know the walk from Kynance Farm to this place like the back of my hand and I could do it blindfold. But I will get off if you're sure you don't mind. Howel's going out tonight with his young lady and he'll be wanting a meal before he goes.'

'Oh, are they going somewhere nice?' Briony was suddenly envious as another long night stretched ahead of her. She had grown very fond of Howel and found herself looking forward to him bringing the supplies each morning bright and early before the children were awake.

'I dare say they'll just go to the local picture house, the Savoy, though the films we get round here are always old ones that have been out for some time. Either that or they'll go to the Jolly Mariner for a drink.'

'Well, I hope he has a nice time.' Briony looked at the envelope in her hand again and cheered up a little. At least she had her mother's letter to look forward to, with all the news of what was happening at home.

Later that evening when all was quiet, she tore the envelope open expectantly, her heart racing. Her eyes flew down the page so quickly that the words blurred into one another, but she was left feeling slightly disappointed. Her mother had never been much of a letter-writer and merely told her that all was well and that Ruth and Mrs Brindley sent their love. There was no mention of Ernie or even if they had had word from him. Sighing, she folded the letter and was just placing it back in the envelope when the door leading from the hall slammed open and Sebastian appeared, his face red with temper.

'Just what the hell do you think you were doing, you little bitch, poking about in my desk down at the funeral parlour!' he snarled.

He was dressed in a dark suit that looked as if it had cost more than Briony had earned in a whole month back home, and the creases in the trousers were so sharp she could have cut her finger on them. Beneath it he wore a starched white shirt and a striped tie, and his fair hair was tight to his head with Brylcreem. He was a handsome man, but with his face contorted with rage he looked ugly and dangerous.

'I don't know what you mean,' Briony defended herself, her head held high. 'The only thing I went into your desk for was to get the ledger that your mother asked me to look at and fetch back here for her.' Inside she was quaking but she wouldn't give him the satisfaction of letting him see that.

'Well, in future keep your nose out of my business,' he said threateningly. 'And don't think I don't know what you're up to, coming here and trying to worm your way into the old girl's affections!'

'I'm doing no such—'

He cut her short, leaning menacingly towards her. 'What's here is all fucking *mine* when anything happens to those two – and you'd do well to remember it,' he spat, and with that he turned and stormed out the way he had come.

Briony was deeply shocked. She shook her head in bewilderment as she tried to think what she had done to upset him so much. She had only been following her grandmother's instructions. As her heart-rate dropped to a more normal level, she sighed. It seemed that she would never be able to do right whilst she was here, but for the sake of her brother and sister, it was something she was just going to have to live with. One thing was for sure, she had just unwittingly made herself an enemy. A very frightening one.

Chapter Twenty-One

First thing the next morning, as Briony was throwing logs onto the fire, there was a loud hammering on the front door. She froze. As far as she was aware, she was the only one up. Should she answer it? Deciding that she didn't have much choice, she strode through the hall and opened the door. Standing on the step was one of the Red Cross ladies she had seen the day before leaving the station with the evacuees.

'Ah, may I see Mrs Frasier please, dear?' she asked with a brilliant smile. There was a little girl standing at the side of her with her head bowed.

Briony stuttered, 'Er, I'm not sure that she is up yet.'

'Yes, I am,' a voice thundered behind her, and there was her grandmother, wrapped in a voluminous dressing gown and with her hair standing on end. 'How may I help you?' She frowned at the woman, not at all happy about being disturbed at such an early hour.

'Well, if I could just step inside?' The woman was in no way intimidated, and Briony wondered if her grandmother had met her match.

Marion Frasier reluctantly allowed her to step into the hallway, where the woman said coldly, 'I noticed that you did not put your name down for an evacuee, Mrs Frasier.'

'That's because I already have three of them!' Marion snapped, making the colour rise in Briony's cheeks.

'Oh really? But I understood from the locals that it was your grandchildren you had staying with you.'

'It's the same thing, isn't it?'

'I'm afraid it isn't.' The woman smiled down at the little girl at her side, who had visibly started to tremble. 'The thing is, we are having trouble finding a place for little Mabel here. Mrs Glover in the village kindly let her stay there last night but as you may be aware she already has seven of her own as well as a little boy she has taken in, so Mabel can't stay there, I'm afraid. I thought, seeing as you have such an enormous house . . . '

'I don't *want* strangers here,' her grandmother said, looking at the child with contempt.

'Well, I'm very sorry to hear that but I'm afraid you don't have a choice in the matter. Everyone who has the room is expected to take an evacuee – and you will of course be paid. Most God-fearing people in Poldak have been only too happy to help, and I doubt they would look kindly on someone with all your advantages who would turn a child away.'

Mrs Frasier became silent as she considered things. The woman had struck a chord when she mentioned God. It wouldn't do if word were to get out among her church friends that she had refused to help a child in need. Briony's thoughts were much more compassionate. As she looked at the little girl, her kind heart went out to her. Mabel seemed so small and vulnerable, and to have to listen to this exchange must have been awful for her.

'I could always drag another bed into Sarah's room,' she suggested, seeing her grandmother's hesitation. 'And I would look after her. You wouldn't even have to see her.'

'In that case, I suppose I shall be forced to take her in,' she sniffed. 'See to it, girl, and just make sure you keep her out of my way.'

'Charitable soul, isn't she? It's people like her who make our job so much easier,' the woman commented sarcastically as Mrs Frasier disappeared back into the room that now served as her and her husband's downstairs bedroom.

Briony smiled at the woman apologetically and said, 'Why don't you both come through to the kitchen. It's nice and warm in there, and I was just about to make a hot drink.'

The woman returned the smile gratefully and gripping the child's hand she followed Briony along the hallway and into the kitchen.

'Thank you for that, dear.' She took a seat at the table as Briony hurried over to pour the boiling water into the teapot. 'I was just beginning to get into a bit of a panic. I have to catch the ten o'clock train back to London, you see, and I still had to find somewhere for little Mabel here to stay.'

'Don't worry, she'll be perfectly all right with us,' Briony assured her, spreading some cups on the table. 'And I'm sorry about . . . er . . .'

The woman waved her hand airily. 'Think nothing of it. I often get that reaction from people. But the children have to go somewhere, bless them. It's hard enough being dragged away from their families without having to stay somewhere where they're clearly not wanted. Still, in this case it seems that all is well that ends well. I'm sure she'll be happy with you.' She then proceeded to take a ration book and a sheet of paper from her bag. Placing them on the table she told Briony, 'All Mabel's details are on there – her home address, et cetera – as well as a stamped addressed postcard so that you can let her mother know where she is staying. My address is there too, should you need it.'

As Briony looked down at the child's bent head she frowned. She could have sworn she had just seen something run across the parting. And then it came to her what it was and she gulped. They were headlice, or nits as Alfie and Sarah called them. The child was crawling with them!

Following Briony's eyes the Red Cross woman rose and gently taking her elbow, led Briony towards the sink out of earshot of the child.

'I'm so sorry, my dear. I see you've noticed Mabel's little visitors.' She looked back towards the child. 'That's one reason I have found her so hard to place, poor little lamb. She's come from a very poor family in the East End and she's one of eight. There were ten but two died apparently, and I'm not surprised after seeing how they were forced to live. The home was little more than a hovel and I'm afraid you may find her clothes will be sadly lacking too. Her father did a moonlight flit years ago by all accounts just after Mabel was born, and her mother is . . . well, I'll just say she earns her keep by rather dubious means if you get my drift? I should imagine the child will be happy to get away from there once she's settled; I shall leave her in your capable hands. But anyway, I'll just finish my tea and then I'll be on my way – unless you have anything you want to ask me?'

When Briony shook her head, she marched back to the table and after swallowing the tea that Briony had poured for her in two gulp she headed for the door, saying cheerfully, 'Goodbye then, my dears. I'll see myself out.' And with that she was gone.

Briony just stood there for a moment wondering what the hell she had let herself in for. Everything had happened so fast that it was only now that the responsibility of what she had taken on began to sink in. Eventually she crossed to Mabel and stooping to her level she really looked at her for the first time as she said, 'Don't you want your tea? I made it nice and milky for you and put lots of sugar in it.'

A skinny arm suddenly snaked out from the sleeve of a very grubby cardigan, and grabbing the cup the child very noisily slurped the contents back in one go.

Briony suppressed a smile, dreading to think what her grandmother would say about her table manners. But then the poor kid had probably never been shown the right way to go about things, so it looked like she had her work cut out for her. First though, she would have to make the breakfast and get the children up for school. Lord knew what they were going to make of their new playmate!

The younger two were actually quite excited when they came down all neatly dressed with their hair shining and their faces scrubbed clean. Briony had briefly explained as she was getting them ready for school, and they were keen to meet Mabel.

'Mabel, this is Alfie and Sarah,' she introduced them, but again she got no response whatsoever. The child hadn't said so much as one word yet.

'What's up wi' her? Can't she talk?' Alfie asked bluntly as he scrambled up onto the chair for his breakfast. Sarah was regarding her solemnly.

'She's probably just feeling a bit shy at the minute,'

Briony excused her as she ladled porridge into their dishes. 'So I want you to be extra kind to her for me and help her to settle in.'

'Will she be comin' to the village school with us?' he asked next as he tucked into his breakfast.

'Yes, she will, but I shall have to come to the school and have a word with the headmistress first to enrol her. For today though she can stay here with me and get used to things.'

The children seemed to accept that, and the rest of the meal was eaten in silence. It was then that their grandmother appeared, and after glaring at Mabel's bent head she told Briony, 'You can take the children to school today.'

It was obvious that she didn't want to be seen with Mabel – until she had been cleaned up at least – but that suited Briony just fine so she nodded. She was learning that it paid to say as little as possible to her grandmother. That way, she wasn't in danger of getting her head bitten off.

There was a mist floating across the fields when they set off twenty minutes later and a nip in the air. It was to be expected at this time of the year.

She saw the children to their classrooms, then, deciding that she might as well get Mabel enrolled whilst she was there, she tapped at the headmistress's office door. Mrs Bracken was a stout woman with a large hooked nose and the most dreadful taste in clothes. But for all that she was kindly.

'Of course we would be happy for Mabel to join us,' she trilled. 'What's your other name, dear?'

'Wilkes,' Mabel muttered. Briony smiled. It was the first word she had heard her say.

'And how old are you, dear?'

'Seven.'

'Well done. Can you tell me when your birthday is?' The headmistress was furiously writing the details into the school register.

'February the fourteenth, I fink.'

'Oh, how charming. That's St Valentine 's Day, dear. Right now I think I have all your details, so we'll look forward to seeing you tomorrow. Goodbye, Mabel.'

Mabel allowed Briony to take her hand and once they had left the school behind, Briony said tactfully, 'We'll unpack your case when we get back, shall we? Some of your clothes might have got grubby on the journey so we'll get them all washed and ironed for you so that they're ready for tomorrow. You can have a bath too and get your hair washed to save you having to have one tonight.'

Mabel looked worried. 'Barf? What – yer mean get *right in* the water? Nah, I don't fink I'll like that.'

Briony was shocked. It sounded like the child had never had a proper bath before, and looking at the state of her, she could quite believe it. Her hair was so matted that it was hard to tell what colour it was, and the dress she was wearing was so faded and worn that it looked as if it might fall apart should she attempt to wash it.

'Oh, you'll love it,' she promised her. 'We'll make it nice and warm so that you can have a play and a splash in it.'

This should be fun, she thought wryly to herself as they moved on. As if I haven't got enough to do! But then she looked at Mabel's pinched little face again and her heart softened. The poor mite looked as if she had the weight of the world on her shoulders and it was up to Briony now to try and make things better for her.

'There we are, just right,' Mrs Dower said some time later as she rolled up her sleeve and dunked her elbow in the bathwater. She had taken to Mabel on sight and was keen to help with her.

'I've still got some of Talwyn's dresses from when she was a little maid, in a trunk up in the loft,' she had told Briony as they unpacked the child's case. There was nothing in there that was even worth washing – just a pile of rags that had been bundled in anyhow. 'I'll get Caden or Howel to climb up and fetch them down, and providing the moths haven't got in, they should be good as new after they've been washed and pressed. She certainly can't go to school in any of these!'

Briony was very grateful for the offer. Sarah's clothes would be far too big for Mabel, who was very small for her age, and she had been wondering what she was going to be able to dress her in. That was one problem solved at least. Mrs Dower also came up with the solution to the second problem when Briony whispered to her that their evacuee had a bad infestation of nits.

'I'll pop back to the farm and grab my nit comb,' the woman said. 'Don't you fret, my bird. By the time I've done with her, she'll be as clean as a whistle.'

Now all they had to do was tempt the lass into the bath, which to judge from the mutinous look on her face was going to be no mean feat.

'Come on then, sweetheart. Do you want to get undressed?' Briony asked as the little girl eyed the water.

She shook her head and crossed her arms protectively as she backed towards the bathroom door.

Mrs Dower blocked it, saying in a wheedling voice, 'Just think how nice and clean you'll feel when you're done.'

Up to now, the child had barely uttered a word and Mrs Dower was beginning to wonder if the cat had got her tongue. But she suddenly shocked them both when she screamed, 'I ain't gonna go in there, so yer can both fuck off!'

Briony's mouth dropped open, but Mrs Dower took control of the situation immediately. She advanced on the child with a resolute glint in her eye and said firmly, 'Oh yes, you are, my little maid. Come on, let's be having you now.'

In front of Briony's startled eyes the woman whipped the child's dress off her before she could protest, leaving her standing there in nothing but a very grimy vest, smelling worse than a sewer rat. She didn't even have any knickers on and both women were appalled to see that the dirt on her body was ingrained, especially on her elbows and her knees. She was painfully thin and her small body was covered in ugly bruises ranging from pale yellow to a deep purple.

Briony's eyes brimmed with tears at the sight of her as she wondered who could ever possibly treat a child like that. But Mrs Dower was on a mission now and determined to get Mabel into the bath if it was the very last thing she did.

'Sometimes you have to be cruel to be kind,' she muttered, and lifting the child, who struggled wildly, she plonked her unceremoniously into the warm water. Mabel immediately began to scream as if someone were attempting to murder her.

'Gerroff me, yer bleedin' old cow.' Her arms and legs were flailing but Mrs Dower ignored her. Lifting a jug that she had put ready, she dipped it in the bath and poured the entire contents over the little girl's head before snatching up a big bar of carbolic soap.

'You'll thank me when I'm done,' she said as she began to rub it vigorously into the matted mess that was the child's hair.

Mabel coughed and spluttered as Mrs Dower worked on, and eventually realising that her strength was no match for the woman's she became still and resigned herself to what she thought of as torture. In actual fact, after a while she quite liked the sensation of being immersed in warm soapy water, but she had no intention of admitting it.

Briony was still reeling with shock following the torrent of abuse that had spilled from Mabel's mouth. She had appeared to be such a quiet, unassuming little girl but she had obviously misjudged her. Goodness knew what Marion Frasier would have said if she had heard her! It didn't bear thinking about. Briony had no doubt whatsoever that she would have given the evacuee her marching orders there and then!

Mrs Dower worked doggedly on, the sweat standing out on her brow until at last she had massaged the soap thoroughly into Mabel's hair. She then took up the nit comb, and to loud complaints from Mabel, began to tug it through the tangled mass. Briony was aghast that so many lice could live on one such small head as the comb came away full time after time.

'Ouch – oohyah – gerroff!' Mabel shouted, but after a time she gave up again as she realised she was wasting her breath.

And to think I thought she was a quiet little Cockney sparrow, Briony thought as her lips finally twitched with amusement.

At last the comb started to come through the hair cleanly. 'That's about got rid of the nasty little mites,' Mrs Dower panted, and she then went on to soap Mabel from head to toe, paying special attention to the particularly grimy areas. Soft pink skin began to emerge from beneath the layers of dirt and Mabel looked astounded as she gazed down at herself. She had always thought that her skin was dark, like some of the black men she had glimpsed at the docks back at home and who had sometimes come to visit her mother – and she felt as if she had suddenly been painted a different colour. She smelled different too, although she couldn't really say she was fond of the smell of carbolic. But she was forced to admit to herself that being clean felt good – even if she wasn't about to share that thought.

Finally Mrs Dower pulled the plug before proceeding to tip large jugs of clean warm water all over her.

'There, doesn't that feel better now?' she said as she lifted the child onto the mat and wrapped a towel about her. Mabel answered by making a face but Mrs Dower merely laughed. 'I can see we're going to have some fun with you!' she chortled.

Once Mabel was thoroughly dried, Briony slipped Sarah's dressing gown onto her. It was too big but at least it was clean and would do until Mrs Dower produced some of Talwyn's old clothes. Briony advanced on her then with a hairbrush, which again elicited squeals and objections from Mabel, and five minutes later it was hard to believe that this was the same child they had dragged into the bathroom half an hour ago. Now that her hair was clean they saw that it was a lovely rich shade of brown. Already it was beginning to curl about her face, and her eyes reminded Briony of soft sticky toffee.

'Oh Mabel, you look *lovely,*' she said softly.

The child scowled. 'Yeah, well, if yer fink I'm ever gonna go in there again you've got anuvver fink comin'!' she answered obstinately.

'Right, well, I'm going back home to pick up those clothes now,' Mrs Dower said as she dried her hands. 'In the meantime, Briony, I suggest you get some food into the child. She's as skinny as my clothes-line.'

Briony ushered Mabel out in front of her and soon the

girl was sitting at the kitchen table with a big pile of ham sandwiches in front of her.

'Are these all fer me?' she asked incredulously, and when Briony nodded she fell on the food as if she were starving. Crumbs flew in all directions as she stuffed one sandwich after another into her mouth.

Briony was both disgusted and saddened all at the same time. It was as if the child were fearful that someone was going to snatch the food away from her. But she didn't say anything. Mabel Wilkes had had quite enough to contend with for one day, and there would be time to teach her better manners when she had settled in a little.

She gave a wry little smile as she went to fetch Mabel a second glass of milk, thinking to herself: I'm going to have my work cut out with this one!

Chapter Twenty-Two

'Ma's sent me over to help you move a bed or something,' Howel informed her as he poked his head round the kitchen door later that afternoon. He glanced curiously at Mabel, who was curled up at the side of the fire looking at the pictures in one of Alfie's comics. 'She said to tell you she'll be over in a minute to start the evening meal. Oh, and she asked me to give you these.'

He handed her a brown paper bag with string handles, and when Briony peeped inside she smiled with delight.

'She's washed and ironed them, but she said to tell you to air them over the fireguard because they might still be a little damp,' he warned.

Briony began to unpack the bag and lay the items on the table. There was a little red pleated kilt and a hand-knitted pale green jumper as well as two small cotton dresses and a pink cardigan. There was also a selection of vests and knickers and a number of pairs of little white socks. They all looked as if they would fit Mabel like a glove and Briony was thrilled with them.

'She's hunting around now 'cos she's sure she's still got a little coat somewhere that might fit her as well,' he went on. 'But she'll bring that over with her when she comes, if she manages to find it. I tell you it's like an Aladdin's cave up in our loft. Anyway, where's this bed you want shifting? I ought to go back and get the sheep down into the side field before it grows too dark. We've had trouble with poachers lately, with meat being so hard to get hold of, and there's no sense in making it too easy for them.'

'Of course.' Briony flushed as she quickly headed for the stairs leading up to their rooms. 'I'm sorry I've taken you from your work.'

'It's no trouble at all,' he answered genially, swiping a lock of his copper-coloured hair from his forehead.

Once upstairs he helped Briony to manhandle a spare single iron bedstead out of another room and into Sarah's, then they carried the mattress through and Briony told him gratefully, 'I can manage now, thanks, if you want to get off. I could have put Mabel in the empty room but I just thought she might be more comfy in here with Sarah, seeing as everything is strange to her.'

He chuckled then. 'Ma was telling me what a mouthful she gave you both when you were bathing her. But she looks so quiet, doesn't she? As if good Cornish butter wouldn't melt in her mouth. Word has it that the woman from the Red Cross would have tried us next if you hadn't taken her.'

'Lucky you, that's all I can say then,' Briony grinned. 'She's like a little spitfire when she gets going.'

'I dare say she's had to be, to survive.' His face was sad

now. 'Ma said her little body was covered in bruises. Who do you suppose would do that to her?'

Briony shrugged. 'I don't know, but she certainly won't be getting any more if I have my way.'

He looked at her admiringly for a moment then turned hastily and left without so much as another word, leaving her to make the bed up with fresh linen.

Dressed in her new finery, Mabel walked to the school with Briony to meet the children at home time. She had said very little when Briony put the new outfit on her, but the young woman noticed that every now and then she would glance down at herself and stroke the little pleated skirt wonderingly. The only thing she was still wearing that she had arrived in were her shoes. Sadly, there was nothing Briony could do about that until she had time to get out to buy her a new pair. They were very down at heel and the soles were dangerously thin, but even so they looked much better after a polish and with a pair of Talwyn's little white socks inside them. Briony had tied her hair back with one of Sarah's ribbons, and every now and then Mabel would raise her hand to touch it self-consciously.

The children bombarded her with questions all the way home but Mabel remained obstinately silent until in the end Briony scolded them, 'Now come along you two and give Mabel a bit of peace. She'll answer all your questions when she's good and ready.' The child walked primly at her side whilst the other two scampered ahead, but she stubbornly refused to hold Briony's hand and Briony wisely didn't try to force her.

Mrs Dower made a delicious shepherd's pie that evening and Sarah and Alfie watched in horrified fascination as Mabel rammed it into her mouth as if there was no tomorrow.

'She's so greedy,' Briony murmured as she stood by the sink with Mrs Dower.

'Hungry, more like,' the woman replied. 'She'll probably be like this for some while, at least till she realises there'll be another mealtime. She's probably had to eat when she could up to now.'

'How awful,' Since rationing had come into force, the selection of food back at home had been sadly limited but Briony was the first to admit that they had never gone hungry, not as this poor little mite obviously had. She promised herself to try even harder with Mabel.

When taking the food through to the dining room where the Frasiers waited to be served, she found the atmosphere so heavy that she could have cut it with a knife, and she was glad that she and the children were banished to the kitchen. Sebastian's expression was grim and his mother didn't look much happier. They had clearly had a row about something – and Briony wondered if it had anything to do with the ledger she had fetched from the funeral parlour. Placing the contents of the tray onto the centre of the table as quickly as she could, she beat a hasty retreat, leaving them to serve themselves.

Just before the children were due to go to bed the wind blew up and a downpour started. The windows rattled in their frames as the rain hurtled against them as if it were trying to gain entry.

'Those poor sheep and cows out in the fields,' Sarah said sadly. 'But at least the pigs can go into their sty and keep dry if they want to.'

'I don't think sheep and cows mind the rain too much.'

Mabel's ears pricked up at the mention of the animals but she didn't say anything and Briony made a mental note to take her along to Kynance Farm to see them just as soon as she could. Living in a city, she had probably had no contact with any before. She had dressed Mabel for bed in a pair of Alfie's pyjamas. Sarah's were too big for her but the little girl hadn't protested. She was still unnaturally quiet but Briony hoped that would pass eventually. She was clearly able to speak, as her outburst in the bathroom had proved!

Deciding that she would clear the table in the dining room whilst the children were quietly sitting in the kitchen, she picked up the tray – but as she was carrying it through the hallway she heard voices raised in disagreement.

'What do you *mean* they used another undertaker?' she heard William Frasier say irately. 'We've known the Thomas family all their lives. Why would they go elsewhere?'

'Because Sebastian said someone else in St Ives offered them a better price.'

'*Rubbish!* We have caskets to suit all budgets,' her grandfather responded, but she didn't wait about to hear any more and instead hurried back to the kitchen. It was the children's bedtime.

Mabel went to bed meekly enough, although she didn't seem too pleased with the idea.

'What time did you go to bed when you were at home?' Briony asked as she tucked the blankets about her.

'Whenever I wanted,' the child muttered.

'But didn't your mum tell you when it was time to go?'

'She was always at the pub by then.'

'I see. Well, after the big day you've had, an early night will do you good.' Briony stroked the springing curls from the little girl's forehead, thinking again how pretty she looked now that she was clean. But she was so frighteningly thin. She had thought that Sarah was frail, but compared to Mabel she looked positively robust! Good fresh air and some of Mrs Dower's lovely home-cooked meals would soon put a little weight on her bones.

She yawned then, realising that she was tired too. I'll tuck Alfie in then I'll have a nice hot bath and an early night myself, she promised herself, and after kissing both of the girls she went on her way.

A sound woke Briony from a dream. She had been dancing with Ernie and as her eyes flickered open she felt cheated. Howel had been in the dream too, smiling at her from the edge of the dance floor as he stood with Ruth. She lay for a moment wondering what it was that had woken her, and then it came again. It sounded as if someone was downstairs in the kitchen. Pulling her dressing gown on she crept along the landing and peeped into Alfie's room. He was fast asleep and snoring gently so she then went to check on Mabel and Sarah. At a glance she saw that Mabel's bed was empty, so hurrying now she headed for the stairs. The house was silent save for the creaking of the boards and the pipes settling, and she guessed that it must be very early in the morning.

Once downstairs she glanced around and stood listening. The sound seemed to be coming from the large walk-in pantry. She crossed to it and snapped on the light – and then her eyes almost started from her head as she saw Mabel kneeling on the floor stuffing the remains of a loaf of bread into her mouth.

'Whatever are you doing?' she gasped. 'You surely can't still be hungry after the massive meal you ate this evening. You'll make yourself ill.'

Mabel's eyes looked huge in her small face but she hugged the loaf to her possessively.

'I *am* hungry,' she said.

'Well, bring it out here, then and I'll spread some butter on it for you,' Briony said calmly.

Mabel inched towards her cautiously, looking like a rabbit that had been caught in a trap. 'Ain't you gonna tell me off?'

'Why should I?' Briony carried the butter dish to the table then held out her hands for the loaf, which looked as if it had been savaged by a pack of wild dogs. 'If you're hungry you only have to say and I'll always get you something to eat,' she added patiently. It was hard to believe that a child could be so hungry that they would resort to stealing dry bread, and her heart ached for her.

'There,' she said when the bread was buttered. 'Now would you like some milk to go with that?'

'Not 'arf!' Mabel was stuffing her mouth so full again that she was making herself gag and Briony had to look away. The sooner she started to teach the child some table manners the better.

At last Mabel gave a loud burp and patted her stomach.

'All full up now?' Briony asked.

'Yes, but I'll still want me breakfast.'

'Of course you will. But come on now. Let's get you back to bed, eh? We don't want you being late for school on your first day.'

She held her hand out but Mabel ignored it as she strode towards the stairs again. Soon she was tucked in once more and Briony headed back to her own room, hoping she would be able to pick up on her dream where she had left off.

She had just dropped off again when a piercing scream rent the air, and once again she awoke with a start. It sounded like Mabel – but what could the matter be now?

She was along the landing in a flash and on entering

the girl's room she saw Sarah crouched on her bed looking fearfully towards Mabel.

The child was tangled in her sheets, thrashing about madly, but she seemed to be still asleep.

'It's all right, sweetheart,' she told Sarah. 'She's just having a nightmare but she'll be fine in a minute.'

'Mabel.' As she leaned down towards the child, Mabel's small fist flew out and she caught Briony soundly on the chin, making her wince. 'Blimey, she can't half pack a wallop,' she told Sarah, hoping to lighten the atmosphere. She shook Mabel gently and suddenly the little girl's eyes flew open.

'Gerroff me . . . gerroff!' she screamed – and then as her eyes settled on Briony all the fight seemed to go out of her and she slumped back against the pillows in a cold sweat.

'It's all right, no one is going to hurt you,' Briony told her soothingly. 'You were just having a bad dream, that's all, but it's over now.'

Mabel gulped deep in her throat as Briony put the bedclothes to rights and then her eyes grew heavy and she turned onto her side and jammed her thumb into her mouth. Sarah had settled back down too and all Briony could do was hope that she might now be able to get a few uninterrupted hours' sleep.

'How's she been?' Howel asked the next morning when he delivered the day's supplies. Looking towards Mabel, Briony lowered her voice and told him what had happened during the night.

'Poor little devil,' he remarked as he stroked his chin.

'I don't know about her, but I don't feel as if I've been to bed,' Briony yawned.

'Well, it's early days but I'm sure she'll soon be all right,' he said confidently.

She hoped he was right. When she had got up that morning she had found Mabel lying in a soaking wet bed, but she didn't tell him about that.

'I've pissed meself . . . I'm sorry,' Mabel had muttered as she cowered against the wall, obviously expecting to be punished for it.

'Oh, we all have little accidents. Don't worry about it,' Briony had responded airily before whipping her off to the bathroom for a thorough wash. There she had met with yet more problems.

'Why do I 'ave to 'ave *anuvver* wash?' the girl had screeched indignantly. 'I only 'ad a bloody barf yesterday!'

'But you have to have a bath or a thorough wash *every* day,' Briony had explained. 'Otherwise you might smell, and then the other children at school might make fun of you.'

Mabel glared at her. 'I didn't 'ave to go to school if I didn't want to when I lived at 'ome. An' if the kids made fun o' me I smacked 'em straight in the gob!'

'Well, I hope you won't be doing that at this school,' Briony said firmly. 'Because you *will* be going regularly now. How else will you learn your lessons?'

'Don't care if I don't learn *nuffin'*.' Mabel crossed her arms and stared at her defiantly, but Briony ignored her. She was willing to be lax on a lot of things with this child, but her schooling wasn't one of them.

Now as Howel watched Mabel slurping her porridge as if it was going out of fashion he remarked, 'Not the most delicate of eaters, is she?' His eyes were twinkling with amusement and Briony sighed.

'That's not the worst,' she confided. 'She swears like a trooper as well. I dread to think what the teachers will do if she starts swearing at them at school.'

Howel changed the subject then when he asked, 'And how are you getting on with Sebastian?'

She grimaced. 'Not very well, to be honest. He came storming in here yesterday and gave me a right telling-off just because I'd brought the accounts ledger back from the funeral parlour as my grandmother asked me to.'

'Don't worry about it, and do yourself a favour and keep out of his way. I know I shouldn't say it with you being part of the family, but he's a right nasty piece of work.'

The conversation was stopped from going any further when Mabel suddenly appeared at Briony's elbow to ask, 'Can I 'ave some more?'

She sounded just like Oliver in *Oliver Twist*, and stifling her amusement, Briony kept her face solemn as she replied, 'Yes, you can, but only if you eat it properly and don't gobble.' Now seemed as good a time as any to start teaching the child some table manners.

'Whadda yer mean?' Mabel asked indignantly.

'I mean you should eat it nicely without slurping. Eat a little more slowly like Alfie and Sarah, and try to do so *silently*.'

Mabel cast a withering look at the other two and seemed on the point of refusing, but then she said in a long-suffering voice: 'All right then.'

Briony refilled her dish and carried it to the table for her, and after she was seated Mabel lifted her spoon and began to eat a little more slowly, taking note of how Alfie and Sarah were eating theirs. She didn't look too happy about it, but it was a step in the right direction.

'Lesson one,' Howel chuckled as he made for the door. 'Have a good day, kids. See you later, Briony. I'll be bringing another load of logs over later for the fire. The weather's on the turn now and you wouldn't believe how cold it can get here with the wind from the sea. Oh, and by the way, Ma sent these over as well. They're some more clothes she dug out for Mabel. The coat she mentioned is in there.' He nodded towards a large bag he had placed down by the door and Briony thanked him.

As the door closed behind him she realised with a little jolt how much she had come to look forward to his visits. He and his mother were the only people she ever got to see who gave her the time of day and it could get lonely here with just the children for company, even though there was enough cleaning to keep her busy for the next year.

Quickly sorting through the bag of clothes, she was delighted to find some flannelette nightdresses as well as the coat. It was navy blue wool and double-breasted and in surprisingly good condition, apart from a little bobbling on the arms. She judged that it might be a little large for Mabel at the moment, but then beggars couldn't be choosers and seeing as the child didn't have one it would do very nicely, for the weather was turning chilly.

'You can write to your mum on the postcard the Red Cross lady left for you when you get home this afternoon and tell her our address,' she told Mabel as she buttoned her into the coat to try it on a short time later. It actually fitted better than she had thought it would and the little girl looked quite smart in it.

Mabel lowered her head and frowned. 'I can't write. Nor I can't read.'

'In that case I'll do it for you,' Briony told her. 'And don't worry, you're only seven. Lots of children your age can't read and write yet.'

Mabel sniffed, clearly not much bothered one way or another, and Briony grinned. This little lady was a law unto herself – and a force to be reckoned with.

Chapter Twenty-Three

'Miss Valentine, might I have a word, please . . . in my office.' Mrs Marshall's face was screwed up so tightly that she looked as if she was sucking on a wasp.

She was the teacher who had been put in charge of the new class that had been set up for the evacuees, and Briony smelled trouble. She wondered what had Mabel been up to now.

She didn't have to wait long to find out.

'I must ask you to see that Mabel Wilkes curbs her foul language in future,' she said primly as she adjusted the steel-rimmed glasses that perched on the end of her nose. They looked as if they were trying to escape and Briony couldn't blame them. Mrs Marshall really was one of the ugliest women she had ever seen, although she had heard that she was an excellent teacher. She had arms like a wrestler that strained against the sleeves of the blue cardigan she was wearing, and a huge bulbous nose.

Briony tried not to stare at the woman's moustache as she asked, 'What has she done?'

'I'm afraid there was an incident in the playground with one of the little girls from the village,' Mrs Marshall said. 'Daisy asked Mabel where she had come from and Mabel told her to f— Well, I don't care to repeat what she said, but it was more suitable for men working on the docks than a little girl. Could you please speak to her about it?'

'Of course I will.' Briony was desperately struggling to keep a straight face. She could just imagine what Mabel must have said.

'Of course I think it's *wonderful* that dear Mrs Frasier has agreed to take the child in,' the woman gushed. 'Especially as she has taken your family in too, and I also understand that some of the evacuees from the inner cities have not been brought up as . . .' she hesitated here as if choosing her words carefully and ended lamely, '. . . as our local children have. Even so, I really think that we must try to maintain our standards.'

'Of course.' Briony was desperate to escape now before a fit of laughter got the better of her. In fact, she was going red in the face trying to contain it. Not that she thought it was funny; she agreed that Mabel's language was unacceptable, but the child was only seven years old after all and she had clearly never been taught any better.

'Leave it with me,' she choked, and rushed for the door before the woman could say any more.

The children were all waiting at the school gates for her and Mabel eyed her warily as she approached, knowing that she was going to be in trouble.

'I only cussed at that Daisy 'cos she said I talked funny – cheeky mare!' she defended herself.

'Well, that's as maybe, but will you at least *try* not to

swear in future,' Briony pleaded, doing her best to sound stern.

Mabel ran her hands down the front of her new coat and sniffed. It was the finest thing she had ever owned and she would have kept it on all day if the teachers had allowed her to.

''S'pose so,' she mumbled ungraciously and at last they set off for home.

Mrs Dower was there when they arrived and the appetising smell of a chicken roasting met them.

'It's a chicken dinner with a cherry pie and custard to follow tonight,' she told them cheerily. 'How does that sound?'

'Lovely,' the children chorused as they took off their coats. Once they had scampered away to fetch jigsaws and colouring books, Mrs Dower told Briony quietly, 'There's been another bomb attack on Buckingham Palace. Remember how the Royal Chapel was wrecked, back in early September? Good job Princess Elizabeth and Princess Margaret Rose were at Balmoral, isn't it?' And then on a happier note, 'Your grandmother brought a letter in for you by the way, while you were at the school. It's over there on the table – look.'

Briony pounced on it, hoping it was from Ernie. She saw at a glance that it was Ruth's handwriting but that was almost as good and she could hardly wait to read it.

'It's from my best friend, Ruth, back at home,' she told Mrs Dower as she tore the envelope open.

'How nice. I dare say she's missing you. Let's hear what she has to say then. It'll take my mind off peeling these sprouts.'

Briony read aloud:

Dear Briony,

I hope you and the children are settling down at your grandparents. There's nothing very exciting to tell you from this end, I'm afraid. We've had some more air raids but luckily nothing too bad up to now. Mrs Brindley heard from Ernie a few days ago and he says he is well, thank goodness, but his letter was so heavily censored that we couldn't make head nor tail of where they're sending him. He did say though that he might get a few days leave soon, so that's something to look forward to.

Everything is the same at work, nothing to report there. It's as boring as ever and you're well out of it. I've seen your mum a couple of times and she seems OK too. I don't half miss our trips to the pictures! It just seems to be all work at the minute. Will you be coming back for a visit soon? It would be lovely if you could time it for when Ernie has his leave. We could all get together again then like old times.

Grandad hasn't been well so I've been going round to help out a bit. His gout is playing him up something terrible! Poor old devil. Rationing is as bad as ever here. What's it like down there? There's no decent clothes to be had in the shops and I'm sick to the back teeth of vegetable soup. Have you heard that the government is on about giving us clothing coupons now? As if things aren't bad enough already.

Anyway, I just wanted you to know that I'm missing you. You will write back, won't you? Have you met anyone tall, dark and handsome yet? Oh – and rich, of course!

Lots of love,

Your friend Ruth xxxxxxxxx

'Who is Ernie?' Mrs Dower asked and Briony blushed to the roots of her hair.

'He's my next-door neighbour's son,' she answered. 'We were brought up together, and me, him and Ruth used to go everywhere together. He's in the RAF now though and his mum Mrs Brindley is worried sick about him.'

'I can understand that.' Mrs Dower shook her head. 'It must be awful for mothers and wives who have menfolk away fighting, never knowing if the dreaded telegram is going to arrive.' She stopped abruptly then as she saw Briony's face crumple and silently cursed herself for being so thoughtless. Hadn't the poor girl received just such a telegram about her father?

'And this Ernie,' she said quickly, hoping to lighten the mood. 'Sweet on him are you?'

'It wouldn't make any difference if I was,' Briony confessed. 'Ruth has adored him since we were at the first school together and she's my best friend. If she thought I had feelings for Ernie, she'd think I'd betrayed her.'

'Oh dear, so you're *both* sweet on him then? That's awkward, but who does Ernie favour?'

'I haven't the faintest idea,' Briony said, and quickly rammed the letter back into the envelope before starting to set the table for dinner.

So that's the way the land lies, Mrs Dower thought to herself. Sounds to me like young Briony has a soft spot for this young fellow but she doesn't want to step on her friend's toes. It seemed a shame, but then things had a way of sorting themselves out in the end. If the lad came back from the war, that was. Everyone knew what a dangerous job the pilots were doing, risking their lives every time their planes took off. She was just grateful that Howel hadn't had to go, although she knew that he had wanted to.

*

Later that evening, when all was quiet, Briony reread Ruth's letter. The unsettled night she'd had with Mabel was catching up with her now and she hoped that tonight would be uneventful.

She grinned when she came to the part of the letter where Ruth asked if she had met anyone tall, dark, handsome – and rich. There was Sebastian, but he was her uncle and he didn't count. Then there was Howel. He was tall and handsome in a quirky sort of way, but he wasn't dark or rich. Still, two out of four wasn't bad, apart from the fact that he was already spoken for by a girl in the village. When she went over the part about trying to get home whilst Ernie was on leave, she sighed heavily. By getting her grandmother to agree to take Mabel on, she had narrowed down the chances of that happening. Who would take care of the children if she were to go home? Mrs Dower was already run off her feet and she certainly couldn't see her grandmother volunteering. Apart from showing everyone how kind she was by taking the Valentine children to school on their first morning there, she hadn't even spoken to them since. Briony had already asked if she could pass on their telephone number so that her mum and Ruth could phone her from the kiosk at the end of the street back home, but she had been told in no uncertain terms that the telephone was there purely for business purposes – so that had put paid to *that* idea.

Briony was concerned that Ruth had said so little about her mum. Ruth had promised that she would visit Lois regularly – and yet in the letter she had said that she had only seen her a couple of times. Briony prayed that her mother hadn't hit the bottle again and that Ruth wasn't keeping the fact from her. Still, Lois did have Mrs Brindley next door, and she had no doubt that their neighbour would be keeping an eye on her mum, which was something at least.

As she glanced around the kitchen, Briony felt a little glow of satisfaction. It looked so different now from how it had when she had arrived. She had scrubbed every inch of it as well as the enormous hallway. The turned wooden banisters now shone, and instead of the musty smell that had greeted them originally, the house now smelled of beeswax polish and of the greenery that she had dotted about in vases she had found beneath the sink. Tomorrow she intended to start on another room if her grandmother would allow it, and hopefully in time she would have the whole house back to how it had been kept in her mother's day. But for now she was tired, so after switching off the lights and placing the guard in front of the fire, she made her way to bed.

Mabel had another nightmare that night. Once again, the stink of urine met Briony full force when she went to wake the girls the next morning, and once again Mabel shrank away from her.

'It doesn't matter. Accidents happen,' Briony said tiredly as the child stood shivering to one side whilst Briony stripped the wet bedding from the mattress again. It was getting harder to dry the washing outside now that the weather had turned damp, and she knew that she would have to try and dry it on the line strung across the kitchen once it had been washed.

'Ain't yer gonna belt me one?' Mabel asked, her eyes looking too large for her small face. 'Me mam used to belt me when I wet the bed back at 'ome. But she didn't bovver to change the sheets. I just slept in 'em till they got dry again.'

'Oh, you didn't wet the bed every night then?'

'Nah, only when the blokes come back an'—' Mabel

suddenly clammed up as Briony looked at her, horrified. What had the child been about to say? She clearly wasn't about to say any more and so Briony didn't push it. The girl would tell her when she was good and ready.

They had only been downstairs a few minutes when Howel appeared with his usual bags of supplies.

Mabel slunk away to the table and kept a watchful eye on him the whole time he was there and once he'd gone she asked, 'Is 'e yer chap then?'

'My *chap*? No, of course he isn't. He's Mrs Dower's grandson. I don't have a chap.'

'Well, I reckon 'e wants to be yer chap. I can tell by the way 'e looks at yer. 'E wants to shag yer.'

'Mabel!' Briony almost dropped the bowl of porridge she was carrying to the table. 'That's an awful thing to say – and you shouldn't even know about such things at your age!'

''*Course* I know.' Mabel stuck her chin in the air. 'That's 'ow women earn money, by lettin' men shag 'em. Me mam told me so.'

Briony was at a loss as to how to answer that, so she clamped her mouth shut, intending to continue the conversation later that day, out of earshot of Sarah and Alfie whose ears had pricked up.

'Well, we'll talk about this another time, shall we?' she choked, trying hard not to show her distress. 'But for now I think we ought to have our breakfast and think about getting you all to school. And Mabel . . . no more bad language today, *please*!'

All day Briony thought of the implications of what Mabel had confided and she felt sick. Could it be that some of the men she'd spoken of had interfered with her? But then Mabel was just seven years old. Surely no man would stoop so low?

She shared her concerns with Mrs Dower when the woman arrived later that afternoon, and the housekeeper listened carefully.

'Perhaps that's why the poor little soul is wetting the bed and having nightmares,' she said tentatively. 'Stands to reason something like that is going to leave scars, doesn't it? Poor little bird. But then we're jumping to conclusions. No doubt she'll tell you the whole story when she's good and ready. Meantime, don't ask questions, that's my advice.'

Briony nodded as she set off to fetch the children. The day was dark and drizzly as she trod over the crisp golden leaves that were swirling about her feet. Gulls squawked and swooped in the sky above her but she hardly noticed. Her thoughts were too firmly fixed on what Mabel had said and she was concerned that if her worst fears were realised and the child had been mistreated in that wicked, vicious way – then brave little Mabel might never get over it.

Martha Brindley stood out on the pavement and stared at the tightly drawn curtains of her neighbour's house. It was well after nine o'clock in the morning now but it didn't look as if Lois was up – yet again. She'd had to pound on the door for the last few mornings to ensure that Lois got to work on time, but it looked as if she was going to ignore her altogether today. Shaking her head, the big woman headed back to her own kitchen tutting with irritation. Her feelings for her neighbour veered between sympathy and annoyance. Of course she was sorry that Lois had lost her lovely husband – but hadn't *she* lost her Clal too? And *she* hadn't hit the bottle, even though the pain of his loss weighed like a heavy stone in her heart. Everyone was being affected by this damn war and they were having to get on with it! But then she would feel guilty for being so unfeeling. After all, Lois wasn't made of such stern stuff as she was, and she knew that she was missing the children dreadfully. If truth be known, Mrs Brindley was missing them too – although she still felt that Lois had done the right thing in sending them to a safer place.

She found Tigger curled up in front of her fire and went to fetch him some food. He seemed to spend more time round at her house now than he did at home; no doubt because he knew that he had more chance of being fed there. Lois didn't bother to feed herself half the time any more, let alone the cat, and seemed to be surviving on pure alcohol. She was the talk of the whole street, not that it seemed to bother her. It broke Mrs Brindley's heart when she thought of what Lois had looked like not so very long ago. Everyone had envied her then but now they pitied her. The weight seemed to have dropped off her bones and her once glorious blonde hair was now scraped back in a greasy ponytail. She never even bothered to wear a bit of lipstick now and yet at one time she wouldn't have dreamed of stepping out of the door without her full war-paint in place.

She bent and placed the saucer of scraps in front of Tigger with tears in her eyes, but then she became aware of someone standing in the doorway and when she glanced up the breath caught in her throat.

Suddenly she was across the room. 'Aw, luvvie. I can't believe it's you!' she cried joyously. 'I thought I were seein' bloody things fer a moment back there.' She was hugging her son to her and he patted her back affectionately.

'No, you ain't seein' things, Mam. It's really me,' Ernie assured her, throwing his kitbag down. 'An' yer goin' to have to put up with me fer a while 'cos this damn leg 'as been playin' up again an' the doc says I've to rest it.' He thumped the offending leg with frustration. 'It ain't never been the same since Dunkirk,' he told her. 'Left it weak, so the doc says, but hopefully I shouldn't need more than a couple o' weeks an' I'll be back in the air.'

Staring up at him and thinking how handsome he looked in his uniform, Mrs Brindley realised how much he had changed in the past year. He had gone off to war as little more than a boy but he had come back to her as a man, and she was proud of him.

'So come on then,' he grinned now. 'Get that kettle on an' then yer can tell me all the gossip, eh?'

'Huh! I don't quite know where to start,' Mrs Brindley grumbled. Despite his cheerful façade, her mother's instinct screamed at her that something wasn't right. She could see the haunted look in his eyes and guessed that he had probably seen atrocities that would stay with him for the rest of his life. War was an abomination. But for now she was just glad to have him home and intended to make the most of every minute they had together.

Over tea she told him about Briony taking the children to Cornwall and she saw his face fall. So I was right then, he has got feelings for her, she thought. Although she loved Briony almost like a daughter she was sad to think of how Ruth would take the news, should she ever find out. Of course it was inevitable that she would, and Martha Brindley was sure it would break the girl's heart. Putting that aside, she went on to tell her son about the drinking problem Lois had developed.

'It would be losing James that has done that to her,' he commented. 'Losing someone close can do funny things to people.' His face crumpled then, and she saw that there were tears sparkling in his eyes. 'My best mate didn't come back from a flight last week,' he told her hoarsely and she knew then that he wasn't just home for his leg; his nerves had been stretched to breaking-point. 'He was shot down over the sea,' he went on huskily. 'No chance of ever recovering his body. I stopped off the train in Ledbury on my way here to deliver a letter he had left with me for his parents.' He laughed then; a hollow sound that held no mirth. 'We do that, you know. Leave letters for loved ones with mates just in case we don't come back. The one I had given him for you must have gone into the sea with him.'

'Oh, lad.' His mother's hand closed over his, and for one of the very few times in her life she was speechless. Words just seemed so inadequate.

'The week before, we were flying over London when the Jerries were bombin' the docks. I managed to get in really close to one of their bombers before I let him have it. So close that just for a second we were looking each other straight in the eye. Then I fired the bombs and next thing his plane was on fire and he was hurtling down into the Thames. It's a terrible thing to kill someone, Mam, even if it's a case of you or him. This war is just so bloody senseless!'

And then the tears came, fast and furious and she was rocking him in her arms as she had when he was a little boy, comforting him with the love and consolation that only a mother can give.

Chapter Twenty-Four

It was early on Saturday evening when Mrs Frasier strode imperiously into the kitchen to tell Briony, 'You are to have the children ready for ten o'clock in the morning. They will be attending the service at the Methodist Chapel with me in Poldak. *That* one can stay here with you. I doubt she's ever walked into a church in her whole life and I can't have her showing me up.' The last was addressed at Mabel, who glowered back at her. She didn't like the missus at all and wasn't afraid to show it.

'But I don't want to go to church,' Sarah said. 'I want to stay here wi' Briony.'

Briony expected her grandmother to object but Marion surprised her when she said indifferently, 'Very well, you can stay here with her. But I must insist that Alfred comes along.'

Alfie opened his mouth to object but then promptly shut it again. He was scared stiff of his grandmother.

Briony gritted her teeth. 'Very well,' she said politely. 'I shall make sure that he is ready.' She had soon realised that Alfie was the only one that her grandmother was vaguely interested in and she knew that it would be pointless to argue. But at least she could keep Sarah with her. The little girl had developed a slight temperature and Briony wanted her to stay in the warm, and try to get her well enough for school on Monday.

On Sunday morning a very reluctant Alfie set off for church with his grandmother and once they were gone Briony began to prepare the vegetables for Sunday dinner. She had taken over the breakfasts and lunches herself now but Mrs Dower still insisted on cooking the Sunday roast and the main evening meal until Briony felt a little more confident.

'Crikey, somebody didn't 'ave a very good night,' Mrs Dower commented when she came in armed with a large goose all plucked ready for the oven. The circles under Briony's eyes were so dark that they looked like bruises and she appeared worn out.

'Actually for once it wasn't Mabel that disturbed me last night.' Briony lowered her voice as she glanced towards the two little girls who were engrossed in playing cat's cradle. 'It was Sebastian. He and that friend of his from London were loading the van with something out of the locked barn and it seemed to go on for ages. Goodness knows what they were doing.'

Mrs Dower frowned. 'Well, I know he stores the coffins in there and I did hear that Jim Tolly from Land's End passed away last night, but I can't see Master Seb fetching a coffin at that time of night. Does your grandmother know about it?'

'I doubt it. She and Grandfather wouldn't hear anything

at the front of the house but my bedroom looks directly down onto the yard so I couldn't help but hear it.'

'Up to no good, I expect,' Mrs Dower remarked as she lit the oven.

By the time Alfie returned from the chapel he was in a rare old mood.

'That were so borin'. We 'ad to sing hymns an' everythin',' he complained, slinging his cap onto the chair.

Mrs Dower grinned before pottering off to set the table in the dining room for the family. Marion Frasier had attended the Methodist Chapel every Sunday morning for as long as she could remember and when he had been well enough her husband William had gone too. Now instead Sebastian would carry his father upstairs to the bathroom each week while the missus was gone, so William could have his weekly bath. When Sebastian was at home, that was. If he was away, Howel would sometimes carry the old chap up if he had time, or William would have to make do with bed baths administered by his adoring wife. Annik Dower knew that it went sorely against the grain for her master. Until his health had failed he had been such an energetic man. His illness had also greatly affected his wife, and sometimes, even more of late, Mrs Dower wondered if she was quite right in the head. Still, as she often told herself, she wasn't paid to wonder so she just got on with whatever she was asked to do.

Now she could hear their voices through the sitting-room door, which Marion had absentmindedly left ajar, and she detected a note of irritation in William's voice as he said, 'You really *must* stop giving him money now, Marion. Our finances will not stretch to funding Sebastian's gambling habits. He's a grown man! If he gets himself into a mess in future, he must get himself out of it.'

Mrs Dower hurried on, her mind working overtime. It sounded as if Sebastian had been tapping his mother for cash yet again. It didn't surprise her. She'd never known him do a hard day's work in his entire life, which was why she'd been so surprised when he joined up. Not that it had lasted long; he'd been back at home in no time with his wounded hand. She had strong suspicions about that injury. After all, how easy would it have been to do that to himself? It was just the sort of stunt he would get up to – although she had no proof, of course. It was just something he had said to Howel one day that had rung alarm bells.

'Worth losing a couple of fingers to be safe back home again, isn't it?' he had sneered. 'But I can still hold *my* head up because unlike you, at least I went and showed willing!'

She knew that his comments had been meant as a slur on Howel, who had stayed at home to keep growing food for the country; without farmers, everyone would starve! She also knew that the words had cut Howel to the quick. But then he'd always been a snide little sod, had Master Seb. His mother had ruined him shamelessly and now she was reaping the rewards.

The family were just finishing their Sunday dinner when there was a loud hammering on the front door. The sound echoed through to the kitchen where Briony and the children were eating their own meal, and Briony quickly rose from the table to go and answer it, wondering who it could be. They didn't get many visitors at The Heights, as she'd discovered since living there. Mrs Dower had gone back home at Briony's insistence. Sunday was supposed to be a day of rest, she had reminded Annik jokingly, and she was more than capable of clearing up on her own.

She opened the front door to find a respectably dressed

middle-aged couple standing on the step. 'Hello, may I help you?' she asked politely.

'I doubt it, but that devil who lives here probably can!' the woman snapped as she clutched her handbag in front of her.

'If you're speaking about Sebastian, I'm afraid he's eating his dinner,' Briony explained, sensing trouble.

'Dinner or not, we want to see him *now!*'

Before Briony's astonished eyes the couple swept past her and into the hallway, demanding, 'So where is he, the scoundrel?'

She opened her mouth to reply just as the dining-room door opened and her grandmother appeared, closely followed by Sebastian.

'Mr and Mrs Pascoe. What are you doing here and what do you want?' Marion Frasier asked pompously.

'You know what we want.' The woman was tearful now as she pointed a quavering finger towards Sebastian. 'We want *him* to tell us where our girl is. She would have had his baby by now, but we still haven't heard a single word from her – and if we don't get some answers today we're going to the police. We've seen neither hide nor hair of her since the day she came here to tell you she was carrying his child, and there's something not right.'

'How *ridiculous!*' Marion spat. 'The girl was more than amply paid to leave and take the bastard she was carrying away from here. I'm still not convinced that it was my son's anyway. She just smelled money and latched on to Sebastian for an easy pay-out.'

'How *dare* you!' The man's face had turned dangerously red and his fists were clenched as he stared at Sebastian. 'Our Jenna was a good girl. Never gave us a moment's trouble she didn't, not till she got tangled up with him!

Even if she had decided to leave, why wouldn't she have come home to collect her things first?'

'I have no idea.' Marion shrugged carelessly. 'She was probably too ashamed to face you again after the generous payment I gave her. And it was on condition that she never showed her face around here again,' she added spitefully.

The couple seemed to deflate like balloons then and Briony felt sorry for them. They were clearly very worried about their daughter and what had become of her.

'Don't you have *any* idea at all where she might be? We just to need to know that she's all right.' The woman stared hopefully towards Sebastian, but he shook his head unfeelingly.

'No idea at all. And as far as I'm concerned it's good riddance to bad rubbish. She was the village tart. The child she was carrying could have belonged to any number of men. Now please leave or it will be me phoning the police. This is harassment.'

The woman opened her mouth to protest but then seemed to think better of it as her husband took her elbow and steered her towards the door, his face set in a grim expression.

'You haven't heard the last of this yet,' he said quietly and then they were gone and Briony closed the door behind them.

'You, girl. Don't just stand there gawping like the village idiot! Get back to the kitchen,' her grandmother ordered before disappearing back into the dining room. Briony was deeply disturbed by the scene she had just witnessed. She felt desperately sorry for the couple who had just left and could only imagine how worried they must be about their daughter. It took her some considerable time to put the incident out of her mind.

*

It was the following morning as Briony was lugging the washing out to the laundry room that a figure appeared around the side of the house – and when she saw who it was, her mouth gaped open.

'Ernie!' The washing basket landed on the cobbles spewing dirty laundry all over the place as she raced towards him, her face alight. 'I can't believe it. I thought I was seeing things for a moment,' she gabbled delightedly as he caught her to him. 'But what are you doing here?'

He laughed. 'Well, I've got some leave so I thought I'd come and see you. Your mum gave me the address and I got into Penzance late last night.'

'But where did you stay?'

'Oh, I found a little place that does B&B down by the harbour so I've booked in for a couple of nights.'

She felt guilty, thinking of all the empty rooms at The Heights, but her grandmother would not have welcomed any of her friends anyway. She and the children were only there on sufferance so perhaps it was for the best.

'Come on in,' she grinned. 'The children are all at school but you'll get to see them later. Meantime you can tell me what you've been doing and about everything that's going on at home.' She noticed he was limping slightly and he'd lost a lot of weight, but other than that he looked fine and very handsome in his uniform although his hair looked as if it had been shorn.

He followed her into the kitchen and let out a low whistle. 'Crikey, this is some house, ain't it?' he said. 'I reckon we could fit the whole terrace back 'ome into this place.'

Briony nodded as she filled the kettle. 'You're right, but most of the rooms here are shut up now.'

The words had barely left her lips when Sebastian strode into the kitchen. 'I thought I saw someone coming up the drive. Who's this then?' He eyed Ernie with an unfriendly expression.

'This is Ernest Brindley. He lives next door to us back at home,' Briony explained.

Ernie was about to say 'How do you do?' and proffer his hand when Sebastian sneered: 'Huh! So we've got to entertain your friends as well as have you lot under our feet now, have we? We're not a charity, you know.'

Ernie fumbled in his pocket and threw a silver sixpence onto the table. 'That should cover the cost of a cup of tea,' he answered scathingly and had the satisfaction of seeing Sebastian flush a dull brick-red.

Sebastian turned his attention back to Briony then as he told her, 'Mother would like tea – as soon as you can find the time, of course.' The last words were loaded with sarcasm but he didn't wait for a response.

Once he was out of the room, Ernie looked towards Briony and asked, 'What the hell was all that about?'

'Oh, I'm expected to earn our keep by cooking and cleaning whilst we're here.'

'You're *what?*' Ernie scratched his head in bewilderment. He had expected to arrive to find Briony and the children living the life of Riley, but that didn't seem to be the case at all.

She quickly told him about where she and the children were sleeping – in the servants' quarters – and of the work she was expected to do, and saw his jaw tighten.

'But that's bloody disgraceful! You're their granddaughter, for Christ's sake, not their skivvy!'

Briony shrugged. 'I don't mind really. Everything has changed since Mum lived here. Most of the male staff have joined up, and between you and me I don't think the family are quite as well off as they used to be. The war has affected everyone. Sebastian is worried that me and the children are after his inheritance, which is absolute rubbish. The second this war is over, I shall be back home like a shot and I won't give this place, or my uncle for that matter, another thought. In the meanwhile though, the children are safer here than they would be at home, that's how I'm able to put up with it.'

Ernie sighed as Briony carried a heavy brown teapot to the table then hurried away again to put a silver tea set on a tray ready for the drawing room.

Once she had served her grandparents with their mid-morning tea and biscuits, she and Ernie sat at the table and chatted as if they had never been apart. The time seemed to fly by. The washing she had dropped was blown about the cobbles, but Briony didn't care. She intended to spend every second she could with Ernie while he was there, and if her grandmother and Sebastian didn't like it they could lump it as far as she was concerned. She made a large cottage pie for lunch and after serving the family she and Ernie sat in the kitchen to eat theirs.

'I shall leave you some money for this,' Ernie told her as he tucked in, thinking what a good little cook she had become.

'Oh no you won't!' Briony was indignant but then she confided, 'That's one good thing about living here. There seems to be no shortage of food like there is back at home.' She then told him all about Mabel and he grinned as she described how foul the little East Ender's language could be.

'I've no doubt you'll whip that young madam into shape,' he said.

Eventually, Briony asked after Ruth and her mother, and he was cautious in his reply. The way he looked at it, there was no point in telling her the truth – that her mother was drunk half of the time now. Briony could do nothing about it whilst she was stuck out here in the back of beyond, and she would only worry herself sick if she knew, so he chose his words carefully and told her that as far as he was aware, Lois was doing fine.

'Me and Ruth went to the pictures the other night to see *Pinocchio*,' he said to change the subject and Briony chuckled.

'But I thought that was for children?'

'We didn't 'ave much choice, but we didn't 'alf miss 'aving you with us.'

Their eyes locked and Briony dragged hers away. It wouldn't do to let Ernie know how much she thought of him, because it would break Ruth's heart.

'I notice there's a little cinema down in Penzance. Is there any chance we could go and see whatever's on there tonight?' he asked. 'I 'ave to get the train back first thing in the morning.'

Briony's heart skipped a beat. She hadn't been anywhere without the children since arriving at The Heights, and the thought of a night out was very tempting. 'I suppose I could ask Mrs Dower if she'd come and keep her eye on the children,' she answered doubtfully. 'But now it's time to fetch them from school. Would you like to come with me? By the time we get back, Mrs Dower should be here to tackle the evening meal and I'm sure she'd like to meet you.'

He nodded as he rose from the table and soon they were on their way with Briony pointing out places of interest to him as they walked. 'That's St Michael's Mount over there,' she said.

Ernie took a deep breath of the clean sea air. 'It's really beautiful 'ere,' he said. 'Sort of rugged ain't it?'

'Oh yes. The children love it.'

Alfie and Sarah squealed with delight when they saw

Ernie waiting at the school gates for them. They launched themselves at him so enthusiastically that they almost overbalanced him.

'How you doin', little 'uns?' he asked affectionately as he bent to their level and gave them a hug.

Mabel shrank into Briony's side and stared at him suspiciously. But then as Briony was fast discovering, she wasn't keen on men at all.

'We're all right,' Alfie said cheerfully, gazing at Ernie's uniform with awe. 'But we miss our mum.'

'Of course you do.' Ernie's face was straight now as Sarah smiled at him shyly. 'And 'ow's my best girl?'

Sarah giggled and took his hand, and soon they were following the cliff path back to The Heights. The sea was choppy and the skies overhead were heavy with the threat of rain, and yet it still managed to look breathtakingly beautiful. Alfie skipped ahead before suddenly coming to an abrupt stop and pointing down to the beach below.

'What are them Army chaps doing?' he asked.

As Briony and Ernie came abreast of him, Ernie said, 'It looks like they're puttin' rolls of barbed wire along the beach.'

'Aw, what are they doing that for? We won't be able to go an' paddle in the sea,' Alfie complained.

Briony and Ernie exchanged a worried glance, both thinking the same thing. But not wishing to frighten the children, Ernie made light of it, saying, 'Well, now the weather is gettin' colder yer wouldn't want to paddle in the sea anyway, and there's still plenty o' sand for you to build sandcastles on.'

'Hmm, s'pose so.' Alfie kicked at a stone, sending it hurtling over the edge of the cliff. 'But they'd better come back an' move it before next summer.' Some gulls that were nesting on the cliff face squawked in protest and flapped into the sky.

'Why do you think they are doing it?' Briony whispered when the children had walked on in front of them again, staring at the points of the wire that were glinting evilly in the fading light. The rolls were like a scar on the landscape; even here they couldn't completely escape the war.

'Probably because the Luftwaffe 'ave been targeting Falmouth, and in case they decide to invade via the sea,' Ernie answered tensely. 'It's just sea defences. But don't worry; you should be all right here. I'm sure they're doin' it just to be on the safe side.'

She hoped that he was right and tried to keep her smile in place, but the sight of the soldiers had seriously unnerved her.

Chapter Twenty-Five

Just as Briony had told him, Mrs Dower was in the kitchen when they got back. The housekeeper greeted him warmly when Briony introduced Ernie, thinking what a dashing figure he cut in his RAF uniform.

'It's about time she had a bit of company her own age,' she told him, smiling fondly at Briony. 'The poor little maid has done nothing but work since she got here.'

'Ah well, in that case perhaps I might ask a favour of you?' Ernie said, licking his lips nervously.

'Ask away, lad.'

'I was wondering if er . . . if you would perhaps watch the children tonight while I take Briony to the cinema. We'd only be gone for a couple of hours or so and I'd bring her straight back as soon as the film finished.'

'I'd be glad to, young man. It would do her the world of good to get out for a while,' Mrs Dower replied. 'But now if you're staying for dinner, you can help lay the table. You know what they say – idle hands make work for the devil!' She winked at him and he grinned as he took off his cap and set to, pleased to know that Briony had at least one friend here.

It was nice to walk down the hill that evening with a whole three hours to herself to look forward to. She had put on her best dress – a cream wool one which fell just below her knees and clung to her curves. It was another of her mother's cast-offs and very plain, but Briony was naturally pretty and the simplicity of the style suited her. She had also put on her best high-heeled court shoes and her red coat, which Ernie thought showed off the sheen of her long black hair. She was even prettier than he had remembered and he had to quell the urge to take her hand as they strolled along. There was a chill wind blowing off the sea which sent Briony's hair flapping out behind her like a cloak and brought colour into her cheeks.

'I wonder what will be on?' she asked chirpily as they headed for the Savoy cinema.

Ernie grinned. '*Goodbye, Mr Chips* featurin' Robert Donat and Greer Garson,' he informed her. 'I 'ad a look at the board outside before coming up to the 'ouse this morning. I'm afraid it's a year out o' date, but yer won't mind, will yer?'

'Not at all.' Briony chuckled and to his delight she tucked her arm though his. 'Howel warned me that we never get the new releases here, but anything beats sitting in the kitchen on my own with a pile of Grandmother's old magazines again.'

There was that name again – Howel! Briony had mentioned him a number of times today and he found himself feeling jealous.

'This Howel,' he began cautiously. 'Nice chap, is he?'

'Oh yes, Howel is lovely,' Briony told him. 'He works so hard, bless him, but he always makes time to have a word with the children.'

'Married is 'e, this paragon of virtue?'

Briony frowned at him. 'No, he's not married as it happens, but he does have a girlfriend in the village.'

'Oh, right.' Ernie felt ridiculously relieved and grinned again into the darkness. It wouldn't do if someone were to come and pinch Briony right from under his nose now!

They enjoyed the film, and once it was over they strolled through the town to the harbour, strangely reluctant to end the evening. There had only been a handful of people in the cinema but Ernie and Briony didn't much care, so long as they were together. The boats that were moored at the quay were dancing up and down on the choppy waves, and once they had left the shelter of the little fishing cottages behind, the wind blew colder, making Briony shudder and pull her coat collar up. Ernie placed his arm protectively about her shoulders and although a vision of Ruth suddenly floated in front of her eyes she didn't shrug the arm away but leaned into the warmth of him. Every inch of her was tingling but she wasn't sure if it was because of the chill mist blowing in off the sea or Ernie's close proximity.

He turned to her, and tilting her chin, he looked down into her eyes. The moonlight made them appear to be almost black and a wave of tenderness swept through him.

'I know yer don't want me to say this,' he muttered, 'but it might be ages before we get to see each other again and I don't want to go away without letting yer know how I feel about yer.'

'Ernie . . . stop!' She dragged herself out of his arms,

suddenly feeling colder than she had ever been in her life. 'We can't do this. We have to think of Ruth. She loves you – she's always loved you and I couldn't bear to hurt her. She's my best friend!'

He spread his hands helplessly. 'I can't 'elp 'ow she feels about me,' he objected. 'I think the world of her too, but only as a friend, and I've never led her to believe any other. It's *you* I have feelings for. I can't force meself to love her just because she thinks she 'as feelings fer me!'

'Oh dear, what a mess!' Briony's shoulders sagged. Ernie was quite right, of course. It was hardly his fault if Ruth had fallen in love with him. But where did that leave her? She felt as if she was caught up in a no win situation. If she admitted to Ernie that she had feelings for him too, she would hurt Ruth. If she didn't tell him how she felt, she would hurt him!

'Look,' she said eventually, 'why don't we just leave things as they are and see how we all feel when this damned war is over? Ruth might have met someone else by then. And even if she hasn't . . . Well, none of us knows what's going to happen, do we?'

'I don't suppose we do,' he admitted, his mouth set in a grim line. No one knew better than he did the risk he was taking each time he climbed into the cockpit of his Spitfire and headed off into the blue yonder to fight the Jerries. 'But couldn't yer just give me a *glimmer* of hope to go away with?'

Making a sudden decision, she nodded. 'All right then, I'll say this: I *do* have feelings for you, and if at the end of the war we both feel the same, then we'll have to admit it to Ruth and be honest with her. I just hope she'll forgive us.'

Even in the darkness she saw his smile stretching from ear to ear and before she knew it he had grabbed her into his arms again.

'That'll do nicely fer now, so how about a kiss to keep me goin'? You wouldn't begrudge me that, would yer?' His face was bending towards her so she closed her eyes, and as his lips gently met hers she gave herself up to the sheer pleasure of the moment. Even through the thickness of their coats she could feel his heart pounding, and she just wished that they could stay that way forever.

Eventually he walked her back through the cobbled streets past the picturesque thatched cottages to the bottom of the hill that led to her grandparents' home, and once there she came to an abrupt stop.

'There's no need to come any further,' she told him. 'I'll make my own way from here.'

'You damned well *won't!*' he protested, but he had forgotten that Briony could be as stubborn as him.

'I damned well *will!*' Her chin lifted as she glared at him. 'It will do your leg no good at all going all the way back up there, and I'm perfectly capable of getting myself back.'

He shrugged, knowing when he was beaten, but then pulled her into his arms again and kissed her gently on the forehead.

'Can I come and see yer early in the mornin' before I catch the train back?'

She nodded. 'I'd like that.' At least she would get to see him one more time, even if it was just for a short while.

She was surprised to find Howel waiting for her when she got back to the house. He was sitting in the chair at the side of the kitchen fire with his feet up on a stool reading the newspaper.

'Had a good night, did you?' he asked pleasantly.

'Yes, thank you. But where's your mum?'

'Thought I'd come and take over from her a while ago to save her walking back too late.'

'Oh!' Briony instantly felt guilty, very aware of his eyes on her as she peeled off her coat. Mrs Dower worked so hard; it had been selfish of her to expect the woman to babysit.

'Have they been good?' she asked, cocking her head towards the ceiling.

'Haven't heard a peep out of them all night. They've been good as gold.'

He had never seen Briony dressed up before and he was amazed at how different she looked. He'd always regarded her as a child, but now he saw from the way the wool dress clung to her that she was very much a young woman. And a very pretty one at that.

'How old are you?' he asked suddenly, before he could stop himself.

'I'm seventeen, although on some days I feel ninety.' She thought it was rather a strange question to ask but decided she could do the same. 'How old are you?'

'Twenty-three next week.'

She was surprised. She had thought he was much older than that although now she came to think of it she seemed to recall Mrs Dower telling her how old he was when she and the children first arrived. An awkward silence followed then until she said, 'Would you like a hot drink before you go?'

'I wouldn't say no.' His eyes followed her as she put milk in a saucepan and fetched some cups and saucers from the dresser. He had always felt easy in her company, but for some strange reason he felt a little shy now.

'I take it that was your boyfriend?' As soon as the words had left his lips he groaned inwardly. His mouth seemed to be running away with itself tonight.

'Not exactly.' Briony sighed as she spooned cocoa powder into the pan. There was never a shortage of groceries here.

Mrs Dower had told her Sebastian always got some for them all when he went to London.

'What does "not exactly" mean? Either he is or he isn't.' Howel had no idea why it mattered, but suddenly it did.

Briony's hands became still as she stared off into space before explaining, 'It's complicated. You see, Ernie, my best friend Ruth and me have all been best mates since we were children. We've always done everything together. But then as we got older, Ruth fell in love with him.' She fiddled with the teaspoon before going on, 'The trouble was, Ernie didn't feel the same about her.'

'Because he had feelings for you?'

Briony nodded miserably. 'And now I feel as if I'm stuck between the devil and the deep blue sea. Whatever I do I'm going to hurt one of them, so I've told Ernie that it's best to leave things just as they are until after the war.' But even as she said it she knew that things had subtly changed tonight, otherwise why would she have allowed Ernie to kiss her?

In truth, Howel knew exactly how she was feeling. He had been seeing Megan Brown from the village for the past two years on and off, and he knew that he had only to say the word and she'd be his for the taking. Until recently he'd been quite content and happy to let nature take its course. After all, Megan was a lovely girl, everyone said so; none better. She was pretty, fun to be with and he knew she'd make a good wife. But for some reason he suddenly couldn't picture himself spending the rest of his life with her, and so recently he'd tried to keep their relationship on a casual footing. Problem was, it was getting harder. Megan was dropping hints about bottom drawers and engagement rings, and he didn't quite know what to do about it. He wondered why everything had to be so complicated. In this neck of the woods it was expected that you would grow up, choose a wife from the local community and live happily ever after.

More than ever, Howel Dower wished that he had never been granted a dispensation from joining up because he was a farmer. He would have happily gone to fight for his country, but there was nothing he could do about it now. People needed feeding! The Frasiers and his family relied on him heavily and he knew that without him, his grandfather would never have managed to keep the two places going on his own. It took the pair of them all their time as it was, and sometimes he worried about his grandmother. Annik never seemed to have a moment to herself but she never complained and was totally devoted to William and now to Briony and the children. Things wouldn't have been so bad if Master Seb had been prepared to pull his weight but he was about as much use as a chocolate teapot, always off on some spree or another. He was gut selfish into the bargain too, but then his grandmother had always said that Marion Frasier had made him that way. And to think that when anything happened to his parents, the whole lot would belong to Sebastian. It didn't seem fair – but then life rarely was.

He waited while the cocoa was heated, and once Briony had poured them each a cup and opened the biscuit barrel he sat at the kitchen table with her. They had both lapsed into silence, each locked in their own thoughts, so once he had drained his cup he stood up and pulled his coat on.

'I'll be off then,' he announced.

'What? Oh yes . . . of course. And thank you, Howel – for keeping your ear out for the children, I mean.' She had been miles away and felt awful when she realised she had almost forgotten that he was even there. He nodded, rammed his cap on and left, and once he had gone she fingered her lips, remembering how it had felt when Ernie had kissed her.

*

As usual, Howel was there bright and early the next morning. The children had scampered off to let the hens out of their coops, a job they had adopted, and now they were scouting round for eggs for breakfast.

He had just entered the kitchen when Ernie followed him in. The two men eyed each other warily.

'You must be Ernie. How do.' Howel held his hand out and Ernie shook it.

'You both timed that well. I've just put the kettle on,' Briony said brightly, detecting a slight atmosphere. She and Howel usually enjoyed a cup of tea together in the morning, but today he shook his head.

'No, I won't stay. I've got a sick sheep back at the farm and I'm waiting for the vet to come out, so I'd best get back.' He dumped the day's supplies on the table then strode back towards the door, adding, 'I'll be back later to chop some logs.' Nodding towards Ernie he left without another word and Briony wondered if he had got out of bed the wrong side. He was usually so cheerful in the morning.

However, she was so keen to spend every second she could with Ernie that she didn't give it much thought. He had breakfast with the children and then walked them all to school with her. They were halfway back when he glanced at his watch and said, 'I'm afraid I shall 'ave to get back to collect me things from the B&B now. Me train leaves in an hour an' if I miss that one there ain't another till tomorrow mornin'.'

Briony secretly hoped that he would miss it, but not wishing to be selfish she told him, 'I'll walk down with you then. I'd like to see you off at the station.'

He didn't object. He was wishing that they could have had a little more time together and wondering how long it might be before they saw each other again.

In no time at all, they were standing on the platform next to the train.

'Right then, I'd best be off.' Ernie swung his kitbag onto his shoulder and placed his cap on as Briony stared up at him. She didn't want him to go; he was a link to home as much as anything, but of course she knew that he must leave.

'You will write, won't you?' she asked as her lip trembled.

'Of course I will, when I'm able to,' he said. 'But don't get worryin' if you don't 'ear anythin' for a while. You know what the post's like.'

'And you will give my love to Mum and Ruth and your mum for me?'

'Of course. And don't you let that grandma of yours get bullying you,' he said sternly.

Already the guard was walking along holding his green flag and slamming the carriage doors, so Ernie bent quickly and pecked her on the lips before hopping aboard. He then pulled the brown leather strap to let the window down and leaned out as the guard blew his whistle and waved his flag.

'Till next time,' he said and she nodded mutely, too full to speak. The train was chugging into life and before they knew it the platform was engulfed in steam and smoke – and it drew away.

Loneliness engulfed Briony as she headed for the exit. She would have given anything to be on that train with him, but she had to think of the children – and the war seemed a very long way from being over yet.

Chapter Twenty-Six

'And you're *quite* sure that they're all well?' Lois stared up at Ernie.

He had only been home in Nuneaton for a couple of hours and it was quite late at night, but Lois hadn't wanted to wait until morning to hear how her family was. Because of damage to the tracks caused by the bombing, Ernie's train had been diverted a number of times and the journey had taken far longer than it normally did – but everyone was getting used to that now. The men who worked on the railways must have felt they were performing a useless task, for each time they repaired a stretch of the line, another section was bombed by the Luftwaffe.

'They're all absolutely fine,' he said, and meant it. 'In fact, I reckon young Alfie 'as put a bit of weight on. The sea air must suit him. And your Sarah looks a picture.'

'It is beautiful there,' Lois answered wistfully. She had loved living in Poldak as a child, with its sandy beaches and hidden coves. 'But how are they getting on with my mother?' she braced herself to ask then.

Ernie averted his eyes and shrugged. 'Fine as far as I could see.' How could he tell her that Briony was little more than a skivvy and that her three precious children were living up in the servants' quarters? It would only worry her and by the look of it she was far from well. In fact, she was a mere shadow of the neighbour he remembered from before he had joined up. Then she had been a curvaceous, glamorous woman – but now that pretty face was drawn and haggard. She was as skinny as a rake as well, but that was hardly surprising as his mother had confided that she seemed to be surviving on alcohol rather than decent meals. He felt desperately sorry for Lois Valentine. She had obviously taken the news about her husband very badly and he was worried that now the children were gone she might just give up altogether, although more than ever now Lois knew that she had done the right thing by sending them away. There had been further raids on Nuneaton since the children had left for Cornwall, one of them far too close for comfort. The Cherry Tree Inn, which had stood on the corner of Westbury Road had taken a direct hit and six houses in Heath End Road had been so badly damaged that the families who had lived in them had been forced to move out. Over one hundred incendiary bombs had rained down on various areas nearby, not to mention the high-explosive bombs that had all but flattened everything they had landed on. People had lost their lives during the raids and Lois was thankful that her children were well out of it.

'Well, thank you, Ernie.' She rose unsteadily from the chair and he noticed that her hands were shaking so badly they seemed to have developed a life of their own. 'I won't keep you any longer but I just wanted to hear that they were all right. Goodnight, all.'

'Goodnight, luvvie.' Mrs Brindley saw her to the door and watched her cross the yard then sighing, she quietly closed the door and drew the blackout curtain across it. 'Poor bugger,' she muttered. 'She don't seem to know if she's comin' or goin' half the time any more. I don't think she'll ever get over losin' James.'

Ernie nodded in agreement.

'So now you can tell me what it's *really* like down there,' his mother said firmly, and she wagged a finger in his face. 'I know you, me lad. An' I know there's more goin' on in that Poldak place than you ever told Lois. So come on, spill the beans!'

And so Ernie told her truthfully about how Briony's grandmother was treating her, and when he was done Martha scowled.

'Bloody old cow! Fancy treatin' yer own flesh an' blood that way. An' callin' her "*girl*"*!* What's the grandad got to say about it?'

'Apparently, Briony gets on well with 'im – when the old woman is out o' the way, that is. It seems to be 'er that's the only fly in the ointment.'

Mrs Brindley's face softened then and she grinned. 'Aw well, if I know Briony she'll handle that old bat. Got spirit, that girl 'as.' She glanced at him out of the corner of her eye then and asked innocently. 'An' was she pleased to see yer?'

'Of course she was . . . we're mates, ain't we?' Ernie answered quickly but he didn't enlarge on it and his mother didn't ask any more. Happen things would work out in the end. She just dreaded to think how young Ruth would handle it if Ernie chose Briony over her. She'd called round once already after work to see if he was back, and the woman had no doubt she'd be round again before the night was out. It was a funny old life, no one could deny!

Briony got all the latest war news from her grandfather, whom she now saw at every opportunity when her grandmother popped out, usually to some chapel function or other. She would make a cup of tea and take it in to him, and they would chat about everything and nothing. When he talked about her mother, which he often did, she would see the regret and sadness in his eyes and she knew how deeply he missed her. She still gave Sebastian a wide berth – which wasn't too difficult to do as he tended to be out during daylight hours. On the evenings when he was at home she had taken to listening to the wireless in the kitchen once the children had gone to bed. She finally felt as if she was getting somewhere with Mabel. The little girl only wet the bed spasmodically now rather than every night, and the nightmares were less frequent too, which was a relief. But she still seemed to have a deep-rooted fear of men – something that Briony found very disturbing.

One evening, Briony decided to have an early night. It was wild and windy outside and she was feeling tired so she had a nice hot bath and after peeping in to check on the children she curled up in bed with a hot-water bottle, a library book and the latest letter she had received from her mother. Sometimes she wondered why she bothered to read them. They all seemed to say exactly the same thing in slightly different words. Even so, they were a link to home and she kept them all together, tied with one of her hair ribbons, in her bedside drawer.

Soon she fell asleep but was woken in the early hours of the morning by raised voices. Knuckling the sleep from her eyes, she struggled up onto her elbow, thinking that it was one of the children before realising that the voices were coming from the kitchen. Her heart leaped into her mouth as she tried to remember if she had locked the back door. She doubted that she had. The Heights was so isolated that strangers in the area were rarely seen, and even in the village people seldom bothered to lock their doors. Pulling on her dressing gown, she crept along the landing and down the stairs.

'Didn't you fucking *hear* me? I told you I'd get it, didn't I?'

It was Sebastian's voice and she stopped dead in her tracks.

'When? The end of never?' a sarcastic voice retaliated. 'I tell yer now, mate. The gaffer won't wait much longer. He's really pissed off, and I don't need to tell yer what that means, do I?'

'Look . . .' Sebastian's voice was wheedling now. 'Just give me another day. I'll have it for you by this time tomorrow. I swear it! I just need to soften the old girl up in the morning when my father is out of the way.'

There was a loaded silence before the other man told him, 'Tomorrer then. But where am I supposed to sleep? I was expecting to drive back tonight, not have to hang around in this dump.'

Briony could hear the relief in her uncle's voice as he said quickly, 'There's a makeshift bed in the back of the barn. It's hardly the Ritz but it'll be better than sleeping the night in the cab of the van.'

'I suppose that'll 'ave to do then.'

Once the back door had closed behind them, she tiptoed down to the kitchen window and twitching the curtain aside, she watched their progress across the yard until they disappeared behind the back of a large van. She thought it might be the one she had seen there before but it was so dark that she couldn't be sure. Time passed and she could hear nothing but the sound of the wind as it battered the house and bent the trees surrounding the yard almost double. Then above the van she saw one of the barn doors that was kept locked opening and she scuttled away back to bed. Sebastian had obviously got himself into some debt again, so no doubt he would be badgering his mother for more money tomorrow. She sighed, because whenever he upset her grandmother, it was Briony and the children who took the backlash of the woman's temper; she had a horrible feeling that tomorrow wasn't going to be a good day.

She had barely settled back into bed when she heard the engine of the van start up and it was driven away. That was odd. Perhaps Sebastian's visitor had decided against staying in the barn after all? Yawning, she turned over and was soon fast asleep.

When she served breakfast to her grandparents the next morning, Briony noticed that Sebastian's chair was empty.

Her grandmother tutted with annoyance. 'Oh, where has he got to?' She looked at Briony and said, 'Go up to my son's bedroom immediately, girl, and tell him that his breakfast is served.'

She never referred to Sebastian as Briony's uncle. It was as if by doing so she would have to acknowledge that Briony was a member of the family. This didn't trouble the girl at all; what did trouble her was the fact that she had no idea where his bedroom was. She had never gone beyond the top of the stairs in the main house.

'I don't know where his bedroom is,' she answered calmly and her grandmother glared at her as if she was a half-wit.

'It's the third door along to the left on the first-floor landing,' she said impatiently.

'Briony couldn't have known that, Marion,' her husband said in Briony's defence.

'Well, she does now. So go and do as you're told – *girl*!'

Briony smiled at her grandfather as she left the room without another word. She'd soon discovered that it was much easier to do as she was told rather than argue.

She mounted the stairs, marvelling again at how grand this part of the house was, and when she came to the bedroom she'd been directed to she tapped at the door. There was no reply so she knocked again, harder this time. Still nothing, so she cautiously tried the door handle. It was unlocked, so she inched the door open just enough to see that Sebastian's bed was still neatly made. Mrs Dower cleaned the family rooms each day and all was neat and tidy.

Briony would have liked to have a nose around, but deciding against it she hurried back downstairs and announced: 'He isn't there and the bed hasn't been slept in, by the look of it.'

'What?' her grandmother spluttered. 'But he *must* be there! He was here at bedtime last night and he didn't mention that he was going out.'

'Perhaps he was called out to deal with a death?' William suggested.

'Well, I didn't hear the telephone ring,' his wife answered.

Briony wondered if she should tell her about what she had overheard in the kitchen and Sebastian's late-night visitor, but then decided against it. It was just as well she did, because at that moment the door opened and Sebastian himself strode in, with a face as dark as a thundercloud. He looked slightly dishevelled and his chin was covered in stubble. There was also a large bruise on his cheek.

'Where have you been? And what's happened to your face?' his mother asked.

'I got called out to collect a body and take it down to the funeral parlour and I hit my face on the side of the hearse as I was loading the corpse in.'

His father stared at him, clearly not believing a word he said.

'Bit clumsy, wasn't it?'

Sebastian shrugged as he took a seat at the table and began to load his plate with bacon and eggs. 'It was dark and I was very tired. But do you mind if I get on with my breakfast now?'

Briony turned and beat a hasty retreat, feeling very much in the way. It was a relief to get back to the kitchen where the children were putting their coats on ready for school.

Sarah had developed a cold and Briony wondered if she should send her, but the little girl insisted that she was well enough and so they set off. Thankfully the wind had dropped but a thick mist had floated in from the sea and they could barely see more than a few feet in front of them.

'I think we'll go through the orchard and cut through the fields today so we avoid the cliff path,' Briony told them as they crossed the yard. 'There's no point in taking unnecessary risks in this fog.'

Once she had dropped the children safely off at the school gates she hurried back the way she had come, but somewhere along the path she must have taken a wrong turn, for eventually she found herself in the yard of what appeared to be an empty farm. This must be the one that Mrs Dower told me about, she thought as she peered through the windows. It was a lovely place and she thought how sad it was that it had been standing empty for so many years. But then she stood and tried to get her bearings before setting off again . . . and shortly afterwards she was relieved to find herself heading towards the orchard.

Howel was in the kitchen unloading the supplies onto the table when she got back, and she told him about her little adventure. The cold air had made her cheeks glow, and with her long black hair shining like coal he thought how attractive she looked.

'Ar, that'll be the Kerricks' old place, Chapel Farm,' he answered. 'Shame it is, but there you go. I don't reckon your grandpa could afford to keep it up. Me and my family lived there at one time till we lost our parents, then the Kerricks took it over for a time. No doubt it will be left empty to go to rack and ruin now.'

'How sad.' Briony had been quite taken with the place. 'Do you think he'd mind if I went and had a look around if I get a bit of free time?'

He shook his head. 'I shouldn't think so. I'll tell you what – I've got an hour free early this afternoon. Do you want me to take you over there before you fetch the children from school?'

'Oh yes please, I'd love that!' Briony responded. She could always jiggle her jobs about, and the way she saw it she was due a little time off.

'Right, I'll call for you after you've served that lot their lunch. Shall we say about one o'clock?'

She nodded as Howel went out into the yard to fetch the logs in while she put the kettle on. He was a little later than usual this morning but she hoped he would make time to stay for a cup of tea.

When they sat together drinking it at the kitchen table a short while later she told him about Sebastian's late-night visitor. 'It's really weird because the man had said that he was going to stay the night in the barn,' she confided. 'And when I first came down they were arguing in the kitchen. It sounded like Sebastian owed money again.'

'Well, you'll soon find out,' Howel said caustically. 'If he does, he'll be trying it on with Mrs Frasier again today.'

A couple of hours later as Briony was mopping the floor in the hallway she heard voices arguing in the sitting room and knew that Howel had guessed correctly.

'And how much do you need *this* time?' Marion Frasier sounded exasperated.

'Er . . . well . . . two hundred pounds.'

'*How* much?' The woman's voice had risen alarmingly.

'I'll pay it back – every penny,' Sebastian said in a wheedling voice.

'Oh, you *will*, will you? And just *how* do you intend to do that? The funeral parlour and the farm are barely making enough money to pay the bills and you said you'd repay the last couple of sums I let you have. No, son, I'm sorry, but this time I shall have to ask your father about it. That's a tremendous amount of money. Gambling debt again, is it?'

Briony didn't hang about to hear any more but grabbed the mop and bucket and went quietly back to the kitchen. It would never do if they thought that she was eavesdropping. Sebastian was asking for two hundred pounds as if it was nothing! He really was the most selfish, odious person she had ever encountered.

Howel called for her at one o'clock as arranged. She had served her grandparents their lunch by then but there had been no sign of Sebastian and she had noticed that William was in an unusually grumpy mood, no doubt after being told of his son's latest debt. But now as she set off with Howel she was in fine spirits and looking forward to her outing.

Chapel Farm stood a mile or so away from The Heights

and as they approached it now she was better able to see it because the weak sun had burned off the early-morning mist. It lay in a small dip, its fields surrounded by drystone walls that put her in mind of a patchwork quilt, and as they walked towards it she thought how pretty it looked with the wild Cornish moors stretching away behind into the distance. It wasn't quite as big as Kynance Farm where the Dowers lived, but the farmhouse walls were built of warm Cornish stone that the sun and sea had mellowed to shades of grey and yellow, and it had a thatched roof. They walked through double gates, at the side of which a large rowan tree grew and Briony recalled Mrs Dower telling her that these trees were planted to ward off evil spirits. A large barn stood to one side of the farmhouse, and as they crossed the yard, Howel informed her that it had living accommodation on the first floor reached by stone steps that led up to a stout oak door. There was also a stable block and a number of pigsties to the other side of it. At the back of the house was an overgrown orchard, the branches of the fruit trees dipping with the weight of rotten fruit. In front of that was what had clearly been a large vegetable patch. Brambles and long grass had encroached upon it now, but Briony knew that without too much work it could be beautiful and productive again. The windows were diamond-leaded and they glinted in the sun as they approached.

'Oh, it's like something off the cover of a chocolate box,' Briony gasped in delight.

Howel ceremoniously opened the door to the kitchen for her; she stepped past him and gazed about. Most of the furniture was still in place but it was festooned with cobwebs and dust now, and the sight made her feel sad. The moths had had a feast of the curtains, which hung in tatters, and the grate was full of ashes that had spewed out onto a tiled hearth. In the centre of the room stood a large oak table with four sturdy matching chairs and either side of the fireplace were two easy chairs that had seen better days. A door in the far wall led into a parlour. Again, most of the furniture was still there and without realising that she was doing it she began to picture aloud how it could look with a little tender loving care.

'This sideboard could be lovely with a good polish,' she remarked as she traced her finger through the thick dust all across it. 'And I think those fire-irons on the hearth are solid brass. They're badly tarnished but I reckon they'd come up a treat with a bit of elbow grease.'

Howel grinned but remained silent as she turned about and headed for a staircase in the corner of the kitchen. Upstairs she found three bedrooms and a small box room that she declared could be just right for converting into an indoor bathroom. The huge wooden wardrobes were old-fashioned but solid and Briony pictured herself cleaning them.

'I'd have flowered curtains and a flowered bedspread in here,' she told Howel in the largest room as her imagination ran riot. 'And I think these beds are brass too. They just need a good clean although I dare say the mattresses would have to be replaced. They're damp.'

Howel chuckled as he leaned against the doorpost and watched her with his arms crossed.

'Thinking of buying, it are you?' he said teasingly and his words brought her back to earth with a bump.

'Of course not. I just think it's a shame for a lovely farmhouse like this to stand empty. Perhaps you and your girlfriend could live here once you get married?'

'I reckon that's some way away,' Howel said abruptly. 'And now if you're done we'd best get back.'

'Oh er . . . yes, of course.' Briony meekly followed him back outside wondering what she might have said to upset him and they made their way back to The Heights in silence.

Chapter Twenty-Seven

As Briony approached the school to collect the children she saw a small cluster of women gathered at the gates. Their heads were bent together and when they saw her, they called her over.

'Have you heard about little Bethany Tiler?' one woman asked. She was the mother of one of the girls in Sarah's class.

Briony shook her head.

'Poor little soul got taken away in an ambulance not an hour since,' the woman told her in a hushed voice.

Briony frowned. 'Oh dear, I hope it isn't anything too serious?'

The woman pursed her lips. 'We hope it isn't either, but rumour has it that the little lass has contracted polio.'

'Oh no!' Briony's hand flew to her mouth. She had heard horror stories about that particular disease, of children existing in monstrous great iron lungs that breathed for them. And of others who were left with wasted limbs and callipers on their legs. 'But isn't that highly contagious?' she said fearfully, and when the others nodded, her stomach did a somersault. 'When will we know if it is that or not?'

The woman replied, 'All I can tell you is that they've taken her to the cottage hospital for now and put her in isolation while they do the tests. A doctor from Truro who specialises in that sort of disease is on his way to look at her and if it's confirmed, they'll move her to the sanatorium where he works.' She tutted, her face a mask of concern. 'If you ask me, I'd say it's probably one of the evacuees from London that's brought it here.' Then suddenly remembering that Briony was caring for such a child, she added apologetically, 'Not that it's their fault, of course, but it's a known fact that polio is rife in the slums.'

The school bell rang then, frightening a moorhen that was perched on the school fence. It flapped away indignantly as Briony waited for the children, trying to keep outwardly calm. She had the urge to take them all home and wrap them in cotton wool until the panic was over, but she knew that this wasn't possible. They would all just have to wait for the results of Bethany's tests and pray that they were negative.

The news when it came three days later was not good. Bethany did have poliomyelitis and had been transferred by ambulance to a sanatorium in Truro. Her parents were distraught after being told that for the duration of her treatment they would not be allowed to visit her, and the headmistress ordered the school to be closed for two days while the premises were given a thorough clean.

Briony and a number of women from Poldak village descended on the school armed with copious amounts of disinfectant and mops and buckets, and they scoured everything within sight. Curtains were taken down and sent away to be washed, and every single wall, chair, desk and floor was thoroughly cleaned. Even the pencils were disinfected. Precious paper that the children had been writing on was burned and replaced with new, and by the end of the first day the smell of disinfectant was so overpowering that Briony could practically taste it. Her hands were red raw with scrubbing but she was happy to do what she could to prevent the infection from spreading. Windows were left wide open as they worked, and the cold wind whipping in from the sea made them all shiver as they tackled one room at a time. Briony was sick with worry. Sarah was still unwell and she was terrified that she might be incubating the awful disease. She had never been a strong child since developing whooping cough as a toddler, and every winter she seemed to catch every cough and cold that was going. She mentioned this fact to her grandmother who grudgingly allowed her to call out the family doctor to look at her.

Dr Restarick was a plump, elderly man with snow-white hair and a bushy white beard who put Briony in mind of Father Christmas. When he arrived he got out his stethoscope and examined Sarah thoroughly, as Briony stood by with her heart in her throat.

Half of the parents in the village were panicking and since Bethany had been diagnosed, the good doctor had been run off his feet.

Straightening, he smiled at Briony kindly, wondering why he had to examine the Frasiers' granddaughter in the kitchen. He would have expected her to be in one of the bedrooms in the main part of the house, with a roaring fire on the go and her grandmother fussing in attendance.

'Of course, it's too soon to be sure but as far as I can tell it's just a nasty chest infection,' he told Briony, hoping to allay her fears. 'I'm going to give your sister some medicine and she should start to feel better in a few days. Meantime I suggest you keep her in the warm and give her plenty of fluids. Does she have a fire in her bedroom?'

Briony looked embarrassed as she stammered, 'Er . . . no, she doesn't.' How could she tell him that she and the children slept in the servants' quarters? It was bitterly cold up there now, although Briony did put a hot-water bottle into all their beds each night before the three youngsters went up.

'In that case I should keep her down here, just for a couple of nights until we see how she is. Do you think you could manage that?'

She nodded. 'Of course. And thank you, Doctor.'

Snapping his bag shut, he smiled before heading for the door to the hallway saying, 'Don't worry about seeing me out, my dear. I might look in on your grandfather before I leave.' And then he was gone, closing the door softly behind him as Briony fussed over Sarah and tucked her blanket snugly about her.

The following morning the children were surprised when their grandmother strode into the kitchen and threw an envelope onto the table. 'That's come for *her*.' Her lip curled slightly as she glanced towards Mabel and then she turned and went out.

Mabel had paled alarmingly and her eyes looked huge in her small face. 'I bet it's from me ma,' she said fearfully. 'Yer don't think she's gonna make me go back, do yer?'

'I shouldn't think so for a minute, but why don't I open it and see? I can read it for you, if you like?' Briony answered gently. The little girl had begun to tremble and knowing what a tough little thing she was, Briony found that surprising. The child had never gone to school regularly back at home in London and now she was only just beginning to learn her alphabet.

When Mabel nodded Briony slit the envelope open and after taking out a single sheet of rather grubby-looking notepaper, she read aloud:

Dear Mabel,

I hope you is ok an behavin yerself. I got yer postcard wi yer address on an it sounds very posh where yer stayin. Fings are much the same ere. The bombin don't get no better but up to now we've bin lucky an ain't bin too badly it. I've met a nice man. Is name is Charlton an e's an American GI so I'm getting plenty o nylons. I'm getting a bit o stick from the neighbours cos e's black but they're just jealous. Ain't eard nuffink from yer bruvvers or sisters but suppose there all right.

Make sure yer be good else I'll tan yer arse when yer get ome. I shan't write again cos yer know I'm no good at writin letters.

Luv Ma x

A look of pure relief swept across Mabel's face as she let her breath out in a long sigh. 'So she ain't sayin' I 'ave to go 'ome then?'

'Not at all,' Briony assured her. 'She's just letting you know that she received the postcard we sent her.' And then she was shocked when Mabel suddenly sidled up to her and placed her small hand in hers. It was the first real show of affection the little girl had ever given her and Briony was touched.

*

Mid-afternoon they heard Sebastian's car pull into the yard and he marched through the kitchen without giving any of them so much as a backward glance. That suited Briony just fine. The atmosphere in the house had been tense to say the least, ever since the night when he had offered to let the man sleep in the barn.

'*No!* You'll have not a penny more!' It was Grandfather's voice, audible through the walls, and Briony could hear the controlled rage in it. She bit her lip in consternation. Arguing like this wouldn't do his heart any good. Mrs Dower had told her that William was living on borrowed time and she felt resentment towards Sebastian for upsetting him.

'You're a grown man now, Sebastian, and it's about time you learned to stand on your own two feet,' the same voice thundered. 'I cannot afford to keep bailing you out, so you'll have to sort it out yourself this time.'

Sebastian's reply was lost.

It was some minutes later that William rang the bell for her and she entered the sitting room to find him wiping the sweat from his brow. He looked very pale and Briony was concerned for him. There was no sign of her uncle and she rightly guessed that he had stormed out because he hadn't got his own way.

'Do you think you could get me a glass of water please, dear?' William asked, and she noticed that his hands were shaking.

'Of course.' She shot back to the kitchen and returned in no time with a glass that she held to his lips whilst he sipped at it.

'That's better. Thank you.' He smiled up at her and she was relieved to see that the colour was seeping back into his cheeks.

'Would you like me to sit with you for a while?' she

offered and he saw the concern in her eyes.

'No, I shall be fine now. Your grandmother has only popped into the village but she should be back any minute.'

'All right. But if you should need me, just ring the bell.'

He stroked her hand and said, 'Thank you, I will.'

She got back into the kitchen just in time to hear Sebastian's car roar out of the drive on two wheels, and hoped that he would stay away for a very long time. How could anyone be so thoroughly self-centred!

The next few days were difficult. Sarah did not improve and on Saturday, Briony took a deep breath, tapped on the sitting-room door and asked her grandmother if she would send for the doctor again.

'Is that absolutely necessary?' the woman challenged her.

'I think it must be if Briony is requesting it,' her grandfather said. 'Go and telephone him, my dear. I'm sure Dr Restarick won't mind.'

Her back ramrod straight, the woman glared at Briony before resentfully going to do as her husband requested.

The doctor was there within the hour, and as he held the stethoscope to Sarah's chest his expression was worried.

'I think we ought to get her into the cottage hospital,' he said, and seeing the fear that flared in Briony's eyes he added hastily, 'I don't think it's polio, but she may be developing pneumonia. Better to be safe than sorry, eh? Now I shall telephone for an ambulance if you wouldn't mind getting a bag ready for her.'

Briony shot off upstairs and packed Sarah's little cardboard suitcase with everything that she thought her sister might need. And all the time she was trying to quell the panic that was rising within her and her heart was beating like a drum.

What am I going to say to Mum if anything happens to her? she asked herself. *I'm supposed to be looking after her!*

The ambulance was there in a surprisingly short time and as Sarah was loaded onto a stretcher, Briony began to cry.

Thankfully, Mrs Dower had just arrived and she patted her arm comfortingly, saying, 'You go with her, my bird. I'll take care of things here and look after the other two till you get back.'

Briony grabbed her coat and followed the ambulance men out after dropping a quick kiss on the housekeeper's cheek. And then the ambulance bells were clanging as it raced towards the hospital and she sat close to Sarah, gripping her hot little hand. Her temperature was so high that it felt as if she was on fire – and Briony was more terrified than she had ever been in her entire life.

She arrived home three hours later after filling in all the admittance forms for Sarah and seeing her settled into a side ward by a young nurse in a navy-blue uniform with a crisp white cap covering her dark curls.

'They wouldn't let me stay any longer,' she told Mrs Dower brokenly as the kindly woman patted her hand. 'But I can go back at six o'clock. That's the visiting time. In the meantime they're going to do some tests.'

Alfie and Mabel were sitting close together, their eyes scared. The three little ones were inseparable now and it felt strange without Sarah.

'She will get better, won't she, Briony?' Alfie asked tremulously.

'Of course she will,' Mrs Dower said brightly, doing her best to keep their spirits up. But inside she was quaking. Only the day before, another little boy – an evacuee who was staying with the Youngs in the village – had been diagnosed with polio and rushed from the cottage hospital to the sanatorium in Truro. What if Sarah had polio too? It just didn't bear thinking about, although Briony had cared for her with a dedication that did the girl justice. All they could do now was wait . . . and that proved to be far more difficult than they had thought.

Chapter Twenty-Eight

Briony was waiting on the steps of the cottage hospital at six o'clock promptly, along with a number of other people who had come to visit patients. She was clutching the latest copy of the *Beano* that she had bought at the local shop, but wasn't sure whether Sarah would feel well enough to read it.

They heard a clock chime from inside and when the door was opened by a nurse everyone surged forward.

Briony tapped on the door of the children's ward, which was kept locked at all times, and soon the same young nurse that she had met earlier opened it and smiled at her.

'Ah, it's Miss Valentine, isn't it?' she said. 'Sister would like a word with you in her office. Please will you follow me?'

White-faced, Briony followed her down the ward past the rows of beds and cots and past the room where Sarah had been put.

The Sister greeted her and motioned her to a seat in front of her desk, and once Briony had perched on the edge of it, the woman steepled her fingers and stared thoughtfully off into space as if she didn't quite know where to begin. Then, taking the bull by the horns, she began, 'I'm so sorry, Miss Valentine, but I can't allow you to see Sarah tonight.' When Briony opened her mouth to object she rushed on, 'Until all the tests are completed we really must keep her in isolation. You have other young children at home, I believe, and it wouldn't be wise to put them at risk too if it is something contagious, would it?'

Put that way, Briony didn't really have an argument and her shoulders sagged with despair.

'When will you have all the results of the tests?' she asked dully.

'Oh, by tomorrow at the very latest and we shall contact you to inform you of the results immediately. I believe there is a telephone at the house where you are staying. Meanwhile I can assure you that Sarah is getting the best possible care and she is as comfortable as could be expected.'

'Thank you.' Briony rose from the chair. She would have given anything for just one peep at her little sister but she could understand why the Sister was being so cautious. It really wouldn't do to put Mabel and Alfie at risk too.

'I'll wait for your call in the morning then,' she said in a small voice. She couldn't see even her grandmother objecting to this one, although she had flatly refused to go to the hospital with her, saying that she was too busy caring for her husband.

'So how is she then?' Mrs Dower asked the second Briony set foot back through the door. On hearing the news, she said sensibly, 'Well, there's no point you making yourself ill as well. And it's not so very long till tomorrow morning. At least we'll know what we're up against then. Just try and keep your chin up, eh?'

It was much easier said than done, and once the children had been tucked into bed, Briony tried to read a magazine to distract herself, but the words kept blurring into one another. When the door suddenly blew open at eight o'clock and Howel walked in with a gust of wind she could have kissed him, she was so pleased to see him.

'I thought you might be glad of a bit of company,' he said, unwinding his scarf from around his neck.

She nodded. 'Oh yes I would, thank you. I can't seem to concentrate on anything. Do you think I should get in touch with my mum and tell her what's going on? I thought we could perhaps send her a telegram.'

'I wouldn't if I were you, not till you know for sure what's wrong with Sarah,' he answered wisely. 'Your mother would only want to come, no doubt – and what would be the point of travelling all that way if no one is allowed to see Sarah?'

'I suppose you're right.' Briony stared into the flames as Howel filled a pan with milk.

'I'll make us a nice cup of cocoa, shall I?' he suggested. 'Mum always reckons it helps you to sleep.'

Briony left him to it. She didn't really want a drink; in fact, she didn't want anything – but she didn't want to throw his kindness back in his face.

'Have you been through to tell your grandparents what the Sister said?' he asked as he bustled about getting cups ready, and Briony realised with a little shock that she hadn't given it a thought.

'Do you think I should?'

He nodded. 'Yes, I do. Your grandpa will want to know at least, I'm sure. Why not go through now before they go to bed and I'll have this ready for you when you get back.'

Briony tapped on the sitting-room door and after shouting for her to come in, her grandmother said snootily, 'Yes? What is it, girl?'

'I thought you might like to know what's happening with Sarah,' she said uncertainly, and when her grandfather nodded, she told them all she could.

'Eeh, poor little maid,' William said sympathetically. 'But at least she's in the right place. Try not to worry, dear. And if she needs anything, you just let us know, right?'

Briony focused on him and avoided looking at her grandmother. Marion was obviously jealous of the affection that had sprung up between them, and Briony sensed that had it not been for him, the woman would have sent them all packing by now, without a second thought.

'Thank you. The hospital said they would ring with the test results in the morning. I hope that's all right?'

'Of course it is,' he assured her. 'Now you go and try to get some rest, and stop fretting. She'll be fine, you'll see.'

Briony was almost at the door when her grandmother suddenly said, 'If it is polio, isn't it highly contagious?'

Briony nodded.

'In that case I shall insist that a bedroom is prepared for Alfie close to ours. I've no doubt Sarah has caught it from that dirty girl you took in! I knew she'd be trouble the moment I set eyes on her.'

'She *hasn't* caught it from Mabel,' Briony answered defiantly. 'And Mabel isn't dirty now. Anyway, we don't even know if it is polio yet. Two of the children from the village school have gone down with it already.'

'Well, there you are then. Even if it wasn't Mabel it was probably one of the evacuees that brought it here. I shall see that Alfie moves into this side of the house tomorrow – and there's an end to it. Oh, and he can eat with us in future too!'

Briony was just too tired to argue and as she left the room she wondered if things could get any worse.

She told Howel what her grandmother had said when she re-joined him in the kitchen and he clenched his fists as anger coursed through him. 'Bloody old sod,' he muttered. 'She was just the same with Seb when he was a kid, apparently. Still is, for that matter! It was always him and never your mother she had time for. I think she's jealous of the girls getting too close to her man, even her own flesh and blood. But never mind, it's not as if he's going to be a hundred miles away, is it? He'll only be just the other side of the door.'

'But he'll hate it,' Briony whimpered as the events of the day caught up with her and tears coursed down her cheeks.

Howel put his arm about her heaving shoulders and hugged her to him, silently cursing Mrs Frasier. Poor Briony, as if she didn't have enough to worry about with little Sarah. But she felt so good in his arms and he knew in that moment why he was no longer so keen on walking out with Megan; he had developed feelings for this lovely girl – for what good it would do him! Once the war was over she'd return to the Midlands and he'd probably never see her again. The thought was depressing.

The next morning, Briony kept the door into the hallway open as she waited for the telephone to ring and at twenty minutes past nine, as soon as she'd got back from school, it finally did.

Racing into the hall she snatched it up and a man's voice sounded down the line. 'Hello. Am I speaking to Miss Briony Valentine?'

'Yes,' Briony managed to squeak and seconds later she placed the phone down again in a daze. Her grandfather had somehow managed to wheel himself out into the hallway and he gazed at her questioningly.

'That was the doctor from the hospital. It . . . it is polio . . . and her chest infection has developed into pneumonia as Dr Restarick feared. They're going to transfer her to the hospital in Truro this morning by ambulance. They . . . they've said that she's very poorly indeed and I won't be allowed to visit her. She'll be all alone. They think that Sarah and the other girl caught it off the little boy evacuee. They were all in the same class, you see.' She began to weep.

'Oh, my dear.' Her grandfather was floundering for something to say that might make her feel better, but he could think of nothing. Words were so inadequate at a time like this. He had found Briony's dedication to her siblings to be commendable and he could only begin to imagine how she must be feeling.

'I . . . I shall have to get word to my mother,' Briony sobbed and he nodded.

'Of course you must. I'll get Howel to go to the post office in the village and send her a telegram at once. Is he here yet?'

'Yes, he's in the kitchen.' Briony was gripping the hall table for support. Her legs felt as if they were going to let her down and a terrible feeling of foreboding had come over her. Suddenly she feared that she might never see her little sister again and the thought was almost more than she could bear.

'Send him in to me, please,' her grandfather told her, taking control of the situation. 'We'll write down what we want to say and he can go and send word to your mother right away. I'll ask Lois to telephone you.'

'*Who* will you tell to telephone her?' Marion Frasier had just appeared from upstairs and as her husband hurriedly explained what had happened, she opened her mouth to object – but then seeing the look on his face she clamped it shut again.

Briony stumbled towards the kitchen. Everything felt unreal and she prayed that she was in the middle of a nightmare. This couldn't be happening. Sarah was just nine years old.

Luckily Mrs Dower had come to the house too, sensing that Briony would be in no fit state to do anything today, and whilst Howel went to speak to William she pressed the girl into a chair and plied her with yet more hot sweet tea. Briony felt as if she was drowning in the bloody stuff but she took it all the same and stared listlessly into the fire.

Lois had just returned from work when the telegram arrived and thankfully had not had time to have a drink. When she opened the door to find the telegram boy standing on the step yet again she wished that she had and her stomach flipped over. She took it from him without a word and stared at it for a moment as if it might bite her before steeling herself and ripping it open. As her eyes skimmed down the page her hand flew to her mouth and then the telegram fluttered to the floor as she rummaged frantically in her bag for shilling pieces for the telephone box. Trunk calls were expensive and she didn't want to get cut off by the pips if she hadn't put enough money into the slot. Mrs Brindley saw her race by her front window in her slippers and without a coat on and scratched her head in bewilderment, wondering what on earth could be going on now?

Lois meanwhile had reached the telephone box. It took two attempts to dial the right number but at last her father answered and she quickly pressed Button A. When her father's voice came down the line once more, she gulped before whispering, 'It's me, Dad.'

'Lois, are you all right, darling?' His voice was so full of concern that it brought tears of regret to her eyes. She had missed him over the years.

'Yes, I am – but what about my Sarah?'

She listened whilst he reported exactly what the doctor had told them and then she choked, 'I'm coming. I have to see her!'

'But she isn't here, darling,' he said gently, as if he was talking to a child. 'And even if she was, no one is allowed to see her. But I promise you we will keep you fully informed of what is happening.'

'But I . . . I can't just do *nothing!*' she sobbed brokenly and he could feel her pain. She had lost her husband and now there was a chance that she might lose one of her children too. He suddenly wished that he could just wave a magic wand to remove the miles that were dividing them so that he could kiss away her pain as he had used to do when she was a little girl.

'Have faith,' he said quietly and she laughed – a dry hollow laugh that chilled him to the bone.

'What good will that do?' she asked bitterly. 'I had faith that James would come back safely to me – and what happened? *He died!* What if Sarah dies too?'

For a moment he was lost for words but then he said, 'I've missed you,' and those three little words healed a hole in her heart. At least her father still loved her.

'I've missed you too,' she answered in a wobbly voice. 'And Daddy . . . I love you.'

'I love you too, darling,' he answered, ignoring his wife who had come to stand beside him and who was tense with jealous disapproval.

'I'll be in touch just as soon as we have any more news. In the meantime, try not to worry.' Afterwards he thought how foolish those last words must have sounded. How could she *not* worry!

But then Marion was reaching for the phone, so he said lamely, 'Goodbye for now, my dear.' And as his wife took the receiver from him and slammed it down, he wished that he could have been stronger.

'You are going to make yourself ill,' his wife scolded as she turned his wheelchair about and pushed him back towards the sitting room. 'Now I want you to sit quietly and listen to the wireless for a while. I have to organise a room for Alfred on our landing. I really cannot risk anything happening to him too. I believe that polio thrives on germs so I want the girl and Mrs Dower to disinfect all the rooms on that side of the house thoroughly.'

He wondered why her compassion could not extend to their granddaughters and Mabel too, but he allowed her to sit him by the fireplace and said nothing. Like everyone else who had dealings with his wife, he knew there would have been no point.

'Do I *'ave* to go an' sleep in that side o' the 'ouse?' Alfie asked tearfully later that night as Briony took him by the hand. He was dressed in his pyjamas and was clutching his rather tatty teddy bear under his arm.

'Yes, you do,' Briony told him. 'Grandmother has your room all ready for you and it's lovely.'

'Well, can you at least still tuck me in?'

She hesitated before nodding. 'Yes, of course I will.' And she would, she decided, even if it meant a fight with her grandmother. Thankfully it didn't come to that, although Marion didn't look at all happy with the idea.

Alfie was to have the room next to Sebastian's and Mrs Dower had been up there for most of the afternoon cleaning it and making the bed up for him.

'See, darling?' his grandmother told him, pointing down the stairs. 'I am just down there if you need me during the night. Grandfather and I have to sleep downstairs now because he can't manage to get up here any more.'

Under other circumstances, Alfie would have been delighted with the room but as it was, he merely sniffed ungratefully. It was at least three times as big as the room he was used to sleeping in and Mrs Dower had lit a fire in the grate to air it out so it was nice and warm now. There was a highly polished wardrobe with a matching chest of drawers, as well as a very high bed in there, and the floor was covered in rugs in muted shades of red, blue and green similar to the ones in the sitting room downstairs. He thought they must have cost a lot of money because they were much nicer than the ones in the kitchen.

When Briony turned the covers back he hopped between the crisp white sheets and she drew them up to his chin as she bent to kiss him.

'Sleep tight,' she whispered, then forcing herself to leave him she walked past her grandmother as if she wasn't even there. She was just too exhausted to argue tonight and anyway, in all fairness, she felt that the woman had a soft spot for Alfie, so hopefully he would be all right.

Her little brother was, in fact, in fine spirits when he strolled into the kitchen the following morning. Briony noticed that he was wearing new grey shorts and a new shirt. She had expected him to be upset but he seemed quite happy with the new sleeping arrangements.

'Look what Grandma gave me to eat in my break at school,' he greeted her, holding out his hand and showing off the Fry's chocolate bar. 'An' she says I'm to 'ave breakfast in the dinin' room wi' her and Grandad this mornin'.'

'Oh, all right.' Briony glanced towards Howel, who shrugged his shoulders.

'You'd better go through then. I'm just about to take the porridge in,' Briony answered and he skipped away as if he hadn't a care in the world.

'So much for lying awake half the night worrying that he might be missing me,' she said wryly.

'Perhaps Mrs Frasier is mellowing in her old age,' Howel chuckled and she sighed, feeling a little peeved that Alfie seemed so cheerful. Not that she'd wanted him to be upset . . . but all the same!

The atmosphere in the dining room was almost light-hearted when she carried the breakfast in on a tray – apart from Sebastian, that was, who glowered at her as she entered. Her grandmother was fussing over Alfie. She had tucked a white napkin into the neck of his shirt and she told Briony abruptly, 'Serve Alfred first. We don't want him to be late for school.'

Alfie seemed to be lapping up the attention as Briony ladled the thick creamy porridge into his dish before leaving the rest of them to serve themselves.

Once back in the kitchen she didn't have much opportunity to think because time was rushing on and she didn't want Mabel to be late for school either. When they got there, however, the teacher was waiting for them at the school gates. She said to Briony: 'We're so sorry to hear about Sarah. Let's hope she makes a speedy recovery.'

Briony blinked rapidly and nodded. The pain of what was happening to her little sister was still very raw and she felt as if she could burst into tears at the drop of a sixpence.

'The thing is though . . .' Mrs Fellows hesitated here, looking decidedly uncomfortable. 'We think under the circumstances that it might be better if Alfie and Mabel didn't attend school for a while. Just until we're sure that they are not incubating the disease too. We're taking all the precautions we can to stop this from spreading. I do hope you understand? But in the meantime I've prepared some work for them to do at home so that they don't fall behind.'

Briony took the sheaf of papers the woman was holding out to her, and feeling like a leper she said goodbye, turned the children about and led them away.

Chapter Twenty-Nine

Neither Alfie nor Mabel seemed particularly perturbed about the fact that they couldn't attend school for a time and Briony made sure to set some time aside each day to help them with the sums and the spellings that the teacher had written out for them.

On Sunday morning she got Alfie ready to go to chapel with his grandmother as usual, and once they had set off she made a pot of tea. After settling Mabel down with some comics to read, she carried it through to share with her grandfather. It had become a ritual and she looked forward to it now.

He was waiting for her when she carried the tray in. 'Put it down there, my girl,' he said 'then come and sit by me and tell me how you're feeling now.'

The first shock and panic about Sarah's illness had worn off now to be replaced by a dull acceptance.

'I'm all right,' Briony answered, but he saw that her

usual sparkle was absent. 'I just hope they'll keep us fully informed of how she's doing. I've heard such terrible stories of the treatments these children get, like the hot cloths they put on their affected limbs. And it seems so cruel that they're not even allowed to see their families. Sarah must think that we've deserted her.'

'Well, you can rest assured that Dr Restarick will make sure that we receive all the details. He's an old family friend and I'd trust him with my life. Also, you have to remember that they're only doing what they feel is for Sarah's own good. And it won't be forever, will it?'

'I suppose not.' Briony handed him his cup and saucer then crossing to the window she stared out across the vast expanse of moorlands. The heather's vivid shades of lilac and purple had faded to dull shades of brown now and it looked drab, just like she felt.

William began to talk of other things then. He had learned that he could hold a conversation with Briony about anything; she was an entertaining and intelligent young woman. He just wished that his wife would give her a chance, but Marion was so wrapped up in Alfie now that she had no time for the other children, which he thought was a shame.

They passed a pleasant fifteen minutes together, but then as Briony was loading the cups back onto the tray, Sebastian came into the room. After scowling at Briony he asked his father, 'Are you ready for your bath now?'

William nodded. He hated having to be carried upstairs each week, especially now that he and his son were on such bad terms after he had refused to give him money again. But then this was the only way he could get a bath, so he supposed he would just have to grin and bear it. Glancing at Briony he winked affectionately and keeping her head down she hurried away back to the kitchen to prepare the Sunday dinner. She heard Sebastian carry his father upstairs then his heavy footsteps along the landing . . . and then there was silence and she got on with what she was doing.

It was almost an hour later when Sebastian appeared in the kitchen with a broad smile on his face, looking rather pleased with himself.

'Ah, there you are,' he said pleasantly. 'I was wondering if there was a cup of tea going?'

She was so shocked that she almost dropped the leg of lamb she was just placing into the oven. Usually he could barely stand to be in the same room as her, so why was he seeking her company now?

'I suppose I could make you one,' she said in a clipped voice as he settled himself at the kitchen table and then as she filled the kettle she asked, 'Is Grandfather back in the sitting room?'

'What? Oh no, actually he asked me to leave him for a while to have a soak – which is why I thought I'd pop down for a cuppa.'

Briony frowned. Knowing how William loathed having to be carried up and down the stairs, he usually wanted his bath over and done with as soon as possible; yet he must have been upstairs for well over an hour already. But then she decided, he was entitled to a soak now and again if he wanted one. She served Sebastian his tea as quickly as she could, barely giving it time to brew. For some reason, that terrible sense of foreboding she had felt when Sarah was taken ill was back again but she couldn't think why.

Sebastian sat there sipping it as if he had all day until Briony's nerves were stretched to the limit and eventually she asked, 'Don't you think you ought to go up and check on Grandfather now? He's been up there an awfully long time and he can't get out of the bath by himself.'

He smiled at her charmingly, revealing a set of surprisingly white teeth. 'I'll tell you what, why don't you go up and check on the old boy for me while I finish this tea?'

Again she was taken aback, but after drying her hands on her apron she headed upstairs. Once she was outside the bathroom door she waited for a second, but hearing nothing she tapped on it lightly. There was no reply so she knocked again, louder this time.

'Grandfather . . . are you all right?'

Nothing – so now she raced back downstairs and bursting into the kitchen she told Sebastian breathlessly, 'He's not answering. I knocked on the door twice and I shouted to him but I couldn't get a reply!'

'What do you mean?' Sebastian stood up and followed her upstairs.

'He's probably nodded off,' he assured her as he opened the door – and then she heard him gasp and she raced into the room only to stop dead in her tracks as she saw her grandfather's sightless eyes staring up at her from beneath the water. She yanked the plug out.

'I'm going to phone the doctor,' She told Sebastian. 'Get him out while I'm gone and turn him on his side.'

Her hands shook as she dialled the doctor's number but eventually she managed to gabble out what had happened to Dr Restarick's wife, who promised her that the doctor would be with her as soon as possible. Briony dropped the phone then and rushed back upstairs. Sebastian had lifted his father from the bath and covered him with a towel on the floor. Dropping to her knees, Briony grasped the dear old man's hand and sobbed, '*Please* speak to me, Grandfather!'

She was still there on her knees when Marion Frasier swept into the room in one of her ridiculous hats, saying,

'Whatever is going on in here?' And then as her eyes rested on her husband she pushed Briony aside and screamed, 'Get out! *Get out*, I tell you!'

Badly shaken, Briony stumbled out onto the landing and somehow got back downstairs and into the kitchen. At last someone rapped on the front door and she flew along the hallway.

'He – he's upstairs in the bathroom,' she stammered as Dr Restarick hurried past her. And then all she could do was wait.

Solemn-faced, he came into the kitchen some half an hour later and sadly shook his head, saying, 'I'm so sorry, my dear, but he's gone. There was nothing I could do. He was already dead when I arrived.'

'What do you mean, he's gone!' Briony shouted incredulously. 'How *can* he be gone? We had tea together earlier on and he was fine. He only went up for a bath!'

'Your grandfather was a very poorly man,' the doctor explained gently. 'His heart was in danger of giving out at any time. I shall write "heart attack" as the cause of death on the death certificate.'

Every instinct that Briony had screamed at her that something wasn't right here. The way Sebastian had come into the kitchen all smiles and friendly as could be when usually he didn't have a civil word for her; the length of time he had left his father in the bath when normally it was over in a matter of minutes – but most of all the look on her grandfather's face when she had found him. He had looked frightened!

'But *surely* you'll be doing a post-mortem?' she said.

The doctor shook his head. 'I don't think there will be a need for that.' He patted her shoulder kindly. 'I'm sorry, Briony. I know what a difficult time this has been for you, what with Sarah taking ill and now this, but you have to try and be strong. Your grandmother is going to need you to help her get through this. She and William were very close. And I happen to know that he was very fond of you too, if that's any consolation.' He turned for the door then and all she could do was watch helplessly as he left. How could she voice her suspicions – and who would listen to her even if she did?

When the second telegram within days arrived at the little terraced house in Nuneaton, Lois stared at it fearfully. She was just having a cigarette in the kitchen with Mrs Brindley.

'Shall I open it for yer, luvvie?' Martha Brindley knew that Lois was already worried sick about Sarah and prayed that it wouldn't contain bad news about the little girl. Lois had already lost her husband and if she were to lose her daughter too, it might tip her over the edge.

Lois handed the telegram over with shaking hands and lifting a knife from the table, Mrs Brindley slit it open and hastily read it.

'It's Sarah, isn't it?' Lois asked tremulously. 'She's died, hasn't she?'

Mrs Brindley took a deep breath and shook her head. 'No, it ain't about Sarah, pet. It's about yer dad. I'm afraid he's passed away. Heart attack, it says here . . . I'm so sorry, but then didn't you tell me some time ago how poorly 'e were?'

Lois nodded numbly. Part of her was relieved that it wasn't Sarah, but another part of her cried out at the injustice of it all. Her father was gone and she had never had the chance to see him again after their long estrangement and tell him how much she loved him face to face. Bitterness towards her mother welled up inside her. They would never have been estranged in the first place if it hadn't been for her, and she said as much now to Mrs Brindley as it all poured out of her.

'Well, happen he knew,' the woman said sensibly. 'An' there's no use cryin' over spilt milk now. It's young Briony as I feel sorry for. She's there in the thick of it.'

'I know,' Lois said dully. 'And now I wonder if I did right sending them all there in the first place. If I hadn't, Sarah wouldn't have caught polio and my father might not have—'

'You can stop that silly nonsense right now!' Mrs Brindley said firmly. 'It's just one o' them things.'

'I wonder if I should telephone my mother,' Lois said then. 'Perhaps she'll want me to attend the funeral.'

'I can't answer that. You must do what yer think is right.'

Lois pulled herself from the chair and walked unsteadily towards her coat which was hanging on a hook on the back of the door. This latest news had knocked her for six and her legs seemed to have developed a life of their own. After checking that she had enough coins for the call box, she told Mrs Brindley, 'I shan't be long. With a bit of luck it will be Briony that answers the phone.'

'Shall I come with yer? You've 'ad a nasty shock,' Mrs Brindley offered but Lois shook her head.

'I'll be fine, but I'd be grateful if you'd wait here till I get back. I don't fancy being on my own at the minute.'

'O' course I will.' Mrs Brindley's eyes were full of sympathy as she watched Lois slip away. What was the saying? It never rains but it pours. Well, that was certainly the case here.

Lois was back within minutes, white-faced and shaking. 'My brother answered the phone,' she said tearfully. 'And he took great pleasure in informing me that I wasn't welcome there. Not even for my own father's funeral! He wouldn't even let me speak to Briony, not for a single moment.' And then at last the dam broke and a torrent of tears flooded down her cheeks.

Mrs Brindley rubbed her arm tenderly. What a family! Poor Lois. For once even she was at a loss for words.

It was getting dark now but still Briony sat, numb with shock. Mr Page and Sebastian had removed her grandfather's body to the funeral parlour earlier in the afternoon in one of the coffins that was stored in the barn, and since then there had been an endless stream of visitors. News travelled fast in such a small community and friends and neighbours were keen to offer their commiserations. It was clear that William Frasier had been a very respected and well-liked gentleman. Mr Page was going to prepare the body for burial, and had told her in hushed tones that she could visit her grandfather in the Chapel of Rest the following day if she so wished.

Once again, Mrs Dower and Howel had been marvellous and had come immediately they heard the news. Briony felt guilty just sitting there letting them do all the work, but Mrs Dower had insisted.

'You just take it easy for a while,' she said in a no-nonsense sort of voice. 'You've had a bad shock, the second this week, and you need to rest.'

And so Briony did as she was told and stared unseeingly at Alfie and Mabel, who were arguing over a jigsaw puzzle.

It was as she was sitting there that an idea occurred to her and she asked, 'Do you think Grandmother will send us away now that Grandfather has gone?'

Mrs Dower paused. She was rolling pastry for a rhubarb

pie on the kitchen table. 'I wouldn't think so,' she said eventually. 'She knows how much you do about the house, and where else would she get anyone to do what you do for such a pittance?'

'She'd be too worried about how it would look to her church cronies anyway,' Howel butted in scathingly as he piled some more logs onto the fire.

'You're right there,' his mother agreed. Sometimes when she saw the way Briony and the children were treated, she felt like asking them to all move in with her at Kynance Farm. But it wouldn't do to be seen to be interfering so instead she made sure that she did everything she could to make it easy for them. She hadn't been in the best of moods as it was today, even before the poor master had died. Howel had calmly informed her over breakfast that he had told Megan that he didn't wish to see her any more.

'But why not?' she had gasped. 'Megan's a lovely, loyal girl and she thinks the world of you. A blind man on a galloping horse could see that from a distance!'

'That was the problem,' he had told his mother. 'It wasn't fair to leave her hoping that we'd be wed when I didn't have the same feelings for her. She deserves better than that.'

'Well, your loss will be another man's gain, you mark my word, you silly young bugger,' his mother had told him stroppily, but he had merely shrugged and carried on with his breakfast. As far as he was concerned it was done with, and the sooner his mother accepted the fact, the better. And now this, on top! Martha thought. First Sarah, then Howel's bombshell – and now the poor master passing! It made her fearful of what else fate might have in store for them next!

Chapter Thirty

William Frasier was buried a week later in the family plot in the little churchyard high on the hill overlooking the sea. It was a bitterly cold day with a nip of frost in the air, and the wind that whipped off the sea had the mourners holding onto their hats and shivering. Even so, Briony decided that it was a nice place to be buried. The quaint little church had been packed to capacity, with some folks even standing outside – and it reinforced to her yet again how highly her grandfather had been regarded. After a fierce row with her grandmother, the children had been left back at the house with Mrs Dower, who was preparing a spread for anyone that wished to return after the funeral. Briony had stood her ground on this one. She didn't think that funerals were a place for children, and eventually Marion had backed down and grudgingly agreed that they needn't attend. Briony was even allowed to sit in the front pew with Sebastian and her grandmother during the service, but she knew that it was only for show. It wouldn't do to be banished to the back of the church, seeing as she was family.

She had heard a few people muttering about her mother's absence, saying how disgraceful it was that Lois hadn't bothered to show up for her own father's funeral, even if they had been estranged for a number of years. Briony was forced to bite her tongue to stop herself from telling them the truth – that her mother *had not been allowed to come*. The day before, she had got up very early and had lifted an envelope from the mat in the hallway, written in her mother's handwriting and addressed to Mrs M. Frasier. She had taken it straight in with the breakfast later, only to see the woman give it no more than a cursory glance, before throwing it into the heart of the flames that were licking up the chimney.

'Huh! It's from *her*!' she had said with loathing, and clenching her hands into fists, Briony had slammed out, leaving her to it. Better that than give her a piece of her mind! The way Briony saw it, they could have been a comfort to each other at this sad time, but Marion was still determined to keep her at arm's length. Briony thought it was stupid. They were both missing William, after all.

Now as the mourners all trailed out of the churchyard leaving the gravediggers to finish their job she walked sedately behind Sebastian and her grandmother. Marion was leaning heavily on his arm. The flimsy black veil that covered the woman's hat was flapping madly in the breeze, but beneath it Briony could see that she was openly sobbing, which only went to show that she must have some feelings at least. Above them gulls and curlews were wheeling in the air and they could hear the crash of the waves on the beach beyond the cliff.

'You will help to serve the food and drink to the mourners

when we get back to the house, girl,' her grandmother informed her coldly in the car on the way home.

During the previous week, Briony and Mrs Dower had methodically cleaned the whole of the downstairs. Dust sheets had been folded and put away, and the furniture and mirrors polished until they gleamed. Carpets had been taken outside and thrown across the line where they were beaten until there was not a spot of dust left on them, and even the library, which Briony had not even known was there, had been reopened. Sebastian had removed his father's wheelchair, storing it in the garage, and the bed was once more upstairs in her grandparents' bedroom, next to the room that Alfie now slept in. Howel had arrived early that morning to light fires in all the downstairs rooms, and as they entered the house they were met by warmth and the pleasant smell of cooking.

Mrs Dower had somehow managed to produce a banquet fit for a king even on rationing. There were hot meat pies and sausage rolls, bread – crusty and fresh from the oven – and a variety of cold meats and pickles as well as home-baked sponges and fruit cakes, and a number of other treats. It had been agreed that the children could attend the wake and they were waiting for Briony as she walked into the hallway, dry-eyed and looking terribly pale. Her grandmother instantly summoned Alfie to her and disappeared off into the sitting room with him, but Mabel sidled up to Briony and placed her small hand in hers.

'Are yer all right?' she asked softly with genuine affection, and this seemed to unlock the hard lump that had formed in Briony's throat. She started to cry.

'Come away into the kitchen,' the little girl urged. 'Yer don't want this 'oity-toity lot seein' yer blubbin'.' She dragged Briony down the hallway, and as she entered the kitchen, Briony saw Howel standing there and just fell into his arms.

Mrs Dower, who was about to carry a plate of ham and mustard sandwiches through to the sitting room, felt something akin to an electric shock suddenly pass through her as she saw the tender way her son was cradling Briony in his arms.

So *that's* why he got shot of young Megan, she thought to herself. He's only gone and fallen for Briony! But the realisation brought her no joy. Briony already had a sweetheart and all she could see ahead was heartache for the silly young sod. Shaking her head, she hurried past them and got on with the job at hand.

Life gradually settled back into some sort of routine. The children had been allowed to return to school, which was just as well because the weather had turned so cold that they didn't venture outside any more unless they had to, or unless they decided to go over to the farm to see Talwyn.

Sebastian seemed to be in a much better mood. Probably because now that his father was gone his mother was able to be a lot more generous with him, Mrs Dower said caustically.

'He always was able to wrap her round his little finger,' she confided to Briony. 'And now the poor master's gone, he's probably bleeding her dry. But it'll all end in tears, you just mark my words. The worm will turn one of these days – and it'll be God help us all when it does and the money's dried up!'

Briony didn't much care. Sebastian was spending even more time away from home now and that suited her just fine.

It was a clear cold night as Mrs Brindley crossed the yard to check on Lois. The air raids had had them scuttling to the safety of the shelter more nights than she cared to remember recently, although there wasn't the same urgency about getting in there now as there had been. Now Mrs Brindley would fill a Thermos flask with tea and make herself a hot-water bottle before she'd even think of leaving the house. 'An' if the buggers wanna bomb me afore I get there, then they can bloody well bomb me,' she was often heard to say.

There were many nights when Lois didn't join her as amazingly, she too had joined the WVS and often spent the nights when the area was raided in some church hall or another, helping those who had been injured or made homeless. Since receiving the news about Sarah, Lois seemed to be staying off the bottle more and more, a fact for which Martha Brindley was thankful. She was still gravely concerned about her friend though. There was barely any meat on her bones from what she could see of it. But then Mrs Brindley thought that was hardly surprising as she ate barely enough to keep a sparrow alive. To make matters worse, Lois had visited the doctor following the death of her father and he had prescribed sleeping tablets to help her sleep. Mrs Brindley didn't approve of them at all. In fact, the way she saw it they were downright dangerous. Lois would pop them in like sweeties and Mrs Brindley had a fear of her overdosing on them. Now, after pushing Lois's door open, she entered the kitchen to find her neighbour sitting at the table staring morosely at some photographs of James and the children. It was clear that she had been crying, and Mrs Brindley sighed. If the raids started again tonight she was going to have a rare old time of it trying to get Lois into the shelter.

'Yer can put those away,' she said with authority. 'No use sittin' blubbin' over what was. We 'ave to get on wi' things as best we can an' thank the good Lord for what we still 'ave!'

'Sorry.' Lois looked at her guiltily as Mrs Brindley shuffled the photos into a pile and shoved them into the sideboard drawer.

'Now then – what 'ave you 'ad to eat today?'

When Lois lowered her head Mrs Brindley sighed again and moving towards the bread bin she said sternly, 'I'm goin' to make yer a sandwich. It'll 'ave to be Spam but I ain't leavin' till you've eaten it. Do yer 'ear me?' She scraped some margarine thinly on the bread, and unbidden her mind slipped back to a time when she had been able to dollop lashings of real butter on as thickly as she liked. It seemed an awfully long while ago now.

Lois grimaced when Martha placed the food in front of her, but she gamely tried to eat it. Mrs Brindley could be a tough old bird at times but for all that, Lois didn't know how she would have got through the last terrible months without her. The loss of her beloved James was like a gnawing pain constantly eating away at her, and that added to the worry of how Sarah was and missing Briony and Alfie made it seem barely worthwhile getting out of bed most days. The tablets the doctor had given her had helped, however, although on a few occasions she had accidentally taken more than she should have and had slept the clock round. She didn't mind. Sleep was her best friend now. When she was asleep, the pain and the constant worry went away and sometimes she just wished that she could sleep forever. She had only just finished forcing the food down her throat when the all too familiar sound of the air-raid siren roared into life.

'Oh lawdy,' Mrs Brindley grumbled. ''Ere we go again. You get yerself into the shelter and take some extra blankets, pet. It's enough to cut yer in two out there. I'll join yer just as soon as I've made us a flask an' some hot-water bottles. We're goin' to need 'em tonight.'

Lois raised her chin and stared back at her defiantly. 'Actually, I think I'll get off up to the church hall in case there are any casualties, if it's all the same to you, Martha.'

'But it's dangerous to be out walkin' the streets when there's a raid on, pet,' the other woman blustered. She was secretly proud of what Lois was doing, but that didn't stop her worrying about her all the same.

'Well, someone has to do it,' Lois shot back, and then her voice softening, she added. 'I know you mean well but I'll be fine. I don't think about my own problems when I'm helping someone else. You go and get yourself into the shelter and I'll see you in the morning. Goodnight.'

Mrs Brindley hovered uncertainly for a moment but then she shrugged and hurried across the yard. You could only help them that would help theirselves, an' if Lois wanted to be difficult an' take risks then that was up to her. On her own head be it; she could only do what she could do at the end o' the day!

In The Heights at that time, Briony was staring critically into her bedroom mirror. Mrs Dower had persuaded her to go to a dance at the village hall with Howel and Talwyn. Social events had been a rare occurrence since the start of the war, but a band from Truro had been booked to play and almost all the young folk from the area were expected to turn out for it. It was a foregone conclusion that there would be far more young women there than men, as most of the boys had joined up. Even so, everyone was looking forward to it – especially Talwyn, who rarely got out to be with young people her own age.

Mrs Dower had altered one of Talwyn's dresses to fit

Briony especially for the occasion. It was a simple style in a deep blue colour, made of heavy cotton and with a sweetheart neckline, short sleeves and a soft flared skirt that swirled about her knees as she moved. Briony had put a wide black belt about her waist but wondered if she didn't look somewhat overdressed. It had been so long since she'd had occasion to dress up that she felt a little strange. She had chosen to wear her black patent high heels with it and brushed her long black hair till it shone and had even applied a little make-up for the first time in months. Now she sighed. There was nothing else she could do so she might as well just go and make the best of it, even if she wasn't in the mood.

Talwyn and Howel were downstairs waiting for her when she entered the kitchen and she flushed slightly as she saw Howel eye her up and down approvingly. He was looking very handsome in a dark suit and a crisp white shirt, and with his hair slicked to his head with Brylcreem she thought how different he looked.

Mrs Dower was fussing over the children and seeing Briony, she exclaimed, 'Why, you look as pretty as a picture! Now get off with you and have a good time. And don't worry about these two tinkers. They'll be good as gold with me.'

Briony put her warm coat on and after giving Mabel and Alfie a quick kiss the three set off. The mist was rolling in from the sea and somewhere far out on the waves a ship's foghorn sounded mournfully in the darkness.

Howel made Talwyn and Briony tuck their arms into his to prevent them from slipping, and in no time at all they arrived at Poldak village hall. As they entered, Briony saw the band tuning up on a small stage at the end of the room. A number of young people were already assembled there, and she saw one girl in particular glaring at Howel; she guessed instantly that this must be Megan, his former girlfriend. She was very pretty – fair-haired with big blue eyes – and Briony wondered why he had ended their relationship. Megan certainly looked nice enough. She took Talwyn to a small cloakroom where they hung up their coats and tidied their hair, and when they got back, Howel had found them a table and got them a drink. He had bought a pint of ale for himself from a small bar, and a shandy for her and Talwyn.

The blackout curtains were firmly in place across the windows and eventually the lights inside dimmed and the band began to play. A young woman who turned out to be the singer took centre stage and began to belt out 'You Are My Sunshine' – one of Briony's particular favourites. Soon Briony was tapping her feet in time to the music and slowly she started to enjoy herself. The dance floor was already full, and when the singer began to croon 'They Can't Take That Away from Me' Howel bowed and held his hand out. As they whirled past Megan, Briony saw the girl's eyes follow Howel hungrily and she couldn't help but feel sorry for her. Even so, she decided that it wouldn't hurt to let her hair down for a change. The only thing that stopped it from being perfect was the fact that she was dancing with Howel and not Ernie – but she tried not to think of that.

Every so often, she dragged Talwyn onto the dance floor. She didn't want the girl to feel left out and she was surprised at what a good dancer she was. Talwyn had a natural rhythm and grace and she was so pretty that every young man in the room watched her as she moved.

The time passed in a flash, and soon it was approaching the end of the evening. When Howel was about to drag her onto the dance floor again, Briony laughed and rubbed at her ankles, saying, 'These damn shoes are killing me! Why not take Talwyn on for a dance? I need to nip to the ladies'.' He obligingly did as he was told and Briony grinned as she noticed that his thick hair had now sprung out from his head again and he had taken his tie off.

When she came out of the lavatory and went to wash her hands, she found herself face to face with Megan, who was combing her hair in the small mirror above the basin.

The girl obligingly moved aside to allow Briony to rinse her hands before saying, 'You must be Briony. Hello, I'm Megan Brown.'

'It's nice to meet you,' Briony said politely, feeling slightly uncomfortable.

'So how long have you and Howel been seeing each other then?' the girl asked next.

Briony's mouth gaped before she stuttered, 'Oh . . . we're not seeing each other. I mean, not in that way. Howel and I are just friends.'

Megan said sadly, 'You might think of him as a friend, but I don't think Howel thinks of you that way. I can't remember a time when he looked at me as he looks at you now.'

'Please . . . you've got it all wrong. I have a young man back at home,' Briony spluttered then added hastily, 'Well, he's not back at home at the moment. He's in the RAF.'

Megan stared at her for a moment, then shaking her head, she walked out of the cloakroom without another word. Briony felt confused. Whatever has given her that idea? she thought. Howel has never been anything other than a perfect gentleman to me. She went back to their table hoping that Megan had believed her.

The singer was having fun with the Andrews Sisters hit 'Oh Johnny, Oh Johnny, Oh!' Briony noticed that Megan had left and as she watched Howel twirling Talwyn around, she felt as if she was seeing him for the first time. He *was* very handsome, not in the classic style like Clark Gable, one of her favourites actors, but in a rugged sort of way. And he *was* undoubtedly kind and dependable. In fact, she wasn't sure how she would have got through these last awful weeks without him. But she was in love with Ernie – wasn't she? Admittedly, they hadn't openly agreed to become a couple, but since his visit they both knew that once the war was over they would be. It was an unspoken agreement. She shook herself mentally and looked away. She had enough complications in her life without adding to them. So why, she wondered, did her eyes keep straying back to him?

Chapter Thirty-One

Once Mrs Brindley had gone, Lois crossed to the sink and fetched out the bottle of cheap sherry she had hidden behind the packet of washing soda. The temptation to take a swig was great, but summoning every ounce of willpower she had, she resolutely poured it away. She would be no good to her children if she allowed herself to become a sot, and she wanted to be there for them when they came home. Her mind drifted back to happier times, and just for a few moments the pain inside subsided and she could pretend to herself that all was well with the world. Any minute now, James would walk through the door and he would take her to bed and she would snuggle into his warm firm body. But first she would peep in on the children and see them all tucked up snug and warm and fast asleep with not a care in the world . . . But then the sound of an explosion close by jerked her back to reality and she shuddered. Her mind was now torturing her with images of Sarah lying in an iron lung, an empty crippled shell of the pretty little girl she had once been, and James dying on the battlefield in thick cloying mud as he called out for her with his last breath. She pushed the images away as she raced towards the front door, snatching up her coat, gas mask and handbag on the way. Some poor sods had copped it already, if she was any judge, so no doubt they would need as many helping hands as they could get up at the church hall.

As she pelted along the road, the sky overhead became black with enemy planes, which blocked out the light of the 'bomber's moon'. And then suddenly there was a whistling sound and before Lois could take in what was happening she was tossed into the road like a rag doll. Stunned, and deafened by the blast, she lay there for a moment, but then lifting her head, she saw the front of a house at the side of her collapse as if it was nothing more than a pack of playing cards. Screams rent the air as a woman, covered from head to foot in thick dust, staggered from the wreckage clutching a small baby in a shawl tightly to her.

'My little girl is still in there,' she cried hoarsely as Lois struggled to her feet. She could hear people running up the hill behind her, but because she was the closest to the woman, she went to her. The fact that the poor shocked woman was close to hysteria didn't make things any easier, and the baby, was wailing loudly.

'My Sarah is still in there,' the woman whimpered, waving a trembling finger towards the house.

Sarah! Lois gulped, then throwing down her bag and her gas mask, she scrambled across the rubble towards the back of the house, which was leaning drunkenly, without even thinking about what she was doing. She soon found herself in what had clearly been the kitchen. By then, her hands and knees were scraped and bleeding, and lumps of plaster were falling all about her but she was oblivious to the pain – and then she spotted a little girl huddling beside an overturned chair. The child was covered in dust and she was clearly terrified.

'Come on, Sarah, sweetheart. We have to get you out of here,' Lois coaxed as she clambered across the bedroom furniture that had fallen down into the kitchen from the floor above. In no time at all she had scooped the sobbing child up into her arms and she was halfway back across the room when there was an ominous rumble – and glancing up, Lois saw the back wall tumbling rapidly towards her.

As Mrs Brindley cowered in the shelter clutching her hot-water bottle, she trembled uncontrollably. She had lived through a fair few air raids by now, but never one like this. The explosions were distant but constant – in the direction of Coventry, she judged – although some had been a little too close for comfort and she knew that more than a few people would be losing their lives this night. She just wished that she could have persuaded Lois to come into the shelter with her instead of going off tramping the streets. The raid had been going on for hours, but as yet there was no sign of it abating. Eventually she risked dragging the shelter door open and peeping out. In the distance a huge pall of smoke rose into the air and the sky was red with flames. The clear, crisp, starry night had made the area an easy target. She shuddered and closed the door, dragging Tigger onto her lap. He usually slept through the raids but even he was nervous tonight and kept flexing his claws and arching his back. The bombs made a whooshing noise as the Luftwaffe released them from their planes, followed by loud bangs that were enough to waken the dead. But all the woman could do was sit there and pray that it might soon be over.

At last, early the next morning the all-clear sounded and when she cautiously inched the door open Tigger shot off in search of a live breakfast. The bombsites all over the town were riddled with rats and mice; they were easy pickings and Tigger took full advantage of the fact. Crossing the yard, Mrs Brindley hurried through the filthy air. A fog of smoke shrouded everything for miles around and fires continued to burn.

Once in the kitchen, she fiddled with the dials on the wireless until at last a voice crackled into being and made a terrible announcement. The whole city centre of Coventry had taken the brunt of the raid; even the magnificent St Michael's Cathedral was gone. It was feared that hundreds, if not thousands, had lost their lives – but as yet it was too soon to know the exact death count. The trams were now no more than mangled wrecks, and hundreds of homes had been razed to the ground leaving countless people with nothing but the clothes they stood up in. The Army were furiously digging amongst the ruins for survivors, and fire engines were struggling to control the blazes which were still burning out of control. The announcer was advising anyone made homeless to go to the nearest church hall, where they would be given food and temporary shelter by the WVS. Already it was reported that there was a mass exodus of homeless people fleeing the city on foot, pushing whatever belongings they had managed to salvage in anything they could find: old hand carts, prams and pushchairs.

As the full horror of what she was hearing struck home, tears began to spill down Mrs Brindley's cheeks. The poor, poor souls! It just didn't bear thinking about. She had a feeling that this night would go down in history.

She was dog-tired now, but after making a pot of tea she decided she would take a mug over to Lois and then try to get a few hours' sleep. God knows, they had all had precious little of it last night. She carried the brimming mug across the yard, trying her best not to spill any, and when she reached Lois's back door she called, 'Lois, are yer awake, luvvie? I've brought yer a brew.' She tried the handle and was relieved when it opened at her touch. Stepping into the kitchen, she blinked as her eyes tried to adjust to the gloom. But it was no good; she couldn't see a thing, so she carefully placed the tea on the wooden draining board and began to open the curtains, letting the early-morning light into the room. She then went to the foot of the stairs and called again. Only silence greeted her, so eventually she climbed the stairs and peeped into Lois's room. Empty. Lois should have been back by now, surely? Deciding there was nothing much she could do, Martha set off back to the comfort of her own kitchen.

She had barely got inside when she heard someone knocking on Lois's front door. Dashing along to hers, she opened it to find one of the firewatchers standing on the pavement. He was covered from head to foot in dirt and grime and looked so weary that Mrs Brindley's heart went out to him.

'Does Mrs Lois Valentine live here?' he asked.

'Aye she does, lad. But she ain't in at present,' Martha answered.

'Then is her nearest an' dearest here?'

'No, the kids are evacuated to their grandparents in Cornwall, an' her old man died some time ago.' Mrs Brindley was worried now. 'If there's anythin' yer need to pass on to the children, yer can tell me,' she said weakly. 'I'm about all they've got now, an' I've been keepin' me eye on Mrs Valentine since the little 'uns went – but as I said, she ain't in at present. She's in the WVS and went off to help last night – and she ain't come back yet. I know 'cos I went round to check not long since.' Her palms had suddenly become clammy and her heart was hammering so hard she was sure he would hear it.

'Ah well, the thing is . . .' The man paused to push his tin hat aside and scratch his head, sending a cloud of dust flying into the air. He was grey from head to foot apart from the whites of his eyes, and even they were red through smoke and lack of sleep. 'The thing is, I'm afraid Mrs Valentine won't be comin' home, missus. She were killed last night, see, tryin' to rescue a nipper from a house that had been bombed further up the Ford. The blast took the front clean off the place, but accordin' to witnesses, Mrs Valentine went in there wi'out a thought fer herself. While she were tryin' to get the child out o' there, the rest o' the house came down atop of her an' she saved the little 'un by throwin' herself over her. The woman were a true hero.'

'My God!' Mrs Brindley's hand rose to her mouth as she stood there in shock trying to take in what he had told her and wondering what else this bloody war was going to throw at them. Lois might have had her faults, God rest her soul, but she had died making theirs a land fit for heroes.

How on earth was she going to break the news to the children?

Chapter Thirty-Two

A cold hand closed around Briony's heart the following morning as she listened to the wireless. There had been a terrible raid on Coventry, lasting all night and causing catastrophic damage and loss of lives. Had her home town managed to escape the attack? Was their mother all right? Her first instinct was to race to the station and get a train back home, but that was out of the question. She couldn't just abandon the children.

'What's wrong?' Howel asked as he came into the kitchen and kicked the door shut behind him. His arms were full of logs and he dumped them onto the hearth. Briony was as white as a ghost and he wondered what could have happened now on top of everything else. She'd certainly had more than her share of bad news to cope with lately, and sometimes he felt that the poor maid was fighting her own war.

'The Jerries have blitzed Coventry,' she told him in a

wobbly voice. 'And it's only a few miles from Nuneaton.'

Without her saying another word he knew that she was thinking of her mother, and crossing to her he placed one arm about her shoulders and gentled the glossy dark hair from her face with the other.

'Your mother will be fine, if that's what you're worrying about,' he told her soothingly.

She stared into his eyes, willing herself to believe him – but somehow she couldn't. That awful feeling was back again and she felt sick inside.

'I have no way of getting in touch with her apart from sending another telegram. What should I do?'

'Absolutely nothing,' he answered calmly. 'If anything was wrong, someone would have telephoned here. And you know what they say – no news is good news, so stop worrying.' Then hoping to cheer her up a bit he asked, 'Did you enjoy yourself last night?'

'Oh yes,' she said, as a brilliant smile transformed her face. 'But I don't think those two did.' She jerked her head towards the door leading into the hallway. 'Your mother told me Sebastian and my grandmother had a tremendous row while we were out. It was so bad that she could even hear it in here.'

'Huh! About money no doubt,' Howel said caustically.

She nodded. 'Yes it was, as a matter of fact. Apparently Grandmother refused to give him any more and he called her all the names under the sun.'

'I dare say he thought she'd be an easy touch once his father was out of the way, but Mrs Frasier seems to be finally coming to her senses. And with her husband barely cold in his grave, poor man.' They sat down together at the table and Briony handed Howel the last slice of jam tart. She was going to bake a treacle one later on. It was as they were sitting there that Sebastian strolled in and glowered at them. He often took the short cut through the kitchen if he was heading for the barn or going to get his car.

'It must be nice to have nothing better to do than sit there eating my food,' he said sarcastically. 'I wonder what I pay you for.'

It was on the tip of Howel's tongue to tell him that in actual fact it was Sebastian's mother who paid his wages, but he decided against it.

Briony, however, positively bristled. 'For your information I only get paid a very small allowance,' she said coldly.

'And you should think yourself lucky to be getting that!' he snarled. 'Sitting here in the lap of luxury scrounging off us.'

'I'd hardly call being shoved up into the old servants' quarters the lap of luxury,' she retaliated. 'And as for scrounging off you – if you brought someone in from the village to do half the work I do about the place, it would cost you easily double what it costs to feed myself and the children.'

That's told him, Howel thought, bowing his head so that Sebastian wouldn't see the amusement in his eyes. It was about bloody time somebody stood up to His Lordship!

Sebastian hovered for a second and if looks could have killed, Howel had a suspicion that Briony would have dropped down dead there and then. But then he seemed to think better of it and striding across the kitchen he went out, slamming the door so hard behind him that it danced on its hinges.

Briony took a deep breath. 'Do you think I was rude?'

'Not at all. Seb is a bully, and it's about time someone gave him as good as they got. I'd do it myself, but I don't want us to be chucked off the farm with no jobs to go to. It would upset everyone. Still, I have to admit there are times when I feel like telling him a few home truths.'

Brushing the pastry crumbs from himself, he then rose from the table, saying, 'I'd best get on. I want to bring the sheep down into the field at the back of the farm today for the winter. They can shelter in the barn then, when the weather turns really bad. See you later. And Briony . . . try not to worry too much.'

She managed a smile, but once he had gone she sat for some minutes staring off into space, picturing her mum all alone at home and praying that she was safe.

In Nuneaton Mrs Brindley stared down numbly at the death certificate that the doctor had just delivered to her. It was still hard to believe that Lois was really dead.

'But what about 'er children? They've already lost their dad,' Mrs Brindley fretted. 'What'll 'appen to 'em now?'

'Aren't they all in Cornwall with their grandparents?' he asked gently.

Mrs Brindley nodded. 'Yes, well, wi' their grandma. Their grandad died recently. What wi' losin' her dad an' her grandad, an' then young Sarah comin' down wi' polio, God alone knows how Briony will cope wi' this on top.'

'Even so, they will have to be informed,' the man told her gravely. 'We will need to know what the family wishes us to do with the body and where they want her to be buried. Is there any way you can get in touch with them?'

'I . . . I suppose I could telephone them. Though Lois 'ad been told she must only get in touch that way in the case of a dire emergency.'

'Well, I rather think this falls under that category, don't you?' His face softened then as he saw how distraught the woman was. She was wringing her hands together and her eyes were full of unshed tears. 'Would you like me to telephone them for you?' he offered.

'Oh, would yer?' she asked gratefully. She had only used the callbox about three times in her life. She bustled away to find the number next door. She seemed to remember Lois telling her she kept it in the sideboard drawer. Sure enough, there it was, and she hurried back and passed it to the doctor.

'I shall arrange for an undertaker to remove her body from the morgue and take it to a Chapel of Rest in Nuneaton as soon as possible. She was a very brave woman,' the doctor said. 'And when I get back to the surgery I shall contact the family immediately. I shall keep you informed. Good day, Mrs Brindley.'

She watched him leave and then rubbed a hand across her weary face. It came away wet with tears. What would happen to the house now? She doubted Briony's grandmother would agree to pay the rent on it – and so the children would have nowhere to come back to after the war was ended. Bloody Hitler! It was all such a mess!

It was Marion Frasier who answered the phone some time later that day. When the doctor who had attended Lois introduced himself and explained why he was calling, her face set into a mask. Even so she was polite and after giving him instructions about the removal of the body, she stared towards the kitchen door. Briony wouldn't have gone to get the children from school yet and so she supposed she might as well go and tell her and get it over with. It was typically thoughtless and inconsiderate of Lois to do such a thing, putting herself at risk like that for strangers – but then she had always been a selfish, headstrong girl. As far as Marion Frasier was concerned, her daughter had died the day she went off with James Valentine. She felt no grief whatsoever about her death.

'I am afraid I have some rather sad news for you,' she said coldly when she entered the kitchen. Briony had just taken the treacle tart from the oven and was placing it on a cooling tray on the table.

'It appears that your mother er . . . well, the doctor I have just spoken to informed me that last night she tried to rescue a child from a house that had been bombed.' The older woman's face betrayed her disapproval. 'And it seems that she didn't even know the family. A wall collapsed on top of her. The child lived, but your mother is dead.'

Briony sat down heavily on the nearest chair as the floor raced up to meet her but she managed to hold herself together as the woman went on, 'I have told the doctor that your uncle will go and transport the body back here so that she can be buried in the family plot. I feel it is what your grandfather would have wished.'

Briony didn't really take in what she was saying. All she could think of was the fact that she and the children had no one now. Or at least no one who cared about them. Her lovely mum was dead! She didn't cry. The pain she was feeling went beyond tears.

'Girl – pull yourself together! Did you hear what I just said? It's time to fetch Alfred from school.'

Even in her shocked state, Briony noticed that her grandmother didn't mention Mabel. It was as if the child didn't exist. But she did, very much so, to Briony and she knew that she must keep going for the children's sake at least. She forced herself to rise from the table and staggered towards her coat. She felt as if she was in a strange sort of bubble, and Marion Frasier's words seemed to be coming from a long way away. Outside, Briony found herself shrouded by a thick freezing fog, but again she didn't even feel the cold as she walked on. She knew the route to the school like the back of her hand by now, which was just as well as her legs automatically took her in the right direction. At the school gates some of the mothers looked at her curiously, but Briony stood apart from them. She wasn't in the mood for small talk today. And then Alfie and Mabel appeared as if by magic, tugging at her hands and smiling up at her. She hadn't even heard the school bell ring and she led them away without a word.

'Is sommat up, Briony?' Alfie asked. His big sister didn't seem to be herself at all.

She stopped abruptly and then bending to his level, she licked her dry lips before saying, 'I'm afraid there is, Alfie. You see . . . our mum has died. She tried to rescue a little girl from a house that had been bombed so she was very, very brave and we must be proud of her.'

Mabel said nothing but looked on in silence as Alfie stared at her in disbelief. 'But – but she can't 'ave! Our dad 'as died too, so who will look after us now?' And then as his lip trembled he began to wail, 'I want me mum!'

His words seemed to release Briony from the strange place of limbo she had been locked in, and now she started crying too and they clung together, united in their grief.

'You'll be fine,' she told him. 'You've still got me and I'll always look out for you.'

'B-but I want me mum!'

'I know you do, sweetheart,' she soothed as she held his shaking little body against her. 'I want her too, but we still have each other. And we'll have Sarah back one day as well, when she gets better.'

It was only then that she became aware that she was kneeling in icy cold mud, and when she stood up she saw that she was plastered from the knee down in it. Not that it mattered. Nothing seemed to matter at the moment after the latest horrendous news they had received.

The only sound to be heard for the rest of the journey was the squawking of the gulls overhead and their sobs, but at last they reached the sanctuary of the house and entered the warmth of the kitchen.

Mrs Dower was there waiting for them. She already knew what had happened, after being summoned by Mrs Frasier, and as she opened her arms Briony went into them, laid her head on the kindly woman's shoulder, and wept.

For the next few days Briony rarely ventured from her room, much to her grandmother's disgust, but Mrs Dower insisted that she be left to grieve. She took on all the household tasks and Howel accompanied the children to school and back without a word of complaint.

All too soon the day of the funeral dawned. Lois was buried in the grave next to her father's. The days leading up to the funeral passed in a blur of pain and disbelief, but now at last Lois was at rest – and Briony prayed that she might find some peace and be reunited with their father. She had died heroically, and the girl was proud of her.

Her grandmother had allowed her to go and see her mother for one last time in the Chapel of Rest, and as Briony had stared down at her serene face, she had seen again a glimpse of the mother she remembered from happier times. Lois looked as if she were merely asleep and so beautiful that it broke her daughter's heart afresh. And yet deep down she knew that her mother could never have survived for long without her beloved husband James. He had been her soulmate, her reason for living.

After the mourners had left the house, following refreshments laid on by Mrs Dower, Briony was ordered into the sitting room where she found her grandmother waiting for her.

'I thought it was time I told you what I have decided about your futures,' the woman told her primly. 'You must be wondering what is going to happen to you all.' She still had on the ridiculous black feathered hat that she had worn for the service, and Briony thought it looked like a big fat spider perched on her head.

'I have decided that you will remain here,' the woman went on. 'It is very difficult to get reliable help in the house so you will continue with your chores. Alfred will be going away to a good boarding school once the war has ended, but he will be known as Alfred Frasier. Valentine is such a ridiculous name! And Sarah . . . well, we shall have to wait and see what she can do. I have received a medical report on her.' The envelope had been addressed to Briony, but Marion had found it on the doormat and taken it away. 'It seems that she is making good progress although one of her legs is badly affected. I've no doubt she will be a cripple and forced to wear callipers, but we will have to cross that bridge when we come to it. I dare say there will be some way that she can make herself useful when she comes back. Isn't that right, dear?' She looked across to the place where her late husband's wheelchair used to stand and Briony realised with a little shock that she was talking to him.

Turning her attention back to Briony, she then went on, 'I have spoken to that . . . *that coarse woman* who was your neighbour in Nuneaton.' Briony knew that she was referring to Mrs Brindley, who had travelled down with Ruth to attend the funeral. They had now gone back to the farm for an hour or two with Mrs Dower, who had kindly offered to put them up for the night, but they had promised to come back later. It was something to look forward to at least and Briony was also hugely relieved to hear that Sarah was making progress. That knowledge was like a tiny ray of light in an inky darkness – something she could cling on to in the gloomy days ahead.

'The house will have to go, of course. There is no point in paying rent on a place that you may never go back to. So I have instructed the Brindley woman to sell anything that can be sold and forward the profits to me. It will go some way towards your keep.'

Briony nodded dully. She just didn't have the strength to argue right now. She doubted that she would have wanted to go back there anyway. The house would be too full of memories and a constant reminder of what they had lost.

'So, unless there is anything you wish to ask me, you may go about your duties now.'

Briony turned and left without a word. Back in the kitchen she sat at the table staring at the piles of dirty crockery that seemed to be stacked on every surface. There was so much of it, and even more still to be carried through from the dining room. She put the big kettle on to boil for the washing-up, then forced herself to go and clear the dining-room table. As she passed the sitting room, she distinctly heard her grandmother chatting away again. It couldn't be to Sebastian; he had left for London shortly after the funeral and she hadn't heard anyone knock at the door. And then it hit her – her grandmother was talking to William again. It felt as if the whole world was topsy-turvy.

After attending to the jobs waiting to be done back at the farm, Mrs Dower arrived back at the house with the children, Mrs Brindley and Ruth all in tow.

The older women looked at the mountain of dishes and

at Briony sitting at the table as still as a statue and instantly took control.

'Right then, Martha,' Mrs Dower said, rolling up her sleeves. She and Mrs Brindley were getting on like a house on fire. 'You take the little 'uns up to the bathroom and get them ready for bed, and I'll set about the washing-up shall I? And perhaps you could put the kettle on, Ruth. I've no doubt Briony would like a drink. I know I certainly would.'

Briony stirred from her lethargy to say 'I'm so sorry, Mrs Dower. I meant to start on the washing-up, but I just sat here thinking.'

'Ah well, there's no shame in that,' the woman told her kindly. 'It hasn't been the easiest of days for you. Between us, we'll soon have this place back to rights in no time.'

'Mrs Dower,' Briony said hesitantly, wondering if she should mention it, 'I heard Grandmother speaking to Grandfather earlier on as if he was still in the room with her.'

'Yes, I've heard her doing it too,' she confided. Tapping her head, she lowered her voice. 'I reckon she's gone a bit doolally! She's been going that way for a while, but I think losing the master has tipped her over the edge. Lord knows where it's all going to end.'

Briony dragged herself to her feet and picked up a tea-towel to help with the drying-up. The way she saw it, things couldn't possibly get any worse.

Chapter Thirty-Three

'Oh Ruth, I wish you didn't have to go back so soon,' Briony told her friend as she clung to her on the station platform the next morning. They had sat up until late the evening before chatting until Howel had walked Ruth back to Kynance Farm to join Mrs Brindley.

'I wish I didn't have to as well,' Ruth answered. 'But I promise I'll come again as soon as I can.' They had had a hellish journey due to German bombing raids on many railway stations and tracks. She kissed her friend soundly and stood aside.

It was Mrs Brindley's turn then and she hugged Briony to her and stroked her silky black hair with tears in her eyes. 'Take care o' yerself, luvvie,' she said in a choked voice. 'An' don't get worryin' about anythin' back 'ome. I'll see to everythin'.' Drawing Briony slightly away from the others, she muttered, 'An' I'll see as anythin' of any sentimental value is stored in my back bedroom fer you an' all till yer get the chance to come an' collect it. Yer know – photos and suchlike. As fer the rest . . . well, I've always prided meself on bein' as 'onest as the day is long, but I'll tell yer now: once I've sold all the stuff I can, I'll be sendin' 'alf o' the money to you fer things you an' the kids might need. Annik's said I can address it to her, as I don't trust that Mrs Frasier not to open your post. It strikes me that oity-toity gran'ma o' yours don't need it. It ain't 'ers by rights anyway. Anythin' as I can't sell I'll give away to the second-'and shop. Will that be all right, luvvie?'

'Of course,' Briony told her. 'But please take anything you'd like first, Mrs Brindley. Like the dresser, for instance. I know you always admired it and I'm sure Mum would have wanted you to have it.'

Too choked to speak, Mrs Brindley nodded but then the train was drawing into the station and once it had stopped, Howel began to lift their bags into the corridor. He put his arm about Briony's waist as Ruth and Mrs Brindley climbed aboard, and once they were gone he led Briony back outside to the waiting trap. This mode of transport had tickled Mrs Brindley pink – but then it was much more common here to see people driving about in them than it was back at home.

As old Meg clip-clopped across the cobbles, Howel glanced at Briony from the corner of his eye. It had started to drizzle and her hair was flat to her head. Her nose was red with the cold too and yet she somehow still managed to look beautiful. Being a Saturday, they had left Talwyn in charge of the children, but now Briony was keen to get back to them. Suddenly she didn't want to let them out of her sight. They were all she had left now, and she didn't think she would be able to stand any more losses. She was clutching the letter that Mrs Brindley had brought for her. It was from the mother of the little girl Lois had saved, expressing her sincere thanks for what Lois had done for them, and Briony would treasure it for always. Because of her mother's bravery there was a little girl back in Nuneaton alive and well who would otherwise have died on that fateful night. Howel knew how proud Briony was of her mother's heroic act, and rightly so, the way he saw it. Even so, he knew that she was still struggling to come to terms with the loss of both her parents, but then that was only to be expected. Time was a great healer and in the meantime he was infinitely patient with her.

Thankfully all was well when they arrived back, but Howel insisted on staying on for a while.

'There's lots of jobs need doing over here, and now seems as good a time as any to tackle them,' he said cheerfully, and Briony felt glad of his presence. For some reason she always felt safe when he was about.

Late on Sunday evening, Sebastian arrived back at The Heights with three of his friends. They had all obviously been drinking and made so much noise that Briony was afraid they would wake Mabel and Alfie. She had been sitting quietly brooding in the kitchen, contemplating what the future might hold for her, when suddenly all hell broke loose.

'Ah, here's my little niece,' Sebastian sneered as Briony appeared in the hallway to see what all the noise was.

One of his friends, a lanky chap with buck teeth and bulgy eyes, looked her up and down appreciatively as he ran his wet tongue across his thick lips.

'I say, Seb old man,' he said in a very la-di-dah voice. 'Where *have* you been hiding this little treasure away?'

Briony squirmed with embarrassment, but before she could say anything Sebastian ordered, 'Get down to the cellar, girl, and fetch up a few bottles of the old man's best whisky. The chaps and I are going to have a few games of cards.'

'Fetch them yourself,' she snapped. 'I'm on my way to bed.'

'Ooh, you wouldn't like a bit of company, would you, darling?'

Briony looked at the man scathingly then turned on her heel and strode away. But her heart was thumping. She didn't like the look of this lot one little bit, and wondered why they weren't in uniform. They'd probably pulled strings to be exempt from service. What would happen if the man was to follow her? Thankfully he didn't, and once she was in bed she lay and fumed. If Sebastian thought she was going to cook breakfast for that lot and wait on them in the morning, he had another think coming!

Sebastian's friends stayed for two days and for Briony it was a nightmare. Marcus, the man who had eyed her up on the night of his arrival, proved to be the biggest nuisance. He would wander into the kitchen at every opportunity, seat himself at the table and leer at her while she tried to ignore him and get her jobs done. With his sharp nose and buck teeth, Briony found him quite repulsive, but it didn't stop him ogling her. She wondered why her grandmother didn't just ask him and his cronies to leave. They had kept everyone awake with their shouting and swearing, and the card games had gone on until the early hours of the morning. But Marion Frasier seemed to be locked in a little world of her own now and hardly seemed to notice what was going on around her.

On the second morning when Briony went into the dining room to set the table for breakfast she found the whole room in a terrible state. She stared about in dismay. Empty bottles had been flung down to roll around the floor, and a glass that had been thrown at the fireplace had shattered into thousands of pieces that were now littered all over the carpet. But it was the smell that was the worst. Holding her nose, she walked towards the table then retched when she saw a pile of vomit on the floor. Whoever had done it had made no attempt whatsoever to clean it up and Briony didn't intend to either.

She flew back to the kitchen and Mrs Dower and Howel who had just arrived looked at her in amazement.

'Whatever has happened now?' Mrs Dower asked as Briony sat down heavily.

'It's . . . it's those *pigs* that Sebastian brought back with him,' Briony said in a rare show of temper. 'One of them has been sick all over the floor in the dining room and just left it – and the place is in a terrible state! I'll tell you now, I'm not cleaning it up. Grandmother can do what she likes about it, but I won't go back in there till it's done!'

Howel immediately strode away to check it out for himself and when he came back he was furious.

'She's right, Ma,' he addressed his mother. 'It's disgusting in there and I don't blame Briony for making a stand. Let the filthy swine who did it clean it up himself.'

'But how can we serve breakfast if we can't go into the dining room?' his mother asked.

Howel shrugged. 'They'll have to go without, won't they? And if Mrs Frasier asks why, we'll tell her to her face.'

Half an hour later, Marion Frasier walked into the kitchen and asked imperiously, 'Why on earth haven't you served breakfast yet, girl? I've been waiting for you to call me!'

'We haven't served breakfast because of the state the dining room is in,' Mrs Dower answered. 'If you're hungry you'll have to eat breakfast in here, but we won't be serving

Master Seb and his visitors till they've cleaned their mess up.'

Marion Frasier frowned, then, like Howel, she went to see for herself what all the fuss was about.

When she came back she said calmly, 'I can understand your reluctance to go in there, Mrs Dower. The girl will have to clean it up.'

'Oh no I won't!' Briony told her defiantly. 'Let those that made the mess do it. And as I've told you before, my name is Briony, not *girl!*'

Her grandmother looked astounded. 'How *dare* you speak to me like that!' she screeched in a most unladylike manner. 'While you are here you will earn your keep, and if I tell you to do something, you will do it! My son is quite entitled to have visitors if he so wishes. After all, this house will be his one day when anything happens to me.'

'That's as maybe.' Briony faced her, hands on hips. 'And I am more than willing to do my fair share of work about the place, as I have already proved. But I will not – repeat NOT – clean that mess up!'

It was then that Sebastian stumbled into the kitchen looking bleary-eyed and unshaven. 'What's all the shouting about? And why is breakfast so blasted late?' He had clearly tumbled into bed in his clothes, still stinking of drink, and Briony looked at him with contempt.

'The breakfast is cooked and in the oven,' she told him. 'If you want some, help yourself, because I won't be setting foot in that dining room again until that vile mess you and your so-called friends made is cleaned up – and that's an end to it.'

'Mother?' He looked towards Marion appealingly and she began to wring her hands.

'I'm afraid that the g— *she* has made her mind up,' she

answered apologetically. 'Perhaps you and your friends could set to and tidy it up a little, darling?'

He was so appalled that his mouth gaped open but Briony wasn't going to hang about to find out what he decided to do.

'Come on,' she said, addressing Mrs Dower and Howel. 'I'm sure that there are lots of jobs that need doing over at the farm. I'll come back here later when the place is fit to be seen again. Oh, and while we're at it' she stabbed her finger at Sebastian now '. . . you can tell that dreadful friend of yours, Marcus, to keep his hands to himself in future. I'm sick to death of him trying to grope me every time he comes within arm's distance.' And with that she stalked out, leaving Mrs Dower and Howel to follow.

They had gone some distance when suddenly Howel began to laugh. 'Did you see the look on Master Seb's face when you laid into him? Why, he was so shocked you could have knocked him down with a feather. He's simply not used to not getting his own way.'

So far, Briony's temper had carried her along but now her footsteps slowed and she glanced at Howel. His shoulders were shaking with mirth and his laughter was so infectious that the anger died away and for the first time since losing her mother she started to giggle. In no time at all, Mrs Dower was laughing too, and when they finally entered the farmyard Caden Dower took off his cap and scratched his old head, wondering what had got into them all. Something had tickled them, that was a fact!

Briony ventured back to the house mid-afternoon to find empty soup dishes and plates piled in the sink. Her grandmother had obviously warmed up the soup that was left over from the day before for their lunch.

It wouldn't hurt them to have to fend for themselves for once, Briony thought before walking through to the dining room. The disgusting mess on the floor was gone although it still ponged a bit, and someone had swept the broken glass up and disposed of the empty bottles. She felt a little thrill of satisfaction. One point to me, she thought smugly as she made her way back to the kitchen. Being away from The Heights for a time had allowed her to put things in perspective, and although she knew that she would never fully get over the loss of her parents, she was feeling a little more optimistic now. Sarah was on the mend, and she had suddenly realised that they wouldn't be stuck here for ever after all. Once the war was over, she and Ernie would be married and she knew that he would have no objections to Sarah and Alfie living with them. Mabel would no doubt have returned to her family in London by then. It was something to hang on to.

She stuck to her word, and that evening Mrs Dower served dinner to the guests in the dining room. Briony was adamant that she wouldn't set foot in the room again until they had gone. They could starve for all she cared.

When Sebastian's guests finally left, Briony let out a huge sigh of relief. Good riddance, she thought as she saw the car they had arrived in pull away. Now that they had gone she had no objections to getting back into her normal routine. She decided to start by giving the dining room and the library a good clean. She tackled the dining room first and then went into the library to start in there. It was as she was wiping down one of the oxblood-leather wing chairs that stood to either side of the fireplace that she saw a small book lying on the floor at the side of it. It looked like some sort of a diary and she flipped it open, thinking that one of Sebastian's friends must have dropped it. As her eyes skimmed the first page, she frowned. There were rows of figures with dates at the side of them relating to funerals that Sebastian had undertaken. Further on were dates and names with sums of money written beside them. She recognised some of the names of the deceased from the ledger that her grandmother had asked her to look at, but there were far more names in this book than there had been in the other ledger. Stuffing it into the pocket of her apron, she decided that she would pass it on to her grandmother. It was really none of her business at the end of the day.

As Mrs Frasier was leaving the dining room that evening, Briony suddenly remembered the book. Taking it from her pocket, she handed it to her saying, 'I found this in the library this morning. I think you or Sebastian must have dropped it. It was on the floor at the side of one of the chairs.' Thankfully her uncle was dining out tonight, and Briony felt that things were returning to some sort of normality. At least she wouldn't have to lock her bedroom door this evening, now that his nasty cronies were gone.

Her grandmother took it from her without a word then began to glance through it. Briony moved swiftly away. The woman didn't smell very nice at all and was still in the clothes that she had been wearing for days – but Briony didn't feel it was her place to say anything.

Howel was reading to the children and Mrs Dower was washing up when she returned to the kitchen. Her heart filled with a warm glow of gratitude as she looked at them. These two kind people had ensured that one or the other of them had been with her constantly since her mother's funeral, and she wondered how she would have got through this terrible time without them. Even so, she knew that they had neglected their own jobs to be there and so now she suggested, 'Why don't you two get off now? I can finish up here.'

'Are you sure?' Howel asked. 'I mean I don't mind staying if Ma wants to get off home.'

'I'll be fine now that the visitors have gone,' Briony assured him. 'But thank you both so much for all you've done for me.' She nodded towards Alfie, who was already dropping off in the chair. 'I reckon I might have an early night once I've tidied up and got these two off to bed.'

Her grandmother had allowed Alfie to sleep back in his own room next to Briony since his mother's death, because he had taken to crying for her in the night.

'I'll just carry this little chap up for you before I go then, shall I?' Howel offered. He swung the child up into his arms and upstairs he laid him in the bed then stood aside as Briony tucked the blankets up under his chin. Alfie's eyes were already closing and she smiled at Howel over her shoulder.

'It's lovely to have him back in this part of the house with us,' she whispered, and side by side they tiptoed from the room, closing the door softly behind them. It was dark on the landing, and as they made their way towards the staircase Briony stumbled. Howel's arms quickly went around her to steady her. She could feel his heart beating and as she looked up into his eyes in the dim light, a strange little tingle went through her. Feeling guilty, she instantly pulled away from him. What was she thinking of? She and Ernie had an understanding, and just because she was feeling lonely she was letting her imagination run away with her. Howel didn't want her. Of course he didn't, and she loved Ernie.

As soon as they got back downstairs, Howel mumbled,

'Goodnight,' and left with his mother, leaving Briony to finish her chores.

Once she was done, she joined Mabel at the side of the fire to read her a little bedtime story and much to her surprise, Mabel scrambled onto her lap and snuggled up to her.

'I like Howel, do you?' the little girl asked sleepily when the story was finished.

'Well, er . . . yes, of course I do. He's very nice,' Briony said, going pink.

'He ain't like the men what did bad things to me back at me mum's.'

Briony's stomach flipped over but she didn't say a word.

'When they did bad things to me they used to give me mum money,' Mabel went on in her own matter-of-fact way. 'Some o' the men used ter go into Mum's room, an' some of 'em would come into mine. When they pushed their things in me it really 'urt an' I used to scream for her to come an' 'elp me – but she never did.' She frowned as the memories flooded back and Briony felt as if her heart were breaking. Poor little mite! She had had suspicions that the little girl had been interfered with after listening to some of her rantings during the nightmares, and now Mabel was confirming it. But it was even worse than she had feared; those men had been stealing the child's innocence and doing unspeakable things to her.

'Well, no one will do bad things to you while you're here with me,' she promised, stroking Mabel's sweet-smelling hair. 'They'd have to get past me first!'

'But yer won't be able to stop 'em from doin' it again when I 'ave to go back 'ome will yer? Couldn't I just stay 'ere wiv you?'

'We'll see.' It was all Briony could think of to say. She couldn't give the child false promises. The future was uncertain for all of them, so they would just have to wait and see.

'I love you,' Mabel said suddenly and the words were so unexpected that tears sprang to Briony's eyes.

'I love you too,' she said, and in that moment she realised that she meant it. Somehow, in the time she had been with her, the little girl had wormed her way into her heart, and it would be devastating to lose her. But would she have any say in the matter if her mother sent for her when, or rather if, the war was ever over? Briony tried to put it from her mind. It was a long way away and she had enough to worry about right now as it was.

Just as she was making for the stairs, she heard Sebastian stumble into the hallway and from the noise he was making it sounded like he was drunk again.

'I want a word with you,' she heard her grandmother say, and clutching her hot-water bottle she stopped to listen.

'An' I wanna little word with you, Mother *dear*.'

Briony shivered at the menace in his slurred words.

'This book – how can you explain it?' Marion demanded. 'There are far more funerals written in here than there are in the ledger that the girl brought back from the funeral parlour – so where has all the money gone from the ones that you haven't accounted for in there?'

'Ah . . .' She heard him pause. 'Well, the thing is – the ones in this book are the ones I *expected* to do, but the people took their business elsewhere.'

'Then why have you written a list of expenses at the side of each entry?'

Again there was a silence until Sebastian stuttered, 'Th . . . they're the prices I was going to charge them if they had used us. But I can't help it if they chose to go elsewhere, can I?'

'Hmm!' His mother clearly didn't believe him, and Briony didn't blame her. Sebastian was lying through his teeth. But then he was good at that.

'But now, Mother, I need to speak to you about another little matter,' Sebastian hurried on, his voice thick with drink. 'The thing is, you see . . . Well, my friends and I had a few games of cards while they were staying here and I lost several times to Marcus. The problem is, he's after me to pay up now – so if you could see your way clear to giving me a little advance . . .'

Briony didn't wait to hear any more but hurried up the stairs. Sebastian was her grandmother's problem, not hers. And thank God for that, she thought to herself. She really couldn't stand the man!

Chapter Thirty-Four

As they raced towards Christmas the sharp pain in Briony's heart at the loss of her mother became a dull ache. It never really went away but she kept herself busy and for most of the time it was bearable now. She had been hoping that Sarah would be home in time to spend Christmas with them, but sadly Dr Restarick had told her that, although the little girl was making progress, she was still some way away from being released. However, Mrs Brindley had forwarded some money to Briony from the sale of the pieces of furniture she had managed to sell, and the girl had been able to buy a pretty doll with blue glass eyes and curly blonde hair, which the doctor had promised he would get to Sarah in time for her to open the parcel on Christmas Day. Howel had found two in a shop in Truro when he had gone there for supplies for the animals and Briony knew that her little sister would love it. The other one was for Mabel. Briony had also bought presents for Alfie as well as the Dowers, and for the last two weeks she had been busy with Mrs Dower making Christmas cakes and puddings with their dwindling stock of dried fruit.

She worried constantly about Ernie. Ruth and Mrs Brindley had heard nothing from him, they told her in their letters, and every day she kept her eye open for the postman, hoping for a letter. Liverpool, London and Sheffield had suffered heavy bombings for weeks now, and whenever she felt down, Briony gave a thought to all the people who had lost their homes. At least she and the children still had somewhere to live, for now at least.

Mrs Frasier was also giving her cause for concern. The woman had taken to wandering off, and knowing how dangerous the cliffs could be, Briony did her best to keep an eye on her. She rarely washed any more and constantly talked to her husband as if he were in the room with her, which sent shivers up Briony's spine. It seemed that Sebastian was taking full advantage of her confused state and Briony often heard him wheedling yet more money out of her. She wondered what would happen when the money finally dried up. He seemed to spend most of his time in a drunken stupor now and poor Mr Page was forced to handle the funeral business all by himself.

'It's not that I mind, you understand,' the kindly old gentleman confided to Briony one day after he had called to see her grandmother. When their business was concluded Briony had given him a glass of sherry in the kitchen and they had had a pleasant chat.

'But the thing is, I'm not as young as I used to be and I've had to call on my son to help me out at times.' Mr Page's son was in his late thirties and had not been able to join up because of poor eyesight. 'He would love to take the business over,' Mr Page told her, 'but I doubt Mrs Frasier would sell it, even though her son has no interest in it now.'

'That's a shame,' Briony said sadly. It seemed that Sebastian's selfishness was impacting on all of them.

Mrs Dower had invited Briony and the children over to the farm to have Christmas dinner with them, but Briony had declined, as much as she would have liked to go. Her grandmother had never said a kind word to her nor shown her a single ounce of kindness in the whole time she had been there, and yet she couldn't bear to think of her spending the day alone. She doubted very much indeed that Sebastian would be there. He spent most of his time away now, only coming home when he needed another hand-out. That suited Briony just fine; the less she saw of him the better, but she couldn't help feeling a little sorry for her grandmother.

Today, Mabel and Alfie were in the Nativity Play at school, and as Briony got ready to go and watch it she smiled to herself. Alfie was one of the shepherds, but Mabel had landed the key role of Mary! Briony just hoped that nothing would upset her, as the little girl was still prone to swear if something went wrong. Only the day before, she had stubbed her toe on the table and cursed, 'Bleedin' 'ell, that 'urt!' before glancing guiltily at Briony. It would certainly cause a stir if she came out with a mouthful during the play, and Briony dreaded to think what the teachers might say.

She was just about to leave when Howel appeared in the doorway looking very nice and tidy, and she raised her eyebrows questioningly at him.

'I'm coming with you,' he informed her. 'You didn't think I'd let my best girl play the star role without me going to see her, did you?'

Briony was secretly delighted although she didn't say anything. Lately Mabel had taken a real shine to Howel and she saw that as a major step forward, considering how afraid of men she had been when she arrived as an evacuee. With very good reason, of course, and Briony still trembled with rage every time she thought of it. Up to now, apart from the one short message she had received from her mother shortly after arriving there, Mabel had heard nothing at all from her – but it didn't seem to trouble the little girl at all. She didn't appear to miss her siblings either, although from what Briony could gather they were all a lot older than her and many of them had already flown the nest before the war even started. Knowing what she did, Briony didn't blame them.

'Come on then, we don't want to be late,' Howel chided playfully, pulling her thoughts sharply back to the present and they set off for the village.

'I'm a bit worried that Mabel's mother hasn't been in touch with her, especially as we're coming up to Christmas,' she admitted as they came to the cliff path.

He shrugged. 'Well, it doesn't seem to bother her. In fact, she has really blossomed since she came to you. You're doing a really good job with her.'

Briony flushed with pleasure. 'She is a lovely child,' she said fondly. 'But I just hope she doesn't come out with something she shouldn't today, that's all. Can you imagine the Virgin Mary giving anyone a load of abuse?'

Howel chuckled as he imagined it, but they needn't have worried. Mabel was on her very best behaviour, and when she sat beside the crib looking like a little angel as the Nativity story unfolded, Briony's heart swelled with pride. Alfie made a fine shepherd too, and after it was over Briony and Howel praised them both.

'You were the bee's knees!' Howel said, ruffling their hair.

'Yes, you were, I was so proud of you both,' Briony

agreed, wishing that Mrs Wilkes could have been there to see the play too. Mabel's mother had apparently never done anything but shout at the girl and scream for her to get out from under her feet, but Briony and Howel always praised her when she had been good, and that made her try all the harder to please them.

Fog had blown in from the sea whilst they were at the school and Briony clutched the children's hands as they made their way home in the eerie atmosphere, afraid that they might stray too close to the edge of the cliff. It was a beautiful walk on a nice day, but in this weather it could be treacherous. They were almost back at the house when Mabel peered through the mist and told them, 'I reckon I just saw someone ahead. I 'ope it ain't a ghost.'

'Grandmother!' Briony said as she looked at Howel, and leaving her to care for the children he hurried ahead.

'Ah, Mrs Frasier.' She was right in front of him now, and far closer to the edge of the cliff than he would have liked. 'What are you doing out here without your coat on? You'll catch your death of cold.'

She gazed at him blankly for a second as he quietly walked towards her and gripped her elbow, leading her onto safer ground.

'I can't find my husband,' she fretted, and despite the fact that she could be a very difficult woman he felt sorry for her.

'Well, let's go and look inside, eh?' he said persuasively. Luckily she didn't protest and once he had shown her back into the sitting room and placed her in a chair by the fire, he went to the kitchen to fetch a hot toddy, and a bowl of warm water as Briony had requested.

His mother was there by then preparing the evening meal, and when he came back she asked, 'Is she all right, lad?'

He nodded but she could see that he was angry. 'Yes – she is now that we've settled her. The poor woman was frozen through! Briony washed her and changed her into a warm nightgown. She managed to persuade her to eat a ham sandwich too. Why doesn't that no-good son of hers show her a little consideration? He can't expect Briony to watch over her all the time. She'd need to have eyes in the back of her head – and she does more than her share as it is. It doesn't seem fair.'

'A lot of things in life aren't fair,' his mother said soberly as she started to stuff the chicken. 'Like this damn war for a start. But we have to get on and make the best of it.' Then, brightening, she looked towards the children and said, 'But I hear we have two little stars in the making here!'

Mabel nodded. 'Me teacher told me I did a really good job o' playin Mary,' she said self-importantly. 'So I've decided when I grow up I'm gonna be a film star like Katherine Hepburn. I like 'er!'

Alfie rolled his eyes. 'Well, I'm gonna be a train-driver,' he declared and the grown-ups smiled.

When the children had scampered away, Howel and his mother were chatting quietly when they heard a scrabbling noise coming from the yard. It couldn't be a fox after the hens, as Briony had shooed them all into their coops for the night before going off to the school. And then they heard a scream – at which Howel almost leaped across the room and yanked the door open, heedless of the light that spilled onto the cobbled yard. Beyond the pool of light was nothing but darkness; he narrowed his eyes and peered about until suddenly a movement over by the barn had him racing towards it. It was a man but he had his back to him, then as he drew closer Howel recognised Sebastian. He had someone pinned against the barn door and whoever it was he had trapped was struggling and whimpering.

'What's going on here?' he shouted, and when Sebastian spun about, startled, Howel saw Talwyn slide to the ground and wrap her arms about herself protectively. Her coat had been ripped open and for a moment Howel was so shocked that he felt as if he had been turned to stone. He could hear his mother and Briony running across the yard behind him and then as the full implications of what Sebastian had been about to do to his little sister hit him, Howel let out a roar like that of a wounded animal and launched himself at the other man, fists flying. The first punch caught Sebastian squarely on the chin and he went down like a dead weight, banging his head on the cobbles. But Howel wasn't finished with him yet and he continued to pummel him.

'*You – dirty – filthy – bastard!*' he ground out.

Sebastian was trying to rise now but each time he did so, another blow sent him sprawling back down. He coughed and spat out a tooth as blood spurted from his nose and mouth, and whilst Mrs Dower dropped to her knees to comfort a sobbing Talwyn, Briony threw her arms about Howel's waist and somehow managed to pull him back.

'Stop it!' she screeched. 'You'll kill him, Howel!'

'Too bloody right I will,' Howel answered as he shook with rage.

Sebastian had scrambled to his feet and now, as the two men confronted each other, Howel caught a whiff of Sebastian's whisky breath. He was roaring drunk – again!

'I'll have the police on you for this, you stinking peasant,' Sebastian grunted as he swayed unsteadily towards the house.

'You do that, man!' Howel bawled. Briony was still struggling to hold him back. 'And when they come, I'll tell them that you were trying to rape to my sister. You know damn well she's like a child that's never grown up!'

'Ah, but her body's that of a woman. She's got a fine pair of tits on her,' Sebastian taunted, blood running down his chin. 'And she's been asking for it for years!'

'Why, *you dirty . . .*' Howel freed himself from Briony's arms and was off across the yard like a rocket to finish what he'd started. Thankfully, Sebastian disappeared off round the side of the house – and just as Howel was within reach of him he flew through the front door and locked it firmly behind him.

'I haven't done with you yet!' Howel yelled as he thumped on the door with frustration. 'You lay one finger on my sister again and I swear I'll kill you!'

'And I haven't done with you, *peasant*,' Sebastian shouted back. 'I'll bide my time but you'll live to regret this, Dower!'

Howel retraced his steps to find Briony and his mother helping Talwyn into the house. Once she was seated, he bent to her level and asked, 'Did he hurt you, my little maid?'

She was trembling like a leaf in the wind but she shook her head, her eyes almost starting from her head.

'That's why she don't like comin' over 'ere when Master Seb's about,' Mabel told them matter-of-factly. 'I've seen 'im try to collar 'er before.'

Howel went towards the door again but his grandmother caught his arm and told him sternly, 'That's enough, Howel. I don't want you to get into trouble with the police. You stay here and look after Talwyn. I'll go and speak to Mrs Frasier – for what good it'll do.'

While she was gone, Briony warmed some soup and encouraged Talwyn to swallow some of it. The buttons on her coat had popped off, as had the ones on her blouse, and Briony shuddered to think what might have happened if they hadn't heard her.

When Mrs Dower came back her face was grim and Briony sent the children upstairs to get washed and changed. They had seen too much already as far as she was concerned, and knowing what Mabel had gone through, she dreaded to think how it might affect her.

'Sacked us, has she?' Howel asked miserably.

Mrs Dower snorted. 'Of course not! Think, lad! Who else would she get to do what we do? You and your grandad alone do the work of four men about the place. No, she says she'll have words with him. And from now on, we'll keep a closer watch on Talwyn.'

She stooped to kiss her granddaughter tenderly on the cheek and asked, 'Are you all right, my bird?'

When Talwyn nodded dumbly she let out a sigh of relief. 'Well, I doubt we'll see much of that one tonight. No doubt he'll go and hide himself away in his room after he's cleaned himself up a bit. But you have to let it go now, Howel. He's had what was coming to him and that must be an end to it. Even *he* isn't stupid enough to try a stunt like that again. Do you promise me?'

Howel nodded reluctantly, and stroking his arm, his grandmother said wearily, 'You get Talwyn home now, and look after her till I get back. God knows what your grandad will have to say about all this. It's enough to give him a heart attack. I think it might be best if we didn't tell him about it, for there's no saying what he might do.'

Howel opened his mouth to object, but then seeing the glint in his grandmother's eye he rose slowly and held his hand out to his sister, who took it trustingly.

When they'd gone, Mrs Dower said heavily, 'I've had my suspicions about the way he's been watching poor Talwyn lately. And I don't mind betting this isn't the first time he's tried it on with her. But you can take it from me: I won't give that waste of skin a chance to touch her again.'

'I'm so sorry,' Briony said tremulously but Mrs Dower shook her head.

'There's no need for you to go apologising,' she told her. 'But just make sure *you* keep your bedroom door locked. Who's to say what that creature will do when he's had a drink! I wouldn't trust him as far as I could throw him, I wouldn't.' She sighed. 'But now come on, this dinner isn't going to cook itself.'

Briony rose without another word and began to chop some carrots, wishing with all her heart that Sebastian would clear off once and for all. Perhaps he would do so when the money ran out, and the way he was fleecing Mrs Frasier, that might be sooner than he thought.

Chapter Thirty-Five

It was 23 December, and as Briony sat wrapping up the presents she had bought she couldn't help thinking of Christmases past. Her parents had never had a lot of money, but they had always made sure that Christmas was a joyous time. She and her father would go out and collect bunches of holly with bright red berries on and place it them in vases along the mantelpiece, and the family would sit together making pretty paper chains that James Valentine would attach to the walls and ceiling. On Christmas Eve they all hung their stockings up above the fireplace and in the morning would troop down together to open them. They had been such magical times, but she knew that they would never come again.

Her eyes strayed across the gifts on the table. She had bought Howel a thick pair of woollen gloves to keep his hands warm while he was working about the farm and a new pipe for Mr Dower. For dear Mrs Dower there was a set of Morny French Fern bath salts with matching soap.

Briony had purchased a simple wooden train set, carved by one of the older men in the village, for Alfie, and Mabel had the same doll she had bought for Sarah. She had also saved up and bought a silk headscarf in a rich royal blue for her grandmother, but she hadn't got anything for Sebastian. From what she could gather he wasn't going to be there anyway so it gave her a good excuse not to bother. There was only Alfie's gift to wrap now – and then another lonely evening stretched ahead of her. She didn't feel like listening to the wireless. The reports on the war were always so depressing and just made her worry about whether Ernie was still safe. There had been no word from him still, but she was trying her best to stay optimistic.

The back door was suddenly flung open and she started – until she saw that it was Howel. The wind was whistling past him and making the flames lick up the chimney as he dragged something into the kitchen before kicking the door shut. And then when she saw what it was, her eyes lit up.

'*A Christmas tree!* How lovely – but where did you manage to get it?'

He leaned against the wall for a moment while he got his breath back, then explained, his eyes twinkling, 'I had to go into the market today to order foodstuffs for the animals, so I picked up one for you and one for our grandma. She's tickled pink with it. In fact, when I left she was putting the baubles on it. Here, look – she sent a few over for you. There aren't that many, but I dare say the kids can make some paper decorations.'

Briony had an overwhelming urge to kiss him for being so thoughtful and generous. The children were going to be thrilled when they saw the tree the next morning.

'I'll go and find you a bucket to stand it in,' he went on.

'And by the time I've done, I reckon I'll have earned a nice cup of cocoa.'

He went back out into the biting wind as Briony walked around the tree admiring it before rushing away to measure out milk in the pan for their cocoa.

In no time at all he was back with a bucket of earth, and once he'd planted the tree in it he asked, 'So where do you want me to put it?'

'Over there by the dresser, I think,' Briony decided. 'We can see it when we're having our Christmas dinner then. Oh, I really don't know how to thank you! This is just such a *wonderful* surprise. But let me pay you for it. You must have had to buy it.'

'You'll do no such thing,' he retorted as he dragged the bucket into position. 'And if you even mention doing that again, I'll be mighty offended. Call it an early Christmas present from me to you and the children.'

'Thank you,' she said softly as she reached out to squeeze his hand. 'You really are a lovely man, Howel.'

He flushed and turned to hold his hands out to the fire as she went to put the pan on to the gas. But not lovely enough, he thought grimly as a picture of Ernie looking handsome in his uniform passed in front of his eyes.

Once he was seated at the table with a fragrant mug in front of him, Briony cut him a generous slice of the jam sponge cake she had baked that afternoon.

'I'm sorry it's a bit plain,' she said. 'I ran out of icing sugar. Some things are hard to get now, even living here.'

He nodded in agreement. 'You're right there, but we're still a lot better off than most of the country, and at least we'll be having a nice fat juicy goose for Christmas dinner. I read in the newspaper that most families inland will be lucky to get an old fowl. Now, how's Mrs Frasier?' he asked then and Briony shrugged.

'I can't make her out,' she said, taking a sip of her drink and then blowing on it as it was boiling hot. 'Sometimes she can talk as lucidly as you and I are doing now, but then at other times she doesn't even seem to know where she is.'

'I reckon losing the master tipped her over the edge.' His face hardened. 'And that swine of a son of hers doesn't help matters. Is he in?'

'I don't think so. I heard him tell his mother he wouldn't be back till the day after Boxing Day.'

'Good!' Howel grunted. 'At least we'll be able to have Christmas in peace. But it just goes to show what sort of a character he is. I mean, who'd go off and leave their mother like that when she's just lost her husband *and* her daughter?' He bit his lip. The daughter he was speaking of was also Briony's mother. He muttered hastily, 'Sorry. I wasn't thinking. I know you must miss your mother too.'

'I do!' Briony said chokily. She stared down into her cup as she blinked back tears. 'But it helps somehow knowing that she's close. I go up to the churchyard sometimes when I've taken the children to school, and . . . and I talk to her.' She added, 'I know she's gone, of course, but it just sort of consoles me.'

'I can imagine it would.'

He would have said more, but at that moment the door creaked open and a sleepy-eyed Mabel appeared, knuckling the sleep from her eyes.

'I 'ad a bad dream,' she said in a wobbly voice, and before Briony could say anything, Howel patted his lap.

'Come and sit with me for a while then,' he encouraged her. 'We'll talk about Father Christmas and all his reindeer, and chase the bad dreams away, eh?'

Mabel pottered over to him and clambered onto his lap,

and again Briony thought what a remarkably nice man he was. And so good with the children too. He would make a wonderful husband and father one day for some lucky girl. Her thoughts suddenly rolled back to Megan's words at the dance hall, *I can't remember a time when he looked at me as he looks at you now.*

Hastily gathering the empty cups, she carried them to the sink and ran cold water over them. Megan was so wrong, she told herself. Howel and I are just friends. He knows that I love Ernie. She wondered then what sort of Christmas Ernie might be having as she wiped down the wooden draining board.

Christmas Day passed as pleasantly as it could do under the circumstances, and Mabel and Alfie were thrilled with their presents. Mrs Frasier had bought her grandson a lovely toy car that Briony guessed must have cost a fortune. It had proper little windows, and the car doors and the boot on it opened, and when he wound it up it zoomed across the kitchen. There were no presents for Mabel or Briony, not that she had expected any. When she served her grandmother her breakfast on Christmas morning, Briony gave her the silk scarf.

'Oh!' the woman said in surprise once she had opened it. 'It's er . . . very nice. Thank you.' It was the nearest she had ever come to being civil to her, and for Briony that was enough. Marion looked so lonely sitting at the enormous dining table all alone that she couldn't help but feel sorry for her.

'You could come into the kitchen and have your Christmas dinner with us, or we could come in here and have it with you, if you preferred?' she suggested.

The woman hesitated for a second as the silk scarf pooled

in her lap, reflecting the light from the window, but then she shook her head. 'Thank you, but we will leave things as they are.'

Briony sighed – but at least she had tried and she could do no more.

It was the day before New Year's Eve when Mrs Dower told Briony, 'There's another dance on at the village hall tomorrow, and Howel wondered if you might like to go with him. It would beat sitting here all on your own and I'd be happy to keep an eye on the children. I can bring my knitting over and listen to the wireless. Be a change from breathing in my husband's pipe smoke.'

Mrs Dower had recently taken to unravelling every woollen garment she could get her hands on, and she used Alfie and Mabel to help her wind the wool into balls for reusing, to knit socks for the troops. 'It makes me feel as if I'm doing my bit for the war,' she confided. Then, staring at her latest efforts, she tutted: 'Trouble is, they're more holey than righteous. Still, what's a few dropped stitches, eh? At least they'll keep our boys' feet warm.'

Briony's first instinct was to refuse the invitation because this Christmas had been the first one without her parents, and she had felt their loss greatly. But then she thought of another lonely night sitting in on her own and accepted. Social events were few and far between, here in the back of beyond, so she knew she should make the most of them.

Howel called for her, looking very dapper in his one and only suit and a crisp white shirt and once Briony had kissed the children goodnight they set off. It was a bitterly cold but wonderfully clear night and a million stars twinkled above them.

'Why is it that there always seem to be so many more

stars in the sky here than there were back at home?' she mused.

He looked up and shrugged. Never having lived anywhere else, he had never known any different. 'Perhaps it's because we're by the sea?' he offered. 'But put your arm through mine now. There's a rare frost on the ground and we don't want you to do the foxtrot before we even get there, which is a possibility in those shoes.'

Briony giggled as she did as she was told, secretly pleased to have a strong arm to hold.

Once again they found far more women than men at the dance, but it didn't spoil their enjoyment. Everyone had a good time. The band were elderly, but good musicians for all that, and those present danced and let their hair down, praying that the coming year might herald the end of the war.

Just before midnight, they all formed a circle and joined hands, and someone switched the wireless on to hear Big Ben in Westminster chime in the New Year. And then the haunting sound of 'Auld Lang Syne' echoed from the rafters of the village hall as they all sang, and Briony felt a choking lump form in her throat. 'Goodbye, Mum, goodbye, Dad, sleep tight,' she whispered. But then everyone was kissing each other and wishing each other a Happy New Year, and when Howel pulled her into his arms she went willingly, glad to feel the contact of another human being.

'Happy New Year, Briony.' His eyes were shining in the dim light and he pecked her on the cheek. And then their eyes locked and before she knew it his lips came down on hers and just for the briefest of moments she responded before suddenly pulling away. What was she thinking of? She loved Ernie. Her lips felt as if they were on fire and her cheeks were burning . . . but then someone else spun her about and kissed her cheek, and she didn't feel so bad. Everyone kissed each other on New Year's Eve, so what was she getting so worried about? It was then that she saw Megan Brown sidle up to Howel and kiss him soundly and she felt a little pang of jealousy.

'Pull yourself together,' she muttered beneath her breath. 'It's just those two glasses of sherry you've had that are making you so silly. Why shouldn't Megan kiss Howel?' Even so, she swung about and waltzed off to the ladies' cloakroom to collect her coat.

Once outside the hall she hesitated. She had had every intention of walking home alone, but everywhere looked so different in the dark and she was afraid that she might stray too close to the cliff-edge. Then Howel appeared – and when he saw her waiting, he sighed with relief.

'Where did you get to?' he scolded, tucking her arm through his. 'I was looking for you and began to worry that you'd gone without me.'

'I was just about to,' she told him stroppily, although she had no idea why she should be annoyed.

'Well, I've found you now,' he grinned, and turning up the collar of his coat he hurried her through the darkness.

On 6 January Mrs Dower was mortified to hear on the wireless that Amy Johnson, the first female flyer who had made history by flying solo to Australia, was missing, feared dead.

'Her plane went down in the Thames, poor young lady. They've found the wreckage, but no sign of her body.' Mrs Dower tutted. 'Who'd ever have thought that man – or woman, for that matter – would fly?' She found the whole concept of air travel incredible.

Briony agreed that it was a great shame, but nothing could

spoil her mood that day because she had finally received a letter from Ernie. Although it was heavily censored, reading between the lines she guessed that he was in Italy. She knew that the RAF had recently bombed Naples as well as some of the Italian bases in Libya, and the idea that he was involved in those raids was frightening.

I think of you all the time when I'm in my plane, he told her. *And it's the thought of coming back to you that keeps me strong. I don't know when I will be home again, but please wait for me.*

I'll wait forever, Briony promised him, and she carried the letter about with her for days in her apron pocket.

The winter was severe and they all began to feel like prisoners, but at last in March the weather took a turn for the better and daffodils and tulips began to push through the earth. Soft green buds appeared on the trees and everything was slowly coming back to life after a long hibernation.

Briony was becoming ever more concerned about her grandmother's health and had mentioned it to Dr Restarick one day when he came to give them an update in person on Sarah's progress. Thankfully, it was good news: the little girl might well be home within a couple of months, although he warned Briony that her sister's leg had been severely affected by the disease.

'Does that mean she will have to wear a calliper?' Briony asked fearfully, and when he lowered his head she had her answer. It seemed unbelievable that the child could be crippled for life, but then Briony supposed that she should count her blessings. At least Sarah had survived, unlike the little evacuee boy from the village who would never be going home.

'And my grandmother?' she asked Dr Restarick now. 'What can I do to help her? She doesn't even seem to know who I am most of the time, although she is more like her old self whenever Sebastian is home.'

'There's not a lot you can do for her, other than keep your eye on her,' the doctor told her truthfully. He was secretly disgusted at the way Sebastian treated his mother and would have liked to take a horse-whip to him. 'But if you get really concerned, let me know and I'll come straight out. I doubt she'd tolerate a nurse coming out to see to her.'

Briony thanked him, and when he was gone she began to make plans for Sarah's homecoming even though it might still be some weeks away. It seemed such a long time since they had seen her, and she intended to guard the girl with her life when she came back.

Her happy mood was marred later that afternoon when Sebastian returned with two of his cronies in tow. She had seen neither of these two before, but she didn't like the look of them at all. They were big burly men who both spoke with a broad cockney accent, and eyed her lasciviously as she served them afternoon tea and cake in the dining room. Sebastian informed her curtly that they would only be staying the one night, so that was something to be thankful for at least. Even so, she kept the children close to her after she had fetched them home from school, and she bolted shut the green baize door leading to the main house. The way she saw it, there was no point in asking for trouble.

Mrs Dower came as usual to cook the main meal and as soon as it had been eaten they heard Sebastian and his friends leave the house.

'I'm praying they'll be gone tomorrow,' Briony commented to Mrs Dower.

'Well, we can live in hope!' the woman responded. She hadn't liked the look of the men any more than Briony had.

Just before she left, she looked at the dwindling log-pile

by the side of the fireplace and asked, 'Hasn't our Howel been over to stock up the logs yet?'

Briony shook her head. 'No. I haven't seen him since he brought the supplies over this morning.'

'That's strange. I could have sworn he said he was coming over to do it this evening. Mind you, he's been getting the sheep back up into the top field all afternoon now the weather's picking up a bit, so one of them might have started to lamb and he wouldn't leave till the ewe had delivered safely.'

Briony wasn't overly concerned. She was more than capable of getting a few logs in if need be. Howel was very reliable and she had no doubt he'd get there as soon as he could, so she went about her work and didn't give it a second thought.

Chapter Thirty-Six

The night was darkening as Mrs Dower looked towards the kitchen window at Kynance Farm and commented to her husband, 'Howel's late back, isn't he? He should have been home hours ago. Do you reckon everything's all right?'

As Caden Dower tapped out his pipe in the hearth he said. 'The boy is a bit late, now you come to mention it. I reckon I'll put my boots on and take a wander up to the top field to see what's keeping him. He might be having problems with one of the pregnant ewes.'

'That's what I thought,' Annik agreed, and her knitting needles began to click furiously again as her husband got ready for the outdoors.

It was pitch black now but the dark held no fears for Caden Dower. He had been working this land since he was a young lad and could have found his way about blindfolded if need be.

Whistling softly, he crossed the yard, but Ben his

sheepdog didn't appear so he knew that his grandson must have taken him along with him to round up the sheep. He headed surefootedly for the top field, keeping a constant lookout for Howel and straining his ears – but all he heard was the sound of the night creatures.

When he reached the top field, Caden hopped over a stile with surprising agility for a man his age, and then hands on hips, he peered ahead. The sheep were grazing, which told him that Howel had completed his job – but where was he? He whistled once again and this time was rewarded when he heard what sounded like a whimper coming from close to the hedge further up the field. Seconds later, Ben came wagging up to him, but knowing his dog as he did, Caden saw that he was upset.

'What's up then, my fine lad?' The old man bent to stroke the dog's coat, and when Ben took off again – limping, he noticed – he followed him closely.

Seconds later, Ben began to bark and as Mr Dower caught up with him he felt as if he had been winded. A dark shape lay in the lee of the hedge, and as he knelt down, he saw that it was Howel and that the young man wasn't moving.

'What the . . .' His words trailed away, and at that moment the moon sailed from behind the clouds and he gasped: Howel was covered in blood.

Mr Dower thrust his hand beneath Howel's shirt and then sent up a silent prayer of thanks as he found a heartbeat.

'You'll have to stay here a while longer, my fine boy, while I go for help,' he muttered to the still figure. 'There's no way I could carry you all the way back to the farm, but I'll be back afore you know it.' And then he was off, running like a hare across the field as he headed for the inn at Poldak. There would be men there who would help him to get Howel safely back home, and he didn't have a moment to lose.

*

Annik Dower wrenched open the kitchen door, heedless of the blackout for now, when she heard a small procession of men crunching across the yard. They were carrying what appeared to be a door.

'What's happened?' she demanded. 'Is someone hurt?'

'It's poor Howel,' her husband answered. 'He's hurt, but don't fret. They telephoned the doctor from the inn when I went for help, and he should be here at any minute.'

The men carried the door into the kitchen, and Mrs Dower's hand flew to her mouth as she saw the state of her beloved grandson. Talwyn had been sitting quietly in a chair by the fire but now she began to rock to and fro, whimpering in distress.

It was clear that Howel had taken a severe beating. Both of his eyes were so swollen that she doubted he would have been able to open them even if he had been conscious, and a deep gash on his cheek was oozing blood. His mouth was swollen too, although it was hard to assess how bad his injuries were because of the amount of blood that was even now drying on his face. He was also deathly cold.

'Lord help us,' one of the men said now. 'Looks like the lousy swines had a go at poor old Ben and all – look!' And true enough, they saw that the old dog was drooping now; there was blood seeping out of his side.

'He'd have attacked them if they were hurting his master,' Mrs Dower said chokily and stood for a moment indecisively, not knowing which of the casualties to see to first. Howel had been just a young lad when they took on Ben, and the dog totally adored him. But then thankfully Dr Restarick strode into the kitchen, asking, 'What's gone on here, then?'

Caden Dower hastily told him all he could.

'Right – well, carry this door through to the sitting room for me,' the doctor ordered, shrugging out of his coat. 'Then I'll have a look at the damage. Meantime, you'd best attend to the dog. He doesn't look in too good shape to me.' It was true. Now that his master was safely home, Ben had slunk into a corner and dropped like a stone, his breathing shallow.

Mr Dower quickly went to him while his wife hovered at the sitting-room door, waiting for news of her beloved grandson.

It was some time before the doctor came out and informed her briskly, 'From what I can see, your grandson has been very lucky. There's no sign of hypothermia. He's got a nasty gash on his cheek which I've cleaned and stitched up, but the rest is only superficial cuts and bruising, although I reckon he'll look as if he's done ten rounds with Joe Louis, come morning. He's got a cracked rib as well. I'm afraid this will mean he's going to be off his feet for a few weeks. He may have some concussion as well when he comes round, but keep him warm, get plenty of liquids inside him and make him rest if you can.' Then glancing towards Caden, who was gently cleaning the blood from his dog's flank, he asked, 'And how's the old boy doing?'

He was shocked to see there were tears shining in the man's eyes as he looked back at him and replied, 'They've stabbed him, I reckon.' There was a tremor in his voice and although he was no vet Dr Restarick dropped to his knees beside him to examine the wound.

'I think you're right.' The dog was clearly in shock now that the crisis was over, and who knew what internal injuries he might have sustained.

'But who would do such a thing?' Mrs Dower sobbed. 'Howel hasn't got an enemy in the world.'

The doctor sighed wordlessly. He didn't have an answer and doubted that the dog would last till morning, although he didn't tell them that.

He rose and after slipping his coat back on, he fumbled in his black bag and handed a small phial to Mrs Dower. 'When Howel wakes up, make sure he takes a few drops of that. It will ease the pain,' he told her. 'And I'll be back as soon as morning surgery is over tomorrow. If you need me before then, don't hesitate to get in touch.'

'I will, Doctor. And thank you.' She saw him to the door then before hastening away to clean Howel up and sit with him.

It looked set to be a very long night.

After Briony had taken the children to school the following morning she hurried back to The Heights feeling slightly concerned. Howel still hadn't put in an appearance, as yet which was very unusual. He was usually up with the lark delivering the day's supplies to her. But then she knew that he had been busy with the lambing for the last few days, so that was probably what had kept him.

When she had served her grandmother breakfast, and helped her to get washed and changed, she was relieved to see no sign of Sebastian and his friends. They were probably lying in bed feeling the worse for wear after a night on the ale, she thought to herself. That suited her just fine. With luck they would drag themselves up and leave, and she wouldn't have to set eyes on them again.

As she was carrying the breakfast things from the dining room into the kitchen, she saw her uncle coming downstairs with his two friends. If they want me to start making them fresh tea and breakfast, they can go and whistle, Briony fumed. However, it seemed that the visitors were more intent on getting away than eating, and as she caught a fleeting glimpse of one of them, her eyes widened. He had a right shiner on him. Served him right! He'd probably opened his mouth too wide to one of the local men. Cornish men were known not to suffer fools gladly, and maybe he'd keep his mouth shut in future.

By mid-morning Briony could contain her anxiety no longer, so after serving tea and homemade shortbread to Mrs Frasier, she set off for Kynance Farm.

As she stepped into the farmyard she waited for Ben to come wagging out of his kennel to greet her as he usually did, but there was no sign of him so she assumed he was out, with either Howel or Mr Dower. Making her way through the chickens pecking in the yard, she tapped on the kitchen door before entering. There was no sign of the menfolk, but the minute she set eyes on Annik Dower she knew that something was badly wrong. The woman's eyes were red-rimmed, although she managed a watery smile.

'Morning my bird,' she said – then promptly burst into tears.

'What's happened?' Briony asked. 'What is it?' It was usually Mrs Dower comforting her, but today it was Briony who placed her arm about the woman's heaving shoulders.

'It's poor Howel,' she sobbed. 'He was set upon last night up in the top field while he was attending to a pregnant ewe, and he's in a bad way.'

'What do you mean *set upon?*' Briony was horrified.

'Just what I say – beaten up. The doctor's only just gone. And that isn't all. Old Ben must have defended his master, and the heartless bullies stabbed him! The dear old boy passed away during the night. Caden is out in the orchard burying him now.'

Briony suddenly felt sick, but holding herself together

she managed, 'And how bad is Howel?'

'Well, thankfully the doctor reckons he was lucky. Lucky, he calls it! He's got a cracked rib and his face is all colours of the rainbow, with the cuts and bruises, but apart from that and a bit of concussion, he should be all right eventually. I'll tell you now though – if I could get my hands on the cowards who did this, I'd strangle them without a second thought.'

'But who on earth would attack Howel?' Briony asked in stunned disbelief. And then suddenly she recalled Sebastian's friend sporting a black eye earlier that morning – and everything fell into place. Sebastian had set this up, she just knew it, in revenge for the time Howel had thumped him after his attempted rape of Talwyn. What was it he had said at the time? *I'll bide my time but you'll live to regret this, Dower!*

As she looked towards Mrs Dower, without a word being exchanged she saw that she was thinking the same thing – but how could they ever prove it?

'Did he see who attacked him?' she asked in a small voice.

Mrs Dower shook her head. 'No. It was dark and they came at him from behind, but he knows there were at least two of them because one held him down while the other beat him up.'

She swiped a tear from her cheek with the back of her hand. 'He seems more upset about losing Ben at present,' she went on, 'but he reckons he did manage to give one of them a good punch at some point, afore he lost consciousness.'

That would account for the black eye Sebastian's friend had been sporting, Briony thought again, but how could she say anything? Sebastian was her uncle, and if Mrs Dower tried to implicate him, she and her family could well be thrown out of their home.

'May I see him?' she asked.

Mrs Dower nodded. 'You'll find him in the second bedroom along the landing on your left. But don't stay too long, my bird. The doctor says he needs his rest. He only came round properly a couple of hours ago.'

'I won't,' Briony promised.

Once upstairs she tapped gently on the bedroom door before inching it open – and then as she saw the state of Howel her breath caught in her throat and she felt like crying. He appeared to be asleep so she tiptoed towards the bed and stared down at him. His face was almost unrecognisable and the stitches stood out on the ugly gash on his cheek.

His top half was naked but the doctor had tightly bound his broken rib. Even his chest and his arms were bruised, and a thin dribble of saliva was trickling through his lips which were bloodied and cracked.

'Oh, Howel,' she whispered tenderly. She took his hand and his eyes flickered open just enough to see her.

'B . . . Br . . .'

'Don't try to talk,' she urged, seeing the effort it cost him. 'Just rest. Do you want anything?'

He raised his other hand, weakly pointing towards the tumbler of water that stood on the bedside table. She slipped her hand gently behind his head and raised it just enough so that he could sip it.

His eyes held hers as he dropped back onto the pillow and suddenly rage took the place of her distress. Had Sebastian been there, she would have set about him herself.

'I'm going home now,' she told Howel. 'But I'll be back later this afternoon. You just concentrate on getting well again, eh?'

He squeezed her fingers and she left the room quickly,

afraid of letting him see how distraught she was.

Anger lent speed to her feet, and she barely remembered making the journey back home. The attackers had beaten her dear friend to within an inch of his life and if Sebastian was responsible for this, she knew that she would never be able to forgive him.

Storming through the kitchen without even stopping to take her outdoor shoes or her coat off, she made for the sitting room and banged the door open without knocking.

Her grandmother had been dozing in the chair and Briony strode over to her, hands on hips, her eyes flashing fire.

'Howel has been badly beaten,' she told her without preamble. 'And I think it was Sebastian's friends that did it.'

Regaining her composure, her grandmother folded her hands primly in her lap. 'And do you have any proof of this, girl?' Her voice was icy and suddenly Briony's shoulders sagged and she deflated like a balloon.

'Well . . . no.'

'Then I suggest you keep your accusations to yourself. You could find yourself in very serious trouble if you go around saying things like that.'

'But I saw one of Sebastian's friends leaving this morning and he had a black—'

'Enough!' The woman held her hand up and glared at her. 'If you continue to talk such rubbish I shall have no alternative but to ask you to leave – and where would you all go then, eh? Your mother is no longer at home waiting for you all now, is she?'

The cruelty of her words hit Briony like a hammer blow, and turning about she left the room without another word. Mrs Frasier had her well and truly over a barrel now – until the war was over and Ernie could take her away from here, at least – and she obviously knew it.

'Oh Ernie, *please* hurry and come home,' she muttered as she entered the kitchen, and then dropping onto the nearest chair, she let go and wept bitterly.

Chapter Thirty-Seven

On a warm morning in May 1941 Alfie hopped from foot to foot as he stared off down the drive.

'How much longer will she be now, Briony?' he asked for at least the tenth time in as many minutes.

His big sister grinned as she gave him a hug. 'She'll be here soon,' she promised. A week ago, Dr Restarick had brought the joyful news that Sarah would be coming home, and ever since then Briony and the children had been in a permanent state of excitement, although Briony's feelings were tempered with anxiety.

Dr Restarick had warned her that Sarah would be forced to wear a calliper on her crippled leg for the rest of her life and Briony wondered how the little girl would cope with that. But still, Sarah was alive and that was the main thing. They would manage somehow.

At last the ambulance turned into the drive leading to the house, and as it came towards them through the canopy of trees, Briony's heart began to flutter. She was longing to see her little sister again, but dreaded having to tell her about their mum. Dr Restarick had thought it best that she didn't know about it while she was in hospital in case it impeded her recovery, but now it couldn't be postponed any longer. Briony would just have to choose her moment.

The ambulance drew to a halt and Alfie and Mabel ran to the back doors expectantly. Moments later they were opened and Briony stared at Sarah. She knew that it was her sister – and yet she scarcely recognised her. Sarah had always been a dainty child but now she looked even smaller than Mabel, and her face was white and pinched.

Briony hovered uncertainly as the ambulanceman lifted the child down before saying cheerfully, 'She's all yours then, miss. Good luck, Sarah.' Then with a friendly wave he placed Sarah's case on the ground and hopped back into the ambulance as Briony wrapped her arm protectively about her little sister. She was so thin that she could feel the bones in her arms through her cardigan. Desperately trying not to look at the ugly iron calliper on her leg she said, 'Come on in, love. Mrs Dower has made you one of your favourite sponge cakes and there are some scones too to have with clotted cream and jam.'

She lifted Sarah's case with one hand and took her firmly by the hand with the other, and as Sarah swung the ungainly crippled leg in front of her, it took Briony all her self-control not to burst into tears.

Mrs Dower and Howel, who was now recovered from his beating, both came to see her later that afternoon and made a great fuss of her, but Briony noticed that her grandmother didn't even enquire how the child was when she took her afternoon tea through to her. It didn't overly concern her. Since the argument they had had following the night that

Howel had been injured, Briony only ever spoke to her when she had to.

She broached the subject of their mother's death as she was helping the little girl to undress that night, and for a moment Sarah stared at her as if she couldn't believe what she was hearing.

'*What?* You mean Mummy is dead too . . . like Daddy?'

Briony nodded as she struggled once again to hold back her tears. 'Yes, she is,' she said, trying to keep her voice even. 'But she died being very brave. She saved a little girl's life and we must be very proud of her.' She had just removed the calliper from Sarah's wasted leg and the sight of it was breaking her heart.

She had expected tears but to her surprise, Sarah's small face hardened and she thrust her big sister away from her.

'It's *your* fault,' she ground out, pointing a shaking finger in Briony's face. 'She died 'cos you didn't care about her. You don't care about *anybody* – that's why you didn't come to see me in the hospital.'

'That's not true!' Briony gasped. 'I wasn't *allowed* to come and see you. If they'd let me, I would have walked a hundred miles to be with you, you must know that!'

Sarah had been quiet all day and it had not turned out to be anything like the homecoming Briony had hoped for, despite everyone's best efforts. Now at last she understood why. Sarah was angry because she had thought no one had cared about her and she had been left to face the terrible treatment they had meted out to her in the hospital all alone.

'Think about it,' she urged as she grabbed Sarah's hands and gently shook them up and down. '*No one* had visitors in there, did they? That's because the disease is highly contagious for a certain time and after that the doctors think that family visits will be too unsettling for the patients. I don't agree with it at all, but I had to obey the rules the same as everyone else.'

Sarah stared at her uncertainly for a moment, and then suddenly her face crumpled and the tears came fast and furious, spurting from her eyes to run in rivers down her pale cheeks.

'I . . . I don't have anyone now then, do I?'

'Oh yes, you do,' Briony said as she hugged the frail body to her. 'You have me and Alfie and Mabel, and I'll always be there for you – *always.*' And they cried in each other's arms at the injustice of life.

For the inhabitants of Poldak life went on relatively normally, apart from the ugly rolls of barbed wire that had been strung along the beaches like some formidable necklace.

Alfie complained about it every time they ventured down onto the beach, which Briony ensured they did whenever Howel had time to carry Sarah down the steps leading to it. The heavy calliper made climbing steps virtually impossible for her, although she had mastered the art of walking with it now and could almost keep up with the others on a straight path.

Briony thought the little girl had been very brave and was inordinately proud of her. She had gone back to school and had already almost caught up with all the lessons she had missed. At last Briony was beginning to feel that the child would be able to lead a comparatively normal life despite the handicap of her withered leg, but only time would tell. For now they just got on with things as best they could and were grateful that they had each other.

Briony had now virtually taken over the running of the house, giving Mrs Dower more time to spend on her farm, but Howel still came daily to deliver the fresh food supplies and Briony continued to wonder what they would do without him.

The weather on this particular July day was wonderful. Cotton wool clouds skated lazily across a pale blue sky and the sun was out in all her glory. The children had just broken up from school for their summer holidays and they were all waiting for the arrival of Ruth and Mrs Brindley, who were coming to stay with them again for a few days. They were all very excited about it and Alfie kept running around to the front of the house to peer down the drive for a sign of them. He still thought of Ruth and Mrs Brindley as his link with his former home, and whenever they wrote to Briony he would make her read the letter out to him at least a dozen times. The only ones she kept to herself were the rare ones she received from Ernie and they were for her and her alone.

'They're comin'!' Briony heard Alfie shout suddenly as he skidded across the cobbles in the courtyard and then he was off running like the wind to meet Caden's horse and trap. As before, the visitors would be staying at Kynance Farm, but they would be spending the days with Briony and the children.

When they entered the kitchen, Mrs Brindley declared, 'By, pet! Yer get prettier every time I clap eyes on yer.' She held Briony at arm's length to look at her. The girl's hair hung down her back like a black silk cloak, and with her sun-kissed arms and shining eyes she was a sight for sore eyes.

'You both look well too,' Briony responded, glancing from Mrs Brindley to Ruth.

Ruth had slimmed down considerably and she'd had her hair styled into a neat chin-length bob that showed off her heart-shaped face to perfection. She was wearing a straight calf-length navy-blue skirt and a short-sleeved white blouse that was trimmed with lace, and Briony had never seen her look so elegant.

Now Ruth's eyes sparkled with mischief as she said, 'Well, happen Mrs Brindley's got a spring in her step because of a certain gentleman.'

'Give over!' Mrs Brindley blushed to the roots of her hair, making her suddenly look quite girlish. 'She's on about Charlie,' she told Briony. 'Yer know? The chap I used to go to school wi' that keeps the allotments. He's took me to bingo an' out fer a drink a few times an' now this one 'ere is hearin' weddin' bells. I keep tellin' 'er we're nothin' more than friends, but will she listen? But anyway, that's enough about me. How are you lot keepin'?'

And so they spent the next hour catching up on all the gossip. Eventually Martha lifted her suitcase and said to Ruth, 'Shouldn't we be gettin' over to the farm now to get settled in? Annik will be expectin' us an' I'm sure Briony 'ere will be wantin' to make a start on the evenin' meal for that lot in there.' She cocked her head towards the hall door.

'But you will come back to eat with us, won't you?' Briony asked, reluctant to see them leave. 'Howel brought a lovely leg of pork over this morning and I've made some apple sauce to go with it. There's an apple pie to follow as well.'

Ruth grinned. Briony knew that apple pie was her favourite. In fact, she'd often declared that she could live on it.

'Try and keep me away,' she laughed as she and Mrs Brindley headed for the door.

'Can we go across to the farm wi' 'em, Briony?' Alfie asked and she nodded.

'Yes, just so long as you promise to come back along the fields and not the cliff path.' The children all scampered off in hot pursuit of the visitors and Briony glanced at the clock before hastily beginning to prepare the vegetables that would go with the pork. If her grandmother's meal wasn't served promptly at six o'clock there would be all hell to pay; the woman was very strict when it came to mealtimes. Not that Briony minded. She had the house running like clockwork now and it gleamed from top to bottom.

The next few days passed in a blur, but all too soon it came to the day before the visitors were due to leave.

'Why don't you two young ones go into Poldak to the picture-house an' 'ave a little time to yerselves tonight?' Mrs Brindley suggested thoughtfully. 'Me an' Annik can' watch the kids, an' a break would do yer good.'

Although it sounded very appealing Briony warned Ruth, 'I think *The Thief of Bagdad* is showing at the moment – I noticed when I went to market the other day. Unfortunately the films are always at least a year behind Nuneaton here.'

'That's all right,' Ruth said cheerily. 'I ain't seen it anyway. In fact, I never go to the pictures since you moved down 'ere. It ain't so much fun on yer own.'

'She scarcely goes out at all,' Mrs Brindley put in. 'She just sits in waitin' fer news of our Ernie an' I've told 'er she's too young to be doin' nowt.'

'So shall we set off then?' Ruth asked hopefully and Briony nodded. The reference to Ruth waiting for Ernie had made her feel very guilty – but what could she do?

Both girls really enjoyed the film, and when it was over they strolled back to The Heights arm in arm through the balmy night air.

'You'd never believe there were a war goin' on 'ere, would yer?' Ruth commented. 'It's so lovely an' peaceful. Not like back at 'ome.' The smile slid from her face. 'I suppose yer read about the air raids back in May? It were awful. They were aimin' fer the munitions factories but they hit Coton Church and an 'undred people died that night. Another 380 lost their homes.' Her face was full of despair as she remembered. 'Makes yer think that this damn war is never goin' to end, don't it? I just worry about Ernie all the time. He could be anywhere right now, flying and being attacked by German planes.'

'He'll be fine,' Briony assured her with a catch in her voice. He had to be because they clearly both loved him.

They had almost reached the drive leading to The Heights when they heard the throb of an engine behind them and stepped to the side of the road. Seconds later, Sebastian's car drew up beside them and the dreaded Marcus wound his window down and looked Ruth appreciatively up and down.

Briony's heart sank. She and Ruth had just spent a lovely evening together but now it looked like this idiot was going to try and spoil it.

'Hello, gorgeous,' he addressed Ruth as Briony stared at him scathingly. He knew better than to try it on with her again. 'Would you like a lift?'

'No, she wouldn't!' Briony said abruptly.

'Hasn't your little friend got a tongue then? Can't she answer for herself?'

'Yes, I've got a tongue,' Ruth said. 'And no, I don't wanna lift. Not wi' the likes o' you anyway, so why don't yer just clear off!'

Marcus looked shocked for a second but then shrugged. 'Your loss, dearie,' he answered like a petulant child that had had its sweeties snatched away. He then wound the window back up and the car screeched away in a cloud of dust.

For a moment Ruth stared after him open-mouthed but then she grinned and said, 'Crikey, ain't 'e just one o' the ugliest blokes you ever clapped eyes on?'

And then before they knew it they began to laugh and they didn't stop until they reached the kitchen.

'Sounds like someone's enjoyed theirselves,' Mrs Brindley said from her seat at the side of the fire. Annik Dower was sitting opposite her and they were enjoying a good old natter and a jug of stout that Howel had fetched from the pub for them.

'We had a wonderful time,' Briony agreed. 'Until we met Sebastian and one of his mates on the way back.'

'Ah well, you just ignore them,' Mrs Dower counselled. 'I dare say His Lordship is just showing his face 'cos he wants some more money off Mrs Frasier. That's all he normally comes back for nowadays.'

Briony nodded as she went to fetch herself and Ruth a glass of lemonade. It was quite clear that the older women were happy with their stout, although goodness knew what state Mrs Dower would be in the next morning. As Briony had discovered in the time she had been there, the dear woman couldn't hold her drink for toffee!

She felt sad at the thought of their friends leaving the next day, but she knew that they would come to see her again whenever they could, and for now she would have to be content with that. All they had to do was get through the rest of the war and then who knew what life might have in store for all of them? One thing she was quite sure of – when it was all over, there was no way she would be staying in this house, for whilst it had offered them shelter it could never be home.

Chapter Thirty-Eight

December 1944

As Mrs Brindley sat enjoying a cup of cocoa before retiring to bed the back door suddenly opened and Ernie appeared carrying his kitbag. She blinked and swiped her hand across her eyes, thinking she must be seeing things. But no, when she looked again he was still there, large as life, looking incredibly tired and limping badly.

'Ernie!' The cocoa went flying and splattered all across the rag rug as she flew out of the chair – and then she was hanging on to him as if she might never let him go, with tears streaming down her cheeks. 'What are yer *doin'* 'ere?' she managed.

'Well – what a welcome,' he teased. 'I can always go away again if yer want.'

'You'll do no such thing,' she said joyously as she pressed him into a chair and started to fuss over him.

'My plane took a hit over Amsterdam and I had to bail

out into the North Sea,' he explained, his face solemn now. 'The old leg took a bit of a battering again but thankfully my parachute opened. My mate Chalky White wasn't so lucky though.' His eyes looked tormented as he remembered. 'He was trapped in the cockpit and the plane went into the drink with him inside it. Luckily there was a British ship nearby and they fished me out before the cold got me and took me on board . . . but they didn't find Chalky.'

'Oh, lad.' His mother could feel the pain coming off him in waves but couldn't help being thankful that he at least had survived. It might have been so different.

'But what about your leg?'

'Oh, nothin' too serious,' he answered lightly. The RAF doc reckons it'll be fine in a couple o' weeks or so now. I've been in a hospital in Colchester fer the last two weeks, where they operated, but I asked if I could do the rest o' me convalescing' at 'ome, so the ambulance drove me up here: they were taking another bloke to Birmingham. But it means yer might 'ave to put up wi' me till after Christmas.'

Mrs Brindley was mortified to hear how close her son had come to death, while at the same time she was thrilled to have him home.

'You just sit there an' I'll make yer a nice 'ot drink,' she told him as she pottered away with a spring in her step. 'We'll 'ave some meat on yer bones again in no time.'

He chuckled. 'Yer make it sound like yer fattenin' me up to 'ave fer Christmas dinner, Mam.'

'Oh, I don't think we'll need to resort to that,' she smiled. 'Charlie never sees me short of a bit o' meat or vegetables, bless 'im.'

'Oh yes – an' who's this Charlie then?' He was amused to see colour flood into her cheeks.

'Yer know Charlie – Charlie Mannering? We used to go

to school together an' he's been keepin' his eye out fer me. Good as gold, 'e's been.'

'Hm!' Ernie watched her flustering about with a twinkle in his eye. If he wasn't very much mistaken his mam had a beau – and good luck to her. There was nothing could bring his father back, more was the pity, but if she could find happiness elsewhere, then so be it. She was too young to spend the rest of her life alone and grieving.

The following evening as he was reading the newspaper with his leg propped up on a stool, the door opened and Ruth stood there. She blinked, much as his mother had done, as if she couldn't quite believe what she was seeing, and then dropping the magazine she had brought for Martha, she closed the distance between them and flung her arms about him.

'Oh, Ernie. I can't believe you're really here,' she whispered incredulously.

He in turn was shocked at the change in her. In fact, when she had first walked in he had barely recognised her. In the two years since he had last seen her, Ruth had grown up. The plump but rather plain girl he remembered had grown into a very attractive slim young woman with clear skin and shining eyes. She was wearing a light wool red coat that showed off her curves, and her fair hair had been cut into a very becoming bob that shone in the light of the fire.

He held her hands and stared at her admiringly, saying, 'Crikey, Ruth, you've turned into a bit of a stunner while I've been away.'

She flushed prettily. 'We all have to grow up sometime,' she said and he could only nod in agreement as she pulled a chair up and sat as close to him as she could. Mrs Brindley had popped to the corner shop, and when she walked back in some minutes later she found the pair chatting away ten to the dozen. They had so much to catch up on.

Placing her wicker basket on the table she said, 'How's that fer a turn-up fer the books then, eh, Ruth? Yer could 'ave knocked me down wi' a feather when 'e strolled in last night.'

Ruth nodded in agreement, her face alight.

'Yes, and he tells me he's going to be here till after Christmas. Perhaps even the New Year. It's wonderful.'

Mrs Brindley grinned as she left them to it and began to prepare the dinner. It looked as if she would be cooking for three tonight because she had a funny feeling Ruth wouldn't be going far from Ernie.

Turning from the safe, Sebastian glared at his mother. 'Where has the money gone that was in here?' he demanded.

Marion Frasier shook her head. 'It's gone. I had to pay the Dowers their wages and some bills with it.'

'So what am I supposed to do then?' he snarled. 'I'm leaving for London tonight and I need some cash to take with me.'

She spread her hands helplessly. 'I can't help you, darling. The banks will be closed now and they won't open again until Monday.'

He slammed the safe door shut and leaning over her, he hissed, 'You're *useless,* Mother. Didn't I tell you that you must *always* keep some cash to hand?'

He began to pace the room as he pondered his predicament. He had to be in London by tomorrow night, and if he didn't have the money he owed . . . He stopped his thoughts from going any further as he stormed out of the room in frustration. And then in the hall, an idea suddenly occurred to him and he took the stairs two at a time. *His mother's jewellery.* The silly old bitch probably wouldn't even miss it, the state she was in now, and it must be worth a King's ransom.

Once outside her room he paused to make sure that Briony wasn't about. She cleaned the whole of the house now but thankfully there was no sign of her so he entered the room and closed the door quietly behind him. He saw the jewellery box on the dressing table straight away and headed for it like a bee to pollen. A number of rings were in the top tray and taking them out, he peered at them. There was the emerald ring that his father had bought for his mother following the birth of Lois. It was surrounded by diamonds and he knew it was valuable, as well as being one of his mother's favourites. There was also a square-cut sapphire that his father had bought her to commemorate his birth, a diamond cluster ring and a ruby one with diamonds set either side of it. He pocketed them hastily and looked into the next tray but he was disappointed. The very expensive necklaces that he had been looking for weren't there. His father had always nagged his wife to keep these very valuable pieces in the safe, but she had always worn them so much that she had preferred to keep them close at hand in her bedroom. But where would she have hidden them? He rummaged through the drawers and then at last he found them beneath her underwear; snatching them up, he began to empty them out of their velvet boxes onto the bed. He reasoned that the diamond one alone must be worth thousands. Once he had pocketed them too he replaced the boxes where he had found them. His mother was so forgetful now that she rarely wore them and when she did discover they were missing he would point the finger at that brat, Briony. Lastly, he scooped up her string of pearls from the bedside table.

Happy again, he stole across the landing and once he got outside he leaped into his car, revved up and sped away without a backward glance.

'Phew,' Briony said to Howel on Christmas night after putting the children to bed. 'I've had a wonderful day but I'm whacked now. Still, I know the children enjoyed it and the tea your mother laid on was wonderful. I don't think I'll be able to eat another thing for at least a week.'

He smiled. He had given Sarah a piggy-back ride all the way to The Heights from the farm and had even helped Briony get the children ready for bed when they got home. But now he supposed he should be going.

'I can't believe Mabel's mother didn't send her anything for Christmas,' he commented as his eyes fell on the children's presents.

'I know,' Briony shrugged. 'Between me and you, I'm getting really concerned about it now. We haven't heard a thing since that first note she sent shortly after Mabel arrived here. In fact, I've written to the Red Cross to ask if they can get in touch with her. I'm beginning to fear that something might have happened to her. But then surely they would have let us know if it had?'

'I would have thought so,' Howel agreed as he headed for the door where he paused to say, 'Night night, Briony.'

'Goodnight, Howel.' Once the door had closed behind him she frowned. Howel hadn't seemed to be his usual cheery self lately and she wondered what was troubling him. But then she set about tidying the kitchen and didn't think about it any more.

'I shall be goin' out wi' Charlie tonight, son. Do you mind?' Mrs Brindley asked Ernie on the afternoon of New Year's

Eve. 'Madge Pinner in Webb Street is havin' a bit of a party an' you're more than welcome to come. Sounds like it's gonna be an open 'ouse to me.'

'Thanks, but I won't bother if yer don't mind,' Ernie answered, patting his leg. 'This is just gettin' right, an' wi' the frost on the pavements makin' 'em like a skatin' rink I wouldn't wanna go me length an' end up back at square one.'

'Well, I dare say young Ruth will be round to keep yer company,' Martha said, admiring her wash and set in the mirror. She'd been saving her clothes coupons for months and had treated herself to a new dress to wear, so she would be feeling like the bee's knees this evening. She wasn't at all guilty about leaving Ernie because he and Ruth had been getting on like a house on fire since he'd been home and now they were inseparable. Apart from going home to sleep and to work, the young woman had spent every minute at theirs so she had no fear that Ernie would be lonely. They might even enjoy a bit of time to themselves, she mused and hurried away to start getting ready. It was a bit early admittedly, but she wanted to look her best for Charlie. He really was very good to her and such a gentleman into the bargain.

'Wow, you look a million dollars, Mam!' Ernie said admiringly when she came downstairs.

Martha Brindley flushed at the compliment. Until recently she had forgotten how nice it felt to dress up, and for the first time since losing her beloved Clal she was beginning to feel like a woman again. She noted that Ruth was already there. She had brought a bottle of port and some lemonade so that she and Ernie could toast the New Year in and she added her compliments to Ernie's.

'You really do look lovely, Mrs Brindley,' she said and Martha beamed. But then there was a knock on the door and she got all flustered.

'Oh dear, that'll be Charlie. Let 'im in fer me, would yer, luvvie? I ain't even got me coat on yet an' I'll be needin' it. It's enough to freeze the 'airs on a brass monkey out there.'

Grinning, Ruth hurried away to let Mr Mannering in, noting that he too had gone to great pains with his appearance. He was wearing his Sunday best suit and his hair was flat to his head with Brylcreem. His eyes were openly admiring when he saw Mrs Brindley and he winked at Ernie.

'I'll tell yer what, young Ernie. I reckon I'll 'ave the prettiest girl in the place on me arm tonight.'

'Oh, get off wi' yer, yer silly old sod,' purred Mrs Brindley. 'It's some years since I've been referred to as a girl, or pretty fer that matter.'

He held his arm out and she linked hers through it then they sailed off into the night as Ruth and Ernie laughed.

'I hope you realise 'e's got a real soft spot fer yer mam,' Ruth warned him.

'I gathered that,' Ernie agreed, with a chuckle. 'An' yer know somethin'? I don't mind at all. In fact it's nice to see 'er 'appy again.'

They then settled down to listen to a tribute to Glenn Miller on the wireless as Ruth made them both a port and lemon. Earlier in the month, Glenn Miller and two companions had set off on a routine flight to France where he was booked to play, never to be seen again. No distress call had been heard and no wreckage had been sighted. Ernie loved his music, 'Moonlight Serenade' and 'In The Mood' being amongst his favourites, and he thought it was a great pity that such a talent had been lost. But then so many lives had been cut short during the war. He took a long swallow of the drink Ruth handed him. He had been thinking of Briony all day and wondered if he might be able to get down to see her before he returned to his unit.

By nine o'clock they were both pleasantly tipsy and Ruth joined him on the sofa and laid her head on his shoulder. He could smell her perfume – he thought it might be Chanel No. 5 – and it felt nice to have someone close to him. He could feel her body heat through the very pretty green dress she was wearing and it felt natural to slide his arm across her shoulders. Sighing with contentment she snuggled closer and again, it seemed the most natural thing in the world for her to softly kiss his cheek. But as she went to do just that, he turned his head and the kiss landed on his lips. Ernie felt desire stir in the pit of his stomach and so did Ruth, and before they knew it they were kissing passionately. When his hand played gently across her breast, she felt her nipple harden and so he gently undid the buttons and rolled his hand across her bare skin. And then somehow they were on the rug in front of the fire undressing each other as the firelight kissed their skins.

Ernie stared in awe at Ruth's naked body as he felt his manhood harden. She really was quite beautiful, but even so he was aware that she was most likely still a virgin so he asked huskily, 'Are you sure yer want to do this, pet?'

She nodded eagerly, her eyes holding his. 'It's what I've waited for all me life, Ernie,' she said softly. 'You must know 'ow much I love you? I've *always* loved you.'

His hand traced down the flat of her belly to the warm moist hollow between her legs, and when his finger slid into her she gasped with pleasure and arched her back. He was tracing little kisses all across her flat stomach and she felt as if they were leaving a trail of fire. At some stage she briefly wondered why she felt no embarrassment. Somehow their clothes had landed in an untidy heap on the floor and this was the first time she had ever been naked in front of a man, after all. And yet, once again, it felt like the most natural thing in the world, and soon her hand dropped to his hardness and she stroked him until he was gasping with desire. Feelings she had never known she possessed were racing through her until, unable to hold back any longer, Ernie slid on top of her, parting her legs with his knees, and then he thrust into her. There was one small cry of pain but then she was rising to meet him and she groaned for more until suddenly they both found release and she felt as if she was floating on a cloud of pure bliss. She wrapped her legs about his waist and sighed with contentment. She was Ernie's now completely, just as it had always been meant to be.

They lay for a while in a tangle in the warm afterglow of their lovemaking but then Ernie suddenly thrust her aside and reaching for his trousers, yanked them on before lighting a cigarette.

'You'd better get dressed,' he told her curtly, and bewildered and confused she began to pick up her clothes.

Ernie squeezed his eyes shut as guilt cut through him sharp as a knife. What had he been thinking of? He and Briony had an understanding. Admittedly he was no saint. There had been quite a few girls since he had joined the RAF, but none of them had meant anything to him. They had just been a way of relieving the tension when he had come back from a flight all in one piece. This was entirely different. Ruth had been pure and he felt as if he had defiled her. He could hear her behind him fumbling as she tried to drag her clothes on, and then she was standing in front of him again and staring up at him with a look on her face that almost broke his heart. She was so trusting and innocent.

'You don't regret it, do you, Ernie?' she asked falteringly. 'Because I don't. I've kept myself for you and it was inevitable that we'd come together some day.'

He looked away, unable to meet her eyes for a second longer. 'I'm sorry. It was a mistake,' he muttered. 'I shouldn't have taken advantage of you like that. It must have been the drink. Let's try to forget it ever happened and go back to how we were before, eh?'

But she shook her head. 'We can never be as we were before, after this,' she told him quietly, hurt evident in her voice. 'I'm yours now for all time.' As the faint echoes reached them of neighbours counting down the seconds to 1945 to welcome in the New Year, Ruth picked up her coat and bag, then left without another word. And it was then that Ernie reached a decision. First thing in the morning, he would return to his unit. Better that than see hope in Ruth's eyes every time he saw her.

At that moment in Poldak, Howel was whirling Briony around the dance floor in the village hall. She was laughing and with her eyes shining he thought she had never looked more beautiful.

'This is getting to be a habit,' she shouted to make herself heard above the band. She had attended the New Year's Eve dance with him every year since she had arrived. It seemed a lifetime ago now and each year as it approached she found herself looking forward to it. The band were playing a lot of the swing numbers that had become so popular, and eventually she held her hands up in defeat and headed for their table.

'Phew! I think I must be getting old,' she joked.

'Yep, twenty-one is a little over the hill,' he agreed as she playfully took a swipe at him. Then suddenly the band stopped playing and everyone crowded onto the dance floor to form a circle as someone switched the wireless on. The haunting chimes of Big Ben echoed around the room followed by the familiar strains of 'Auld Lang Syne' and then she was in his arms and as she stared up at him she knew that he was going to kiss her.

Hastily pecking him on the cheek, she yanked herself free, saying brightly, 'That's it then, the party's over. Shall we head for home?'

He was staring at her as if he was seeing her for the very first time and he nodded abruptly. She had just helped him to reach a very difficult decision.

'Of course. I'll just go and get our coats.'

She chewed on her lip as she watched him march away with his back as straight as a broom. When he returned, he handed her her coat and helped her on with it. Then she followed him meekly from the hall.

The wind momentarily took her breath away, but Howel didn't pause to wait for her or offer her his arm as he usually did. She found that she was almost having to run to keep up with him, which was no mean feat in high heels, and eventually she gasped, 'Howel, slow down, *please.* Is something wrong?'

He slowed his pace but kept his eyes straight ahead. 'No, nothing's wrong, but I've reached a decision tonight.'

'Oh?'

'I've decided that once the war is over, I'm going away.'

'But you can't!' she said, unable to keep the shock from her voice. 'How would your parents manage without you? And where would you go?'

'I wouldn't go until there was some chap back from the

war ready to take my place. And as for where I would go . . . well, the world is my oyster. I've seen nothing but this place, so I think it's time I stretched my wings a bit. I can turn my hand to most things so I can go where the fancy takes me and work where I will.'

'I see.' But she didn't see at all. It should really make no difference to her, she knew. Once the war was over, she would marry Ernie and she would leave this place too. So why then, she wondered, did the thought of him leaving hurt so very much?

Chapter Thirty-Nine

In April 1945, word reached the British public that the last German forces had been expelled by the Finnish Army. Two days later, the Italian dictator, Benito Mussolini, was captured near Lake Como by Italian partisans whilst trying to flee to neutral Switzerland. On 28 April he was shot, and the other fascists who had been captured alongside him were taken away and executed. The bodies were then transported to Milan and hung in one of the city's main squares for a gruesome public display.

'This is the turning point,' Annik Dower said sagely. 'We've got the Nazis well and truly on the run now.'

Briony could only pray that she was right.

And then on 30 April, Hitler finally realised that all was lost, and not wishing to suffer the same fate as Mussolini, he committed suicide with his new wife, Eva Braun.

As word of his death was broadcast, the British people flew into a frenzy of excitement.

'It's only a matter of time now,' Mr Dower said stoically, echoing his wife as he sat listening to the wireless whilst sucking on his pipe.

It was during these momentous events that Briony received a letter from Mrs Brindley.

Dear Briony,

I hope as this won't come as too much of a shock to you but I wanted you to be one of the first to know that me and Charlie Mannering have decided to get wed. We've been walking out for a while as you're aware, and we've decided that life's too short to spend alone. I know he can't never take the place of my Clal and I also know that I won't ever take the place of his late wife Vera, but we get on well together and we've decided to try and make a go of it. I hope you'll be pleased for us and not think too badly of me. As soon as we have a date booked for the wedding I'll let you know. We'd be tickled pink if you and the children could make it. It may not be till the summer as we've still got a lot of decisions to make, like where to live for a start off, seeing as we both have a house but I dare say it'll all come out in the wash.

Also I need to let you know that Ernie is home again. He's got another infection in that leg of his, but he'll be down to see you just as soon as he's able. Thank God the war is over for him and I pray that it will soon be over for all of us,

Lots of love to you all,

Martha Brindley xxxxx

Briony's heart was thumping as tears of joy flowed down her cheeks. Ernie was safely home and for now that was all that mattered. She clutched the letter to her. And Mrs Brindley was getting married again! Briony thought it was wonderful news and intended to write back to her that very day to tell her so. But oh, how the time was going to drag now until Ernie arrived . . .

On 8 May everyone gathered around the wirelesses in their homes and listened intently as the Prime Minister, Winston Churchill, made an announcement to the nation from the Cabinet Room at Number 10.

He told them all in his wonderful and dramatic way that the ceasefire had been signed at 02.41 at the American headquarters in Rheims. The act of unconditional surrender was to be ratified in Berlin that day, but in the interests of saving lives the ceasefire had come into effect the day before. War in Europe was finally over.

In London, crowds dressed in red, white and blue congregated outside Buckingham Palace to cheer as the King and Queen with the two princesses came out onto the balcony. Hours before, tens of thousands had listened intently to the King's speech, which was relayed by loudspeaker to those who had gathered in Trafalgar Square and Parliament Square. Even after night fell, hordes of people continued to converge on some of London's great monuments, which had been floodlit especially for the occasion. All around Britain, fireworks lit up the sky and effigies of Hitler were burned on hundreds of bonfires. Street parties were organised everywhere in a spirit of jubilation and Poldak was no exception. The very next day, trestle tables were laid all down the centre of the High Street and Union Jack flags and red, white and blue bunting was strung from lamp-post to lamp-post. The womenfolk produced pasties and saffron cakes as if by magic, whilst the men rolled out barrels of home brewed beer. A piano appeared and soon someone was thumping out the favourite tunes of the day.

The party was in full swing when Briony suddenly became aware of someone standing close behind her. Turning round, she found herself face to face with Ernie.

She gasped. She had been talking to Howel, but now as Howel saw who the visitor was he strode away. Briony didn't even notice. Her eyes were fixed on Ernie and she thought how strange but wonderful it was to see him in civilian clothes. He was leaning heavily on a walking stick but apart from that he appeared to be unscathed.

'Oh, Ernie!' She launched herself at him, almost unbalancing them both.

'You look well,' he said politely, aware that people were watching them curiously.

'Oh, I am. I'm fine. Especially now that *you* are here! But how long can you stay for?' she asked all in the same breath. It felt as if this wonderful day just couldn't get any better.

Glancing around he told her, 'I'm afraid I need to catch the two o'clock train, so this is just a flying visit. But is there somewhere we could talk . . . in private?'

Her smile firmly in place, she took his elbow and led him towards the clifftop walk. Mrs Dower and Howel would keep their eye out for the children, although they were having such a good time she doubted they would get into any mischief.

The clamour of the party gradually receded until there was nothing but the calls of the gulls and the waves crashing on the beach to be heard.

Ernie was strangely subdued, but then Briony supposed that the long journey had taken its toll on him; she wasn't overly concerned. It was just so good to see him.

Eventually she drew him into the shelter of a large oak

tree and as they sat down on the bench beneath it she asked, 'So how are you?'

'Very well, thank you,' he answered stiltedly.

She stared at him as he squirmed uncomfortably, and suddenly he burst out: 'Look, Briony, there's no easy way to say this so I'd best just get it over with. The thing is, when I was at home over Christmas and the New Year, Ruth an' I . . . Well, we got a bit carried away and we . . . yer know?' He gulped, avoiding her eyes. 'Anyway, I went back to my unit and tried to forget that it ever happened but when I got sent home again a few weeks ago because of this . . .' He gestured at his injured leg . . . 'I found out that Ruth was pregnant.' He rushed on, 'So the long and the short of it is, I got a special licence and we were married last week.'

Briony stared at him blankly, a sick feeling in the pit of her stomach. The future she had planned for herself and the children had been snatched away with just a few words. And yet . . . she loved Ruth and was glad that Ernie had done the right thing by her.

'I see.' She forced herself to remain calm. 'Then I suppose I should congratulate you. You didn't really have a choice, did you?'

Now he looked more uncomfortable than ever as he mumbled, 'Actually, I did. But the funny thing is that when I went back to my unit after Christmas I realised that I had deep feelings for Ruth, the same as she had for me. I suppose I always have had, deep down. But we were kids and somewhere along the way I developed a crush on you. I hope you understand, Briony. Ruth was sad because she couldn't ask you to be her matron of honour at the wedding, but it was a very simple affair and we didn't have much time for planning. She insisted I come and tell you personally, though. She's that sort of girl, see? Thoughtful and kind.'

Briony saw the love he had for his new wife shining in his eyes and her spirits sank further. But then she had only herself to blame. She should have agreed to be his girl when he had asked her all that time ago, instead of telling him they must wait until the war was over. Well, the war *was* over now – for everyone else, at least. She would just have to battle on and decide what she and the children were to do.

Suddenly she just wanted him to be gone. Everything had changed in the space of a few minutes and now she needed some time alone to get her head around it. 'I hope you'll both be very happy,' she forced herself to say, and she saw the relief flash across his face.

'Thanks, Briony.' He held out his hand and she took it. He struggled to his feet then, and leaning heavily on his stick he told her, 'I ought to be going. I'm not so quick on my pins as I used to be.'

'I'll walk with you to the road,' she offered, and as they set off she suddenly asked, 'Where will you both live now?'

'We're at Mam's at present, but when she marries Charlie we're takin' over the house an' she's movin' into his home. And don't get worrying about Tigger, mum and Charlie will be taking him with them. Ruth's a bit worried about having a cat around a new baby, see?'

It seemed that everything had fallen into place for them all, but she wouldn't have wanted it any other way. Ruth deserved happiness after all her years of devotion to Ernie, and hopefully she would find it now as his wife.

'Goodbye then,' Briony said. 'It's wonderful news about the baby.' They had reached the road leading into Penzance and the railway station. 'Tell your mother and Ruth I'll get to see them just as soon as I can – and good luck, Ernie.' They shook hands formally and she turned about and headed back to the party.

Howel was watching out for her, and when she reappeared she was aware of him staring behind her for a glimpse of Ernie. He raised his eyebrows questioningly when he saw that she was alone, but she didn't enlighten him. Howel had already informed her that he would leave just as soon as there was someone to take his place on the farm, so why should she share her humiliation with him – or anyone else, for that matter?

Chapter Forty

The war in Europe was over, but in the Far East it raged on. On 6 August 1945 the world's first atomic bomb was dropped on Hiroshima in Japan by a B-29 Bomber. It flattened the city. Approximately 80,000 people were killed instantly and a further 35,000 were injured; many thousands more would die agonising deaths over the next decade and beyond from the effects of the fallout. Three days later, a second atomic bomb was dropped, this time on Nagasaki – a major shipbuilding centre. The Japanese had no weapon that could match the destructive power of that now wielded by the Allies so at last, on 16 August, Emperor Hirohito's permission to surrender was formally given.

As news filtered through, celebrations all across the land erupted once more. Soldiers danced the congo down Regent Street in London, and bonfires were lit on headlands all along the coast of Great Britain. Briony went out to see the sight that might never be seen again, and it put her in mind of a gleaming necklace suspended high above the beaches.

It still felt strange to see the lights of Penzance and Poldak glowing in the dark after the years of darkness. But even now she continued to feel as if she was still fighting a private war in a darkness of her own. Only the night before, she had overheard Sebastian ranting at his mother again; he was probably after yet another hand-out but funds must surely be running low now. All the years she had lived here, it had been the same scenario.

To her dismay, she had got up this morning to find her grandmother still sitting in the chair. Marion clearly hadn't been to bed and she looked so ill and confused that Briony couldn't help but feel sorry for her.

Lately, Mrs Frasier had taken to wearing evening gowns and long silk gloves that reached right up her arms. They were terribly out of date and Briony suspected that they were the ones she had worn when Lois and Sebastian were children. From things her own mother had told her, Briony knew that her grandparents had enjoyed an active social life back then, so she presumed that she had dug the dresses out from somewhere. They hung on her thin frame now and smelled of mothballs. This, added to the unpleasant odour of her unwashed body, was not a nice combination – but what could she do about it? She could hardly drag her off to the bathroom and force her to wash. She'd fetch a basin filled with warm water and try to clean her up – unless the woman tipped it over, as she had done before!

Even so, Briony was concerned enough to telephone the surgery. Dr Restarick had called at The Heights earlier that morning.

'There doesn't seem to be anything physically wrong with your grandmother,' he had told Briony after examining the old lady. 'But you've probably already guessed that she is suffering from senility.'

'Oh, I see. So what can be done for her?' Briony asked anxiously.

'Nothing, I'm afraid. As she deteriorates she's going to need round-the-clock nursing. Either that or there are homes where she could go.'

'Oh!' The news hit Briony like a hammer blow. There was no way she could see Sebastian caring for his mother – and that left only herself, with occasional help from Mrs Dower. There had never been any love lost between herself and her grandmother, but she was still family at the end of the day – so what was she to do?

Briony was still pondering the dilemma now as she stood staring at the flames from the huge bonfires painting the night clouds orange. Now that the war was over she had planned to find somewhere for her and the children to live, and a job so that she could support them. But now it looked as if she might have to stay here for a while longer. There was nothing to go back to Nuneaton for, and the children were happy and settled. Alfie, now a bright-eyed mischievous ten-year-old, spent every moment he could helping Howel on the farm, and Sarah, who had turned out to be very bright academically, was already planning a career as a teacher. The Red Cross were still trying to locate Mabel's mother, but as yet without success. Briony tried not to think about that too much. The child was part of the family now and shadowed Alfie everywhere he went. He was obviously her hero and Mrs Dower often joked that they were meant for each other. Briony knew that if Mabel went back to London, Alfie would be devastated, because he adored her too – which was why she tried to push thoughts of the girl leaving to the back of her mind.

Heaving a big sigh, she went back the The Heights. She would speak to Sebastian about his mother's condition when he chose to put in an appearance again before making a decision about their futures.

Over the next weeks the young men who had gone away to fight the war slowly began to return, some still in uniform, others wearing ill-fitting standard issue 'demob' suits. Even without the suits the boys returning home were easily recognisable because of their pale faces and short back and sides.

Women waited with their hair freshly curled, and dolled up in their Sunday best – and the excitement in the air was palpable. Others, less fortunate, sat at home and wept for the loved ones who would never return.

And then in mid-September, Martha Brindley wrote to say that Ruth had given birth to a baby girl, three weeks premature.

She's a right bonny little thing, and both mother and baby are doing well. They're going to call the lass Molly. My first grandchild! Our Ernie is like a cat that got the cream. He can't do enough for the baby. He's got a new job, working in the post office and seems happy as Larry though his leg still gives him gyp. But at least he came home, which is more than a lot did. Me, Charlie and Tigger are settling in at his house and he treats me like a queen, so I can't grumble. We were sorry you couldn't make it to the wedding but understand why, what with your grandma being ill and having the children to look after. Still, let's hope we see each other again soon, eh? There'll always be a welcome here for you all.

Briony had been wondering how she would feel when she got the news that Ruth's baby had arrived, but surprisingly she felt nothing but joy for them all. As yet, she still hadn't told anyone about Ernie's marriage but now for the first time she felt that she could do so when the time was right.

Ernie was a part of her past now, and for the children's sakes she had to look to the future.

On a cold blustery morning in late November as Briony was clearing up in the kitchen, she glimpsed a figure through the window walking slowly up the drive. There was something about it that looked vaguely familiar, although for the life of her she couldn't put her finger on what it was. She shrugged and carried on putting things away. It was probably one of Sebastian's friends, although most of them usually arrived after dark in flashy cars or in large vans that they then unloaded into the locked barn. She had still never so much as set foot in the place and had no wish to do so, because of the coffins stored there. During the summer the smell issuing from inside when she walked past had almost taken her breath away, and she dreaded to think of the rotting haybales that must be causing it. She knew that there was little chance of her uncle cleaning it out and she simply avoided going anywhere near it. No doubt Sebastian was up to no good, but as long as he left her and the children in peace, she didn't much care. They merely tolerated each other, and that suited her just fine.

She was just about to begin washing up when a shadow passed the window. Wiping her hands on her apron she crossed to the door and opened it . . . and when she saw who it was standing there, the world seemed to rock and she had to grasp the door handle for support.

She screwed her eyes tight shut, but when she opened them again he was still there – and now she began to cry, great shuddering sobs that shook her whole body.

'Dad!' And then they were in each other's arms and he was cradling her tenderly. By some wonderful miracle, James Valentine had come back to them – and she knew that

she could face anything life cared to throw at her now.

After hauling him over the doorstep they stared at each other, both shocked at the changes they saw. When he had gone away Briony had been a pretty young teenager, but standing before him now was a very beautiful, mature young woman.

She in turn saw a gaunt man who barely resembled the handsome, healthy father she had held in her heart – apart from his eyes, that was, which were still that wonderful deep blue colour that had always reminded her of a summer sky. He was dressed in the familiar demob grey pinstripes and his hair, which had once been jet-black, just like her own, was now snow-white. He was so thin that he looked almost skeletal, his skin was sallow too and he looked frail and ill, but she didn't care. Now that he was home she would soon make him well again.

'We . . . we got a telegram telling us that you were missing, presumed dead,' she managed to stutter.

'I was in a Japanese prisoner-of-war camp called Changi, in Singapore, until a few weeks ago, and there was no way of getting word to you,' he told her, still clinging to her hand. It was as if he was afraid that if he let her go, she might vanish into thin air.

She shuddered. The newspapers had been full of the atrocities men had been forced to endure in those places, and now she understood why he looked so ill.

'Oh, Dad!' She led him to a chair and made him sit down, suddenly wondering if he knew about her mother's death. How was she going to tell him?

But as if reading her mind he said quietly, 'I went back home. It was quite a shock, I don't mind telling you, to find someone else living in our house. But Ernie and Ruth next door found me and let me stay with them until I was strong enough to come here.' His eyes welled with tears then as he told her, 'They filled me in on everything that's happened.'

'You know about Mum then? And Sarah having polio?'

'Yes. I thought you might show me where mum's buried in the churchyard when you have time so that I can visit it and take some flowers. But first I have to find somewhere to stay locally and get myself some clothes. It seems Mrs Brindley gave all my stuff to the WVS when she emptied the house for you, and all I have at present is what I'm stood up in.'

Perplexed, Briony chewed on her lip. There was no way her grandmother or Sebastian would allow James Valentine to stay here, despite the fact that there was plenty of room, and yet she hated the thought of them being separated again.

The kitchen door barged open then, and Mrs Dower bustled inside – but seeing that Briony had a visitor she said hastily, 'Oh sorry, my little maid. I didn't mean to interrupt.'

'It's all right,' Briony answered. 'Mrs Dower, this is my father!'

The woman looked flabbergasted. '*What*? Is it really you, Mr Valentine? I thought you had been killed.'

'We thought he had, but he's been in a prisoner-of-war camp in Japan.'

'Well, bless my soul!' the woman spluttered as she came forward with her hand outsretched and a broad smile on her face. 'Welcome home, my dear! It's nothing short of a miracle!' Then, eyeing him up and down, she said sympathetically, 'I didn't recognise you for a minute there. You must have had a bad time of it.'

The haunted look in his eyes gave her the answer.

'But where will you be staying?' she asked solicitously. 'I can't see that one in there letting you stay here. She has never forgiven you for taking Lois away, as you already know.'

'Oh, I dare say I'll find somewhere in the village that will put me up,' he said tiredly.

'You'll do no such thing,' she told him bossily. 'You can come and stay with us at Kynance Farm. By the look of you, you need feeding up and a damn good rest, Mr Valentine.'

He looked slightly embarrassed. 'Well, that's very kind of you, Mrs Dower, and I really appreciate the offer, but I wouldn't want to put you to any trouble.'

'If it was any trouble, I wouldn't have asked you, would I?' she said stoically. 'And please call me Annik. Is your luggage down at the station?'

'Well, actually no. As I was just saying to Briony before you came in, I have to find some clothes from somewhere, which won't be easy with them still being on ration. It's been quite a shock, getting used to England again after all this time. I'd forgotten how chilly it can get.'

'I can help you out there and all,' she smiled. 'I reckon you're about the same height as Howel so he can loan you some togs to tide you over – though looking at you, they'll hang off you like a clothes-prop. But it's nothing that a bit of good homemade Cornish food can't put right.'

Glancing towards Briony, who was alternating between sobbing and laughing, she beamed.

'It's good to see that lovely maid of yours so happy,' she said with great affection. 'She's had more than enough to put up with since you went away. Still, let's hope this is the start of happier times for all of us.'

But the happier times came to a halt temporarily when Sebastian suddenly strolled into the kitchen, saying, 'Did I see someone coming down the drive a short wh—' He stopped abruptly – as recognition dawned – and his mouth drew into a thin line.

'What the hell are *you* doing here, Valentine?' he hissed.

'I don't know how you've got the nerve to show your ugly face here! I thought you were dead – you certainly look half-dead – and I hope you haven't come here expecting free lodgings too!'

Something in Briony snapped, and her hands balled into fists as she ground out, 'How *dare* you say that! I have *never* had free lodgings off you, even though this is my grand-parents' house. I've done the work of two women since I came here, and have been treated as a skivvy. What's more, your mother has our ration books, which covers the cost of our food. I've told you this before! You are lucky to have us here!'

'Women looking for work are two a penny,' he shot back. 'And mind your mouth, young lady, or you just might find yourselves out on the street.'

'Throw her out, and we'll go with her!' Mrs Dower told him hotly. 'And then what will you do, eh? Who will farm the land and look after your mother?'

His mouth clamped shut at that, and she nodded. 'That's right, you ungrateful devil, you just think on! And don't you dare say a word about James. He's a hero, unlike some filthy cowards I could mention, and he'll be staying with me!'

Dark colour flooded into Sebastian's cheeks and turning about he strode away with his hands clenched.

Satisified, Mrs Dower turned back to James, saying, 'That told him, didn't it? But come on now – forget about your so-called brother-in-law. A little drop of my fish soup will keep you going until I can get you settled back at the farm. You look all in. Then Briony can bring the children over to see you on their way back from school.' She grinned, imagining their faces when Sarah and Alfie saw the father they thought they had lost forever. It made her believe that there was a God, after all, although He had sorely tried her belief through the war.

Chapter Forty-One

James never came to The Heights again, but Briony frequently visited him at the farm and slowly he began to resemble the man he had been before he went away to war. He could only eat small amounts, due to years of starvation and disease, but he eventually gained weight and grew a little stronger, although Briony would see that haunted look in his eyes again and know without him saying a word that he was thinking of the comrades who had not survived the camp, and of his beautiful wife Lois, another victim of the terrible war. Mrs Dower fussed over him like a mother hen, not allowing him to do any work as yet, although she would always encourage him to go out for a gentle stroll to the churchyard, which he did frequently, to visit his wife's grave and talk to her.

The war was well and truly over, but rationing was still strictly in force. Thankfully the people of Poldak had not suffered from lack of food, although for some time they had been forced to find alternative fuel for their fires since coal had become like gold dust. But then they counted themselves lucky, and everyone knew that it might take many years for the country to get back on its feet.

Even so, as Christmas 1945 approached the children were excited. Alfie and Sarah had been overjoyed to see their father and even Mabel had taken to him. But then James had always had a way with children.

'Just one more week to go,' Briony said. She was rolling pastry at the table for some early mince pies when she noticed that Mrs Dower seemed rather preoccupied.

'Is anything wrong?' she asked, clapping her floury hands together.

'Yes, my bird, there is.' Annik Dower sniffed to hold back tears. 'Howel informed me and his father that as soon as Christmas is over, he's going to talk to some of the lads who've returned safely to Penzance, to see who's best suited to take his place on the farm. He'll be off then. But there you go,' she said on a sob. 'My grandson is a grown man, and if he's made his mind up, there's nothing I can do to stop him. It's going to break all of our hearts.'

Briony felt as if someone had thumped her in the stomach. 'But how will we manage without him?' she asked, unable to keep the distress from her voice.

Mrs Dower shrugged sadly. 'Same as all the other women had to manage without their menfolk when they went off to war.'

That night, when she sat alone in the kitchen, Briony's mind ticked over the news. Somehow she couldn't imagine life without Howel in it now. She had got used to seeing his cheery face each morning and had always known that he would be there for her in a crisis. And who would take her to the dances in Poldak when he was gone? Admittedly she had more than her fair share of admirers, especially since the young men had started returning from the war – but none of them could hold a candle to Howel as far as she was concerned.

Sighing, she started to switch off the lights downstairs and it was then that the familiar sound of raised voices reached her from the sitting room. Sebastian was harassing his mother again. Briony hurriedly climbed the stairs in the main hallway, hoping that she wouldn't be heard, picking up a pair of high-heeled shoes on the way. Mrs Frasier had a habit of dropping her clothes wherever she took them off these days, and there was often a trail leading to her bedroom. Briony decided she would light the paraffin stove in her grandmother's bedroom as she did each night for her, to heat the ice-cold room, and then leave them to it.

Sebastian was simmering with anger as he stared down at the bank-book his mother had just handed him.

'What the fuck do you mean, this is all that's left?' he raged.

The old woman's head wagged from side to side in distress. 'It's true,' she said shakily. 'That bit and the income from the funeral parlour and the farm is all we have now.'

Sebastian was incensed. What was he supposed to do? He owed money left, right and centre – and this piddling amount wouldn't last him for five minutes. Turning on his heel, he slammed out of the room and stormed up to his bedroom. A little later, he heard footsteps on the landing – his mother going to bed, no doubt. And that was when it came to him in a blinding flash.

He was the sole heir to all that his mother owned – and with her out of the way, everything would be his. Trouble was, there wasn't a lot of money left – but there was the house, which he knew was worth a small fortune, and if it were to burn down with his mother in it, he would get the insurance money. He could sell the funeral business and the farms then, and he need never set foot in this back-of-beyond place again.

Hurrying downstairs, he poured a large whisky into a cut-glass tumbler, then going back upstairs he tapped softly on his mother's bedroom door. Just as he had hoped, there was no reply: she must have gone to the bathroom, so quick as a flash he emptied a handful of her sleeping tablets into the whisky and stirred them in.

When she came back she found him waiting for her with a contrite look on his face. 'I'm sorry I shouted at you earlier, Mother,' he said as she padded towards the bed. She peered at him suspiciously as he handed her the glass. 'Look, I've brought you a nightcap to make amends.'

She hesitated, but he thrust it towards her, saying, 'Come on, or I shall think you haven't forgiven me.'

After clambering into bed she took it from him and downed it in three swallows, shuddering slightly at the strong taste.

'Thank you, son.' She smiled sweetly at him. 'I've always known you are a good boy really.'

Her grey hair was standing on end and she had done the buttons on her long cotton nightdress up all wrong. She looked like a witch but he kept his smile firmly in place as he tucked the covers about her.

'Goodnight, Mother.'

'Goodnight, my little boy. Sleep tight.'

He had to stop himself from grinning. *You* certainly will, he thought as he stepped out onto the landing. Now all he had to do was wait for the deadly mixture to take effect.

*

It was little more than an hour later when Briony was woken by the sound of crying. She had only just dropped off but she knew instinctively that Mabel was having one of her nightmares. Bless her, they happened very infrequently now but Briony suspected that she would never be completely free of them. It was hardly surprising, after what the little girl had gone through. She woke the sweating child gently, then after giving her a reassuring cuddle she told her, 'I'll just pop down to the kitchen and fetch you a drink of water. How about that, eh?'

Mabel sniffed tearfully as Briony, barefoot, made her silent way down into the kitchen, where she snapped the light on. It would have been hard to say who was the most startled as she almost collided with Sebastian, who was heading for the green baize door.

'What on earth are you doing in here in the dark?' she asked, then as she spotted the can of paraffin in his hand, she went on. 'And what are you doing with that?'

'Oh I er . . . thought I'd refill the heater in Mother's room before I turned in.'

'But you know I always do that before I go to bed and have done ever since we couldn't get enough coal.'

His temper erupted. 'Always interfering, aren't you?' he spat. 'Just go back to bed and mind your own business, girl.'

'No, I won't!' Every instinct she had was telling her that something was seriously wrong. Since when had Sebastian ever done any menial chores? And why was he suddenly waltzing about the house with a can of paraffin?

'Give that to me,' she said boldly, holding her hand out, but he slapped it away as he finally lost control.

'You *nosy* little bitch,' he ground out as he grasped the

neck of her nightgown and pressed her back against the table.

'Y-you're going to do something bad, aren't you?' she whispered tremulously.

He laughed; a cold hard sound that echoed around the kitchen.

'I certainly am. I'm going to burn this bloody house down with all of you in it, and then I'm going to play the part of a grieving son and uncle, and claim all the lovely insurance money.' He was enjoying seeing her frightened now and couldn't seem to stop himself from going on as she tried to free herself.

'But that's *murder*,' she choked.

He nodded. 'And it won't be my first if you'd care to look in some of the coffins that are stacked at the back of the barn,' he giggled. 'And this . . .' He held his injured hand up before telling her, 'I did this – and do you know why? Because I didn't want to be a dead hero. Though I'll tell you now it takes some guts to shoot yourself! But it will all be worth it soon. I'm finally going to get what's rightfully mine and get rid of you lot all in one go.'

'You're mad,' she croaked as she overturned one of the kitchen chairs in an attempt to get away from him. It crashed onto the stone flags but he seemed oblivious as he looked around for something to quieten her with. And then he saw just the thing. Lying at the end of the table was the heavy marble rolling pin that Briony had used earlier.

Dragging her with him, he lifted it as she pleaded, 'Please don't do this. Think of the children upstairs.'

She was fighting him as best she could, but it was soon clear to her that her strength was no match for his and she began to cry.

He lifted the weapon then, and just before he brought it

crashing down on the back of her head she thought she saw madness shining in his eyes . . . and then there was nothing but blackness.

Briony crumpled to the floor like a rag doll and after checking that she was unconscious Sebastian snatched up the paraffin can again and headed upstairs. His mother was out for the count, just as he had known she would be, and he smiled with satisfaction before beginning to sprinkle the paraffin about. He splashed some up the curtains and onto the rugs and then the bedding, then with an evil grin he moved to the small heater and tipped it over. The fire must look like an accident. It was common knowledge now that his mother was barmy, and by the time anyone discovered the fire he would be long gone and they would think that she had knocked the heater over accidentally. The flames instantly began to lick at the carpet then the curtains, and soon the bedclothes were alight too. But his mother slept on, impervious to the danger she was in. He watched unmoved as the flames snatched greedily at her eiderdown and once he was quite sure that the fire had a hold he picked up the paraffin can and ran from the room. There was no time to lose now.

He had just started down the stairs when the sole of his shoe came into contact with something slippery, and just before he fell he glanced down to see one of the long silky gloves that Marion Frasier had taken to wearing lying on the carpet. His arms flailed wildly and the can flew out of his grasp as he tried to right himself . . . but then his legs went from beneath him and he was tumbling down the stairs head over heels to roll and land in a broken heap by the hall-stand.

Chapter Forty-Two

Howel kept pace with Mabel as the child ran across the frozen hillocky grass. She was barefoot but so distraught that she didn't even seem to notice the pain.

'We *must* go quicker,' she panted as her nightgown billowed out behind her like a sail. Behind them, Mr Dower and James were struggling to keep pace with them but failing miserably.

Already a pale orange glow shone in the sky beyond the orchard in front of them and Howel's heart sank into his boots. *What if we're too late?* he asked himself, but desperation drove him on and at last they were in the yard. Some of the upstairs windows had already imploded with the heat and smoke was billowing out of them. Broken glass was shining like diamonds amongst the cobblestones, and it scrunched beneath his boots. For now all Howel could think about was getting into the kitchen where Mabel had told him Briony was lying unconscious.

'You wait here now,' he ordered the frightened child, and when she went to disobey him he caught her arm and shook her roughly. 'I mean it,' he shouted, but thankfully his father and James caught up with him then and he pushed her towards them.

'I'm coming with you,' James said through gritted teeth in a voice that told Howel he meant every word and as Mr Dower hugged Mabel against him, the two men rushed towards the kitchen door.

'You get Briony, I'm going up for Alfie and Sarah.' The electricity no longer worked and James fumbled through the darkness towards the stairs leading to the servants' quarters. Smoke was billowing and he knew that he could not afford to waste a single minute. Snatching a handkerchief from his pocket, he put it across his nose and mouth and then he began to shout, '*Sarah . . . Alfie*, where are you?' He was flinging doors open as he went and at last he saw Sarah sitting up in bed, her eyes terrified as she hugged the blankets to her.

'Wh-what's happening? An' what's that funny smell?' she asked as her father felt his way towards her.

'Don't worry about that for now,' he soothed. 'Just do as I tell you, there's a good girl.' He snatched up the calliper that was lying on the floor at the side of her bed before hoisting her up with his other arm. The smoke was getting thicker now and he was beginning to feel light-headed, but he knew that if he lost focus, they would all be burned to death. 'Which is Alfie's room?' he shouted once they were out on the landing again.

'That one there.' She pointed and he kicked at the door with his foot. It sprang back to bounce off the wall behind it, but not before he had seen Alfie cowering in a corner.

'Come on, son,' he said, trying to keep his voice calm.

'Grab hold of the back of my shirt and whatever happens – don't let go.'

Alfie was so frightened that for a moment it appeared that he was not going to obey, but then James roared, *'ALFIE, DO AS YOU'RE TOLD – NOW!'*

He had already lost his wife and nearly his own life and sanity in the hell of the camp, but he was determined that he was not going to lose his children too. If he did, he would have nothing left to live for. It was only the thought of coming home to them that had kept him alive during those nightmare years.

Alfie sprang forward and soon they were at the top of the stairs. Sarah buried her head in her father's shoulder, crying softly, her arms tight about his neck and James told her, 'Come on, pet, we're almost there now.'

At last they were at the foot of the stairs and as James started across the kitchen with his precious bundles the green baize door suddenly blew inwards and flames leaped hungrily into the room, consuming everything in their path.

'Just a few more steps, that's it,' James panted encouragingly. His strength was failing now but he pushed himself on – and suddenly they were in the yard and after the heat inside, the cold air hit them like a fist.

Howel was leaning over Briony, who was lying on the cobblestones, and James heaved a sigh of relief before pitching forward, overcome by the smoke.

'I've got to go back in for the old lady,' Howel gasped when he was sure that Briony was breathing, but his father grasped his arm.

'It's too late, lad.' Caden Dower nodded towards the kitchen door. Flames were clearly visible in there now. 'You'd not even make it to the hallway. All we can do is wait for the fire brigade now. They will have been alerted when we set off from the farm, so they shouldn't be too much longer now.' And so the little group stood shivering with shock and cold and watched helplessly as the beautiful old house burned in front of them.

'So,' the village bobby said to Briony sometime later as she sat wrapped in a blanket in Mrs Dower's kitchen. 'Do you know where Mr Fraiser is now, miss?'

She winced as she tried to shake her head. She had a lump the size of an egg on the back of it, but Dr Restarick had assured them that she was fine, although she would probably have a throbbing headache for some days to come and would need to rest.

'I should imagine he was going to get away and make out that he knew nothing about it.' Briony had told the policeman everything, including what Sebastian had said about there being bodies in the locked barn. The police from Penzance were already back at The Heights, looking to see if there was any truth in it. The barn remained intact; the flames had not had a chance to reach it.

'D-did they manage to get my grandmother out?' she asked now.

The constable cleared his throat and said tactfully, 'The fire brigade are still there trying to bring the blaze under control. Rest assured they'll do all they can.'

Briony dropped her head as tears splashed down her cheeks. She and her grandmother had never got along – Marion Frasier had not allowed it – but even so she didn't deserve what her son had done to her. No one deserved to die like that. But then, Briony thought, she herself had a lot to be thankful for. Apart from smoke inhalation, her father was all right and so were Alfie and Sarah, thanks to the heroism and quick thinking of young Mabel.

The little girl had explained that after waiting for Briony to return with a glass of water following her nightmare, she had crept downstairs to see what was keeping her and had heard and seen what Sebastian had done to her. Realising that she was no match for him, she had then raced all the way to Kynance Farm to raise the alarm, so in everyone's eyes she was the heroine of the hour.

'You've been a very brave girl indeed,' the policeman told her kindly. 'Were it not for you, you might have all been trapped in the fire.'

Mabel blushed self-consciously. She thought of Briony and the others as her family now and was just grateful that she had been able to get help to them in time.

Mrs Dower had gently bathed her feet, which were almost cut to ribbons, and they were throbbing nicely now, although she found it strange that she hadn't felt the pain until the crisis was over.

Satisfied that he had all the information that he needed for now, PC Tredwen snapped his notebook shut and rose.

'Well, I think I ought to leave you good folk to get some sleep now,' he said. 'There's nothing more we can do at this hour, but I'll be over in the morning when we know a little more. Are you sure you can cope with all these extra people, Mrs Dower?'

'We'll cope just fine, Daveth,' she assured him. 'Where else would they go? They're like family now.' Annik had known Daveth Tredwen all his life, for he had been a school pal of Howel's.

And so PC Tredwen headed back to the house on his motorcycle while Mrs Dower pottered about making cups of cocoa, fussing over them all and giving her husband and grandson a proud and loving hug.

*

Next morning at about nine thirty, the constable returned, and after stepping into the kitchen where all the adults were assembled he removed his helmet and told them solemnly, 'I'm afraid the fire brigade were unable to rescue Mrs Frasier. Mr Page removed her body this morning,' he paused then before going on, 'along with the body of her son, Mr Sebastian Frasier. They've been taken down to the funeral parlour.'

'*What?*' Briony could hardly believe her ears. 'But what was Sebastian still doing in the house? Why didn't he leave?'

'It appears that he somehow tripped and fell down the stairs whilst trying to get out,' PC Tredwen informed her. 'His neck was broken.'

Briony was stunned. It seemed that Sebastian's wicked plan to claim the insurance money and kill them all had led to his own death.

'And the house?' she whispered.

He shook his head. 'I'm afraid it will have to be demolished, Miss Valentine. The fire brigade did all they could, but the damage is extensive and the building is unsafe.'

'So what will happen to us all now then?' Mrs Dower asked fearfully. She and her family were only tenants, after all, and it now looked as if they might lose their home too.

'Mrs Frasier's solicitor has been informed of what has happened and he assures me that he will be in touch within the next few days.' Daveth Tredwen paused then before adding, 'My colleagues also discovered two more bodies stored in coffins in the back of the barn. One was the skeleton of a young woman, the other was that of a man.'

Briony suddenly remembered the night she had heard Sebastian arguing with the fellow who had come to collect money from him from London. She had thought it strange after hearing Sebastian offer him a bed for the night to then see Sebastian driving the man's van away. Could he have killed him and dragged him into the barn before hiding his body away? It seemed highly likely. It would also explain the terrible smell that had issued for a time from behind the locked doors. She shuddered involuntarily at the thought of it.

'I don't mind betting the woman will be identified as young Jenna Pascoe, the lass from the village Sebastian got pregnant,' Mr Dower said darkly. 'Poor girl, her parents are going to be devastated. They always thought it wasn't right, the way she just disappeared. I thank God our granddaughter escaped his clutches. But what else did you find in there? Sebastian always kept that place under lock and key and no one were ever allowed in there.'

'I'm not surprised,' the constable said wryly. 'It seems he had a right little set-up going on. At this point we can only assume that he had people looting abandoned properties in London during the bombing, and also getting hold of black-market goods. He would sell the stuff on, making a nice tidy profit. But of course we will be investigating further.'

'That would account for all the vans coming and going in the early hours of the morning,' Mrs Dower said, as everything began to fall into place. 'And to think that something like that was going on right under our noses – and we didn't have a clue! It was his mother's fault. She spoiled that boy from the moment he was born, and she turned him into the monster he became. Just think – he murdered his own mother, after years of extorting money out of her. He was a rotten apple, all right.'

After the constable had gone, the adults all sat trying to digest what had happened.

Mr Dower said sorrowfully, 'It looks like we might have

to retire sooner than we thought, Annik. Howel is going off, aren't you, my lad, so we'll have to find somewhere to rent for us and young Talwyn.'

'I shall have to look for somewhere for us too,' James put in. He and his family couldn't impose on the Dowers' hospitality for too much longer anyway. They had been kindness itself but they were packed into the farmhouse like sardines. Even so, he had a lot to be thankful for. His family had survived the fire, although it might have been a different story altogether had it not been for young Mabel.

'Well,' Howel said then, ever the practical one, 'life has to go on the same for now until we know what's happening. The animals still need seeing to, so I'm off.'

Throughout the morning, as news of the tragedy spread through the village, neighbours turned up with clothes that their children had grown out of, and miscellaneous gifts for the Valentines. They guessed that they would have lost all their possessions in the fire, and wanted to show their support.

Briony couldn't believe how thoughtful everybody was, and it struck her then just how much she was going to miss living here. The children were kitted out in no time and were off helping Howel about the place, cheerful as ever, and thankfully no worse for their ordeal.

For the next few days, Briony helped Mrs Dower to run the house and did as much as she could. Then one cold morning, there was a knock on the door and when Mrs Dower opened it she found the woman from the Red Cross standing on the doorstep.

Mrs Dower ushered her inside and after making her a cup of coffee, called Briony to come and join them in the kitchen. The woman had called to give her a message.

'I'm afraid I've come to tell you, Miss Valentine, that despite our best efforts we haven't been able to contact Mabel's mother, Mrs Wilkes. We discovered that her house had been bombed during the Blitz and neighbours informed us that she went off one evening with an American GI and hasn't been seen since.' She sighed. 'Given the circumstances we have had to find a place for Mabel in an orphanage in the East End. I thought I might take her with me today and start the journey as soon as possible. There doesn't seem any point in delaying any further.'

Horrified, Briony looked towards her father with tears in her eyes and instantly he took control of the situation.

'There will be no need to do that,' he told the woman firmly. 'Mabel can stay with us.'

The woman blinked in surprise. 'Do you mean as a temporary measure?' she asked.

James shook his head. 'No, not at all. I am quite prepared to adopt her if need be.'

'Why, how wonderful!' The woman beamed. 'If only all the orphans I am having to deal with could have such a happy ending. I will have to speak to Mabel first, of course, to see how she feels about it.'

Mabel was duly fetched from the farmyard where she had been happily collecting eggs, and she stood in front of the woman looking fearful. Was this it? Was she being made to go home to her mother?

When the woman told her that her mother was missing, the girl showed no reaction whatsoever – but when she then put James's suggestion to her, the child's face lit up brighter than a summer's day.

'*Yer what?* Yer mean that I can stay wiv Briony and the rest of the family fer always?'

The woman smiled kindly. 'Yes, dear, if that's what you

want. Of course there will be paperwork to be done and the adoption will take a while to go through, but I see no reason why it shouldn't. Miss Valentine has clearly done an excellent job of looking after you, so I see no problems at all.'

Mabel let out a whoop of delight and launched herself at Briony, who chuckled as she hugged her.

'This is just gonna be the *best* Christmas ever,' Mabel declared, and despite the trauma of the last few days they all smiled with her.

Epilogue

It was the day before Christmas Eve when Mrs Dower arrived back from the village with her husband driving the trap. Her shopping basket was full, and another box of groceries was stowed on board. There were a lot of people to cook for this year, and although they were all concerned about their futures, the kindly woman was determined to make an effort for the children.

'I just heard a bit of good news in the village shop,' she said, looking towards Howel, who had come home for a mid-morning cup of tea.

'Oh yes, and what would that be then?' he asked, helping himself to a couple of ginger biscuits to dunk in his mug.

'I heard that Megan Brown has just got engaged to young Robbie Penhallow. Didn't you all go to school together?'

'We did that.' Howel smiled. He had felt guilty about letting Megan down, but now it seemed that she had found happiness with someone else. He was pleased for her.

Megan deserved someone who would love her, and if he remembered rightly, Robbie had always had a soft spot for her even when they were at infant school. He had recently returned from the Army and Howel hoped that they would be happy together.

Briony was watching him closely for his reaction and was surprised to see that he looked relieved. The strange thing was, she was too – although she had no idea why . . .

It was shortly after lunch when a car drew up on the drive in front of the farm and a smart elderly gentleman stepped out, carrying a large leather briefcase.

'It's Mr Briggs, Mrs Frasier's solicitor,' Mrs Dower said, flying into a panic. 'Show him into the front parlour, would you, Briony? We can't receive him in the kitchen.'

Briony couldn't help but grin as she rushed off to do as she was told. Mrs Dower kept a very tidy house usually, but with so many people there it was difficult to keep it as spick and span as she liked.

'Ah, you must be Briony Valentine,' the gentleman said as she opened the door. 'Miss Valentine, could you spare me a few moments of your time?' He peered at her over the gold-rimmed glasses perched on the end of his nose.

'Of course, would you come this way?' Briony answered politely as she showed him into the parlour. She introduced him briefly to Mrs Dower, who then tactfully withdrew.

Once Mr Briggs was seated, he took a sheaf of papers from his briefcase and said quietly, 'I would like to say how sorry I am about the recent terrible fire and the loss of your grandmother and uncle, Miss Valentine.'

When she inclined her head he went on, 'I am here today to inform you of where you stand.'

Confused, Briony frowned. Whatever could he mean? Where she stood?

'The thing is,' he continued, 'Mr Sebastian Frasier was the heir to The Heights and all the worldly goods of his parents following their demise. But of course, he perished in the fire too. I believe that his sister, your mother, sadly lost her life in the war – which means that legally, you my dear young lady, you are the next blood relative. The inheritance will pass to you.'

Briony stared at him like a simpleton, scarcely able to take in what he was saying.

'B-but there's nothing left to inherit,' she croaked eventually. 'The house is gone. And I know that grandmother didn't have a lot of money left. That's what she and Sebastian were always arguing about and why he burned the house down, so that he could get the insurance money. That is what he told me.'

'Ah, but that isn't quite the case,' the solicitor told her. 'Yes, the house is gone admittedly, and unfortunately your grandmother had let the insurance lapse so there will be no recompense there. But there is still the undertaking business, as well as the land and two working farms to take into consideration. Should you wish to put another tenant into Chapel Farm and allow the Dowers to continue here at Kynance Farm, I think you would find you would have a very comfortable income. Alternatively, you could sell everything and be a very wealthy young woman indeed. Land is at a premium now that the war is over.'

Briony could only stare at him dumbly as his words sank in.

He then rose and told her, 'I can see that this has come as a shock to you, my dear. Perhaps you would like some time to think about it, and when you decide what you would like to do, get in touch with me then with your instructions.'

But suddenly everything was blindingly clear and she said eagerly, 'Actually, Mr Briggs, I think I know *exactly* what I'd like to do – so could you perhaps take some instructions now?'

'Of course.' He sat down again and after taking a notepad and pen from his briefcase he began to write down everything that she told him.

'So what did Mr Briggs have to say?' Mrs Dower asked when the solicitor had left and Briony had rejoined her in the kitchen.

'Oh, he just wanted to tell me that Grandmother had let the insurance on the house lapse, so Sebastian did what he did for nothing.' She kept her fingers crossed behind her back as she was telling the tale. But then she wasn't really lying, the way she saw it. She just wasn't telling the whole of the truth. That could wait for Christmas Day.

'Well, bless me!' Mrs Dower was shocked. 'So the old lady died all for no good reason. But then she was going senile, so let's hope she wouldn't have known anything about it.' She reached for the bottled plums and the subject was dropped.

Christmas Day dawned bright and clear, and despite the cloud they were living under everyone seemed to enjoy it. The gifts that Briony had so carefully chosen and wrapped had perished in the fire, but no one minded, not even the children. They were just glad to be alive.

Mrs Dower did them proud with the Christmas dinner. There was a turkey as well as a leg of roast pork with crispy crackling and all the trimmings, followed by a Christmas pudding that she had made with a secret hoard of raisins and had had soaking in brandy for weeks.

When it was over, James and Mr and Mrs Dower all settled beside the fire to listen to the wireless, and doze, and Briony asked Howel, 'Do you fancy a walk? There's something I want to talk to you about.' The children and Talwyn were all happily engrossed in a game of Ludo, so she doubted they would even be missed.

He looked at her curiously for a moment wondering what she had in mind, but then he nodded and went to fetch his coat.

Once outside, she slipped her arm through his and steered him in the direction of Chapel Farm.

'Where are we going?' he asked, but she just grinned and carried on walking.

When the farm came into view she paused to look down on it in the hollow and said quietly, 'It's in a lovely spot here, isn't it?'

'It certainly is,' he agreed and they walked on. Once they'd passed beneath the rowan tree and crossed the farmyard, Howel took the kitchen door key from beneath an upturned flower pot and let them in.

'So what are we doing here then?' he enquired as he looked about at the cobwebs and the dusty furniture.

'I thought we could talk here without any interruptions,' Briony explained. Then, brushing off two of the kitchen chairs with her mitten, she motioned him to sit down and placed herself opposite him. 'The thing is,' she said softly, 'this farm is mine.'

'What?' He stared at her incredulously, wondering if she had finally taken leave of her senses after all she had been through.

'It's true,' she assured him with a nervous giggle. 'That's what Grandmother's solicitor Mr Briggs came to tell me. Now that Sebastian is dead, I am the nearest blood relative left to Grandmother so I get to have his inheritance. The farms, the land, the undertaking business and the house – for what's it worth – are all mine now.'

She watched a muscle in his cheek begin to work then as she rose and looked around.

'I've decided that I'm going to live here,' she told him then. 'Dad can have the rooms above the stables to give him some privacy and I know he'll love working here. He always did want to work outside in the fresh air. I shall have to make a few alterations, of course; this sink will have to be replaced for a start-off.' She screwed her nose up as she stared at the cracked butler's sink beneath the window. 'But then we could fill this one with fresh herbs and stand it just outside the kitchen door so that the smell of them wafts into the kitchen in the summer. And oh . . . the other thing that I need to tell you is that I've had Mr Briggs sign Kynance Farm and the land with all the livestock on it over to your parents. I think they deserve to be able to call it their own after working so hard on it for all these years, don't you?'

She saw the shock register in his eyes but she wasn't finished yet. 'I've also instructed Mr Briggs to have the undertaker's business valued and then to sell it to Mr Page's son Johnny at a reduced price. Mr Page told me some time ago that he wished to retire so that he could spend more time in his garden, and after all his years of devoted service to my grandparents, I felt that was the least I could do. The money from the sale of that business will then give me the funds to purchase some livestock for this farm. What do you think?'

When he was capable of speech he choked, 'Well, it doesn't really matter what I think, does it? You seem to have everything worked out.'

'Oh, but it *does* matter,' she said sweetly. 'Surely you'll want to choose your own animals? I don't know anything about it or what to look for, do I? One sheep or one cow is just like any other to me.' She had come to realise how much Howel meant to her, and why she had been able to accept Ernie marrying Ruth so well, when Howel had told them all that he was going away and she had been forced to try and picture her life without him in it. She knew now beyond a doubt that what she had felt for Ernie had been no more than a childhood infatuation. But what she felt for Howel was an enduring love, one that would last forever.

'What do you mean – *choose my own animals?'* he asked, still puzzled. And at last she did what she had been longing to do, and crossing to him she sat down on his lap and put her arms about his neck before kissing him softly on the lips. She was thankful that he didn't attempt to push her away. Not now when she had finally realised just how very much she loved him.

'This farm will be in the name of Mr and Mrs Dower too,' she informed him with a twinkle in her eye. 'You didn't think I'd attempt to take a farm on without a husband to manage it, did you?'

'Is that a proposal?' His eyes were alight with love now and she could feel his heart beating against hers even through the thickness of their coats.

'Well, I'll certainly expect you to make an honest woman of me,' she pouted. 'I don't think my father would be too pleased if I told him we were planning to live in sin.'

'In that case, I suppose I shall have to accept.' He kissed her then and she knew that she would never forget this day, not for as long as she lived. But eventually she clambered off his lap, saying, 'Come on then, let's go and tell everyone our news – and, of course, let your parents know that they're landowners at last.'

And hand in hand, they headed for Kynance Farm. Briony's war was finally over.

Acknowledgments

My love and thanks as always to the wonderful team at Constable & Robinson.

Special thanks to Victoria, my brilliant editor, Sheila, my lovely agent, Joan, my wonderful copy editor, and Laura, my fantastic publicist, for all your support and faith in me. xx